Alex took Meg's arm and whipped her around to face him, forcing her to meet his implacable gaze.

"You go too far," he said in a low voice that carried the faintest hint of a threat. "It is my responsibility to see you safe tonight. So do as I say and stay well away from those men."

She lifted her chin defiantly. "I don't know what you are talking about."

His eyes flared, and he tightened his grip on her arm. "Don't press me, Meg."

His voice was deep and liquid and seemed to wrap around her. She knew she shouldn't provoke him, but he brought out a mischievous side long forgotten. Lifting one brow, she asked, "Or what?"

Before the taunt had left her mouth, she was in his arms again and jerked firmly against the broad chest she'd just admired. She gasped. His eyes were hooded, his expression dark and full of promise.

"Or I will prove to you just how innocent you are, my sweet, and how very little control you have over a man and a man's desires."

He lowered his head. Slowly. Inch by heart-stopping inch. Giving her every opportunity to object.

She could hear the fierce pounding of her heart. His mouth was so close. If she were breathing, their breath would have mingled in the cool night air. But Alex's mouth moved over hers, and G̶o̶d̶ ̶h̶e̶l̶p̶ ̶h̶e̶r̶, ld not stop him.

Also by Monica McCarty

Highlander Untamed

HIGHLANDER

A Novel

A Ballantine Books Mass Market Original

Copyright © 2007 by Monica McCarty
Excerpt from *Highlander Unchained* copyright © 2007 by Monica McCarty

Published in the United States by Ballantine Books, an imprint of The Random House Publishing Group, a division of Random House, Inc., New York.

BALLANTINE and colophon are registered trademarks of Random House, Inc.

This book contains an excerpt from the forthcoming mass market edition of *Highlander Unchained* by Monica McCarty. This excerpt has been set for this edition only and may not reflect the final content of the forthcoming edition.

ISBN 978-0-345-49437-5

Cover illustration: Craig White

Printed in the United States of America

www.ballantinebooks.com

OPM 9 8 7 6 5 4 3 2 1

To my mom, for all those trips to the library, and for the bags of books from garage sales and flea markets; and to my dad, for the countless chair-lift spelling tests and for the early lessons in editing. Do you still have that red pen? And to both of you, for the gift that keeps on giving . . . a top-notch education.

To Maxine and Reid, who may not always understand why Mommy is busy and can't play, I love you both very much. (But you better be reading this twenty years from now. If not, put the book down. On second thought, that goes for you, too, Dad.)

Acknowledgments

I've been very fortunate to have some wonderful and extremely talented people around me. I'd like to thank them.

First to my editor, Charlotte Herscher, who saw the real Alex even before I did. You were right. Thank you for showing me the light.

Thanks to the team at *Wax Creative,* especially Emily Cotler and Claire Anderson, for designing my beautiful website at www.MonicaMcCarty.com. (With a special thanks to Julie for the referral.)

Thanks to Jami and Nyree, who, as with the first book, read many, many versions of this story. You guys are the best. What would I do without you? And to Tracy, for helping me work through the revisions. It still amazes me that one of my favorite authors has become such a good friend.

Finally, thanks to my husband, Dave, for cooking all those dinners while I was under a deadline—and to Reid and Maxine for eating them. I love you all.

Part One

Chapter 1

He was going home.

Alex MacLeod urged his mount faster down the narrow path. The powerful black destrier responded with a sudden burst of speed through the densely wooded forest, as if this were the first mile and not the hundredth. The grueling pace Alex set three days ago had only intensified as they neared their final destination. He knew that he was pushing his men, but they were accustomed to—nay, thrived on—such rigor. They had not become the most feared band of warriors across the Highlands by suffering complacency. His brother, Rory MacLeod, Chief of MacLeod, had summoned Alex home for an important mission. His chief needed him, and Alex would not delay.

Rory's message was circumspect and brief, but Alex knew well what it meant. The opportunity he'd been waiting for loomed. And Alex was ready. Battle-hardened, honed as sharp as the edge of his claymore, and primed for whatever task his brother sought to impart upon him.

Nearly three years had passed since he'd last set eyes upon the jagged, rocky shorelines of Skye and the for-

bidding stone walls of Dunvegan Castle—the stronghold of the MacLeods for nearly four hundred years. He
hadn't intended to be gone for so long. But in the most
brutal and primitive of conditions, living the life of an
outlaw, Alex had found his calling.

He was at his best on the battlefield. It was the only
place where he could quiet the demons, the restlessness
that drove him. But the years of constant battle could
not dull the fire that burned inside him. If anything, the
flame burned even hotter.

For now the battle had moved close to home.

Home. A wave of something akin to wistfulness
washed over him. Alex rarely allowed himself to think
about all that he'd left behind. His family. Peace. Security. Such things were not for him. His destiny, he knew,
lay in a different direction.

Charging into a clearing, he slowed, giving his men
time to catch up. His squire, Robbie, pulled up beside
him. Not yet ten and seven, the lad was already on his
way to becoming a skilled warrior. Living by the sword
did not leave much margin for error. Boys quickly became either men . . . or corpses.

Robbie was breathing heavily, and sweat poured
down his face, but Alex knew the lad would rather take
a dirk in his gut than admit he was tired.

"Will we make it, do you think?" Robbie asked.

Alex caught the direction of his gaze. "Before the
rain?"

The lad nodded.

Alex looked up through the curtain of trees at the
darkening skies. A storm was brewing, and if the thickened air and dense black clouds were any indication, it
was going to be a fierce one. He shook his head. "Nay,

lad. I fear we'll get a good soaking." Wiping the sweat from his own brow, he added, "One that we all could use."

The boy made a face, and Alex felt a rare tug of amusement. There had been precious little to laugh about lately. It would not be the first time they'd traveled in treacherous weather. And at least this time they were not dodging the king's henchmen.

They rode for perhaps another mile before Alex's ears pricked at a faint sound. He hadn't kept the Reaper at bay the past three years only by his skill with a claymore; he'd learned to trust his instincts. And right now those instincts flared.

Reining in his mount, he raised his fist in a silent command for his men to follow suit. The band of warriors immediately ground to a halt behind him.

A soft breeze pushed the stray leaves scattered across the forest floor in a gentle rustle, and with it carried the almost imperceptible sounds of a cry.

Alex met the hard stare of his chief guardsman. "An animal?" Patrick asked.

Alex shook his head. "I don't think so." He held perfectly still, listening again. He knew he should just move on; he had a job to do. But before he could order his men on their way, he heard another cry.

This one more distinct.

More distinctly feminine.

Damn. He couldn't ignore it now. His brother's words flashed in his head: *Keep your identity hidden.*

Alex shook off the reminder. Not many would recognize him after so many years. He'd changed. War had hardened him, and not just in spirit.

Do not delay. . . .

There would be no delay.

This wouldn't take long.

Feeling the familiar surge of blood rush through his veins as his body anticipated the coming battle, he swung his destrier around to the south and plunged into the trees, leading his men in the direction of the screams.

Right before the sky broke open, unleashing its torrential fury.

It was going to rain. Perfect. Meg Mackinnon pulled the wool *arisaidh,* the full-length plaid she'd wrapped around her for protection from the elements, more firmly around her head and once again cursed the necessity for this journey. They'd only just begun, and already she was dreading long days on horseback, navigating the treacherous tracks of the drovers. Even had her father been able to arrange one, a carriage would have been useless along these paths. The "road" from the Isle of Skye to Edinburgh was barely wide enough to ride two abreast. The cart that carried their belongings had proved to be enough of a burden on this rugged terrain.

Meg had at least a week of discomfort left before her. It would take them that long to reach Edinburgh, where she must begin in earnest her search for a husband.

She felt the familiar flutter of anxiety when she thought of all that was ahead of her. Her father had entrusted her to find the right man for her clan; she would not let him down. But the responsibility inherent in her decision weighed heavily on her. The pressure at times could be stifling. A wry smile touched the edges of her mouth. Perhaps a week of travel wasn't long enough.

Yet part of her couldn't wait until it was all over. It would be a relief to have the decision made and behind her. Of course, then she would be *married*. And that brought a whole new bundle of anxieties.

Meg sighed deeply, knowing she couldn't have put off the trip to court any longer. Her father's recent illness had made that very clear. Without her help, her brother's place as chief would be challenged. The corbies had begun to circle the minute her father had taken to bed with a mysterious wasting ailment. Her once hale and hearty father, the powerful Chief of Mackinnon, had lost nearly two stone and was still too weak to travel.

Meg glanced over at her mother riding beside her and felt a pang of guilt for dragging her so far from home. It was difficult enough for Meg to leave her father and brother; she couldn't imagine how her mother must feel.

"I'm sorry, Mother."

Rosalind Mackinnon met her daughter's gaze with puzzlement. "Whatever for, child?"

"For taking you away from Father at a time like this." Meg bit her lip, feeling the need to explain. "I just couldn't bring myself to accept—"

"Nonsense." Her mother cut her off, a rare frown marring her beautiful face. "Your father is much better. A trip to court is exactly what I need. You know how I love all the latest fashions, the latest hairstyles,"—she smiled conspiratorially—"and all the latest gossip."

Meg returned the smile. She knew her mother was only trying to make her feel better, though she did love going to court. Meg, on the other hand, hated it. She never fit in the way her mother did. Partially, it was her own fault. She did not share her mother's enjoyment of frippery and gossip and was not very good at pretending otherwise. But this time, she swore she would try. For her mother's sake, if not for her own.

"Besides, I'll not have you marry a man you do not love," her mother finished, anticipating the apology Meg had been about to make.

Meg shook her head. Rosalind Mackinnon was a hopeless romantic. But love was not the reason Meg had refused the offer of marriage from her father's chieftain. The offer that, had she accepted it, would have dispensed with the need for this trip.

But Meg's choice of a husband was dictated by unusual circumstances, and Thomas Mackinnon was not the right man for her. He was an able warrior, yes, but a hotheaded one. A man who reached for his sword first and thought later. Meg sought a strong warrior, but a controlled one. Equally important, she needed a clever negotiator to appease a king with growing authority over his recalcitrant Highland subjects. Tensions between the two ran high. The time of unfettered authority by the chiefs was waning. She must find a husband who could help lead her clan into the future.

But lack of political acumen was not the only reason she'd refused Thomas. She also sensed too much ambition in him. Ambition that would put her brother's position as the next chief in jeopardy.

Above all, she needed a fiercely loyal man. A man she could trust.

Love was not part of the bargain. Meg was a realist. She admired the deep affection between her parents, perhaps even envied it, but recognized that such was not for her. Her duty was clear. Finding the right man for her clan came first. And second.

"I don't expect to be as fortunate in marriage as you,

Mother," Meg said. "What you and Father have is rare."

"And wonderful," Rosalind finished. "Which is why I want it for you. Though just because I love your father does not mean I always agree with him. In this, he asks too much of you," she said with a stubborn set to her pointed chin. As Meg had never heard her mother speak against her father, it took a moment to register what she was saying. Her mother shook her head. "You already spend far too much time with your nose in the books."

"I enjoy my duties, Mother," Meg said patiently.

But her mother continued on as if she hadn't heard. Scrunching up her tiny nose, she shivered dramatically. "All those numbers. It makes my head swim just thinking about it."

Meg covered her smile. Now that sounded more like her mother. She never could understand Meg's fascination with mathematics or scholarly pursuits in general. Meg derived great pleasure from working with numbers. There was something satisfying in knowing there was only one right solution. And learning had always come easily for her. Unlike it was for her brother, she thought with a sharp pinch in her chest.

"And now he expects you to sacrifice your future happiness," her mother lamented, as if a daughter marrying for the good of the clan were anything out of the ordinary. When, in fact, Meg choosing her own husband—albeit one who met certain criteria—was the oddity.

"Truly, Mother, it is no sacrifice. Father asks nothing of me that I don't want myself. When I find the right man to stand beside Ian, he will be the right man for me."

"If only it were that easy. But you cannot force your heart to follow your head."

Maybe not, but she could try.

As if she knew what Meg was thinking, Rosalind said dismissively, "Don't worry. Just leave it to me."

Warning bells clanged. "Mother . . . you promised not to interfere."

Her mother stared straight ahead with a far too innocent look on her face. "I don't know what you are talking about, Margaret Mackinnon."

Meg's eyes narrowed; she was not fooled one bit. "You know exactly—"

But her words were lost in the violent crash of thunder as a deluge of rain poured from the skies. The ground seemed to shake with the sudden fury of the storm.

Her mother's terrified scream, however, alerted Meg to the fact that the shaking was from more than just a storm.

Still, it took her a moment to comprehend what was happening, so suddenly had it begun. One minute she'd been about to take her mother to task for her matchmaking ways, the next she was in the midst of a nightmare.

Out of the shadows, like demon riders on the storm, the band of ruffians attacked. Huge, savage-looking men in filthy shirts and tattered plaids, wielding deadly claymores with ruthless intent. They seemed to fly from the trees, surrounding Meg's party in all directions.

Her cry froze in her throat, terror temporarily rendering her mute. For a minute, she couldn't think. Watching helplessly as the dozen clansmen her father sent along to protect them were locked in a battle of untempered ferocity against at least a score of brigands.

Her blood ran cold.

There were too many of them.

Dear God, her father's men had no chance. The Mackinnon clansmen had immediately moved to protect Meg and her mother, circling them as best they could in the confined area. And one by one, they were cut down in front of her.

Meg gazed in rapt horror as Ruadh, one of her father's chieftains, a man she'd known her entire life, a man who'd bounced her on his knee and sung her songs of the clan's illustrious past, was unable to block the deadly strike of a claymore that slid across his belly, cutting him nearly in two. Tears sprang to her eyes as she watched the light slowly fade from his gaze.

Her mother's scream sliced through the terror, jolting Meg from her stupor. The moment of panic dissolved in a sudden burst of clarity. She gathered her courage, with only one thought: protecting her mother.

Heart pounding, Meg leapt down from her horse and grabbed the dirk from Ruadh's lifeless hand, his fingers still clenched around the bloody hilt. The weapon felt so heavy and clumsy in her hand. For the first time in her life, she wished she hadn't lingered so long indoors with her books. She had no experience with weaponry of any sort. She shook off the bout of uncertainty. It didn't matter. What she lacked in skill she would make up for in raw determination. Clasping the dirk more firmly, she moved to stand before her mother, ready to defend her.

They'll have to kill me first, she vowed silently.

But a bit of her bravado faltered when another of her father's men fell at her feet. The way it was going, it might not be long before they did. Only six of her father's men remained.

The *arisaidh* had slid from her head, and rain streamed down her face, blurring her vision. The pins holding back her hair were long gone, and the wavy tendrils tangled in her lashes, but Meg hardly noticed, focused as she was on the battle. The battle that was tightening like a noose around them, as their circle of protectors quickly diminished.

She bit back the fear that crept up the back of her throat. Never had she been more terrified. But she had to stay strong. For her mother. If they were to have a chance to survive.

Meg's action seemed to snap her mother from her trance, and she stopped screaming. Following Meg's lead, she slipped down from her horse. Meg could see her hands shaking as she pulled Ruadh's eating knife from his belt.

Meg turned, and her chest squeezed to see the resolve on her mother's face. To see the direness of their circumstance reflected in her gaze. Even drenched, her hair and clothes a sodden mess, Rosalind Mackinnon looked like an angel—albeit an avenging angel. Though she was forty, her beauty was undiminished by age. *Dear God, what would these vicious brutes do to her?* Meg swallowed. *To them both?*

Though Meg knew her mother must be thinking the same thing, her voice was strangely calm. "If you see an opening between them, run," she whispered.

"But I can't leave you—"

Her mother cut off her protest. "You will do as I say, Margaret." Meg was so shocked by the steel in her dulcet tone that she simply nodded. "If you need to use the knife, strike hard and do not hesitate."

Meg felt an unexpected swell of pride. Her sweet, gentle mother looked as fierce as a lioness protecting her cub. There was far more to Rosalind Mackinnon than Meg had ever realized.

"I won't," she said, feigning courage. But what chance did two women, and two particularly diminutive ones at that, have against such strength and numbers?

A filthy, hulking ruffian lurched for her mother. Without thinking, Meg stabbed his arm. It was a good effort. At least three of the ten inches sank deep in his skin, opening a wide gash in his forearm. He roared in pain and backhanded her across the face. Stunned by the blow, she lost her grip on the dirk and it dropped to the ground, where he promptly kicked it out of her reach.

Meg's hand instinctively covered her wet cheek, soothing the hot sting.

"Bitch," he spat. "You'll die for that." He turned, lifting his claymore in a deadly arc above her head. Her mother moved to defend her, slicing his shoulder with the eating knife. Easily blocking the blow with his forearm, he shoved her mother harshly to the ground. Meg watched in horror as her head landed squarely on a rock, connecting with a dull thud.

Horror rose in her throat. "Mother!" she screamed, rushing to her side. Meg shook her listless body, but her eyes wouldn't open. *Dear God, no!*

She sensed him, or rather smelled his rank stench, approaching behind her. Anger unlike anything she'd ever experienced flooded her with rage. He'd hurt her mother. Grabbing the knife that her mother had dropped, Meg turned on him, surprising him for a moment. She stabbed him again, this time aiming for his neck. But he was too tall, and without leverage, she managed only to nick him.

She'd lost her advantage.

A vile expletive ripped from his mouth. She felt his enormous dirty hands on her as he grabbed her and tossed her to the ground. His hard black eyes fixed on her. A sneer curled his lip, revealing coarse brown teeth. Shivering with revulsion, she huddled in a ball as he started toward her.

"I'm going to enjoy this, you little hellcat."

Meg scooted back in the mud, but he kept coming. Laughing. She could feel the heavy pounding of her heart in her chest. She glanced around, but there was no one to come to her aid. Those who remained of father's men were locked in their own battles. She grabbed fistfuls of mud in her hands and tried tossing them in his eyes, but this only made him more furious.

They couldn't die. What would happen to Ian? She felt the hot prickle of tears in her eyes. Without Meg and her mother, there was no one to protect him. *Think,* she told herself. *Use your head.* But the logic and reasoning she'd always relied on failed her. There was no escape.

In the black glint of his merciless eyes, Meg saw only death.

Please, she breathed.

And in the skip of two long heartbeats, the answer to her prayer exploded through the trees on a fearsome black warhorse.

A knight. Nay, a warrior. Not in shining armor, but in the yellow cotun dotted with bits of mail that identified him as a chieftain—though his size alone would have set him apart. Even without his padded war coat, Meg knew he would be one of the largest men she'd ever seen. Tall and muscular, with a chest like a broad shield. As if forged from steel, every inch of him looked hard and forbidding.

And dangerous.

A trickle of fear slid down her spine. For a moment, Meg wondered whether she'd merely exchanged one villain for another.

Their eyes met and held. She gasped, startled by the most crystalline blue eyes she'd ever beheld, set in a face of rugged masculinity partially hidden beneath the heavy stubble of a week-old beard.

The entire exchange lasted only an instant, but she quickly read the absolute command in his gaze. A look that was oddly reassuring despite his ferocity.

For the first time, she noticed that he was not alone; perhaps half a dozen men had ridden in behind him. A more fearsome band of warriors she could not imagine. To a one they were strong, well muscled, and utterly ruthless looking. *Broken men,* she knew with an instinctive certainty. Men without land or a clan who roamed the Highlands as outlaws. Yet for some reason, they did not inspire her fear. Her eyes returned to the warrior. Because of their leader? she wondered.

With no more than a tilt of his head and the dart of his eyes, the warrior issued his orders. His men moved as a unit, swiftly taking their positions with the discipline of Roman centurions and an ease that certainly belied their rough appearance.

Despite their lesser numbers, Meg knew without a doubt that the tide of battle had just turned. This man would not be defeated. Only a fool would challenge him.

With his men in position, the warrior headed directly

for her. Finally realizing that something was wrong, her attacker glanced over his shoulder. The horrible laughing stopped. Taking advantage of the distraction, Meg ran to her mother's side, gently dragging her back toward the trees, nearly sobbing with relief to see that the color had returned to her cheeks and her eyes had begun to flutter. All the while, she kept her eye on the man who was their savior.

He reached over his shoulder with one hand and drew an enormous claymore from the baldric slung across his back as if it weighed no more than a feather, though the blade alone would have reached to her chin. Still using only one hand, he raised it high above his head, wielding the weapon with remarkable ease, and landed a heavy blow to the ribs of her attacker. Meg heard the crunch of bone as the villain crumpled to the ground.

The warrior leapt off his mount, then pulled a dirk from the scabbard at his waist and unhesitatingly drew his blade across her tormentor's throat. Relief washed over her. She should regret the loss of life, but she could not. Their eyes met, and she felt a connection so strong that it startled her.

"Thank you," she mouthed, too shaken to sound the words.

He acknowledged her gratitude with a nod. Then, with a fierce war cry—the words in Erse, which she could not make out—he raised his sword and charged headlong into the fury of the battle, wielding the blade with deadly finesse and accuracy, cutting down all who stood in his path. Her stunned clansmen rallied behind him.

As she attended to her mother as best she could,

Meg's gaze flicked back and forth to the battle taking place all around them.

And to the warrior.

His strength and skill were truly awe-inspiring.

Feeling oddly detached from the mayhem surrounding her, Meg stared in horrified fascination as he killed three men with steely efficiency. Each movement was a precision death stroke. For such a large man, he moved with surprising grace. Like a lion. Two ruffians attempted to corner him, striking at him from either side. He raised his claymore. The blade flashed above his head like a silvery cross before the crash of steel on steel sounded as he deflected their blows one after the other. The brigands were skilled fighters. Working in tandem, they landed blow after blow. Surely he must be tiring? But the warrior seemed to be enjoying it, as if the added challenge only invigorated him.

Using his claymore with one arm to hold back one man, he wielded his dirk with the other, dispatching the second man with ease. Furious, the remaining villain rushed at him. Sliding to evade him, the warrior lost his footing and skidded in the mud, enabling the other man to knock him down. Meg gasped, holding her breath, as the villain prepared to deal his death blow. But in the most brave, or reckless, display of daring she'd ever witnessed, the warrior waited until the claymore was mere inches from his head before slipping his dirk in the ruffian's gut and rolling deftly to the side.

Stunned, Meg watched as he sprang to his feet.

Almost instantly, another ruffian attempted to take him from behind.

"Watch—" Even before Meg had time to shout a

warning, her warrior spun and plunged his dirk deep into the other man's side.

The warrior seemed indestructible, as if nothing could touch him. But there was something to his prowess that went beyond strength and skill. The battle seemed to consume him. He fought like a man without fear of death. Not recklessly, he was too controlled for that, but with unfettered purpose. An edge of danger hovered over this untamed warrior that she could not ignore.

It didn't take long for the remaining ruffians to recognize the futility of their endeavor. Scattering like bugs from beneath a rock, they fled.

The warrior looked around as if to assure himself that she was safe. Their eyes met again. Meg felt as though she'd been struck by a bolt of lightning; every nerve ending prickled with awareness. Her mysterious warrior was more than simply handsome. His features were the fodder of legends, classically handsome yet ruggedly masculine at the same time. Wavy brown hair, its true color obscured by the dampness, hung in a blunt line just past his chin, setting off a strong, squared jaw. Rain streamed down a broad forehead, along the curve of his high angled cheekbones, and over a finely chiseled nose. Though his mouth was set in a tight line, his fierce expression could not hide the full, sensual shape of his lips.

But it was his striking blue eyes that held her. Ice blue. Like a frozen loch in the darkest winter. Their color made more intense against the deep tan of his golden skin. Yet when he looked at her, it was not a chill she felt, but warmth that started at her neck and spread all the way down to her toes. He seemed to see right through her with a hawklike intensity that stole her breath and sent her pulse racing.

He made her feel nervous . . . unsettled . . . vulnerable. Unfamiliar feelings that increased her wariness. With one last hesitant look at the warrior, Meg returned to attending to her mother.

The rain had stopped. The battle was over.

When the cowards turned to run, Alex motioned two of his men to follow to make sure they didn't return. The others he instructed to tend to the wounds of the injured and dispose of the bodies as best they could. But it wasn't until he'd gotten an initial report from Patrick that Alex knew he had a problem.

Mackinnons. Damn. Powerful bad luck to have come to the aid of a neighboring clan from Skye. At least no one appeared to have recognized him. But he knew the longer he lingered, the more chance there was for questions to form. Despite the beard, it wouldn't be long before someone noted his uncanny resemblance to the infamous Chief of MacLeod. His brother cut a wide path around these parts.

They should leave.

His gaze slid back to the lass. She was ministering to the woman he'd initially thought dead but appeared to be slowly regaining consciousness. In between soothing the woman with soft words, the lass set her men about making order out of chaos with the smooth efficiency of a general. Horses were fed and watered, the cart that was carrying their trunks was righted, and arrangements were made for returning the injured and killed to Dunakin.

For one so young—she couldn't be much past twenty years—she appeared to be handling the aftermath of the attack admirably.

More than admirably, actually. Her composure under the circumstances was remarkable. From the first moment he'd seen her, she'd impressed him with her courage. Riding in, he'd caught the very end of her attempt to stab the man who was attacking her. For such a wee thing, she'd managed to inflict some damage. When the fiend had gone after her, Alex's reaction had been instantaneous. He'd killed without hesitation. He had no mercy for men who harmed women. The coward deserved to die a far worse death than the swift one he'd been granted.

Of course, her courage wasn't all that he'd noticed.

When she gazed up at him with wide green eyes that dominated her tiny heart-shaped face, he found himself unable to look away. Warmth spread through him, and he'd felt the stirrings of something that had been absent inside him for a long time. Desire.

His interludes with women over the past few years had been about satisfying the needs of his body; he had neither the time nor the inclination for anything else. But standing there, with her hair plastered to her head and rain streaming down her face and clinging to her long lashes, she looked like a drowned wood nymph. Sweet, vulnerable, and achingly lovely. And Alex felt the unmistakable pull of attraction. Attraction that now, after the fighting was done, had taken on a new potency.

He took the opportunity to observe her as she ministered to her mother. She was nothing like the flamboyant beauties who usually attracted him. Her beauty was more refined, less obvious. If it weren't for those remarkable eyes, he might not have bothered to look closer. And it would have been a tragedy to miss the delicate turn of her cheek, the tiny pert nose, or the soft, lush curve of her mouth. His eyes lingered on her lips.

Damn, she was lovely.

And innocent.

His thoughts right now, however, were anything but innocent. They were filled with vivid passionate images of naked limbs and soft, silken heat. Of releasing the pent-up energy that lingered in his body from the fight. Perversely, he hungered for her innocence. As if her purity could wipe away the ugliness that surrounded him.

What was he doing? After what she'd been through . . . He shook off the strange yearning. He'd wanted to protect her, not capture her like his marauding Viking ancestors for his own pleasure. The primitive life of an outlaw had left its mark.

He took a few steps toward her, intending to see if she was all right. But at that moment, the woman she was tending sat up, enabling Alex to see her face for the first time. His step faltered. Damn. The Mackinnon's lady. He looked back to the girl, seeing the resemblance. The lass must be his daughter.

He averted his face. Rosalind Mackinnon would know him.

He could dally no longer. Alex turned and ordered his men to be ready. Much to the relief of the Mackinnon guardsmen, he had offered the services of three of his men to travel with them until replacements arrived. The lass and her mother would be safe.

His job was done.

He mounted his destrier and turned to leave, unable to resist looking back at her one more time. Alex was not a man to be distracted by a lass. But there was something about this one. Perhaps it was because she reminded him of everything he'd left behind. Family. Hearth. Home. Things he hadn't yearned for in a very long time. Her natural beauty was a stark contrast to the death and destruction he'd been surrounded by for the last few years.

His eyes fastened on hers, and he could see her hesitation, sense her wariness. As though she wanted to say something but was perhaps a little frightened. *Of him.* The truth struck him hard. Gazing around at the bodies scattered across the forest floor, he supposed he couldn't blame her.

But he didn't like it. Didn't like it at all.

He'd just saved her, yet she looked at him with fear in her eyes.

This was what he did. It wasn't pretty, but war never was.

Anger rose inside him and coupled with his primitive response to the lass made his blood run even hotter. He was tempted to give her reason for her fear. To pull her into his arms and reap the spoils of victory from her soft lips. But he hadn't fallen that far from civilized. Yet.

"Ready, sir?" Robbie asked, looking at him strangely.

Alex shook off the lustful haze and forced an evenness to his tone that he did not feel. "Yes," he answered. "We've delayed long enough."

Without further hesitation, he turned and rode away. And didn't look back.

Chapter 2

Holyrood House, Edinburgh, July 1605

Court was exactly as she'd expected: pure torture. Meg had tried, but she would never fit in. At Holyrood House, nothing was as it seemed. Intrigue, innuendo, subtlety. They might as well have been speaking Greek. No, wait, she understood Greek. They might as well have been speaking Arabic, Meg amended. She would never be able to understand the language of courtiers. Only two weeks and already she couldn't wait to leave and return to her beloved Skye. But not yet. Not until she found what she'd come for.

As she'd done every night since her arrival, Meg stood with her friend Elizabeth Campbell near the doorway of the great hall—a position that afforded her the best vantage into the room—carefully surveying the crowd of courtiers swarming about the palace of James VI of Scotland, now James I of England.

King James had been ruling Scotland from Whitehall for almost three years now, but you wouldn't know it by looking at the number of people who flocked to the palace each night. Edinburgh was still the center of power in Scotland, with or without the king. Instead of the king, the hordes of sycophants now sought favor from Lord Chancellor Seton or his privy councillors. *Like bees to honey,* Meg thought wryly. Behind the plush velvets and fine brocades of their elaborate court dress, each person in this room was here with a purpose. To a one, they wanted something from someone: power, position, intrigue, or, like her, a husband.

Acknowledging that unfortunate truth, she forced herself to scan the room again in the vain hope that she'd missed something, or rather someone, the first time around.

"Any new prospects?" Elizabeth asked.

Meg turned to her friend and shook her head. "No." She didn't bother trying to hide the frustration in her voice. Elizabeth was well aware of Meg's trials in her ongoing search for a husband. "I think I've been introduced to every unmarried man in Scotland between the ages of twenty and fifty."

Elizabeth smothered a giggle behind her gloved hand. "Don't forget Lord Burton. He was sixty-five if he was a day."

Meg grimaced. "You're right. I stand corrected."

"Give your mother some time," Elizabeth teased, patting her hand. "I'm sure she'll find you any number of potential suitors."

Meg tried not to groan. Her mother's attempts at matchmaking were anything but subtle.

"It could be worse," Elizabeth added sympathetically. "At least she finds the handsome ones."

Meg sighed and shook her head, acknowledging the truth of the statement. Her mother was quite predictable in that fashion. Certainly Meg was not immune to a handsome countenance, but extremely handsome men made her wary. She knew firsthand how easy it was to lose your senses in the twinkle of a charming smile. Relying on attraction was a recipe for disaster. But she didn't have the heart to discourage her mother, as she seemed to take such pleasure in her task.

"Indeed, if handsome fops were what I was looking for, I'd be back on Skye by now." Meg bit her lip and looked around furtively, relieved that no one had overheard her. She'd spoken bluntly again. Yet another of the reasons she didn't fit in well at court. Except with Elizabeth. She didn't seem to mind Meg's propensity for frankness. Elizabeth and her brother Jamie were the only good things about coming to Edinburgh. She'd met them two years ago on her first appearance at court and she'd been friends with them ever since.

"You've certainly met your share of them," Elizabeth agreed. "But with your list of requirements in a husband, I fear you are going to have to expand your search."

Meg lifted a brow, intrigued. "How so?"

Elizabeth's eyes danced. "Perhaps one man is not enough."

Meg would have laughed if it didn't feel as though Elizabeth might be right. Already two weeks gone, and she was no closer to finding a husband than when she'd first arrived. Her task was proving much more difficult than she'd originally anticipated. It almost made her understand why marriages were arranged by fathers. Initially, she'd considered herself fortunate to choose her own husband. Now, however, she wasn't so sure. Less than a month remained before they must return to Dunakin in preparation for Michaelmas. Yet despite the urgency of the situation, try as she might, Meg just couldn't muster up the proper enthusiasm for the task at hand.

As if to prove her point, a man not much taller than her, dressed head to toe in shiny white satin with his trunk hose puffed out as wide as a pumpkin, strode by with a gallant bow in her direction. It wasn't a secret that Meg sought a husband, and her fortune attracted plenty of interest. She forced a smile to her lips and acknowledged his attentions with a small nod, all the while knowing that he would never do. Ticking through her mental checklist of requirements, she just couldn't picture this man leading her braw Mackinnon warriors into battle at her brother's side.

Unfortunately, he was quite typical of the Lowland gentlemen who frequented court. Lowlanders bore closer resemblance to Englishmen than their Highland countrymen. The king's disdain for Highland "barbarians" was well-known, which in part had compelled this trip to court—to broaden the scope of her search for a husband to include influential men connected to King James's government.

But how was she supposed to find a man of strength and valor in this garden of preening peacocks?

Not for the first time, Meg's thoughts slid back to the copse of trees and to the mysterious warrior who'd rescued her. As handsome as Adonis, with the prowess of Ares. Both qualities unnerved her. But perhaps even more unnerving was the realization that she'd been attracted to the man. *Despite* his too handsome face and what she'd witnessed on the battlefield.

He was not at all the sort of man she typically found attractive. His size, for one, was too overwhelming. Big braw men made her . . . well . . . nervous. She frowned.

Actually, now that she thought about it, everything about him was overwhelming. From his fierce, handsome face, to his unfettered fighting skills, to his blatant masculinity.

Still, she could not forget him, which given the task at hand was disconcerting to say the least. It was an odd experience for her. Meg was not at all the sort of woman to be distracted by a pleasing countenance. She knew better.

It was ridiculous. She didn't even know who he was, and as she usually did her best to avoid consorting with outlaws, she would most likely never see him again. Her subtle attempts to glean more information about him from the men who'd accompanied them through the forest had been unsuccessful. From their silence, she was even more certain that the men were outlaws. They asked no questions and answered just as many. A more circumspect escort she could not imagine. Even learning their names had been a challenge. They claimed to be Murrays, a name she knew that many MacGregors had assumed after their clan was proscribed. Could her warrior be a MacGregor? It wouldn't surprise her. But what were MacGregors doing so close to Skye?

Of course, his identity, or lack thereof, only added to the mystery, which no doubt explained her illogical fascination with a man she knew nothing about.

Except that he saved us. And perhaps that was all she needed to know.

She'd been surprised, and disappointed, that he'd left without speaking to her. She wished she'd found the nerve at least to thank him. She should have put aside her qualms, marched over there, and done it right away. But truth be told, she'd been more than a little bit frightened. The controlled frenzy of his fighting had taken her aback.

She'd been too aware of him and too unsure of herself.

She consoled herself that it was probably just the unusual circumstances she was responding to. A Greek god riding to the rescue at the last moment would make an impression on anyone. Even someone as otherwise levelheaded as Meg.

Unfortunately, however, she did not have the luxury of a fairy tale. She needed a real man, not a mythical one. And soon. The thought of returning to Dunakin empty-handed was a sobering one. Her father would be disappointed. And disappointment was the one thing Meg could not bear.

She'd delayed her decision long enough. She could not allow thoughts of her mysterious warrior to distract her from her duty any longer.

"You have that far-off look in your eyes." Elizabeth spoke, startling Meg from her reverie. "Daydreaming about your handsome rescuer again?"

Her cheeks heated. Not for the first time, she wished she hadn't confided quite so many details about the man who'd rescued her. She covered her embarrassment with a frown. "I don't daydream."

"But you were thinking of him?"

Meg gave her friend a sharp look. Elizabeth was not easily put off. "Very well. Yes. I was thinking about him."

"It's so romantic," Elizabeth said, sighing dreamily.

Meg rolled her eyes. "You sound like my mother. But I assure you, there was nothing romantic about it." She couldn't quite repress the shiver as her thoughts flew back to the melee in the forest. "It was awful. We were very lucky to escape with our lives, and Mother with only a knot on her head. So many others weren't as fortunate," she said, thinking of Ruadh and the other Mackinnon warriors who'd lost their lives that day.

"I'm s-s-sorry, Meg. I didn't m-m-mean to s-s-sound insen-n-nsitive. I can't im-m-magine what you w-w-went through."

Meg heard her friend's stammer and felt horrible for making her anxious. Elizabeth rarely stammered around her, as she did when in company with others she felt less comfortable with. She took Elizabeth's hands and forced a bright smile on her face. "What happened is in the past, and I must look to the future. And an outlaw, no matter how heroic, is not the man for me."

If only she knew who was.

Finding a suitable husband shouldn't be so difficult. A warrior her clansmen would follow into battle. A skilled negotiator to pacify the Privy Council. A man of integrity and loyalty to support her brother. But it *was* difficult. With each day that passed, it had become more and more clear that there was only one man who might be suitable: Jamie Campbell, her best friend's brother.

Elizabeth gave her hands a little squeeze. "Don't worry, Meg. You will find the right man. Or perhaps you already have?" she asked hopefully. It was no secret that Elizabeth wished Meg to marry her brother.

"Perhaps," Meg replied with an encouraging smile.

In many ways, Jamie Campbell epitomized the type of man her father entrusted her to find. Cousin to Archibald "the Grim" Campbell, Earl of Argyll, Jamie could not be better connected. The Campbells were the most powerful clan in the Highlands, thanks in large part to

Argyll's influence with the king. Jamie had something of his wily cousin in him, and Meg knew that Argyll was becoming increasingly reliant on his young cousin both to exert his influence at court and to enforce his authority in the Highlands.

By virtue of his extraordinary height and natural command, Jamie also had the makings of a great leader. Only two years older than Meg at four and twenty, Jamie still possessed a young man's build. But in a few years' time, when he added girth to his frame, he would be a formidable man. A strong, powerful man who would be more than capable of defending Dunakin.

And most important, Jamie was a man of integrity, honor, and unswerving loyalty.

He seemed the perfect choice.

But something still held her back. His youth, perhaps? And his connection to Argyll would be viewed by many Highlanders as a black mark against him. In some quarters, the name Argyll was as reviled as the devil. Clan Campbell's power in the Highlands had not come without dispute or the shedding of blood. MacGregor blood in particular.

All of a sudden, she felt Elizabeth's elbow jabbing her ribs. "Hold on a minute. I think I've found him for you. The perfect man."

Meg muffled an unladylike snort and followed the direction of Elizabeth's dreamy gaze. At first she thought Elizabeth was talking about Jamie, but then another man moved into her view. He had his back to her, though she had to admit, it was a very impressive one. Beneath the heavily embroidered silk of his black doublet, Meg discerned broad shoulders and well-muscled—exceedingly well-muscled—arms. Her pulse jumped. His powerful legs, clad in fitted black venetians, left no doubt of his strength. In a room of colorful satin and silk, he stuck out for his dark masculinity. Even standing next to Jamie, who was a good five inches over six feet, he dominated the room. Although perhaps an inch or two shorter than Jamie, he appeared much larger owing to the solid muscle of his frame.

"Who is he?" Meg asked in what she hoped was an appropriately nonchalant tone.

"I haven't seen him in years," Elizabeth answered. "But I'm almost certain that it's Alex MacLeod."

Meg raised a brow and tried not to get ahead of herself. "Brother to Chief Rory MacLeod of Dunvegan?" Rory Mor was one of the most revered chiefs in the Isles and a longtime ally of her father's. An alliance with the MacLeods would be an excellent one.

Elizabeth nodded.

Vaguely, Meg recalled a gangly youth with sun-drenched blond hair and a heart-stopping lopsided grin. Many years ago, Alex had accompanied his brother to the Highland games held at Dunakin Castle one spring. Though Meg was too young herself, she recalled that he sent many female hearts a-patter at Dunakin with that grin.

She frowned, suddenly remembering something else. Meg hoped seeing Alex again wouldn't be too awkward for her friend. At one time, Elizabeth was to have married Chief Rory Mor.

Confident that Elizabeth was showing no signs of discomfort, Meg returned her attention to the new arrival. It was odd how still he stood. Stone still. Watchful. Completely vigilant of his surroundings. Like a soldier. There was something in his stance that gave her a whisper of trepidation.

Her brows drew together across her nose. "I've heard nothing of Alex MacLeod in years."

"Neither have I," Elizabeth said. "It's strange, isn't it?"

"Very," Meg agreed, always intrigued by a mystery.

Jamie saw her and smiled. He pointed in her direction and started heading toward her. The man turned, and anticipation prickled at the back of her neck as a strong, rugged profile and, moments later, a breathtakingly handsome face came into view. She gasped. Piercing blue eyes pinned her to the ground.

Her heart dropped to her feet.

She would know those ice blue eyes anywhere.

It was him.

Her warrior.

She should have recognized the battle-hardened physique. Admittedly, he looked different. But a shave and a haircut could not disguise the man who'd haunted her dreams.

Without the beard, the true masculine beauty of his face was revealed to startling perfection. His features combined the refined edge of the MacLeod's Norse ancestors with the raw masculinity of the Celt. Tanned to a dark bronze, his skin gave proof of time spent outdoors beneath the hot summer sun. The hard angles of his cheeks and square jaw were exactly as she remembered. Now, bereft of whiskers, she could see the slight cleft in his chin and smattering of small scars across his nose and cheekbones. Another thin scar cut through his left brow, lending a wicked edge to an otherwise almost too perfect face.

She was surprised to discover that his hair was more blond than brown, much lighter than she'd expected. It reflected the light like a golden halo.

Though there was nothing angelic about this man.

The dark expression on his face took her aback. His gaze swept over her without a flicker of recognition. A shadow of uncertainty stole through her consciousness.

It *was* the same man . . . wasn't it?

Bloody hell, Alex thought. *It's her.*

The woman Jamie Campbell couldn't stop talking about, his "Meg," was the one Alex couldn't seem to forget. He should be furious to find her here. If she recognized him, with one careless word—especially to Jamie—she could shatter a carefully constructed plan, making his task much more difficult. But anger wasn't what he felt.

Hell. If Alex weren't so disciplined and focused on the task at hand, he might have even thought it was a flicker of pleasure.

Apparently his body had no discipline, because it responded right away. The same intense attraction he'd felt that day in the forest hit him hard. It was odd. She was not the typical sort of woman to inspire instant lust. But damned if that wasn't what he felt. Raw, unbridled desire. Desire that coiled like a fist inside him and would not let go.

She looked different, which wasn't surprising since the last time he'd seen her she was soaking wet. Now, instead of a simple Highland *arisaidh*, she was gowned resplendently in her court finery, though the pale yellow color of her dress did not flatter her incredible ivory skin. He looked a little closer. Nor did the gown seem to fit too well; it hung shapelessly on her dainty figure.

Her hair was lighter brown than he'd realized. Rather than tumbling loose around her shoulders in enticing damp tendrils, she had it arranged in a tight, severe knot at the back of her head. But it was more than just the change of clothes and hair. Her expression was different. The serious-looking woman staring at him looked nothing like his vulnerable wood nymph.

Still, he had no doubt it was the same lass. The tiny, heart-shaped face and enormous soft green eyes were unmistakable.

As was the heat that surged through him the moment their eyes met.

He quickly turned his gaze, but not before he saw the look of shock on her face, followed quickly by recognition. *Which was definitely a problem.* Knowledge of his presence so near Skye only a few weeks ago could lead to questions with which he'd rather not have to contend.

He would not let anything, or anyone, interfere with his mission. Certainly not one wee lass, no matter how hot she fired his blood.

Alex had been sent to court on behalf of his brother, Rory, and the other Island chiefs, to discover what he could about the rumor of a second attempt by the king to colonize the Isle of Lewis with Lowlanders. The Lowland colonists, the so-called Fife Adventurers, had been repulsed from Lewis once before. It was Alex's sole purpose to ensure that if they tried again, they would fail again.

"Colonize" was the king's euphemism for displacing Highlanders and stealing their land. Convinced that the Highlands were an unmined source of riches with which

to fill the ever insatiable royal coffers, the king had en-
acted a series of laws intended to divest the clans of land
they'd held for hundreds of years.

In many ways, the fate of Lewis was a bellwether for
the rest of the Isles. Rory and the other Island chiefs realized that if the king was successful in colonizing the Isle
of Lewis by supplanting Highlanders with Lowlanders,
their lands would be next.

Alex's reasons were more personal.

Knowing that the Lowlanders at court would be suspicious of any Highlander in their midst, the plan had
been to distance Alex from Rory, including circulating
rumors of a falling-out between the brothers. Alex's absence for the last few years had worked in their favor. It
also had provided an explanation for his being at court.
Posing as a mercenary looking for hire, recently returned from fighting with the Irish gallowglass, the elite
mercenary warriors, under the famed Irish Chief of
O'Neill, Alex hoped to learn information from the type
of men who might be hired to protect the colonists of
Lewis.

This mission was Alex's chance to strike hard at the
king's injustice and to redress an old wrong in one fell
blow.

He would not fail.

Meg Mackinnon could make things difficult for him.
Especially since she appeared to be close to one of the
men he was targeting for information—Jamie Campbell,
the Earl of Argyll's cousin and right-hand man. If there
was a plan to colonize Lewis, you could be sure Argyll was aware of it. The greedy bastard undoubtedly
had a hand in it.

Befriending Jamie was a key part of Alex's plan.

Though admittedly Jamie was different from the lad he remembered. Harder. Not easily duped. Alex could see why Argyll had begun to rely on his young cousin to enforce his dubious policies in the Highlands. It was a shame, Alex thought. Though nearly eight years his senior, Alex had always liked the lad. But Alex's interests had changed, and now he and young Campbell were at odds. Although he'd prefer it if Jamie didn't realize that fact. Which brought him back to the Mackinnon lass.

Keep your identity hidden. His brother's warning that he not let anyone know he had traveled to Skye was coming back to haunt him. Still, he could not regret coming to her aid, even if it had made his task more difficult. He would just have to convince her that she was mistaken as to his identity.

Now. Before she had the opportunity to voice her suspicions.

Alex allowed Jamie to lead him across the hall to where she stood with Jamie's sister, Lizzie.

He could feel the Mackinnon lass's eyes on him as they approached, studying him with an intensity that would have put an eagle to shame. Avoiding any signs of recognition, he checked her with his gaze, hoping to embarrass her. But she appeared completely unrepentant to have been caught blatantly staring.

Apparently, Meg Mackinnon was not the sort of woman to back down. But Alex wasn't overly concerned. He could be persuasive. Very persuasive. He hardened his expression, keeping his mind focused on the task at hand—and not on her troubled little face.

The closer he drew, the more he sensed her wariness. He was used to his size eliciting a certain amount of consternation among the lasses, but he knew she had even more reason to fear him. She'd seen him in the heat of battle. He didn't want to frighten her, but he realized that a certain amount of caution on her part would be beneficial to his goal. Perhaps if she were a little off balance, she would be less confident in her memory.

It wasn't until he was standing right in front of her that he realized she was even smaller than he'd thought. The top of her head wouldn't even reach his shoulders. Behind the stiff stomacher, farthingale, and voluminous skirts, she was a wee slip of a thing. So frail, she looked as if she might break. But he knew the frailty was deceptive. He'd seen her courage.

He could probably span her waist with his hands, and he had a sudden urge to prove it. He yearned to wrap his callused palms around the silky, soft skin of her waist and hips, lifting her over his hard . . .

He nearly groaned. Living like a monk had obviously addled him, making him lose focus. In his youth, he'd been insatiable. But like many of the things in his carefree youth, the regular bedding of lasses had given way to steely determination and undaunted purpose. So focused on his task, he'd didn't have much time for anything else. Clearly, he'd been too long without a woman; the faint scent of roses that wafted from her hair was doing strange things to him.

Jamie began the formal introductions. After so many years of living in virtual squalor, most nights without a roof over his head, Alex found the pomp and ceremony of court maddening and the social niceties absurd. Court was about the last place a warrior wanted to be. But he had a job to do, so he would set aside his distaste. For the moment.

He could still feel the heat of her gaze on his face. She

was trying, not very subtly, to get him to look at her. Clearly, she found his lack of response vexing. Out of the corner of his eye, he could see her lips purse. She looked so charmingly befuddled, he fought a strange urge to laugh.

When it was her turn, and Alex was forced at last to acknowledge her, she looked him squarely in the eye and said, "We've met before."

Forthright, he realized.

Indeed, her frankness took him momentarily aback. It was not a characteristic he typically associated with ladies at court or with one so young.

And there was no mistaking the undertone of challenge in her voice. Though he admired the direct attack, given that she had to lift her chin to prodigious heights just to look at him, he also found it somewhat amusing.

"I'm surprised you remember," he said. "You were but a child the last time I enjoyed the hospitality of Dunakin."

She frowned, and adorable little lines appeared between her furrowed brows. "But that's not—"

He cut her off by addressing Lizzie. "It's good to see you again, Lizzie."

The poor girl blushed to her roots and murmured something unintelligible. Apparently, Elizabeth Campbell had not lost the extreme shyness that he remembered from when she was a girl.

Jamie must have noticed Meg's confusion at Alex's casual greeting, because he explained, "Alex and his brother were fostered with our cousin Argyll. My sister and I spent quite a bit of time at Inveraray Castle in our youth, as did Alex's sister Flora."

"And if I remember correctly," Alex said to Lizzie,

"you and Flora were always underfoot. Scampering around getting into some sort of mischief." His mouth quirked at the memory of the pretty flaxen-haired child who'd traipsed after his willful wee hellion of a sister. It had been too long since he'd seen Flora, he realized. He wondered if she'd fulfilled her earlier promise of beauty. He hoped so. With a temper like hers, she'd need it. Lizzie was still pretty, in a quiet, understated fashion. Much like her friend.

"Flora?" Meg asked.

"My youngest sister." At her look of surprise, he explained, "She lived with my stepmother, Janet Campbell, Argyll's aunt, after our father died."

"Then your sister is—"

"Argyll's cousin also, yes," he finished. It was hardly a connection he could forget.

Alex turned back to Elizabeth. "How long has it been, Lizzie?"

"O-o-ver fi-i-ifteen y-years," Lizzie stammered, her cheeks flaming.

Meg had finally turned her gaze from him and was watching her friend struggle with barely concealed distress. Her gaze flickered back to him as if trying to gauge his reaction. Alex felt his annoyance grow. What the hell did she expect, that he would laugh at her friend?

Yes, he realized with a start. Knowing the vicious tongues at court, he imagined that was the typical reaction to Lizzie's stammering.

"Fifteen years ago?" Meg interjected smoothly—obviously she'd done this more than once. "You truly were a child, Elizabeth." She turned to Alex, fixing him with those enormous eyes. The effect was instantaneous. *God's breath,* he could drown in those luminous depths.

Up close, he could see the smooth translucence of her skin and the soft green of her eyes, fringed by long feathery lashes. He felt a powerful yearning to touch her. To brush his finger across the delicate curve of her cheek and see if it was as unbelievably soft as it looked. This time, he was the one who was staring. "Are you recently arrived at Holyrood, then, Laird MacLeod?" she asked, breaking his trance.

Despite his temporary fixation, Alex didn't miss how the Mackinnon lass adroitly took control of the conversation, protecting her friend from further embarrassment. From the look of barely concealed adulation on Jamie's face, he realized it as well.

Alex was not unaffected. Lizzie had found herself quite a protector. He shook off the twinge of admiration. He should be focusing on Jamie Campbell and not Meg Mackinnon. He had no time to be distracted by a lass, no matter how intriguing.

Alex nodded. "I only arrived yesterday."

"Where from?" Meg asked not so innocently. "Skye?"

All vestiges of convivial thought fled. He gave her a hard look, one meant to stop further questions. "No." His voice must have sounded harsher than he intended because she took an almost imperceptible step back. In a somewhat softer tone, he asked, "And what of you, Mistress Mackinnon, have you been at court long?"

He could tell that she wanted to press the matter but thought better of it. "Just two weeks."

Jamie, apparently not liking what had essentially become a private conversation, made a possessive move toward Meg and took her hand, giving it a comforting squeeze. "Meg and her party were attacked on the way to court," he explained.

Alex lifted a brow in feigned surprise. "How unfortunate. You were not harmed, I hope?"

Meg looked him straight in the eye again. He couldn't help but admire her fortitude. "No, though six of my father's men were killed, and my mother suffered a blow to the head. They would have killed us all, but we were fortunate to have been rescued by a mysterious band of warriors."

"Fortunate indeed," Alex agreed. The way she was watching him didn't bode well. He tensed. She was going to say something—

"Actually," she said with a provoking little smile, "the leader looked remarkably like you."

Damn. Alex quickly masked his flash of anger with a chuckle, as if she'd just said something incredibly amusing. But he didn't miss the slight sharpening of Jamie's gaze.

"Though I'd like to take credit, Mistress Mackinnon, I'm afraid you must be mistaken. You know what they say around here—all of us barbarians look alike."

She didn't laugh; rather, her study of his face intensified.

Jamie frowned.

Alex knew he'd better think of something fast. Suddenly, it came to him. "Actually, it sounds more like something my brother might do. We look much alike, don't we, Jamie?"

Jamie studied him carefully and finally nodded. "Yes. Very alike."

But Alex could see that the damage had been done.

Jamie's suspicions had been aroused. Alex would have to tread carefully.

"Hmm," Meg said, "I'm sure that's it." But he could tell she did not believe him.

"These outlaws have grown too bold," Jamie said. His face darkened, and for a moment Alex had a glimpse of the ruthless man he would become. "Broken men are a scourge upon the land. Threatening innocent women," he said indignantly. "I'll hunt down every last one and see them pay."

Alex fought to control his temper. *Your cousin is already doing a fine job of it.*

He was relieved when Meg decided not to further press the matter of his identity. "How long will you be at court, Laird MacLeod?"

"Not long," he answered truthfully. Once he found what he'd come for, he would be gone. "I hope to have my business concluded soon and be on my way."

"Are you here, then, on behalf of your brother?" she asked.

Her tenacity was almost awe-inspiring. If he weren't so furious with her, he'd applaud. But she'd done enough damage for one day. "No."

"Alex is a soldier," Jamie explained. "Only recently returned from Spain and Flanders."

"Oh!" Meg exclaimed, her eyes wide with surprise.

Alex watched as understanding dawned. Somehow, he knew what her reaction would be.

Disappointment flickered in her eyes. Those damnably entrancing eyes.

The news that he was a mercenary soldier had done what he could not—stopped her questions. She no longer studied his face but turned her attention back to Jamie. A subtle rejection, and a surprisingly effective one.

He should be relieved. But when they took their leave, and her gaze slid over him with barely concealed regret, he was almost sorry about the need for the ruse.

Chapter 3

The next evening, Meg found herself in exactly the same place she'd been for the last two weeks. But tonight there was a discernible difference. *He* was here.

Unfortunately, she was not the only one to have noticed.

She excused herself from the circle of ladies and moved toward the open window overlooking the rose garden, hoping the fresh air would help clear her head. He'd only just arrived, and already she'd heard more than enough about Alex MacLeod. Even if she wanted to forget him, it would be nigh impossible.

There was only one thing the ladies at court liked to gossip about more than a handsome man, Meg realized: a handsome *unmarried* man. Add a hearty dose of rugged Highland masculinity, a touch of the forbidden, a dash of mystery, and the subject proved absolutely irresistible. As was evidenced by the not so minor sensation created by Alex's arrival at Holyrood.

Speculation was rife about the nature of his business at court. Not a few ladies Meg had spoken to hoped he was in search of a wife. She didn't have the heart to disillusion them. They would find out soon enough.

He was a mercenary. A sword for hire looking for a job. A man with no loyalties.

Meg didn't want to believe it.

She almost wished he were an outlaw. At least then she could believe that he was a man of principle, fighting for something he believed in. That he'd chosen to use his considerable skills to barter to the highest bidder was some heavy tarnish on his shining armor, to say the least.

What was it about Alex MacLeod that so intrigued her? That *still* intrigued her despite what she'd learned of his profession?

More than once tonight, she'd caught herself unconsciously seeking him out. He wasn't difficult to find. Head set high above the rest, a shock of golden brown hair glistened in the candlelight. His wide shoulders and dark clothing set him apart, as did the strength and power that radiated from him. He appeared remote, untouchable. An inscrutable expression fixed eternally on his handsome face.

He didn't belong here. He was a Highland warrior in the midst of Lowland courtiers. But it was the courtiers who suffered from the comparison. He was like a great tawny lion holding court among a sea of silk-clad parrots.

Women flocked to him, but he seemed to show no particular favor toward any one. Including Meg. He hadn't looked at her all night. It didn't bother her. Truly. She could hardly expect to compete with the steady stream of beautiful women throwing themselves at his feet. Not that she wanted to, she assured herself.

But she knew that for the lie it was when he tossed back his head and laughed at something his companion said. The smile on his face stopped her heart. She drank in the sight of amusement transcending the darkness that normally shaded his expression. There was the smile that she remembered from his visit to Dunakin long ago; she'd wondered where it had gone.

Surely it was a sin to be that glorious? When her gaze shifted to see which lucky woman had brought a smile to his face, Meg was shocked to discover that he was talking to her mother.

Turning back toward the night air, Meg shook her head, a wistful smile playing upon her lips. She didn't know why she was surprised. Rosalind Mackinnon was exceptionally beautiful and charming, two qualities to which Meg could hardly lay claim. Meg's features were perfectly acceptable, even pretty in the proper perspective, but downright bland compared with the vividness of her mother's. Rarely did Meg pay much attention to her appearance; it simply wasn't that important to her. Her mother had tried to get Meg more interested in clothes, hair, and other feminine accoutrements— repeatedly—but most of the time, Meg was too busy to bother. As for charm, well, her oft blunt tongue precluded any suggestion of that.

Her lack of courtly accomplishments had never concerned her before. It was highly disconcerting to realize that they did so now.

She barely had time to ponder the meaning of her strange melancholy before a familiar voice sounded in her ear.

"Margaret, look who I've brought for you to meet. Our delightful neighbor from Skye."

Meg cast a cautious glance over her shoulder, only to see her beaming mother bearing down on her with a stone-faced Alex pulled along in her wake. That was quick, Meg thought with reluctant appreciation, even for her mother. Unfortunately for Meg, it was too late to hide.

She didn't miss the horrified look on her mother's face when she noticed Meg's gown. Meg looked down. What was wrong with orange?

Bravely, she stood ready to face the torture. She could only imagine what nefarious schemes her mother had concocted. Finding a handsome Highlander at court—from a powerful neighboring clan nonetheless—had probably sent her into a tizzy of excited wedding preparations. But Meg could not fault her for her good intentions—or for her taste, for that matter. Rosalind Mackinnon wanted a fairy-tale marriage for her daughter, whether Meg agreed or not. And a fairy tale always included a handsome prince.

She sighed, resigned to her fate. If it was any consolation, Alex appeared no more eager for this meeting than she. She wondered what her mother had said to get him over here. Meg almost felt sorry for him. With a lesser man, she would have. She knew what it was like to be caught up in the determined machinations of her mother's schemes. Ever since Meg had begun in earnest her search for a husband, Rosalind Mackinnon had elevated the role of matchmaker to an art form. But she was sure Alex MacLeod could take care of himself. Even against a worthy foe like her mother.

Meg bowed her head slightly in greeting. "Laird MacLeod."

Her voice sounded steadier than she felt. To put it bluntly, the man flustered her. Simply standing beside him made her pulse race. Once again, she was uncomfortably aware of the vast difference in their sizes. She had to tilt her head back just to look at him. Though, admittedly, it was worth the effort. He really was quite magnificent. And imposing. He made her conscious of her own vulnerability, but at the same time, never had she felt so safe. An odd duality to be sure.

He answered with a curt bow. "Mistress Mackinnon."

Meg turned to her mother to explain. "I had the pleasure of making Laird MacLeod's acquaintance last night."

Her mother's brows lifted just a little too much to be believable. "You did?" Her eyes sparkled with mischief. She turned to Alex with a soft, chiding rap of her fan on his arm. "Why, you never mentioned it."

Alex frowned, obviously confused. "I believe I did—"

"I was just telling this dear boy about our misfortune on the road," her mother interrupted blithely.

Only her mother could call a man of at least thirty years standing well over six feet a "dear boy"—and mean it.

"But didn't he tell you?" Meg's innocent smile mirrored her mother's as her gaze shifted to Alex. "Laird MacLeod knows all the details of our attack."

"He does?" her mother asked, and this time her surprise was genuine.

Meg could swear she saw a muscle clench in Alex's jaw. Proof of his deception, perhaps? She held his gaze as she answered her mother. "Yes, I told him all about it last night."

His gaze sharpened, as if she'd surprised him. She

might enjoy prodding him, but Meg was not fool enough to voice her beliefs to her mother.

"Did the laird tell you that he was a soldier?"

Amazing, Meg thought. Her mother would have made an excellent inquisitor.

"We could use more men like him in Skye protecting our roads, especially near Dunakin, don't you think, Meg?"

Meg murmured something, trying to cover her acute embarrassment. Her mother was never one for subtlety. Though Meg supposed neither was she.

Her mother continued, completely unabashed, "It's a beautiful evening for dancing, isn't it, my laird?"

"Would you care to dance, my lady?"

Meg smothered her sudden snort of laughter with a cough. The flash of dry wit was unexpected, but delightfully so. She gave him an appreciative grin, and their eyes met in a moment of shared understanding that was strangely affecting. There was more to this forbidding soldier than met the eye.

Undeterred, her mother flashed a saucy smile. "Me?" She tapped him playfully with her fan again, as if he were a naughty schoolboy. "Oh, you're a horrible tease. I'm much too old for dancing. But . . ." She turned her eyes on Meg.

Alex didn't pretend to misunderstand this time. "Mistress Mackinnon, would you care to dance?"

Meg hesitated. There was something about Alex MacLeod that gave her pause. Just as had happened last night when he'd stood so close and his spicy masculine scent enveloped her, her body came alive with awareness. Whenever she was near him, she felt as if every nerve ending were set on edge. Waiting. Anticipating. For what, she did not know.

But she didn't like it.

On the other hand, her mother was probably already fast at work mentally compiling the guest list for the betrothal and picking out the color for Meg's elaborate bridal gown. Truth be told, if Meg stuck around much longer, Rosalind would probably ask Alex which color he preferred. At this point, dancing was likely her only means of escape from a potentially even more embarrassing situation.

One dance—surely there could be no harm in that?

Nodding her acceptance, Meg allowed Alex to lead her to the dance floor for a reel. Her hand slid into the bend of his arm, and she fought the urge to pull it back as if shocked. His muscles flexed beneath her fingertips. *Dear God, he was strong.* And hard as a rock.

Her heart beat a little faster.

He placed his hand on her back to guide her toward the dance floor, and a swift jolt surged through her. Her skin felt branded with his touch. She could *feel* him.

Meg flushed, and a strange heat spread over her. The force of her response was unsettling. What was wrong with her? She'd danced with many men, but never had she felt every touch, every movement, as powerfully as she did now. Alex MacLeod was dangerous. He made her mind race with things she'd never thought of before. Intimate things. Longings she'd thought buried.

They formed a small circle with another couple, and the reel began. Every time they came together and clasped hands or his hand fell firmly on her waist to turn her through the steps of the energetic dance, Meg felt a shock of pure heated awareness. She had to fight hard to concentrate on the dance steps, unable to get her mind away from the warm tingle that radiated from under his possessive hold.

Peeking out from beneath her lashes, she took the opportunity to study him closer. She could see the evidence of a hard life in the fine lines around his eyes and the thin scars peppered across his nose and cheeks, the telltale marks of a warrior. The slight dent in his chin and the strong angle of his jaw made him appear hard and forbidding. But his lashes were long and thick, and together with his sensual mouth, they softened an otherwise implacable face.

His expression, as always, was inscrutable. She wondered what he was thinking. Could he tell how affected she was by his touch?

Meg bit her lip. She hoped not. Unlike him, she was not accomplished at hiding her thoughts.

The sooner this dance was over, the better.

This dance was a mistake.

Alex had successfully avoided Meg Mackinnon all night, until Rosalind Mackinnon had sunk her teeth into him. That woman could teach his men something about dogged determination.

He could feel the weight of Meg's gaze upon him as they danced, and as he'd done throughout the long evening, he forced himself not to return her stare. She looked like an inquisitive little kitten with her big eyes and tiny face, and every time he looked at her, something inside him shifted.

Touching her was pure torture. He'd never been so damn aware of just how much touching there was in a reel. Each time he held her tiny hands in his or placed his hand on her waist to guide her through the steps, he didn't want to let go. The soft curve of her waist fit neatly in his palm. Too neatly. He longed to caress every sweet inch of her. To slide his hands over her breasts, down her hips, and around her backside, exploring every delectable curve. She was slight, but the feel of her hips hinted of a voluptuousness well hidden under her farthingale.

But it was the sight of her small white teeth nibbling on her plump lower lip that sent shards of lust bolting through him. His groin swelled with heat. The erotic movement cracked the cool reserve he'd struggled to maintain. The primitive desire he'd experienced on the battlefield came rushing back full force. He ached to taste her. To pull her into his arms and feel the press of her body against his. Each time he touched her, the narrow space between them seemed to crackle with anticipation. It would be so easy to lean down and cover her soft mouth with his, to run his tongue along the crease, to slide it in . . .

Hell. He was half-hard already. He took a sudden interest in the gilded wall over her shoulder.

The music had slowed, providing an opportunity for conversation that he wasn't sure he wanted. Breaking the silence, she said, "You don't have to worry, you know. I'll keep your secret."

His eyes fell to hers, betraying nothing. "What secret?" That he wanted to ravage every inch of her with his mouth? To leave her panting with need? To bring out the passion hiding under her serious façade and hear the cry of his name on her lips as she came apart in his arms?

"I *know* it was you who came to our rescue."

That secret. A small perverse part of Alex was pleased by her certainty, if not by her persistence. A corner of his mouth lifted in a half-smile. "I can see you've inherited your mother's tenacity."

She looked surprised, as if she'd never recognized the similarity before. A shy, adorable grin lit her features, wiping away all vestiges of the strain and worry that seemed fixed on her expression.

She should look like this always, he thought. Whatever burden she carried—and he was sure that she did carry one—was too heavy. He'd found himself watching her, wondering what made her look so serious. She was young and lovely, she should be having fun. Yet there was a maturity to her bearing that was at odds with her years.

But, he reminded himself, it wasn't his concern.

"Thank you," she said.

He hadn't meant it as a compliment, but she knew that.

"And that wasn't an answer," she reminded him.

"Was there a question?"

She gave him a chiding look. "It was implied. But if you insist, I shall spell it out: Was it you who came to our rescue?"

"You seem to think so."

"I *know* so."

"And how can you be so sure?"

"I'd hardly forget the man who saved my life."

Alex smiled at her indignant expression. "As much as I'd like to take credit for doing so, I'm afraid I cannot. *If* this man resembled me as much as you say he did, it must be my brother."

"So you said last night," she said dismissively. "But as

I said earlier, you can keep your secrets." She paused, and a gleam of something that made Alex nervous appeared in her eye: curiosity. "Though I do wonder why it should matter if you were in Lochalsh. Unless there is a reason you don't wish people to know you were near Skye?"

Damn, she did have a nimble mind. Meg Mackinnon was considered something of an oddity at court, "unusually bookish" was the term he'd heard bandied about. A euphemism for a smart woman that was intended to be unflattering. *Lowlanders were such fools*, he thought with disgust. If he was going to spend a lifetime with one woman, he'd make bloody well sure she was intelligent. "You have a suspicious nature, Mistress Mackinnon. Why should it matter if I were so near my home?"

"Why indeed. It is only natural that you would wish to see your brother after being gone for so long. He is your chief."

It was on the tip of his tongue to say something. To advance the rumor that he and his brother had suffered a falling-out. But for some reason, he did not want to lie to her any more than was necessary. Perhaps he'd already guessed how she would react to the news.

"It wasn't necessary. My brother will be arriving at court in a couple of weeks to present himself to the Privy Council," he explained, biting back his resentment at another of the king's onerous requirements to keep his Highland subjects in line—forcing the chiefs to present themselves in Edinburgh each year to account for their "good" behavior like naughty little children.

"Hmm," she said, but it was clear she did not believe him.

Alex feared his denial was merely whetting Meg Mackinnon's appetite for more. "Very well, you've found me out, it was me."

Her eyes narrowed, studying him. "You're just saying that."

He shrugged. "Does it matter? You are convinced you are correct, and I have just admitted as much. Isn't that what you wanted?"

Her brows furrowed. "No. Yes."

He smiled. "You can't have both."

She looked so frustrated, for a moment he considered admitting the truth. Though he barely knew her, he sensed he could trust her. But he could not risk it; he must stick to the plan. For now.

"How long have you been gone?" she asked.

"For some time." Before she could ask any more questions, he asked, "And what of you, Mistress Mackinnon? What brings you to court?"

He expected her to blush and murmur some excuse. But her wide green eyes met his without artifice. The color really was extraordinary. Soft moss green with tiny flecks of gold. He'd never seen their like. Nor could he recall ever paying so much attention to a woman's eye color before. It wasn't usually the first thing he noticed.

She considered him for a long moment. "May I be frank?"

He nearly chuckled. Could she be anything else? "Aye, of course," he murmured, hiding his amusement.

"What brings most young women to court?"

Alex stared at her, not bothering to hide his bemused admiration. Such candor was refreshing. He'd known the truth, though he hadn't expected her to admit it. Jamie Campbell had been only too eager to inform Alex of her purpose for being at court, presumably in an effort to discourage Alex from any interest he might have in the lass. Jamie had made her situation quite clear. She'd been sent to court to find a husband to help support her brother. A situation made imperative by the recent illness of her father. While at Dunvegan, Alex had been informed of the Mackinnon chief's recent illness, but Alex had forgotten that Meg's brother was said to be simple. He remembered how quickly she'd jumped to Lizzie's defense, and he suspected it was something she did quite often.

According to Jamie, Meg had been groomed to run the clan's lands. An enormous undertaking for one so young, Alex realized; no wonder the lass looked so weary. She pushed herself too hard. At some point, it was going to be too much. And now she must find her own husband? For a father to allow his daughter such a say in her choice of husband certainly spoke well of her good sense. But Alex suspected it also had contributed to the level of anxiety he read in her manner.

Despite his political differences with Jamie Campbell, Alex admitted that she could do much worse.

Meg Mackinnon, though tempting, was not for him. He'd do best to remember it.

"So it is time to find a husband?"

She was watching his reaction intently. "I'm afraid so."

"Why are you telling me this? It's not something young ladies usually admit."

A wry smile turned her mouth. "It's not exactly a secret. There is no point in hiding what is common knowledge." She lowered her voice conspiratorially. "I find it helps weed out the unsuitable candidates."

I'd imagine so. "A practical approach."

She beamed. "Exactly!"

Meg was nothing like the coy, jaded ladies who inhabited court. She was a breath of fresh air, like the warm, salty sea breeze that blew across Dunvegan. "And have you found anyone who is suitable?" he asked, more interested in her response than he wanted to admit.

The tiny lines appeared between her brows again. " 'Tis more complicated a decision than I anticipated."

She looked so discouraged, Alex found himself wanting to ease her worry. He wanted to make her laugh. He couldn't recall having that feeling in a long time.

Bending down, he whispered in her ear, "Ah, but you have one thing on your side that assures your success."

"What's that?"

"With your mother helping, I don't think you have anything to worry about."

Meg laughed. He was teasing her. This enormous, forbidding warrior was trying to make her laugh. And when he smiled back at her, really smiled at her, Meg realized something very disturbing. She could lose herself in this man.

The pure magic of that sensual smile shot like an arrow straight into her gut. For an agonizing moment, Meg was unable to look away, unable to contain the small excited flutter in her heart. His appeal was undeniable.

The music stopped, and she realized his hand was at her waist. He should have released her. But instead his hand pressed deeper against her, drawing her infinitesimally closer. She drew in her breath. His thumb stroked her lower back. She should pull away, but she couldn't move.

Their eyes locked, and against her better judgment her heart did an involuntary flip. It was that same intense look he'd given her on the battlefield. A look of desire. When he leaned closer to her, Meg gasped, thinking he meant to kiss her right here on the dance floor. In front of hundreds of people. And the worst part was that she didn't care.

As his face moved closer, she could see the crystal clear blue of his eyes and the soft golden tips of his eye-lashes. For a moment, she could feel his warm, spicy breath on her cheek.

But it was a whisper—not his mouth—that swept across her ear.

"You're lovely when you smile, you know." The words were not posed as a question. His voice was deep and rough, sending chills up her spine, leaving no doubt as to his sincerity. Nor could she deny the pleasure his words brought. He found her attractive.

Self-consciously, she lowered her lashes, not knowing how to respond. Unlike her mother, Meg was not used to receiving compliments or engaging in the flirtatious banter of court. Her tendency to speak her mind had scared off many a suitor, but Alex did not seem at all put off by her frankness. In fact, she sensed that he admired it. The realization warmed her.

"You look much like your mother, but—"

Meg stiffened and instinctively pulled back, knowing what he was about to say. A dull ache of disappointment throbbed in her chest. How could she be so foolish to think even for a moment that he would find her attractive? She smiled crookedly and finished for him: "But not the same."

"No," he said definitively. "Not the same."

Of course not. She wasn't surprised by his words, just by how much his honesty hurt. A twinge of longing pinched in her chest. What would it be like to be beautiful and admired?

He must have seen something on her face because he started to say, "That's not what I meant—"

But the next dance began, and Meg jumped at the opportunity to escape. She felt ridiculous. For a moment, she'd been foolish enough to think he might be interested in her. But Alex MacLeod would never desire a plain wren like Meg. That he didn't shouldn't come as such a surprise. She would never be beautiful like her mother, so long ago she'd given up trying. But she'd rather not have it pointed out so bluntly. It wasn't important, she told herself.

"You'll have to excuse me. I see Elizabeth and Jamie and must speak with them at once." She couldn't hide the overbrightness of her reply. Like a coward, she dashed away before he noticed her surprised hurt.

For a moment, she'd been distracted. She'd allowed herself to relax her guard. But even if she wanted to attract someone like Alex MacLeod, he would never want someone like her. He had his pick of the beautiful, willing women in this room. And Meg was none of those.

She hated this feeling of vulnerability. This feeling that he'd opened up a part of her that she'd fought hard to repress. Meg had devoted herself to her family, to her clan. Through hard work and sacrifice, she'd carved out an unusual place for herself in managing the Mackinnon lands. She liked the responsibility she'd earned. It should be enough.

But Alex MacLeod made her remember girlish longings she'd fought hard to forget.

Chapter 4

❖

Jamie intercepted her flight from the dance floor with a glass of claret. Despite his youth, he managed to look quite forbidding with a grim expression on his face.

"Are you all right? Did Alex say something to upset you?"

Obviously, he'd been watching her. Meg shook her head. "No. Of course not," she said, taking the glass from him.

"Alex MacLeod seems to be creating quite a bit of interest around here."

Meg heard a sharp edge to his voice that sounded suspiciously like jealousy. Not for the first time, she realized that Jamie was no longer a youthful companion, but a man, with a man's pride. "Has he?" she asked airily.

But Jamie wasn't fooled. He studied Alex with an assessing gaze. "You seemed fairly certain last night that it was Alex who helped your clansmen fight off the attack in the forest."

Absolutely sure. But Meg held her tongue. For some reason, Alex MacLeod didn't want anyone to know about his role in rescuing them from the attack. Fine. She supposed she owed him at least that much for helping them. Keeping her suspicions to herself was a small price to pay for the lives of her mother and her clansmen. Besides, she didn't relish listening to Elizabeth's teasing if she were to discover that Alex was Meg's mystery warrior. Heaven only knew what her mother would do with the information. Meg repressed a shudder. Alex MacLeod could keep his secrets. Though she did wonder why he chose to do so.

"I hope I didn't embarrass him. I never should have said anything. Now that I've had a chance to look at him closer, I can see it wasn't him," she said firmly. "I was mistaken." Meg felt a sharp pang of guilt for the lie and for how easily it slipped from her tongue. She, who never lied.

Jamie studied her face and seemed to be satisfied. "It does seem more likely that it was Rory. Alex has absented himself from Skye for many years."

She circled the rim of the glass with her finger. "Really?" she asked, careful not to sound too interested.

She could feel Jamie's eyes on her, watching her intently. "Yes. Apparently, Alex and Rory had a falling-out some time ago."

Her eyes flew to Jamie's face. This time she couldn't hide her surprise. "Did Alex MacLeod tell you that?"

He shook his head. "No. It's just another rumor being bandied about court. But it has the ring of truth to it. Rory was said to be unhappy about his brother fighting for the O'Neill. Alex is Rory's designated successor, his *tanaiste*. Or rather *was* his *tanaiste*. Rory claimed that Alex's allegiance belonged to him. And only to him."

It did. Meg could never consider a man who did not do his duty to his clan. Family loyalty was of utmost importance.

She felt a fresh stab of disappointment, reminiscent of

the reaction she'd had last night upon learning that the man she'd spent hours thinking about the past few weeks, her gallant knight in a yellow cotun, wasn't what she'd thought. She bit her lip, unable to forget the strange hurt she'd felt. He wasn't suitable, even if he was interested in her—which he obviously wasn't. She should have listened to the little voice in her head. The voice that warned he was wrong for her.

Hadn't she seen it for herself? Wasn't that what had troubled her that day in the forest? Every inch a battle-hardened warrior, he was a man born with a sword in his hand. Fighting consumed him. He wasn't hotheaded like Thomas Mackinnon; he was far too disciplined for that. But he teetered overly close to the edge of danger for her conservative sensibilities. She needed a stabilizing force, not a warmonger who would be off fighting someone else's wars.

If there had been any question as to his suitability before, there couldn't be now. If Alex MacLeod wasn't loyal to his own brother, how could he be to hers?

She shouldn't be so disappointed.

But she was.

She'd romanticized a man she knew nothing about. That was precisely the problem with succumbing to the dubious charm of attraction. Meg was surprised at herself. She usually had more sense. But when he'd looked at her with such soul-piercing intensity, she'd felt something so powerful that she'd responded without her usual deliberation.

Which only proved what she already knew. She must choose a husband with her head and not with her heart. Once before, she'd succumbed to the lure of a handsome face and the fierce pounding of her heart, and it had ended in disaster. She would never let that happen again.

Why was she even thinking about this? He wouldn't want someone like her. He'd danced with her because her mother had forced him into it. She didn't know what had provoked her to tell him of her search for a husband. Maybe she'd meant to discourage him. Not that he needed discouragement.

"Did you ask him about the rumors?" she asked.

Jamie nodded. "I did. He didn't deny it, but said it was none of my damn"—he cleared his throat—"business."

Meg shifted her attention back to Jamie, gazing at him thoughtfully. "Why are you telling me all this, Jamie?"

He shrugged. "I just thought you should know."

He was doing his best to look indifferent, but Meg realized her obvious interest in Alex MacLeod had perhaps had the unintended consequence of damaging Jamie's still youthful pride. It was a situation she must rectify.

"Loyalty is of the utmost importance to me, Jamie," she said truthfully. "You and Elizabeth have been nothing but true and loyal friends to me. I value your friendship greatly."

Jamie didn't bother to hide his pleasure. "I'm pleased to hear it. I just didn't want you to be disappointed."

I already am. With effort, Meg returned his smile. "How could I be? I don't even know the man."

"I thought I did, but Alex has changed much since the last time we met."

"How long ago was that?"

He thought for a minute. "Five, maybe six years ago.

Though he left my cousin's service over fifteen years past."

"Time enough for anyone to change."

"Alex is nothing like I remember. The years have hardened him. He's no longer the teasing youth always quick with a smile. Believe it or not"—he indicated with a quick flick of his head—"he used to be the lighthearted one."

Meg would have found it hard to believe except for her memories of his visit long ago and the glimpse of teasing she'd seen on the dance floor. She wondered what had caused him to harden.

Jamie paused reflectively. "Rory was the serious one, Alex more an instigator. But they were always close. Strange to think that so much could have changed. But I suppose as Alex grew to be a man, it would be difficult to be the younger brother of a legend like Rory Mor— Rory the Great."

Alex MacLeod didn't strike her as the type to be lost in anyone's shadow—no matter how broadly cast. He was too much in control. Too confident. Too much a leader in his own right. But Meg kept her opinions to herself.

Her gaze slid to Alex, and she was surprised to find him watching her. Or, rather, glaring at her. He looked almost . . . angry. There was something dark and frighteningly primitive in his eyes. The heated intensity of his gaze coiled around her and squeezed, taking her breath away.

It was a look of raw possession. Possession that spoke to her in a language she'd never heard before. Of desire, passion, and lust. For a moment she felt helpless, caught in his powerful trap. His eyes held her, just as surely as if he'd reached out across the room to claim her with his arms. She hated that she couldn't look away.

But he did. His eyes shuttered. And before she could catch her breath, he broke the connection, turned on his heel, and left the hall. Leaving her reeling.

What did this man do to her? He knocked her senseless merely by looking at her.

"Is everything all right, Meg?" Jamie asked, concerned. "You look as white as a sheet."

She took a long gulp of her claret, allowing the sweet liquid to calm her racing pulse. "I'm fine. Perhaps a little hungry, that's all."

Jamie offered her his arm. "Will you allow me to see you to the dining room?"

Meg fought the urge to look around for Alex. *Let it go, Meg. He's not for you. You need a man like . . . Jamie.*

Jamie was the answer. He was where she should concentrate her efforts. Then why was she vacillating? It wasn't like her to procrastinate. But there was so much at stake if she chose wrong. It was too important a decision to rush to judgment. She needed proper time for deliberation and analysis; but time was the one thing she didn't have.

She'd always thought of her father as invincible, but his recent illness had shown her just how fragile life could be. How everything could change in an instant.

She should have known better. A vivid memory flashed before her eyes of one hot spring day when the course of her life had changed just as quickly.

Meg ran to the library with her hand over her mouth, trying to contain the laughter bubbling inside.

She'd just been swimming with the village children in the loch, and Ian had made himself a crown of buttercups and dubbed himself King of the May. Ian was always doing funny things to make them laugh. She was eager to tell her mother. She'd been so sad lately; surely this would bring a smile to her face. The door was open, and the sound of her mother's tears brought her to a dead halt.

"She's sure?" her father asked.

Meg heard the muffled sounds of her mother's sobs.

"No more children," her father echoed. "No more sons." Meg could hear the crush of disappointment resonate in his voice. "Who will be chief when I'm gone?" he asked, almost as if to himself.

That is strange, Meg thought. Ian, who else?

"Ian will never be able to manage on his own," he said.

And with his words, Meg was forced to acknowledge what she'd fought so long to ignore. Something inside her knew that fifteen-year-old boys shouldn't be making crowns of buttercups and dancing around a tree.

"I'm sorry," her mother choked.

"Shush, my love. There'll be no more of that. We'll think of something. But men are hard to find in our family. If I had a brother, uncle, cousin, anything . . . No, Ian is the only possibility. But even if I name Ian tanaiste, his succession as chief will be challenged. If not from within the clan, then from outside when I am gone." She heard her father sigh, the sound ripe with disappointed resignation. "If only Meggie were a lad, she'd make a fine chief."

Meg could still feel her heart breaking for Ian. Her big, strong, handsome older brother who was kind and sweetly innocent. Who cared that he didn't read or do his sums as well as she did? Or that he was sometimes awkward around strangers? Meg loved him the way any girl would love her older brother. Perhaps she even loved him a little bit more, because he needed her so badly. She was his buffer from a cruel world. But she could not protect him from everything. He understood so much more than people realized. He knew when he was doing something wrong or lacking. The hardest part was watching his growing frustration as he tried to please her father.

If only Meggie were a lad, she'd make a fine chief. It was that offhand comment that had sparked the beginnings of a plan. She would help Ian. For the last ten years, she'd dedicated herself to the clan, to learning the business of managing the lands and handling the financial concerns of Clan Mackinnon.

But she needed to find a man who would stand beside her brother where she could not in his dealings with the king's men and who would fight beside him if need be. A clan was only as strong as its chief. When her brother inherited, their land would be at grave risk from attack by more powerful clans—clans that constantly sought more land to provide for their ever increasing numbers. Her father's guardsmen were no longer young, they might not be able to protect Ian's position, so Meg's choice of husband was crucial.

With her help and her husband's support, Ian would make a fine chief. Ian was her father's *tanaiste,* his designated successor. That position was his by right of birth, but vestiges of tanistry from the old Brehon Laws made some think it could be challenged. On Skye, he was derisively known as "Ian Balbhan." Ian the Dumb. She despised the epithet and had done her best to shield her brother from others' cruelty.

And from her father's disappointment.

Her chest tightened with the pressure of expectation. She'd worked so hard to prove to her father that it could be done. She had to do the right thing. There wasn't room for mistakes. Really, there was only one choice.

And it was up to her to make it.

So much for fairy tales. No one was going to ride in on a white horse and make her decision easy for her.

Alex MacLeod was not for her. She was attracted to him in a way that she never had been attracted to a man before. But it did not matter. She would not let it interfere with her decision. He was a mercenary. A warrior. A man of the past. Men like Alex harkened to a bygone era. A time of feuds and forays and the unfettered authority of the chief. The role of the Highland chief was changing. No longer just a warlord, he must also be prepared to deal with the king and his men.

She needed a man to put the king's men at ease. Alex was a threatening presence the moment he walked into the room. Every inch a Highland warrior, he was exactly the type of powerful man these Lowlanders feared.

She took a long look at Jamie, who stood patiently beside her, not allowing her thoughts to slide back to the forbidding man who'd just exited the hall. The man who threw her emotions into a tumult.

Taking a deep breath, she placed her hand on the crook of Jamie's arm. This time, there was no shock.

The lean muscle beneath her fingers did not elicit wild, uncontrollable emotions.

She was tired of this charade. Meg was out of her element at court, and she knew it. Jamie Campbell was the most logical choice for a husband.

There was only one decision she could make.

Chapter 5

Alex left the hall unaccountably edgy, if not down-right angry. And the worst part was that he didn't know why.

After slipping outside the palace gates, he started down Vai Regius, the Way of the King—a cobble-paved road recently constructed by King James that stretched between Holyrood and Edinburgh Castle. Although he'd made no effort to hide his departure, he was care-ful to make sure he wasn't followed. Most people seemed to have accepted his story about being a merce-nary looking for work, but Highlanders were always viewed with suspicion. He'd take no chances.

Alex was late. He was supposed to be meeting his squire, Robbie, at the White Hart Inn to report what he'd learned so far, but he'd been delayed. Delayed by a wee enchantress with big green eyes. Instead of observ-ing the king's men to gather more information, he'd found himself watching Meg's conversation with Jamie Campbell with increasing frustration. He'd seen some-thing in her eyes. . . .

He suspected she'd made her choice.

But, he reminded himself, it didn't concern him. Alex had made his own choice a long time ago, and it didn't involve taking a wife. His future was uncertain at best and short at worst.

He'd been tempted to go to her after his awkward compliment on the dance floor. She'd misunderstood, but he realized that he'd hit on a vulnerability when he'd made an unwitting comparison with her mother. Rosalind Mackinnon was undeniably a beautiful woman, but so was her daughter. Everything about her was . . . endearing. Irresistible softness to a man who'd known only hardship for so long. Didn't Meg realize how lovely she was? *No.* It suddenly occurred to him that she almost seemed to go out of her way not to emphasize her beauty, hiding herself beneath ill-fitting clothes and unflattering hairstyles. Even he had almost missed it.

The flash of hurt in her eyes had unsettled him deeply. *Hell,* he thought with frustration. *She* unsettled him. Meg was the first woman in four years to make him think about anything other than revenge, justice, and atonement.

He'd do his best to steer clear of her.

As he neared the city, the pungent stench of excrement burned the back of his throat. The vile cesspool of intrigue and corruption that permeated court seemed to have spilled onto the streets. Literally. *And they think we are barbarians,* he thought with disgust. At least Highlanders don't toss waste out their windows to run in open sewers with merely a warning shout of "Gardyloo!"

The smell was revolting, and on a warm night like tonight, unbearable. Even to a man who was used to the primitive conditions afforded the life of an outlaw, the filth of Edinburgh was nearly inconceivable.

He used the edge of his cloak to smother the stench.

The faint scent of lavender still clung to the wool, courtesy of his brother's wife, Isabel, he supposed. Upon his arrival at Dunvegan, she'd threatened to toss most of his clothing into the fire, relenting only after he'd agreed to allow her to see to its washing.

The sweet reminder from home made him even more anxious to leave this woe-begotten place. Court was a necessary but unwelcome stop to gather information before he set course for the Isle of Lewis. If the rumor of a second attempt by the Fife Adventurers to colonize Lewis proved correct, Alex would ferret out whatever information he could to help his kin, the MacLeods of Lewis, thwart the incursion. But Lewis was where the real battle would be fought . . . and won.

If he could leave for Lewis right now, he would.

One step at a time, he reminded himself. But damn, he was eager to begin. Preventing the king from claiming Lewis would be a resounding victory for the Island chiefs, but in helping his kin, the MacLeods of Lewis, Alex would finally have the chance to right a wrong that had shadowed him for five long years.

He knew he trod a treacherous path. If he were caught, here or later on Lewis, his actions could well be construed as treason.

But it was worth the risk.

Because of that risk, his brother had tried to stop him, but eventually Alex had persuaded Rory that no one else would suffice. Alex had both position and familiarity with court, as well as access to Jamie Campbell and other important political leaders. And as for his ability to lead the battle on Lewis, it had taken two hours on the lists with Rory—ending only with Isabel threatening to separate them by dousing them both with cold water—to convince his brother of Alex's readiness.

Initially, Rory had wanted to lead the rebellion himself, but there could be no question of that. Rory's first duty, as chief, was to his clan. He had to placate the king, at least nominally.

Alex didn't.

He'd never envied Rory his role as chief. Unlike his brother, Alex was free to follow his conscience and his own sense of justice. He'd done precisely that for the last three years. Not long after leaving Dunvegan, Alex had joined with a handful of dispossessed warriors who used to go by the name MacGregor. King James had turned the MacGregors into outlaws on their own lands—hunted like vermin, persecuted, and jailed without cause. Forbidden on pain of death even to call themselves MacGregor. The injustice and atrocities perpetrated by the king sickened him, and it wasn't long before Alex had become the leader of the proscribed men. Fighting his way across the Highlands, he'd found a modicum of peace.

The ten o'clock drum sounded. He quickened his pace through Lawnmarket, keeping to the main streets and avoiding the maze of narrow wynds and closes that permeated the city. After turning left on West Bow, he wound down the steep hill into Grassmarket. A thriving marketplace, Grassmarket also had the dubious distinction of being the place where public executions were held. Not an area of town frequented by courtiers. Alex was hoping to minimize the possibility of seeing someone from the palace.

Having reached his destination, he opened the door of the White Hart Inn and had to duck his head to pass

through the doorway. Musty air and the scent of un-
washed bodies accosted him. The main room was small
and poorly lit, holding perhaps a score of patrons who
were scattered about at small tables; a few stood near
the bar area, where a "luckie" alewife stood ready to
dispense her brew. He ordered a tankard of grozet from
a serving maid and passed through to another chamber,
this one slightly smaller than the first. Low ceilings continued, and Alex repeatedly had to stoop beneath the
wooden beams as he crossed the room.

Screens of brown paper separated the tables, offering
a semblance of privacy. After quickly locating Robbie,
Alex slid in opposite him on a wooden bench, facing the
door. He was pleased to see that the lad had followed his
direction and secured a table in the back corner of the
room, minimizing the potential for prying ears.

His squire looked relieved to see him.

Amused by Robbie's obvious concern for his welfare,
Alex said, "So eager to see me, lad? Apparently, I've
been negligent in my duty. I'll have to see that your
training is stepped up when I'm done here."

Robbie blanched, then ventured a tentative grin when
he realized that Alex was only teasing. He cranked his
head around a few times and whispered, "I don't much
like this place." He wrinkled his nose. "The entire city
smells something horrible."

Neither do I. But it would do no good to mollycoddle
the boy; they had a job to do. So instead Alex asked,
"Any problems?"

With so many of the king's men about, Edinburgh
was a dangerous place for a MacGregor. Normally, Alex
would have his squire with him at court, but he couldn't
take any chances that the lad would be identified.

Robbie shook his head. "No, my laird."

"Patrick and the others?"

"They're ready."

"Good." While Alex discovered what he could at court, Patrick and the rest of Alex's warriors would blanket the taverns and alehouses frequented by mercenaries and soldiers, listening for rumors of any forces leaving for the Isles. Robbie would take messages back and forth between Alex and his men. His youth and comparatively less imposing stature would make it easier for him to slip in and out unnoticed.

"Have our friends arrived?" Robbie asked in code, referring not to friends, but to the Lowland scourge intent on sailing for Lewis.

"As we expected, not all of them could make it."

Robbie's eyes lit with understanding. The absence of key Lowland gentlemen at court supported the rumor that the Fife Adventurers were gathering for a second attempt on Lewis.

"Will they be traveling this summer?" Robbie asked.

"I don't know yet. But if they want to be settled by winter, they will have to leave soon. I hope to have more information by the end of the week."

Robbie nodded.

Alex cast his gaze around the room, making sure they were not the subject of undue attention. "We will meet again on Saturday a week hence. We should be able to speak more freely then."

"Where?"

"Beyond the city gates. A place called Sheep's Heid Inn. Have you heard of it?"

Robbie shook his head. "No, but I'll find it."

"It's situated at the eastern edge of Holyrood Park, at

the rear of archer's seat, in the village of Duddingston. Wait for me. I don't know what time I'll be able to slip away."

Alex gave him a hard look. Robbie was quick with a blade, but so many things could go wrong. "Have care, Robbie. The city can be a dangerous place for a lad on his own."

The boy couldn't hide his pleasure, proud to have drawn his laird's concern. Alex didn't know what had come over him. A week at Dunvegan with his brother and wife, and he had grown soft. But attachments and war, he knew, didn't mix.

Unbidden, his thoughts slid back to the wee green-eyed enchantress.

Robbie slid off the bench and stood up. "And you have care as well, my laird."

Alex chuckled. "Get out of here before I decide to step up that training now."

Robbie flashed a jaunty grin and left before Alex could make good on his word.

Leaning back on the bench, Alex took a moment to relax as he scanned the room and its occupants. Taverns and alehouses were the great equalizers. Perhaps a dozen men from all strata of society mingled in apparent ease and drunken camaraderie. A couple of men slid into the compartment in front of him. Wedged into the corner and hidden in the shadows, Alex doubted they could see him. But neither could he see them. He was just about to stand up to leave when one of the men began to speak in Erse with a brogue that identified him as a Highlander.

"You'll get no more money from me until the job is done."

"But I lost most of my men in the first attack," the second man complained. "I'll need to find replacements before I can try again."

A Highlander also, Alex realized.

"That is not my concern. You were paid well for your skills." The man's voice rose in anger. "Skills that were obviously exaggerated if you could allow a group of vagrants to defeat you."

"These were no vagrants, but trained warriors. I've never seen any man fight like their leader. He fought with the strength of five men."

The first man snorted his disbelief. "So you've said. But that doesn't explain how a handful of men defeated a score of your cutthroats."

"It won't happen again. It was bad luck that they came upon us as they did. I'll finish the job, but it might take some time. It will be more difficult finding an opportunity in Edinburgh."

Alex heard the loud bang of a tankard slammed on the table. "Which wouldn't be necessary had you done the job right in the first place. I don't want to hear your excuses. Just get it done. Now. Or 'tis you who will be the hunted."

That the men had some foul purpose in mind was obvious, but there was something else about the conversation that bothered him. A feeling. They could have been speaking about the attack on the Mackinnons. Alex had assumed the attack had been random. But what if it hadn't been? Could someone have been after Meg or her mother? But why? For what purpose?

Alex shook his head. He was being ridiculous. There was nothing in the men's conversation to tie them to the attack on Meg. It was surely just a coincidence.

He turned back to his drink but could not quiet the persistent niggle of uncertainty. Was it too much of a co-incidence? Could there have been another attack foiled in the Highlands by a group of skilled warriors?

The men stood up to leave. Alex slid out just enough on his bench to get a look at them. The first man was thinly built and of average height, with dark hair and sharply pointed features. His nose was long with a slight hook, and his eyes were deeply set with hooded lids. The second man had his back to him. He was large and heavyset, with scraggly dark red hair. Both men wore simple leather breeches and jerkins. Neither one seemed familiar, but Alex hadn't seen all the attackers that day. Some of the villains had scattered quickly.

He was being foolish. Meg Mackinnon was a distraction he couldn't afford. His sole focus must be on his mission. He took a final swig of his ale and set his tankard forcefully down on the wooden table.

But what if . . .

Alex cursed. He didn't want to be drawn into the web of Meg Mackinnon. He *should* just walk away. But he just couldn't ignore the sliver of suspicion. He'd keep an eye on her for a while, just to make sure. But as soon as he allayed this unreasonable concern, he intended to for-get all about Meg Mackinnon.

Chapter 6

❖

Now that she'd made her decision, Meg was anxious to have the matter resolved. Jamie had given her every indication that he intended to offer for her, and she intended to give him every opportunity to do so. But in the past few days, she'd seen very little of him.

Once she had secured a proposal, she could return to Dunakin Castle and the Isle of Skye. She'd been away from her father and brother for too long. Not to mention that she would have hours of reports to go over when she returned. But she knew that wasn't the only reason she was so eager to leave Holyrood. Meg wanted to distance herself from Alex MacLeod and the strange feelings he aroused in her. Try as she might, she could not get the blasted man out of her head. It was embarrassing, really. She had always been careful to approach things logically, never allowing emotions to rule her head. But she couldn't forget the way he'd looked at her or the way it felt when he'd had his hands—his very large, capable hands—on her. And neither could she forget the strength of her reaction to him or how much it had hurt when he'd found her appearance lacking.

It didn't matter.

She'd made her decision. It was Jamie and not Alex MacLeod she should be worrying about.

When Jamie had not met them for a morning walk around the gardens as he usually did, Meg hadn't been concerned. But when he'd skipped the midday meal, she'd wondered what could be keeping him. Jamie was usually so attentive, it was odd to have seen so little of him. Elizabeth mentioned that he'd received a missive from their cousin the Earl of Argyll this morning and had gone to discuss something with Lord Chancellor Seton. But she hadn't heard from him since.

But it was her mother who truly gave Meg cause for concern. She was definitely up to something. Rosalind had spoken to Jamie earlier and had the look of a contented cat afterward. And it was her mother who had pointed her in the direction of the lord chancellor's apartments.

Meg was not at all familiar with this wing of the palace—the section housing the apartments of Lord Chancellor Seton and his Privy Council. At court, unlike at Dunakin with her father, Meg did her best to avoid political discussions. She could see both sides of the issues facing her Highland clansmen and their Lowland adversaries, but at Holyrood there was no place for rational discourse. At Holyrood, it was all about power. And the king's was greater than it had been in over one hundred years, since the fall of the Lordship of the Isles in 1493 to James IV. Change was coming for the Highlands, whether the chiefs wished it or not.

To prosper, the Mackinnons must learn to navigate the treacherous maze of Lowland government.

She strode purposefully down the corridor, methodically stopping to peer in each lavishly decorated room as she passed. Like the rest of the palace, the rooms had gilt-encrusted walls, heavily carved ceilings, and sumptuous jewel-toned velvets upholstered on the furniture. The king had been in debt for most of his reign, but his palaces showed no evidence of frugality.

Most of the chambers were empty, but a few, like this one, were occupied. Meg quickly scanned the men converging in the small antechamber for a tall man with a healthy head full of dark auburn hair. Not such an easy task in a palace full of Scotsmen.

Yet despite the profusion of red-haired men, something about Jamie stood out. It wasn't just his size or handsome countenance. That realization took her aback. Jamie was actually quite handsome. She frowned. Odd that she'd never really noticed before. In some ways, Jamie was like a brother to her, as Elizabeth was like a sister. The three of them spent a great deal of time together. In addition to literature and philosophy, they discussed land administration, clan tensions, and politics. The Campbells were both open-minded and well-informed. She knew the way Jamie's mind worked. She understood him. And he understood how hard she'd struggled to prove herself. Jamie would help her brother, leaving her free to manage the clan lands. Ian's position would be protected with Jamie as her husband.

Moreover, Meg genuinely liked Jamie Campbell. And he was fond of her.

It would be enough. More important, her father would be thrilled with her choice.

Meg had just about given up her search when she heard voices coming from a room that she'd overlooked at the end of a dark corridor. She lifted her heavy skirts and hurried toward the sounds. Pausing at the entrance of a small library, she anxiously searched through the group of men gathered to pass the afternoon with the time-honored masculine pursuits of drinking and gaming.

And at last she found him, seated at a table, playing cards with the person she most wanted to avoid—Alex MacLeod. She fought the urge to turn right around. By now, she should have grown accustomed to his presence. But the effects of proximity to the man had not lessened one whit. Meg struggled to control the race of her pulse and the overwhelming sensation of heightened awareness that seemed to flow simply from being within a hundred paces of him.

Determined not to be affected, she turned immediately to Jamie. "Jamie, here you are. I've been looking for you."

Befuddled, Jamie said, "I'm sorry, Meg, was I supposed to meet you someplace?"

"No, but there is something I would like to discuss with you." Her eyes flicked to Alex. "In private, if you don't mind."

Alex looked annoyed by her interruption. He leaned back and crossed his arms. His bulging muscular arms, folded across his broad chest, strained against the fabric of his thick doublet. Her mouth went dry. Such a raw display of manly power left her in a bit of a stupor. She'd never noticed how alluring arms could be. What would it feel like to be enfolded by those strong arms and crushed against that hard, broad chest?

"As you can see, Mistress Mackinnon, Jamie here and I are in the middle of a hand of maw," he said, indicating the cards before him. He glanced around meaningfully. "Surely your discourse can wait."

Jamie frowned at Alex. "Of course we can take a break—"

"That's all right, Jamie," Meg interrupted. "I don't mind waiting." Now that she'd found Jamie, she didn't know exactly what she planned to say. She bit her lip. How exactly did one let a man know one was willing to accept a proposal that had yet to be made?

She felt Alex's gaze upon her. His eyes were fixed on her mouth. They darkened, and suddenly self-conscious, Meg pressed her lips closed.

She stood beside the table in silence, trying—albeit unsuccessfully—to be inconspicuous in a room bereft of another feminine form. If she'd taken the time to look around before entering, she might not have been so hasty to barge in.

Rather than inadvertently catch any of the curious glances that flickered her way, Meg attempted to follow the play of cards. Although maw was the favorite card game of King James's court, she preferred games of logic like chess. There was too much luck involved in cards.

It wasn't simply being the only woman in the room that was bothering her. It was precisely *who* was in the room.

The men assembled were the elite of Scotland's kingless government, those left in charge while the king wooed his new English subjects. Secretary Balmerino stood talking with Comptroller Scone and Lord Advocate Hamilton. The Marquess of Huntly, one of the "Great Lords," was playing chess with the sole privy councillor from the Highlands, Kenneth Mackenzie. Several other privy councillors were dispersed throughout the room. The only men missing were Lord Chancellor Seton and the justice general—the Earl of Argyll—the other Great Lord.

These men were the rulers of Scotland—subject to the

king's directives, of course. Although Meg was aware that on occasion the king's writ did not always run all the way to Scotland. Doubtless it was far easier to ignore the words of a king relegated to paper hundreds of miles away than it was to deny the king in person.

Overwhelmingly, with the notable exception of the two men before her and the Mackenzie chief, the men were Lowlanders. Jamie Campbell's presence among the men could be explained by his close connection to his cousin Argyll, but what was Alex doing here? She would not have thought that the brother of a Highland chief would be sympathetic to the king's Lowland leadership. And she knew enough of the clan feuds on Skye to realize that the MacLeods and the Mackenzies despised one another. Alex's brother, the chief of MacLeod, had killed the Mackenzie's father and older brother a few years back.

So why was a Highlander, and a mercenary to boot, socializing with his enemies?

Meg's eyes widened at a disturbing thought. Unless they weren't his enemies.

Alex was furious at Meg's interruption. This was the closest he'd been to the king's minions, the de facto rulers of Scotland, since he'd arrived. It had taken quite some maneuvering to insinuate himself among these men. But Meg Mackinnon had rendered all of his efforts for naught.

At every turn, she seemed to place an obstacle in his path. First, voicing her suspicions of his presence near Skye to Jamie, then taking his mind from his mission last night and embroiling him in a murderous plot overheard at a tavern, and now barging into a room in the midst of conversations he'd hoped to hear more of.

His lack of progress over the last week was frustrating. There was much to be gleaned from careful observation, but he'd hoped to catch at least a stray comment or two. But so far, he'd heard nothing of the Isle of Lewis or the Fife Adventurers.

Mayhap the silence said it all.

The king's men were wary of him, and justifiably so. His task would require finesse. He did not want to overplay his part as the hired sword arm on the outs with his brother. But subtlety required time, a luxury he did not have. If he was going to discover any useful information, Alex knew he was going to have to take some risks.

He peered over the edge of his cards at Meg. She was doing her best to appear oblivious, but he could see by the slight flush on her cheeks and the brightness in her eyes that she was uncomfortable. Good. So was he. The lass had become a thorn in his side for more reasons than one. She drove him to distraction. Her mere presence toyed with his senses. Did she have to smell like damn roses all the time? And did she have to chew on her lip with that adorably pensive look on her face? He could almost hear her mind work. Worse, he found himself wondering what she would say next. He couldn't concentrate on anything else when she was in the room.

The most innocent of movements or gestures seemed sensual and provocative when she made them. Captivated, he watched as she repeatedly attempted to tuck away a stray lock of hair that had loosened from its taut moorings, her dainty fingers drawing attention to the long ivory line of her neck and the tiny pink shell of her ear. He wanted to tear out the pins that bound her hair and bury his face against her neck and hair, inhaling the sweet fragrance that he knew would be intoxicatingly intense. He'd run his mouth along the smooth soft velvet of her neck, take her tiny ear between his teeth, and kiss her until she writhed in his arms. And he wouldn't stop there. He felt the blood rush to his cock; he stiffened, imagining all that he'd like to do.

"Do I have a smudge on my face?" she asked.

Her question snapped him from his lust-filled trance, but the ache in his groin would not be so easily dismissed. He was hard as a damn rock. "No. Why?" His voice sounded rough, even to his own ears.

"You're staring at me."

Only Meg would be so innocently blunt. Alex nearly flushed like some besotted squire and not a man with enough experience, more than enough experience, to know better. What the hell was the matter with him? Holding his expression impassive, he carefully lifted one brow. "Am I? I didn't realize. Nice of you to point it out."

But Meg either missed or chose to ignore the sarcasm. "And you had quite a furious expression on your face," she added primly. "You're liable to scare people half out of their wits if you don't temper those dark looks."

"I'll try to remember that," Alex said dryly.

Jamie looked decidedly smug. Tossing him a fierce glare, Alex dared him to crack a smile.

Since she'd apparently ruined his chances of overhearing anything of import right now, he might as well do what he could to allay his other concern. Her safety.

Alex tossed another card on the table and glanced over at her. Briefly.

"Have you had word about whether they have captured any of the men who attacked you?"

She shook her head. "No. My father is certain they've

left the area." She beamed at Jamie. "Thanks to Jamie, his cousin sent his men to aid in the search. They've scoured every inch of Lochalsh, but to no avail."

I'm sure they have, Alex thought. He knew from experience how thorough Argyll's men could be. "Did you by chance recognize any of the men who attacked you?"

She appeared taken aback. "Should I have?"

Alex shrugged.

"No. I'd never seen any of the men before." Her eyes narrowed. "You can't be thinking that someone attacked us on purpose?"

Once again, Alex found himself impressed by her quick thinking. "It did cross my mind."

"You've been too long at battle, my laird. You see war in places where it is not."

Alex's temper flared. Not because she was wrong, but because she just might be right. Had he grown so distrustful that he was seeing trouble everywhere?

"What reason would someone have to attack Meg and her mother?" Jamie asked.

Alex had considered this issue most of the night. He had a few theories. "It's no secret that Mistress Mackinnon has a large fortune."

"The men who attacked us were not interested in my fortune. If they had been, they would have tried to abduct me. But the cutthroats were intent on killing, not on taking hostages."

"What of feuds?" Alex asked. "Is your father at war with anyone?"

She shook her head. "The past few years have been peaceful. Nothing more than a few exchanges of cattle with the MacDonalds."

Alex's fingers tightened around his glass, the only outward sign of the turmoil inside him unleashed with the name MacDonald. But as much as he'd like to lay blame at his enemy's feet, Meg was right: Lifting cattle was no cause for the murder of women.

"If you had been there"—she paused meaningfully— "you would have seen it for yourself. This was a random attack perpetrated by brigands, nothing more."

"Unfortunately, it's all too common an occurrence in the Highlands," Jamie said. "Do you have reason to believe it was not a random attack, Alex?"

Did he? A vague discussion of a murderous plot in an Edinburgh tavern hardly qualified. He shook his head. "No."

Jamie stared at him for a long moment before turning back to Meg. "Perhaps you should exercise a bit of caution just to make sure."

Meg laughed. "If someone intended me or my mother harm, court would be the last place they'd try anything. There are people everywhere. I long for a bit of privacy." She smiled sweetly at Jamie. "Besides, I have you to look after me."

Alex stiffened. His entire body rebelled at the idea of another man protecting her. But it was clear what she'd decided, though Jamie had not yet realized it.

Jamie shifted uncomfortably in his chair. "Yes, well, about that, Meg. It seems I may be gone for a bit." Obviously not concentrating on the play of cards at the table, he errantly tossed out a knave of trumps, which Alex scooped up. "I must leave tomorrow on some business for my cousin Argyll."

Business that Alex suspected had something to do with the Fife Adventurers' plan to invade the Isle of Lewis. Upon receiving the letter from his cousin Argyll this morning, Jamie had gone immediately to the lord chancellor's chambers. Alex had tagged along. Something was going on, and he intended to find out what.

Meg's face fell. "But you can't go now, not when I—" She stopped what she'd been about to say, but Alex could fill in the blanks. Not when she'd decided on Jamie. "How long will you be gone?" she asked instead.

"A few days, perhaps one or two longer. MacLeod here has agreed to escort your mother, you, and Elizabeth over the next few evenings." Jamie's words were uttered with the reluctance of an extracted tooth. It was clear he did not like the idea of Alex escorting Meg anywhere.

"That won't be necessary," Meg said quickly. "I'm sure Laird MacLeod has other obligations that require his attention. I daresay we will be fine on our own for a few days."

Alex locked his gaze on hers. "I'm afraid it has already been decided."

"What do you mean?"

"Did I mention that your mother suggested the arrangement?"

Meg groaned.

Alex could commiserate. Rosalind Mackinnon was a force of nature. Somehow he'd found himself the conscripted escort of three ladies without uttering a word. But he supposed this would give him an opportunity to keep an eye on Meg and assure himself that the attack in the forest was as random as she thought.

He didn't know whether it was the prospect of Jamie leaving or Alex staying that had Meg so upset. But she was clearly agitated by the news.

"No wonder she . . . ," Meg said, more to herself.

"No wonder she what?" Alex asked.

"Nothing," she said quickly. "But how did my mother even know of your leaving?" she asked Jamie.

"By chance, your mother intercepted us in the corridor on our way here," he explained. "She brought up the masque—"

"You will be gone for the masque?" Meg sounded so crestfallen, Alex felt a strange urge to sweep her into his arms and soothe her obvious distress.

"I'm afraid there is no avoiding it," Jamie answered apologetically. "I'll not make it back from Argyllshire by the end of the week."

Her shoulders sagged. "Are you sure you have to leave right now?"

Alex could hear the strain in her voice. The burden of her decision was clearly a weight she wanted lifted. The urge to offer her comfort intensified. At that moment, she seemed fragile and very young.

"Unfortunately, it cannot be avoided, Meg. You know my cousin. Argyll will not be put off."

"Well, it appears that it has all been decided," she said truculently. "I will see you upon your return."

"But I thought you wished to speak to me?" Jamie said. "We are just about done here."

"Apparently, it will have to wait." She was angry, though at whom, Alex didn't know. Shoulders rigid, she turned on her heel and flounced out of the room.

The easy sounds of conversation that had died down when Meg had entered the room returned upon her swift departure. They finished the game, but Alex didn't like the way Jamie was watching him.

Alex stood up to leave. He'd get no information here,

and he had another possible source to explore. But Jamie stopped him.

"What did you hear?" Jamie asked, his voice steely.

Alex considered his former friend with calculated interest. Jamie had guessed that there was more to the story than Alex had let on. Campbell was unusually cunning for his age, though with Argyll for a mentor, he shouldn't be surprised.

He decided to tell him the truth. "Nothing specific." He recounted the conversation he'd overheard at the tavern.

"You're right. It's not much to go on." Jamie paused thoughtfully. "You're sure they were Highlanders?"

"Yes."

"There was no mention of women?"

Alex shook his head. He'd asked himself these same questions all night. "Most likely it's a coincidence."

"Undoubtedly," Jamie agreed. "Lawlessness is endemic in the Highlands. I'm sure Meg and her party were not the only travelers to be attacked recently."

Both men were silent, mulling the situation, neither one completely convinced. Alex would wager Jamie was thinking the same thing he was: *What if they were wrong?*

"I'll stay," Jamie said. "My cousin's errand can wait."

Alex gave a snort of laughter. He knew Argyll. "And what will you tell him? That you are refusing to do his bidding because of a conversation overheard in a tavern?"

Jamie clenched his jaw, saying nothing.

Alex realized that Jamie Campbell was going to be a problem for him. Thus far he'd taken Alex at his word, but he didn't know how much longer Jamie would continue to do so. He'd begun to suspect that Jamie was just as interested in keeping Alex close as the other way around. Jamie was already suspicious. It would be disastrous if Jamie found out Alex's true purpose at court and thought it his duty to warn his cousin. If the Island chiefs were to have any success in defeating another attempt to colonize Lewis by the Fife Adventurers, Alex could not let that happen. Since it was becoming clear that Alex would get no information from Jamie, it would be best for his mission if Jamie left court.

"Go. I'll guard her with my life," Alex said, realizing that he meant it.

Jamie's gaze sharpened. "What interest do you have in Meg Mackinnon?"

Alex wiped all expression from his face. "None."

"You want her."

He didn't bother to deny it. "Who wouldn't?"

Jamie looked at him oddly. "So you find Meg attractive?"

The corner of Alex's mouth lifted at Jamie's jest. It took him a moment to realize Campbell wasn't joking. "Of course. Don't you?"

Jamie looked troubled. "Yes, but at court Meg is not revered for her beauty as much as she is known for her unusual intelligence and frank manner."

Alex scoffed, "Blind fools."

Jamie's mouth lifted in a half-smile. "In this we are in agreement." But his smile soon faded, and his eyes turned wintry. "But you'll do nothing about it, because you know you have *nothing* to offer her."

Jamie's words hit him like a blow to the chest. He clenched his jaw but otherwise gave no indication of their impact.

"I intend to marry her," Jamie said. "Do you offer the same?"

No. And for a moment, Alex regretted it. Striding to the door, he said, "I'm sure she'll be very happy."

The worst part was that he knew it was true.

An hour later, Meg had still not found her mother. *Coward,* she thought. Hiding from her own daughter. Returning to her chambers, she passed by the servants' quarters and happened to glance down the corridor just as a large man exited through a doorway.

She froze, recognizing the tall, muscular frame. Alex MacLeod. But what was he doing in a servant's room? A vague, uneasy feeling swept over her. She had her answer a moment later when a pretty, blond, and very buxom serving maid came out of the room after him, calling him back.

She felt as if the wind had been knocked out of her. It shouldn't matter if he chose to dally with a serving girl, it was hardly unusual, but the dull throbbing in her chest told her that it did. The irony was too perfect, reminding her of another time she'd seen a man she'd wanted to trust dallying with a maid.

Ewen Mackinnon, the son of her father's oldest chieftain and as handsome as the summer solstice was long. So easily he'd charmed the naïve sixteen-year-old girl she'd been with passionate kisses that left her breathless and consumed by emotions that erased all thought of everything else. Even her duties had suffered as she'd devised ways to slip away and meet him. They'd talked of marriage, of a family, of a future. But she'd been a fool.

One afternoon, rather than helping her father with the accounts, she'd pleaded a headache and then snuck from her room to find Ewen, hoping for more of his exciting kisses. Instead, she'd stumbled upon the man she'd thought to marry seducing a housemaid in the stables.

> The girl giggled prettily and slapped his hand away from her round bottom. "But what about Meg Mackinnon? I hear you intend to marry her."
>
> "I do. And you'll be my leman. She could never satisfy me like you do."
>
> The girl seemed to ponder his offer. "Don't you find her pretty?"
>
> "Meg?" He laughed cruelly, and Meg felt her heart crumble at her feet. "That little bland wren? Too bad she's not more like her mother. But one day soon, when I get rid of that idiot brother of hers, she'll make me chief."

The knowledge that Ewen had pursued her only for his ambition and how easily she'd succumbed to his charm was a bitter lesson. But one well learned.

The pain of that moment came back full force as she watched Alex with his pretty maid. The girl's cheeks were flushed as she giggled and batted her eyelashes flirtatiously. Meg felt a pang of envy, for a moment wanting to be the type of woman who inspired lust. Alex smiled, whispered something in the girl's ear, and patted her fondly on the rump as if to shoo her away. But the pretty maid would not be dismissed so easily. When Alex ignored her subtle invitation, the girl grew bolder. She rose on her toes to drape her arms around his neck, stretching against him like a cat and squishing her plump breasts against his leather jerkin, begging not so subtly for his kiss. Meg felt as if she were watching some horrible, intimate charade. She couldn't breathe, waiting for confirmation of what she desperately didn't want to believe. She must have made a sound because his gaze shot around and their eyes met.

Silent accusation fired back and forth. She felt exposed, raw. Certain that he could see right through her. See the hurt and disappointment wallowing inside. She hated that he could see her vulnerability. Meg was a rational woman; she knew she had no claim on him. Unlike Ewen, Alex had never sought her out.

His face darkened with fury. But what did he have to be angry about? That he'd been caught? And though she'd done nothing wrong, Meg felt a trickle of alarm.

Snapping the connection, she turned and sped down the corridor, wanting nothing more than to put distance between herself and Alex MacLeod.

She hadn't taken more than a few steps before a hand snaked around her waist and she found herself swept up in his arms and pulled against the granite wall of his broad chest. She'd never heard him coming.

Meg was frightened, but not too frightened to notice how hard and warm his body felt against hers. Or how wonderful he smelled. Like soap and spice with a hint of myrtle. His arms locked around her like steel bindings. She couldn't move, even if she'd wanted to.

"What are you doing?" His voice shook with fury. "Spying on me?"

She tried not to cower under the onslaught of his rage, though any fool would have been terrified. She forced her spine straight and dared to meet his gaze. Or glower, actually. "Of course not," she said indignantly. "You were not exactly inconspicuous."

"Why is it that everywhere I turn you are there? What are you doing in this part of the palace?"

Meg felt her ire rise. "What right do you have to question me?" She lifted her chin. Perhaps it was the wrong thing to do. Their faces were so close, she could see the flecks of gold on the edges of his eyelashes. Surprisingly thick and curly eyelashes. His startlingly blue eyes bored into her. She could see every tiny scar peppered across his ruggedly handsome face. If anything, the small imperfections only increased his attractiveness, giving proof of his life as a warrior, especially the thin scar that sliced across one brow that gave him a decidedly devilish edge—and made something inside her quiver. But most of all, she was deeply aware of his wide mouth only inches from hers.

"Answer me." His voice was low and rough and oddly hoarse, as if he were in pain.

"I was looking for my mother. I might ask you the same question. Why are you here?"

"It's none of your damn business."

She felt oddly deflated; part of her had hoped he would deny it. "You're right, it's not. And what you were doing is quite obvious. You may dally with whomever you wish, wherever you wish," she said thickly, her throat tightening. "But next time, you might choose not to do it in the open, where anyone might see you."

He pulled her even closer. "When I want advice from you, my sweet, I'll ask for it."

Heat seemed to radiate through her. She could swear she felt the fierce pounding of his heart against hers. The pulse at his jaw twitched. Every muscle in his body tensed with restraint; he seemed to be holding himself by a very thin thread.

Her own breathing was shallow and erratic. She was deeply conscious of the heavy rise and fall of her chest against him. He held her so tight, her breasts swelled high over her stays. A warm flush spread over her when she realized her nipples had hardened against him. Every part of her body felt heavy and achingly sensitive.

Tension crackled between them. His gaze dropped to her mouth. *Dear God, he was going to kiss her.* The strength of her desire rose high inside her, threatening to erupt, but she struggled to tamp it down. Her duty lay with Jamie. Her voice, when it came, was ragged. "Let go of me."

From the expression on his face, Meg could see his shock. Without another word, he released her. This time Meg ran.

Chapter 7

"Margaret, stop fidgeting."

"Ouch!" Meg cried, trying to evade the torture of her mother's comb raking through her mop of tangled curls. The night of the masque had arrived, and with it the fulfillment of her promise to her mother. *A promise made under duress,* Meg thought crossly. "I'm not fidgeting. I don't know why I agreed to this, especially after your part in arranging our escort for the evening."

"You agreed because you want to make your mother happy," her mother said. "And it will make me happy to see to your hair and wardrobe tonight." She sighed dramatically. "You are a beautiful girl, darling, if only you'd attend to your appearance the way you attend to the rents."

"The rents are important, the way I wear my hair isn't," Meg answered patiently, as if this were the first time they'd had this conversation rather than the hundredth. "And you can see how much trouble it is to tame this unruly mess."

Her mother shook her head with disbelief and attempted a stern expression, failing miserably. It was impossible for her mother to ever look sharply at anyone. "I don't know why you are so upset about our escort for the evening. Alex MacLeod is a perfectly delightful man."

"I'm upset because you promised not to interfere. Besides, your efforts are all for naught. I've already decided that if he asks, I'm going to marry Jamie."

Her mother frowned. "But you don't love Jamie. I've seen the way you look at Laird MacLeod. You are obviously attracted to him. All I've done is arrange it so that you can spend some time with him. You should be thanking me."

Meg's cheeks heated. Her mother was far too observant. "I'm not blind, Mother. I'll admit he's handsome—forsooth, who wouldn't? But there's a difference between physical attraction and true sentiment. Besides, he has no interest in me."

Her mother put down the comb and crossed her arms. "Fiddlesticks."

Meg's eyes widened. For her soft-spoken mother, that was akin to a curse.

"You *are* blind if you can't see that Alex MacLeod is far more than a handsome face. He is a laird in his own right, brother to one of the most powerful chiefs in the Highlands, a commanding presence, a warrior of obvious skill, intelligent, and witty. And more important, he can't seem to take his eyes off you."

"You're imagining things," she said, tamping down the swell of pleasure that her mother's words inspired. "For heaven's sake, Mother, he's a mercenary. He sells his sword to the highest bidder."

"Well, you have more than enough gold to bid."

"Mother!"

Her mother lifted her pointed chin in a remarkable

imitation of stubbornness. "We could use a good warrior at Dunakin."

"We need more than a good fighter. What of loyalty? Have you not heard of his falling-out with his brother? How could I trust his loyalty to Ian?"

Rosalind waved her hand as if Meg's concerns were meaningless. "Gossip."

Meg couldn't hide her frustration, especially since her mother seemed to be voicing the very thing she herself refused to consider. She could not risk her brother's future, her clan's future, on an unknown. After all, what did she really know about Alex MacLeod?

He was a man with questionable loyalties who'd arrived at court under an air of mystery and subterfuge. Why did he not want anyone to know he was near Skye? Why was he socializing with men who should be his enemies? And why had he been so quick to accuse her of spying on him? He was hiding something, of that she was sure.

Admittedly, he was an exceptional warrior. He had all of a warrior's command and natural authority, without the usual arrogant swagger. But although his leadership skills might have impressed her on the battlefield, she didn't know whether he had the cunning to lead her clan into the future in dealing with the king's men. And most important, would he stay loyal to her brother, or would he try to claim power for himself? There was something else that bothered her. She sensed something simmering under the surface, something that he struggled to contain. Alex MacLeod was a man of dangerous passions.

She couldn't trust him. Not enough to risk her brother's future and her own. Nothing had changed. Jamie was still the only choice. "Stop interfering, Mother," she said sharply. "I know what I'm doing."

Her mother's eyes welled with tears at Meg's harsh tone. "I'm sorry, darling. I only want you to be happy."

Meg took one look at her mother's face and panicked. This was precisely what had gotten her into this situation of being trussed up like a Christmas goose in the first place. Unfortunately, Meg suffered from the same malady as her father—she could not stand to see her mother weep. *Please, darling, just this once,* Rosalind had beseeched. So instead of her usual refusal when her mother offered to help her with her wardrobe, Meg had given in.

She took her mother's hands and gave them a squeeze. "I know, Mother, forgive me. I know you only want what's best for me. I will be happy. With Jamie."

Her mother opened her mouth to argue, but Meg cut her off.

"I think we'd better call for Alys if we have any hope of being ready in time."

She could tell her mother wanted to say more, but thankfully she nodded and called for the maid.

After seemingly hours of prodding and poking, Alys finished pinning the last curl in Meg's new hair arrangement and stepped back. Meg was berating herself again for agreeing to this foolery when she heard her mother gasp. She spun around. "What's the matter?" Her hands went to her head. "Is it that awful? I told you this would be a waste of time."

Her mother's hands covered her cheeks, and her eyes were wide with awe. "Margaret . . ." She paused, continuing to stare at her. "You look beautiful."

Meg smiled, knowing how prone her mother was to

dramatic exaggerations—especially when it came to the accomplishments of her children. "Oh please, Mother," Meg dismissed, turning to look at Elizabeth, who'd just entered the room. But Elizabeth, too, looked shocked.

"But you do look beautiful, Meg," Elizabeth said. "Truly, I've never seen you such. You're positively radiant."

Uncomfortable with such unusually sincere compliments, Meg felt her cheeks grow hot. "Nonsense." How much could a new hairstyle and gown matter? Still, she couldn't resist a quick peek in the looking glass.

The woman who met her gaze was nearly unrecognizable. For once, her unruly curls were tamed and fastened becomingly at the back of her head. Alys had allowed a few of the more golden brown curls to dangle down her back and shoulders. A slight dusting of powder on her nose hid her less persistent freckles, and the pink remains of her embarrassed blush still swept her cheeks.

Her eyes, wide with wonder, seemed to dominate her face. In comparison, the rest of her features looked unusually delicate: her chin tiny and pointed, her slight nose upturned, her mouth a soft pink bow. The combination lent her face a fragile vulnerability that Meg would have previously thought impossible.

In honor of the masque tonight, Rosalind had chosen a simple silk gown in a shade of moss green that matched her eyes exactly. Dispensing with the bolster and farthingale, the soft folds of the dress hugged her slim figure and emphasized the gentle swell of her breasts rather than flatten them as did the stiff bodices and ruffs of her typical court attire.

The woman staring back at her in the glass looked more like her mother than she could have ever dreamed

possible. Meg actually looked . . . pretty, she realized
with shock.

She didn't know what to say. She'd never had the
time, or never allowed herself the time, to devote to her
appearance. It had never mattered before. But at that
moment, she realized that it was more than her duties
keeping her from taking an interest in her appearance—
she'd been scared. Scared to discover that it might not
make a difference.

Emotion gathered at the back of her throat. "Thank
you, Mother," she said with a grateful smile, leaning
over to kiss Rosalind's soft cheek.

Her mother returned her smile, tears of joy shining in
her eyes. "You're welcome." But being a mother, she
couldn't keep from adding, "Though I wish you had not
fought the obvious for so long." Rosalind studied her
daughter. "I think tonight you might be surprised how
much the bit of effort pleases you."

And only minutes later, as much as Meg wanted to
deny her mother's words, she could not. Rosalind was
right, Meg was pleased. Excessively so.

When Alex MacLeod strode into the small salon to escort them to the masque and literally stopped in his
tracks, for the first time in her life, Meg felt beautiful.
There was no confusing his attraction this time. The blatant admiration that widened his eyes was well worth
the hours of tedium. Although clearly surprised by the
change in her appearance, interestingly, he did not seem
as shocked as Elizabeth.

He stared at her for much longer than was polite.
Long enough for Meg to grow uncomfortable. She fiddled with the carved bone handle of her fan, significant
because she *never* fiddled. His eyes darkened with inten-

sity as his gaze traveled slowly from her head down the length of her figure, lingering an embarrassingly long moment on her breasts, taking in every inch of her new ensemble. A shiver of awareness followed in his heated wake. When their eyes locked, she felt a jolt. Shocked by the flash of white hot desire revealed in his gaze.

But he seemed, well, angry. His mouth fell into a hard, straight line. A muscle in his cheek began to twitch. Even dressed in the elaborate court attire, his entire body tensed as if prepared to battle. Alex MacLeod looked every bit the fierce and predatory Highland warrior as he had that day in the forest.

Whatever was the matter with him?

With one last burning glance, he turned to her mother and offered her his arm. Meg frowned. He was acting very strangely indeed.

Alex fumed in silence. The tenuous control he held on his restraint had been stretched to its limits. With each minute of this blasted masque that passed, his anger intensified. He tried not watching her, but it didn't help. He was only too aware of every damn lascivious coxcomb hanging all over her. A small army of men had surrounded Meg, with her mother and Elizabeth nowhere to be seen. Where the hell were they, anyway? Didn't they know not to leave an innocent lamb alone among a pack of starving wolves?

You'd think the men at court had never seen a beautiful woman before.

Used to solving problems with his sword, Alex found it difficult to maintain the illusion of civility. He wanted nothing more than to smash a few of those lust-filled leers focused too often on her surprisingly generous bosom.

Meg Mackinnon was testing his patience, and other parts of him as well. He was as restless and edgy as a caged lion. Resisting his instincts was frustrating for a man used to living by them.

From the first moment he'd walked into the salon tonight and seen Meg, he'd realized what was going to happen, and it had enraged him. He'd known how these men would react, because he'd reacted the same way. With a warm rush of lust.

She looked like a damn goddess with her cascade of soft curls, her wide, innocent eyes, and her soft red rose-bud of a mouth. But it was the gown that made him half-crazed. For the masque, the usual stiff bodices and wide skirts had given way to softer, more flowing gowns. Meg's gown hugged her body, revealing her high, firm breasts, tiny waist, and slim, narrow hips.

He no longer had to imagine the shapely curves she hid under her courtly armor, he could see every lush inch of her for himself. He clenched his fists and swore. But so could everyone else. His wee bookish nymph had a sensuality that left his mouth watering.

Bloody hell! Why did it have to be tonight that she unveiled her beauty for all the world to admire? She'd always been popular with the older men for her wit and considerable fortune, but adding beauty had impossibly sweetened the pot. Tonight, both young and old sought her out. But it was the former that worried Alex. Lord knew what kind of trouble she could find herself in with an overzealous young admirer. The same sort of trouble she'd nearly found with him in the corridor.

He should be focusing his attention elsewhere. So far,

he'd seen nothing to suggest that Meg was in any danger. The conversation he'd overheard in the tavern must have been a coincidence. Alex told himself that since he'd agreed to act as escort, it was his duty to watch over her, as inexperienced as she must be with men— especially these men. But he was spending far more time keeping an eye on Meg and her aggressive suitors than he was in keeping an eye out for Lord Chancellor Seton.

The only good thing to come out of the near debacle with Seton's serving maid in the corridor a few days ago had been the news that Seton intended to attend the masque tonight. Alex had flirted with the maid in the hopes of learning more, but apparently she was the only servant in the palace who didn't listen to the conversations going on around her.

Yet in other ways she'd proved a surprisingly aggressive creature. Indeed, he'd been trying to uncoil himself from her viselike tentacles when he'd caught sight of Meg. He'd reacted without thinking, turning his discomfort at being caught in a compromising situation onto her. He'd seen the flash of hurt in her eyes and wanted to explain, but he had his mission. Holding Meg in his arms had been a mistake, but one that he could not regret. She'd felt too damn good.

But the small tease of pleasure had only made his hunger deepen.

He caught himself staring at her again. She'd changed, but she hadn't. Her hair might be more artfully arranged, but she still wore the same matter-of-fact, pensive expression. An expression entirely without artifice. That alone made her stand out and made her infinitely more attractive than the jaded courtiers who surrounded her. There was no pretense with Meg Mackinnon. It was one of the things he most admired about her, her confidence and ability to speak her mind.

But tonight there was a subtle difference in that expression. She looked more relaxed than he'd seen her before. Happier. It was the carefree young girl he'd sensed lurking beneath the serious façade. He'd wanted to see her laugh and smile. Just not with other men.

She smiled at something the man next to her whispered, too close to her ear for Alex's comfort, and the pure radiance of that smile transformed her face beyond mere loveliness. He couldn't look away. He was mesmerized by the bewitching glint in those soft green eyes, the amused wrinkle in the small upturned nose, and the gentle curl of that pink bud mouth. He ached to taste her, to press her close to him again, and to discover whether she tasted as impossibly sweet as she looked.

His groin tightened painfully.

Meg moved with such an artless, guileless grace. Movements that were all the more seductive for their rarity. She might never have the flamboyant beauty of her mother or his sister-in-law, Isabel, but though more understated, it was equally entrancing.

Unfortunately, now he was not the only one to notice.

Out of the corner of his eye, he saw her tip her head back and laugh at something one of her admirers said. An admirer who was standing much too close and couldn't keep his damn eyes from falling to the deep valley between her breasts. The pounding started in his ears, and all Alex could see was red.

He'd had enough. His wee little seductress needed a severe talking-to.

*   *   *

Since the moment of their arrival in the hall, a noticeable buzz had trailed Meg's every move. She found herself thoroughly, and surprisingly, enjoying her newfound popularity. She'd never lacked for suitors—her fortune alone would compel many men to seek her hand—but tonight she detected a subtle difference in the intensity of their interest.

They did not want her just for the power and position she would bring them with an alliance, they wanted *her*. It surprised her that the difference mattered.

Meg felt a trickle of apprehension along the back of her neck. She'd been aware that Alex was watching her—he was so blatant, it was impossible not to be—but when he came storming toward her with a savage expression on his face, she decided that perhaps it would be prudent to avoid him. He was in a black mood, and she suspected that for some reason he blamed her. Though she couldn't imagine why. She turned to one of the gentlemen at her side, accepted his arm, and started to move away. Only to find Alex had managed to cut in front of her to block her path.

That trickle turned into a full-fledged flood. She didn't like the way he was looking at her. Not one bit. But, she reminded herself, she hadn't done anything wrong.

"Excuse me," she said in a surprisingly calm voice. "I was just about to take some air with—"

"Good idea," he snapped. "I'll take you. Lord Maxwell here won't mind." He grabbed her arm and started pulling her toward the balcony. Lord Maxwell appeared to mind very much, but he didn't have the gumption to argue. Meg peeked out of the side of her lashes and noticed Alex's taut mouth and clenched jaw. There was also the fact that his shoulders were twice as wide and he had at least eight inches of height on Lord Maxwell. She supposed she could hardly blame the poor man for standing aside. It was as if Alex had claimed her and dared any man to oppose him. She shook off the feeling. That was ridiculous.

For a man of his size, Alex moved with a surprising grace. But being pulled along beside him, she found it a struggle to keep up with his long, powerful strides. A burst of cool air smacked her senses as she exited the hall. The night air was a welcome reprieve from the stagnant heat of an overcrowded room. After glancing around to see that they were alone, she brusquely shook off his hold. He seethed beside her, but she refused to be intimidated. Even if he did outweigh her two times over. At least.

The realization took her aback. Though he looked every bit as forbidding as he had that day on the battle-field, she did not fear him. No matter how angry he was, she knew that he could never harm her. Even when he was furious, Meg felt safer with him than she'd ever felt with anyone before.

The knowledge both pleased and emboldened her. She turned to face him, toe-to-toe. "That was very rude," she pointed out, resisting the urge to stick her finger in his chest. "Whatever is the matter with you? You've been glowering at me all night. You can't still be angry about what happened the other day. I told you I wasn't spying on you. I'm sorry for interrupting your little tryst, but really, you can't blame me for walking down a corridor."

He didn't say anything for a moment but simply stared at her, piercing her with the heated intensity of his gaze. Somehow, she managed not to squirm.

"I'm not angry with you," he said finally. "I'm simply attending to your welfare."

Meg couldn't help it, she let out a little snort of disbelief. "And was I in some kind of danger?"

Obviously, he didn't like the flippancy of her response, because he took a step closer. An intimidating step closer. Close enough for Meg to feel the warmth of his body and see the tiny silk fibers on his black peascod doublet. His chest was a wall of granite. This man was built to dominate. Though the knowledge sent a perverse thrill through her, Meg knew she had to stand her ground. Drawing up every inch of her diminutive frame, she squared her shoulders, refusing to cower before him.

"Flirting like that, you could have been," he said flatly.

Incredulous, she gaped at him. "You can't be serious. Me, flirting? How dare you criticize my conduct! I was not the one kissing a serving maid in the open for everyone to see."

He was obviously struggling to control his temper. His arms stretched taught along his side, and he looked up to the heavens as if asking for patience. "I was not kissing her," he said through clenched teeth.

She turned away and made a sound, surprised by the painful twinge in her chest. Gazing up at the starry sky, she was keenly aware of the man standing next to her. The sinfully handsome face, the soft, shiny waves of dark golden hair that just grazed the top of his collar, the tall, powerful physique, the strength she felt beneath his callused warrior's hand.

But Meg knew it was far more than simply physical attraction that she was responding to. It was his utter command over everything around him. Alex was a man who made her feel wonderfully feminine. His dominance was strangely reassuring; he had a subtle way of taking charge just by his presence of authority and strength. When she was with this man, she felt as if nothing could harm her. Her problems did not seem so insurmountable. She did not feel so alone. With Alex, she could relax.

He let out a long sigh. "It's not what you think."

For some reason, she sensed that he was telling the truth. Even hurt and angry, she remembered his gentle rebuff of the pretty maid and his attempt to unwind her arms from around his neck. "Then what was it?"

His face went blank. "It's none of your affair," he snapped. Then, more kindly: "It has nothing to do with you."

His honesty hurt. He was right, Alex MacLeod had nothing to do with her.

She felt a suspicious burning behind her eyes, but she quickly put a grip on those unwelcome emotions. Meg never cried. But it seemed that ever since she'd met Alex, so much of what she'd thought she knew about herself had changed. She could read Latin, Greek, and French, could run an estate as well as any man, but at her core she was just as vulnerable as anyone else. She'd tried to hide from her emotions, but they'd found her. "You're right," she said with a catch in her voice. "It is none of my affair, but neither do you have any right to interfere in my business. From now on, I'll thank you to mind your own."

He took her arm again and whipped her around to face him, forcing her to meet his implacable gaze. "You go too far," he said in a low voice that carried the faintest hint of a threat. "It is my responsibility to see you are safe tonight. So do as I say and stay well away from those men."

She lifted her chin defiantly. He had no right to order her about. And her conduct tonight was beyond reproach. He'd taken his duties well beyond the scope of an escort. "I don't know what you are talking about."

"Don't you? You play a dangerous game. Those men will eat an innocent like you for breakfast."

She laughed. The pulse appeared in his jaw again, but Meg didn't heed the warning. "Surely you jest? I've known most of those men for years. They are quite harmless, I assure you. I was merely enjoying myself. You might try it sometime." She paused, daring to add, "And how do you know I'm innocent? You presume much, my laird."

His eyes flared, and he tightened his grip on her arm. "Don't press me, Meg."

She didn't miss the intimate use of her Christian name, but there was no mistaking the threat this time. His voice was deep and liquid and seemed to wrap around her. She knew she shouldn't provoke him, but he brought out a mischievous side of her long forgotten. Lifting one brow, she asked, "Or what?"

Before the taunt had left her mouth, she was in his arms again and jerked firmly against the broad chest she'd just admired. She gasped. Not from shock, but from the realization of how much she liked being pressed against him. Of how she savored the sensation of her breasts and hips molded against the hard length of his body, of melting against him, of being secured in his arms. A wave of heated awareness shuddered through her.

His eyes were hooded, his expression dark and full of

promise. "Or I will prove to you just how innocent you are, my sweet, and how very little control you have over a man and a man's desires."

In his eyes, she saw the very depths of his desire. The lust, the need, the hunger.

For me. This fierce warrior, who held himself so aloof and remote, wanted her. And her body responded, softening.

Time stood still. The masque, the sounds from the hall, her responsibilities, all fell away. There was nothing left but the two of them alone in the moonlight. He lowered his head. Slowly. Inch by heart-stopping inch. Giving her every opportunity to object.

She could hear the fierce pounding of her heart. His mouth was so close. If she were breathing, their breath would have mingled in the cool night air. Her eyes felt heavy, begging to close. Desperately, she fought the magnetic pull of warmth and desire that beckoned from his seductive form. She'd been kissed before, and it had nearly led to disaster. But Alex's mouth moved over hers, and God help her, she could not stop him.

A whisper. A breath. A warm scent of spice and then the barest, sweetest touch. A touch that sent a shock wave rippling through her body. Every inch of him was hard, unyielding male, but he startled her with a gentle brush of his mouth. She felt the softness of his lips for only an instant before he raised his head, leaving her with a tightness in her chest and a sharp yearning for more.

It was a kiss of aching tenderness that packed unexpected strength. With one swift touch, something inside her shifted, exposing a part of her best left buried. She didn't want to feel. She wanted to do what was right and

marry Jamie. Not dream of a fierce warrior with unknown loyalties. A man whose very nearness tossed her
into a state of confusion.

It was all wrong, she wanted to cry out in frustration.
She wanted him to be rough and brutish, to make her
not want him. To prove the validity of her decision in
choosing Jamie. She didn't want this gentle warrior who
kissed her as if she were the most precious jewel in the
world.

She stared at him, breathing fast through softly parted
lips. Not knowing what to think. In truth, he looked just
as stunned as she did.

I let him kiss me. I must be losing my mind. She'd
played with fire, but she'd never expected to be burned
by tenderness.

"Why did you do that?" she asked dumbly.

He released her and took a determined step back. "I
don't know."

"Well, don't do it again."

"On that account, you have nothing to fear."

For some reason, the absolute certainty of his tone
made her feel worse.

The sound of the balcony doors opening was a welcome
reprieve. The woman who appeared, however, was not.

Bianca Gordon was the most empty-headed, selfish
woman at court. And probably the most beautiful—
which was convenient, since that happened to be her
favorite subject. She epitomized the classical ideal of
beauty: flaxen hair, eyes the sparkling blue of the sea,
and refined features. But her disposition did not match
her lovely features. Her father was the powerful Marquess of Huntly, and Bianca made sure everyone knew it
and bowed accordingly.

Wanting to escape and still annoyed by Alex's presumption in lecturing her on her conduct tonight, Meg took a step backward, her mind churning. Alex must have read her intentions.

"Don't you dare, Meg," he warned in a low voice.

Meg ignored him and flashed Bianca a brilliant smile. "Bianca Gordon, how nice to see you!"

Bianca looked perplexed. Meg had never welcomed her company before. "Meg, what have you done to yourself?" she asked rudely. Her eyes narrowed as she took in Meg's hair and dress. "Why, you look pretty."

Meg's voice was honey sweet. "How kind of you to notice. But of course, I could never be as beautiful as you, Bianca."

Bianca nodded with all the confidence of a queen accepting homage, obviously pleased to have the attention focused back on her.

Meg turned to Alex. "Bianca, do you know my neighbor from Skye, Laird Alex MacLeod? He's been simply begging me for an introduction."

Meg swore she heard Alex hiss.

Bianca beamed eagerly, fluttering her long lashes. "How do you do, my laird."

"My lady," Alex murmured, bending over her proffered hand.

Despite the threatening glower Alex threw her, Meg said, "Alex, didn't you just say that you were looking for a partner for the next set of dances?"

Before Alex could strangle her—if his expression was any indication of his intent—Meg started away. She looked back over her shoulder and met Alex's glare. "Enjoy your evening, you two."

That should occupy him for a while. Meg felt better

already. She would not let one brief kiss from an over-bearing laird, no matter how unsettling, ruin her night.

Alex didn't know whether to throttle her or stay as far away from Meg Mackinnon as possible.

After being foisted off on Bianca Gordon—as vain and insipid a woman as he'd ever met—he decided on the former. But that kiss made him reluctant to get anywhere near her.

Kissing Meg had been a mistake.

She'd felt so soft and sweet in his arms, the temptation had been nearly overwhelming. Still, he would have resisted if she hadn't pushed him to the breaking point. The thought that she might not be as innocent as she seemed slammed him with a wave of possessiveness unlike anything he'd ever felt before. His iron control had snapped as easily as a dry twig. He'd wanted to ravage her senseless but found the primal instinct tempered by an unexpected wave of tenderness. He'd moved slowly, giving her every opportunity to stop him. If only she had.

The moment his lips touched hers, he knew she'd never known a man's passion. But by God, she would have known his if he hadn't felt as though the wind had been knocked out of him. The honey taste of her and the soft tremble of her mouth had sent an ache of such sublime perfection to his chest, he'd pulled back, leveled by the force of it. It hadn't been lust at all, but something altogether unfamiliar and far more powerful.

Not even an hour of listening to Bianca Gordon's silly prattle could dampen the memory. That one little taste had irrepressibly whetted his appetite for more. He didn't trust himself not to taste her again, and this time nothing would stop him from delving into the sweet recesses of her mouth and tasting her deeper. So rather than seek her out, to vent his anger or his lust, he did what he should have been doing the entire night and resumed his search for Lord Chancellor Seton.

After a quick examination of the adjoining antechambers, Alex returned to the hall, joined a group of men discussing King James's containment of the borders, and casually scanned the crowd for Seton. The sight that met his eyes made his blood run cold.

Meg had blatantly ignored his warning. If anything, her circle of admirers had grown, though Alex couldn't help noticing that her attention seemed focused on one man in particular.

She'd defied him, though it shouldn't surprise him. Meg Mackinnon challenged him in a way no woman had before. Normally, it might even amuse him. But right now, all he could do was force himself not to storm over there and smash his fist into the face of the man with whom she was engaged in deep conversation. An intimate conversation. Alex gripped the stem of his goblet tighter as the brazen fool leaned over and whispered close to her ear.

Abruptly, he put down his claret, excused himself from the group of men, and headed straight for Meg. His anger had taken on an entirely different edge, one consumed by an emotion so foreign that he almost didn't recognize it. *Bloody hell,* he was jealous.

From the costume and mask the man wore, Alex realized he was the master of the revels for tonight's performance. There was something else vaguely familiar about him, but Alex was too focused on Meg's bewitching smile to ponder it further.

So focused that he almost walked right into Lord Chancellor Seton. Mumbling an apology, Alex watched as Seton moved to exit the hall. This was just the opportunity he had been waiting for. He had to take it. Pushing aside his jealousy and the compulsion he felt to tear Meg away from her admirer, Alex turned to follow Seton. The lord chancellor was almost to the doorway; in a minute, he would disappear into the corridors. Alex took a few steps after him and swore, unable to resist one more glance across the room at Meg.

It was a mistake.

His entire body drew taut as he watched the man trail his fingers seductively down Meg's arm, his knuckles brushing the full roundness of her breast. From the sly smile that curved the bastard's mouth, Alex knew he had done it on purpose. Seton temporarily forgotten, Alex started back toward Meg, rage surging through his veins. Alex was going to kill him.

The sly smile hovered on the edges of his memory.

Alex had almost reached Meg when the man's identity hit him. The blood drained from his face. As if he could feel the weight of Alex's stare, the man turned and confirmed what Alex had already known. He would never forget the flat eyes of his enemy.

The last five years faded away, and Alex stood on the bloody corrie under the looming majesty of the great Cuillin mountain range, catapulted back to the day that would be forever branded into his conscience.

The promise of blood permeated the morning mist. His warriors were eager for battle. It was so close now, Alex could almost smell it.

It was his first command, and Alex swelled with pride in the responsibility he'd been given. Not only would he lead his brother's men, the MacLeods of

Dunvegan, but he would also lead their kin the MacLeods of Lewis. Both branches of the clan had joined forces to fight the MacDonalds.

They hunted their quarry from the giant shadow of the great Cuillin mountain range. The kinsmen, descendants from the sons of Leod, numbered near fifty warriors strong. A large group, yet they moved soundlessly up the grassy path, climbing ever higher into the looming mountain above them.

Alex lifted his hand, signaling the men to halt. He motioned for two of his luchd-taighe guardsmen, his cousins John and Tormod from Lewis, to follow him. The three powerful mail-clad warriors took a few cautious steps forward, then got down on their bellies, slithering forward to peer over the edge of the hill.

The sight below them was not a pretty one for a MacLeod. Their prey—the despised MacDonalds— were celebrating a successful foray below them. The stolen cattle that the MacDonalds had lifted during their bloody raid on his brother's Bracadale lands grazed peacefully in the corrie along the grassy banks of the fairy pools.

The bucolic scene fired Alex's already smoldering anger. He was responsible for watching Rory's lands while his brother was away. Even now, the brazen fools celebrated while still on MacLeod lands. Alex fought to control his anger, for this raid had occurred under his first command.

It was time to teach the thieving bastards a lesson.

With a fierce battle cry that pierced the quiet morning like the high-pitched wail of the Banshee, the

MacLeod clansmen charged down the hillside and fell upon the unsuspecting MacDonalds.

The battle had begun.

The blistering sun moved slowly across the cloudless midsummer sky. After hours of relentless fighting, Alex and his men had long ago lost any advantage of surprise.

At the head of the battle, Alex faced Dougal MacDonald, leader to leader, champion to champion.

Blood saturated the crushed grass below Alex's feet, making it difficult for him to move and maintain his footing. Sweat pooled behind the heavy mail and spewed off his weary limbs with each shattering stroke that he met of his opponent's blade.

His grip on his claymore was starting to slip.

His vision clouded with perspiration that dripped from his brow. He fought to breathe through the overwhelming stench that filled the heavy air. The pungently sweet smell of death had long ago drowned out the fresh scent of heather.

Alex was tiring. His opponent sensed it and swooped in for the kill. Alex met the powerful force of Dougal MacDonald's stroke, and a shuddering pain exploded up his arm. His fingers loosened, and his claymore suddenly lifted from his hands. It flew through the air like a gleaming silvery cross and landed with a dull thud well away from him. Shocked by his disarmament, he turned back to find the point of his enemy's blade pressed firmly at his throat.

"Surrender," Dougal warned. "Call off your men or we'll slaughter them like the swine that they are."

Alex glanced around at the carnage surrounding him—a bucolic landscape no longer. Bodies littered the once peaceful corrie. Blood tinged the clear waters of the fairy pools a gruesome crimson. A few of his men were still fighting. Some, like him, were caught. No matter. While there was still breath left in his lungs, he would fight. He'd never willingly face the shame of surrender.

He spat at Dougal's feet, clenching the dirk still in his hand. "I'll never surrender to a MacDonald whoreson."

Dougal MacDonald appeared pleased with Alex's words. He nodded to two of his men standing across the corrie and smiled.

In horror, Alex realized Dougal had motioned to the two men who held his captured cousins John and Tormod. Alex lashed out in protest and tried to pull away, but it was too late. His cousins tumbled to the ground in a horrible thud, gulleted—the dirk slashed across their throats so deep, there could be no doubt that they were dead.

"Shall we try again?" Dougal asked pleasantly. "Surrender, or I will give my men leave to kill them all."

The taste of defeat bitter on his tongue, Alex turned to the rest of his men. His pride had killed his cousins, it wouldn't kill the rest of them. "Throw down your arms," he said hoarsely. " 'Tis over."

The pipers had longed ceased playing as Alex and the surviving MacLeods were bound and led away— prisoners instead of victors.

Twenty-two of his clansmen were left dead in the "Corrie of the Foray."

Dead under his command.

And now the man who'd murdered his cousins and held Alex prisoner for those long months afterward stood not twenty feet in front of him, with his vile hands on Meg and a familiar gloating smile twisting his mouth. At one time, that smile had held the power to make Alex lose control, but no longer.

Alex's face was a mask of ice while rage festered inside him like an open wound. Every instinct cried out for battle, to avenge his cousins' deaths, to raise his sword and crush Dougal MacDonald into the ground. He struggled to contain that hatred rising inside him, threatening to erupt. Hatred that would turn this glittering hall into a melee of death and destruction. But he would never allow Dougal MacDonald to see his anger.

Slowly the shock ebbed, replaced by cold certainty. Alex would have his retribution; he and Dougal would cross swords again. But not here. This was not the place.

There was only one way to atone for his past, and that was to help his cousins defeat the incursion by the Fife Adventurers. Seeing Dougal had done one thing: It had brought back the importance of his mission full force, reminding him of why he'd driven himself so relentlessly the last five years. All the fighting, all the toil, had been to bring him to this point.

Nothing would divert him from his path.

His gaze shifted to Meg, and he could see the hesitancy in her gaze, as if she realized something had changed. It had. He'd allowed himself to be distracted by a green-eyed enchantress. Lust had made him temporarily lose his focus, but it would not happen again. Hell, he'd had a chance to follow Seton and had wasted it on jealousy.

Meg Mackinnon was not for him.

With one last deadly glance at Dougal, Alex turned on his heel and headed in the direction he'd last seen Lord Chancellor Seton. His mission was all that mattered. It had taken Dougal MacDonald to remind him of the stakes.

Alex would find the information he needed to help save his kin, the MacLeods of Lewis.

Or die trying.

Chapter 8

Meg was trying to stay focused on the man before her. If she hadn't already decided upon Jamie, perhaps she would be more attentive. By all accounts, Dougal MacDonald would be a good match—the MacDonalds controlled a considerable portion of Skye—but something about the man rubbed her the wrong way. He was physically imposing, nearly as large as Alex, and attractive enough, she supposed. On the surface, he seemed quite charming. But beneath the flattery and warm smiles, Meg detected a ruthless glint in his hard blue eyes.

But her wariness where Dougal was concerned wasn't the only reason she was distracted. Her thoughts kept sliding back to Alex. Where was he? She'd wanted him to leave her alone, to stop confusing her . . . or had she? His expression when she'd left him with Bianca had been priceless. It was no less than he deserved for his high-handedness; he had no call to order her about. But Meg had immediately regretted her actions when she saw how stunning they looked together on the dance floor. Alex had made no secret of his unwillingness to partner with Bianca, but Meg had felt a twinge of something suspiciously like jealousy all the same.

He had no right to dictate to her, no right to kiss her. A kiss that had lingered on her lips long after he was done. She knew she should stop thinking about it; it was a momentary lapse, that was all.

Realizing her gaze was wandering again, she forced her eyes back on Dougal. He was looking at her expectantly, and she realized he'd asked her something. When she asked him to repeat it, he leaned closer, much closer than was necessary. She tried not to show her discomfort. After all, she was hardly an expert in courtly flirtations.

"I was sorry to hear about your father's illness," he repeated. "I heard there was some trouble." At her obviously confused look, he continued, "With the issue of his successor undecided and all."

Her eyes narrowed, surprised that the grumbling of a few of her father's men would have reached the Mac-Donalds. She smiled thinly. "I'm afraid you are misinformed. My brother is my father's *tanaiste*."

He smiled indulgently. "But his, uh . . . limitations . . . make the situation uncertain, do they not?"

Meg fought to control her temper. "They do not."

Perhaps realizing that he'd overstepped his bounds, he at once turned contrite. "Of course. Of course. I could see for myself on my stay at Dunakin last month that the rumors of Ian being a half-wit were greatly exaggerated."

Meg stiffened, but he didn't seem to notice.

"And I suppose if you were married, if you had a strong husband . . . maybe even one whose lands closely border your own?"

Pretending that she didn't realize he was talking about himself, she forced a smile. She'd thought his visit to Dunakin soon after her father's recovery odd, but now she realized it had been with a purpose to woo her for marriage.

When she didn't respond, he said, "Walk with me outside. I yearn to see whether you are as beautiful by moonlight as you are by candlelight."

His finger trailed down her arm. Meg could not repress an involuntary shiver of distaste at his touch, but she literally flinched when his finger grazed her breast. Had he done that on purpose? She looked at him sharply, but his gaze revealed nothing. Now Meg was becoming very uncomfortable. "Perhaps later," she said, keeping her voice light. "I've just returned from taking a turn outside."

"With Alex MacLeod?" he snapped.

"Yes," she answered, surprised that he'd been watching her so closely. "Do you know him?"

"You might say that."

She didn't like the tone of his voice. "Do you know him well, then?" They couldn't be friends; the MacLeods and the MacDonalds had generations of enmity between them.

For an instant, the thin veneer of charm cracked beneath the divulgence of a snide smile. "You might say we lived closely together at one time. But you can ask him all about it, he's heading this way. With the devil nipping at his heels, I'd say by that black look on his face."

Meg looked over her shoulder to see a furious-looking Alex bearing down on them quickly from across the room. Intuitively, as she'd never inspired such an emotion before, Meg recognized his jealousy. Misplaced though it might be.

Then suddenly, when almost upon them, he froze. His

eyes locked on Dougal, and his eyes flashed with such intense hatred that she felt scorched in its wake. Alex looked as if he could kill him. But it was his expression only moments later, utterly devoid of emotion, that truly scared her. He looked cold and determined. And so remote that she knew he'd moved beyond her reach. Turning on his heel, without sparing her another glance, Alex strode away in the opposite direction. Away from her. Almost as if he no longer wanted anything to do with her.

Something was terribly wrong.

Her only thought was to go to him, to help, to see what could have caused such desolation. And such hatred.

Meg forgot all about Dougal and pushed her way through the crowd, heading toward Alex. But before she could reach him, he'd disappeared. She turned around helplessly, searching the sea of inquiring faces gawking at her. But he was gone.

She had to find him. For Meg knew that if she did not, he might just slip beyond her reach forever.

Dougal MacDonald hid his outrage beneath a lazy smile as he watched his intended bride flee the hall, scampering after Alex MacLeod. She'd seemed oblivious to the whispers that followed or to the fact that she'd just abandoned him in the middle of the room. Abandoned him for his nemesis, which made it even worse.

His spies at court had of course informed him of MacLeod's presence, but Dougal hadn't been aware of his interest in Meg Mackinnon. Nor of hers in him. It was a complication, but not one that worried him greatly. Complications were easily taken care of.

He smiled, this time with pleasure. He'd beaten Alex MacLeod before, he'd do it again. And this time, he would show no mercy.

Even if Dougal didn't want her for himself, a Mackinnon with a MacLeod was an alliance that could never be allowed to proceed. The battle for dominance of Skye between the MacLeods and the MacDonalds had endured for centuries. Placing the Mackinnon's lands in either hand would lead to an imbalance, one that Dougal intended to secure for himself.

Originally, he hadn't intended to marry the chit himself. He admitted to being pleasantly surprised tonight when he'd first caught sight of her. His little pigeon was much improved from the last time he'd seen her. Dougal was almost looking forward to the bedding. His expression hardened. But if she dared embarrass him like this again when they were married, she would feel the brunt of his anger. He would not be shamed by any woman.

Wooing Meg Mackinnon was proving more of a challenge than he'd anticipated. She was unusually intelligent for a woman and would not be easily duped. Dougal admired her spirit. He would put it to good use in the bedchamber, but he would never allow it to get in the way of his plans.

One way or another, Meg Mackinnon would be his wife.

For the first time since he'd arrived at court, Alex could see his mission laid out clearly in his mind. And refocusing on the task at hand, and not on a pair of enchanting green eyes, was already yielding results. He could scarcely believe his good fortune.

By the time Alex had forged his way out of the

crowded hall, Lord Chancellor Seton was nowhere to be found. Cursing the wasted opportunity, and the spark of jealousy that had led to it, Alex looked around, only to see someone just as important leaving the hall and starting down the corridor: Secretary Balmerino—one of the original twelve Fife Adventurers from the first attempt to colonize the Isle of Lewis a few years back. Given the secretary's previous involvement, Alex knew that his sudden appearance at court was significant.

Alex made the quick decision not to look for the lord chancellor, but to follow Secretary Balmerino, hoping that one might lead to the other.

Living as an outlaw for the past few years, Alex had depended upon stealth to evade capture by the king's men. He was used to moving soundlessly, to hiding under brush, to blending in with the landscape. But blending into the background at court was an altogether different proposition. In circumstances such as these, his size definitely worked against him. There weren't too many places he could hide. It wasn't difficult to be inconspicuous near the hall with all the people milling about, but as the secretary approached the corridor leading to the presence room, the crowds had thinned considerably, and Alex had to drop back farther and farther, trying to keep as much distance between them as possible without losing sight of him.

He also had to make sure he wasn't being followed. Once, when he'd been forced to slip into a room to avoid the sound of approaching voices, he thought he'd lost the secretary. But a few seconds later, a muffled cough pointed him in the right direction.

Not taking any more chances, Alex drew closer, silently willing the secretary not to turn around. He would be hard-pressed to convince Secretary Balmerino that he wasn't following him. As a precaution, he'd studied the layout of the palace; but unlike in the wild, in the palace escape routes where he could slip away unnoticed were limited. Being caught spying on these men would be tantamount to treason. Alex had been imprisoned once, courtesy of Dougal MacDonald, and he was not eager to repeat the experience. But he'd known the risks when he volunteered for the job.

When Balmerino continued past the presence room to a dark, deserted corridor at the rear of the palace, Alex breathed a sigh of relief. The alcoves that lined the hallway would provide some measure of protection. About halfway down the hall, the secretary entered a small antechamber, and Alex's suspicions were rewarded. The secretary had led him directly to Lord Chancellor Seton and his cronies and, finally, to the conversation that Alex most wanted to hear.

The one that he hoped would send him on his way to the Isle of Lewis.

The king's dream of colonizing Lewis, and later presumably the rest of the Western Isles, was founded on the false belief of hidden riches in the Isles that lay merely awaiting his plunder. After a series of laws aimed to divest Highlanders of their land, the king had "leased" the Isle of Lewis—land that rightly belonged to the MacLeods of Lewis—to a group of Lowlanders, mostly from Fife, who were willing to take up the challenge.

King James had hoped to establish a settlement of Lowlanders at Stornoway, the largest village on the Isle of Lewis, and eventually to build a trading port. But Alex's kin Tormod and Neil MacLeod, with the secret

help of some of the Island chiefs, had successfully
burned and pillaged the interlopers back to Fife.

The "Gentlemen Adventurers from Fife," as they
called themselves—*making it sound like some damn ex-
pedition rather than a conquest of their countrymen,*
Alex thought—had returned with their tails between
their legs to a furious and humiliated king. A king who
Alex knew would do everything in his power to ensure
that a second attempt was not the same resounding defeat as the first.

Alex, on the other hand, would do everything to ensure otherwise. He'd be damned if he'd just sit back and
watch the king steal his cousins' land and fill it with
bloody Lowlanders. But he knew that his reasons for
helping his kin went even deeper. His cousins' deaths on
the battlefield at the hands of Dougal MacDonald four
years ago still weighed on him. He now had the opportunity to make amends.

Tucked into one of the small alcoves that lined the
corridor, Alex was doing his best to conceal his large
frame in a small area—with limited success. Should
someone quit the room unexpectedly, he risked almost
certain discovery.

But it was a risk he had to take.

From his position to the side of the door, he could not
see directly into the room, but he could hear enough to
make out the gist of their conversation. Already his
muscles were complaining from the effects of being
confined—he'd been forced to suffer through the seemingly endless idle chitchat before they'd finally broached
the subject he'd been waiting for.

Despite the discomfort, it was well worth the wait.

He recognized the commanding voice of Lord Chancellor Seton. "Rest assured you will have your ships, Secretary. The king has pledged to do all he can to ensure the success of your endeavor. Are your men ready?"

"At the king's command, my lord chancellor. Even now my men are in Fife awaiting word, readying the colonists and stockpiling provisions. By the time the king's ships arrive, we'll be ready."

"Excellent. How many colonists will you bring this time?" the lord chancellor asked.

"Perhaps four hundred persons, including fighting men, craftsmen, builders, and women."

Alex exhaled, relieved to hear at last the direct confirmation of a second attempt by the Fife Adventurers to take Lewis. Now if only he could learn *when*. . . .

"As long—"

Alex heard something. The faint sound of footsteps drew his attention down the corridor, preventing him from hearing the rest of the lord chancellor's words. Someone was coming.

The scent of danger sent the familiar rush of blood surging through his veins. He drew out his dirk, and the long, sharp blade gleamed in the soft candlelight. Stealthily, he unfolded himself from the alcove and started walking down the dimly lit corridor toward the approaching footsteps and away from the room, hoping to put as much distance between him and the open door as possible. Just as the intruder was about to turn the corner, Alex slipped into the shadows of another alcove, every nerve set on edge, waiting. He half expected to see that Dougal had followed him.

Once the reflexive urge to kill Dougal MacDonald had dissipated, Alex realized that Dougal's presence at court was not likely to be a coincidence. Although the

MacDonalds claimed to be a part of the alliance of chiefs that had banded together to protect the Isle of Lewis from invasion, Alex didn't trust them. Dougal MacDonald would bear close watching. If the MacDonalds planned to deceive them, Alex intended to know about it.

The footsteps were light, too light for a man.

He cursed, immediately recognizing the tiny form of the person who turned the corner. Meg. He didn't know whether to be furious at her untimely interruption or thankful that it was only her. He'd never met a woman so eager to bear the brunt of his anger. She didn't have the good sense to leave him alone. Slipping the dirk back into his belt, he stepped out of the darkness into her path.

She jumped back, startled. Then, realizing who it was, she put her hands on her hips and scowled. "What are you doing hiding in the shadows like that? You scared me half out of my wits."

"Which are apparently in limited supply," he quipped. She gasped with outrage, which he ignored as he grabbed her arm to pull her around the corner and out of immediate sight. Seeing her again triggered all the emotions he'd vowed to put behind him as he'd stormed out of the hall. He wanted to press her up against the wall and punish her for distracting him. For frustrating him. For making every damn inch of his body hard and throbbing with need. "Or do you make it a practice to follow men down dark corridors?" he asked. There was an edge to his voice that he knew was a result of seeing her with his enemy. The image of Dougal MacDonald touching her still burned too vividly in his mind. As did the urge to wipe it away.

"Not usually," she said crisply, lifting her adorable chin. "But I did come to find you. You seemed disturbed back in the hall—"

Alex tensed. She was venturing into dangerous territory.

She paused, heeding the subtle warning. She bit at her lip anxiously, measuring her words. "I was worried. I could tell something was wrong." Her hand settled on his forearm. Despite the thick velvet of his doublet, a surge of warmth spread through his body from her touch. It hadn't been that long ago that he'd held her in his arms, and the memory proved a powerful one.

But Alex didn't want her comfort. He wanted to put her out of his mind.

He vowed to remain detached, but her small upturned face looked so damn lovely. Those beseeching green eyes, wide with concern. Her thin arched brows drawn together in a delightful wrinkle above her tiny tilted nose. Even in the soft light, he could see the sensual line of her delicate lips. A wave of possessiveness hurled over him. *Mine.* But she wasn't, nor ever could be. He fought the primitive urge to cover her mouth with his, to claim her, and to eviscerate all vestiges of Dougal MacDonald from her memory.

Hell. He dropped her arm and stepped purposefully away from her. "You don't take advice very well," he said darkly. "I warned you to have care."

"Advice?" She quirked a brow sarcastically. "Don't you mean orders? And no, I don't. Do you?"

Alex refused to bite. "You had better get used to it if you intend to marry."

She pressed her lips closed and said nothing, but Alex caught the flash of defiance in her eyes.

His eyes narrowed. "Or is that one of the criteria for
a husband? A man who will let you do as you please."

"Of course not," she retorted.

Alex's gaze slid over her indignant face, but he suspected he'd hit upon at least a partial truth. Meg had
carved out an unusual position for herself, and from all
accounts she relished her responsibilities. Responsibilities he doubted she was eager to give up.

He studied her upturned face for a long moment. "If
you think Jamie Campbell will be led around by his
nose, you do not know him very well."

"You have no right to talk to me like this. My marriage is no concern of yours."

Alex noticed that she hadn't argued with his premise—
she intended to marry Campbell. It riled him more than
he wanted to acknowledge. "You're right," he said
curtly. "You shouldn't be here. I could have been anyone." His mind harkened back to the conversation he'd
overheard in the tavern. "These darkened corridors are
no place for a woman alone. It's dangerous." *I'm dangerous.* "If you cried out, no one would come to your
rescue."

Though she tried to hide it, Alex saw the flicker of apprehension cross her face. "You'd never hurt me."

"How can you be so sure?" He bent his head, unable
to resist the urge to inhale her intoxicating scent, a mixture of roses and a subtle feminine perfume all her own.
Her lips were softly parted, and he could hear her uneven breathing. Caught up in the irresistible lure, he slid
his thumb over the frantic pulse on her neck as his
fingers brushed the side of her velvety smooth cheek.
Her body trembled at his touch, and the knowledge
that she wanted him only fueled his hunger. His body

hammered with need. It took every ounce of his resolve not to feed it.

He stepped back. "What do you want from me?" he asked roughly, dragging his fingers through his hair.

"Nothing," she replied automatically.

"I think you do."

He could see the hot blush stain her cheeks, and she looked flustered. "I told you I was worried."

"As you can see, there was no cause for concern. Return to the masque."

Despite the curt dismissal, she didn't budge an inch. "Why did seeing Dougal MacDonald anger you so?"

Alex stilled. Meg had a way of peeling off the layers and cutting right to the core. He schooled his features into a model of indifference. "The MacLeods and Mac-Donalds are enemies."

Clearly, his explanation did not satisfy her. Not only was she direct and to the point herself, but she had an uncanny ability to appraise those around her in the same way. Never before had he met another woman who was so confident in her ability to see the truth. "Is that all?" she asked patiently.

"Isn't that enough?"

"You didn't answer my question."

"Return to the masque, Meg. But take my advice. Stay away from Dougal MacDonald. He is not the man for you."

Damn. Alex heard sounds behind them, coming from the direction of the antechamber. If the lord chancellor and the secretary found him here, he risked someone asking questions about what he was doing lurking in a secluded corridor so close to the door of a secret meet-

ing. Nor did he trust Meg not to blurt out the same
question.

He had to stop her from talking.

A floorboard creaked behind him. They were coming
this way. He had to do something. He didn't have a
choice. There was only one thing to do. What he'd
ached to do since the first moment he'd seen her. He'd
finish what he'd started on the balcony.

"Why—"

But her words were cut off when, without warning, he
pushed her back against the wall, screening her face
from the curious men intent on discovering the source of
their interruption and them from hers. He didn't want
her to see who had been in the room. He knew her; she'd
ask too many questions.

"What are you doing?" She tried to pull away, but he
held her firmly in his grasp.

He wrapped his hand around her small waist, turning
her slight body into his. His body reacted instanta-
neously. He nearly groaned with the erotic sensation of
her hips molded snugly against the crook of his pelvis.
Relief pulsed through his body. His cock rose hard
against her. No doubt she could feel the proof of his desire even through her gown. Did her body dampen for
him? The erotic thought only fueled his agony.

He heard her sharp intake of breath. The gaze that
met his was not quite so self-assured. Alex's lips curled
into a slow, dangerous grin. Those beautiful green eyes
fringed with sooty black lashes widened at the hard evidence of his arousal.

The delicate arches of her brows peaked atop a worried forehead, an expressive compliment to the small
wrinkle furrowing her tiny nose. She tipped her head

back to meet his stare, and her loose curls tumbled lower down her back.

"You should have just let me walk away," he said, lowering his head.

"You're going to kiss me again," she blurted out.

Alex chuckled. *Always so damn blunt.* "Aye, but this kiss will be nothing like the first." He tipped her chin and looked deep into her confused eyes, feeling the impossible lure of destiny. He'd been waiting too long to have her lips beneath his, to slide his tongue into the sweet recesses of her mouth, to taste her passion. And to unleash his own. His body strained to feel her pressed against him, responding to his kiss.

This time there would be no holding back.

The dark, sensual promise of his words coiled inside her. *Dear God, he was going to kiss her.* And this time it would not be so gentle. Her body felt taut with anticipation, and her heart fluttered wildly in its small cage. *Anticipation,* she acknowledged. But this wasn't what she'd wanted when she'd come after him . . . was it?

Meg had seen his expression in the hall and simply reacted. Her only thought had been to find him and discover what had caused him pain. Tonight, she'd caught a glimpse of the dark turmoil simmering beneath the surface. She'd seen him angry before, yes, but nothing like the raw emotion she'd witnessed when he'd looked at Dougal MacDonald. But for a moment, before the cold, murderous rage set in, there had been a bleakness in his gaze of such immeasurable pain, it had cut her to the quick. It was as if he'd bared a tiny window of his soul.

He always appeared so remote and untouchable. A

fierce, indestructible warrior in complete control of everything around him. But seeing Dougal had caused a crack, even if only a temporary one, in that wall of reserve. Alex wasn't detached at all, she realized. He felt things very strongly, more than she ever would have guessed.

So she'd gone after him. But she'd sought only to comfort him, not end up in his arms. No matter how much her body claimed otherwise.

He'd been furious that she'd followed him. For a moment, she'd had the fleeting feeling that she was disturbing him. But his anger had quickly dissolved into an emotion far more terrifying. Passion.

He pulled her tight against him, enveloping her with the force of his overwhelming masculinity. Masculinity that no longer felt like a threat. All she could think of was heat and strength. She *should* feel vulnerable, pinned between the cold stone wall at her back and the hot muscular wall of his chest. But instead she felt a rush of excitement, a sensual thrill of pure feminine pleasure. Alex MacLeod was built to dominate. But he wasn't overpowering her. As much as she'd like to claim otherwise, Meg was not helpless to resist. She could resist, she just didn't want to.

God help her, she could feel every inch of his long, hard body pressed against her. She shuddered, suddenly aware of one very long, hard part in particular, intimately wedged against her stomach. The overwhelming evidence of his arousal sent a rush of heat pooling in her breasts and stomach and between her legs. She felt his passion as her own.

Half-hidden in the shadows, the lean, handsome lines

of his face were fixed in a taut mask of desire. His ice blue eyes bored into her, almost as if he were silently challenging her. He'd laid down the gauntlet, forced her to acknowledge the strength of his desire and dared her to accept. He nudged his hips against her just a little closer, so there could be no mistaking his intent. Meg's breath caught high in her throat. The slight friction had set off a thousand tiny bursts of awareness. Her body tingled where they joined, as if awakening from a deep slumber. It felt like nothing she'd ever felt before. It left her . . . wanting.

What was he doing to her? He hadn't even kissed her, and she had never been more intimately aware of the wicked cravings of her body.

After what seemed like an eternity, though it had been only seconds, he cupped her chin in his fingers and lifted her mouth to his. He brushed his lips against hers, just as he had on the balcony. And just as before, Meg's heart stopped, feeling the sharp yearning for something more. He seemed to be waging an internal battle, looking deep into her eyes for the answer.

Apparently he found it, because he kissed her again, this time harder. His lips covered hers with a raw, possessive hunger that took her breath away. No longer reverent and gentle, his mouth was warm and demanding, moving over hers with a skill that demanded her response. His lips were achingly soft, the masculine taste of him divine. Of wine and spice and dark desires.

Awash in sensation, she dissolved in his arms, succumbing willingly to his exquisite plunder. Her body sighed with relief. She'd been fighting desire and attraction for too long. His kiss had shattered whatever fragile barrier had existed to protect her from the truth. There was something so right, so perfect, in the feel of his mouth on hers.

She could no longer deny it. And neither could he. The fierce pounding of his heart against hers told her that he was just as affected as she.

His strong hands covered her body, roaming over her back and waist with a firm caress as if to memorize every inch of her, leaving a trail of fiery sensation in his wake. He skimmed over her hips and cupped her bottom, nudging her ever closer, moaning when he found that perfect fit.

A sound of voices down the corridor, not that far away, startled her. She protested against his mouth, and Alex lifted his head, breaking the kiss. Her breath came hard as their eyes met in the darkness.

"Someone's coming," she whispered in a breathy voice that seemed not her own.

"Ignore them," he said in a tight voice. "Perhaps they'll leave."

Meg knew that hidden in the shadows they could not be seen unless someone was almost on top of them. The voices drew nearer. She broke their stare and lifted up on her toes, attempting to look over his shoulder. As if he knew what she planned, he lowered his mouth to hers again, preventing her from doing anything other than reveling in the exquisite feelings wrought by his mouth moving over hers in a slow, sensual dance.

She would have forgotten all about the sounds, but a voice called out, "Who's there?"

Alex's body tensed. She might not have noticed if she hadn't been practically molded to him.

"Giggle," he ordered with his mouth still pressed against hers.

Appalled, she pulled back her head. "What!"

"Do you want them to see you? Just do it."

Meg did her best imitation of a simpering maid and tried to laugh. Apparently, it wasn't good enough, because Alex rolled his eyes and slid his fingers under her arm. Meg gasped with shock, only to giggle in earnest when he began to tickle her.

It worked. Meg heard a man say "find a chamber" and "tryst." The sound of voices retreated, punctuated by the firm slam of a door only moments later.

Meg's cheeks burned when she realized what those men had thought and could have seen. But something wasn't right. Questions began to form. With the masque going on tonight, this part of the palace should be deserted. Who were those men? One of the voices had sounded familiar. She turned to study Alex, realizing that he was watching her with a strange expression on his face. He never had explained what he was doing lurking in the shadows. She opened her mouth to question him, but, sensing her transient thoughts, Alex pulled her closer, driving all lucidity from her mind as his mouth came down on hers again.

Meg gasped at the unexpected invasion of his tongue. She heard his groan as he plundered the soft recesses of her mouth with the warm, seductive stroke. For a moment she stilled, not sure what to do. This couldn't be proper. Nothing that felt this wantonly delicious could be. But the intense sensations shooting through her body soon brought her past the point of caring.

Her body felt liquid, dissolved in the dark heat of his

mouth and tongue. He stroked deeper and deeper, until anticipation filled every part of her body. His mouth moved over her jaw and down her neck as he ravaged her with heated kisses that sent her skin aflame.

A soft moan of pleasure escaped her lips. Meg couldn't believe the throaty sound had possibly come from her. His mouth moved across her chest, achingly close to the edge of her bodice. Her body softened in response, melting deeper into his hold. She could feel the hard chisel of his muscles crushing her body to his. All that warmth. It was going to her head, she felt so dreamy.

She'd never felt like this before. Helpless. Mindless. At the utter mercy of a force much stronger than rationality. What had she done, unleashing something she could not control? All she could do was respond, melting against him, giving herself over to the heat that flamed between them.

Slowly, tentatively, she reached up and grabbed his shoulders to steady herself, but perhaps also because for some strange reason she yearned to feel his strength under her fingertips. To test his impossible hardness, to see whether he burned as hot as she. He did. His shoulders were as hard as rock. Her hands spread across their wide breadth and slid down the steely muscles of his arms. Instinctively the muscles flexed, and Meg felt the strange urge to pull off his doublet. To see the bare layers of hard muscle under her fingertips. God he was magnificent.

Touching him only made her want more. Drunk with wanton urges, she couldn't get close enough. Stretching up against him, she pressed her breasts to him and her nipples strained against the granite wall of his chest. For a moment, she even wondered how it would feel to rub herself up and down against the hard naked planes of his chest. Skin to skin.

As if he could read her thoughts, his kiss grew more demanding, deeper, harder, wetter—as if he sought to devour her. The rough stubble on his chin tore the soft skin around her mouth. His hips circled against her, pressing her back even harder against the wall. His hand came up to cup her breast, and Meg moaned again, delirious with pleasure.

The massive evidence of his arousal pressed into her stomach, demanding. An odd wave of heat gushed below her abdomen. Heavy with desire, she felt a strange urge to move against him, to rub her tingling flesh against the rigid column pressed so firmly against her, to ease the restlessness quivering uncontrollably in her body. The world had seemingly spun out of control, and Meg fought to hang on.

Meg was innocent, but not ignorant. Inquisitive by nature, she understood what happened between a man and a woman—privacy was not a Highland way of life. She'd also sought to further her education by studying the mating habits of animals. She'd never dreamed that her body would compel her to the deed. But she wanted him deep within her, filling her with his heat. Surely she was wicked, and that she craved him between her legs would assuredly send her to eternal damnation. But, oh, what a way to fall.

Through the haze of pleasure, her mind sounded caution. He was not the man for her. But her heart urged him on, knowing that nothing could be more right than kissing him, making love to him.

This was how it felt to lose control.

The bubble burst. One lucid thought brought her back to reality. What was she doing? It was too much: his fervor, her inexperience. The intensity of her own response.

This was passion at its most terrifying extreme. This was passion unlike anything she'd experienced before, the type that could make her lose her head. The strength of her desire for Alex was nothing like what had come before. Her heart hammered with sudden panic, with a sudden fear of the loss of control.

Ewen's handsome, smiling face swam before her eyes.

Only once before had she allowed emotions to cloud her judgment, but it had been a lesson well learned. The mistake with Ewen had nearly cost her everything. She couldn't let it happen again.

The reversal of emotion that came over her was startling in its intensity. It was as if all of the hot waves of passion surging through her veins had suddenly turned to shards of ice.

She couldn't do this.

Without thought but to escape, in one swift movement she brought her knee up hard against his crotch, as her father had taught her to do if she ever found herself in such a circumstance.

She was free. Alex hunched over and uttered what was surely the most vile expletive she'd ever heard. His face contorted. Meg bit her lip, feeling a wave of remorse. Her father had not mentioned this amount of pain.

She moved cautiously back out of his reach, sucking in air, trying to retrieve her breath. Surely she must look ravaged, with her mussed hair and bruised lips. But she didn't care. She had to get out of here.

"What the hell was that for?" he moaned, his voice hoarse.

"I wanted you to stop."

"You might have said something first."

"I . . ." Mortified, she put her hand over her mouth, realizing she hadn't even tried to push him away. She'd simply reacted. Overreacted. "I'm sorry," she whispered, tears building behind her eyes, threatening to break.

Shaking, whether with panic or still blistering desire she did not know, Meg turned and fled toward the sanctuary of her chamber.

The urge to spill the contents of his stomach passed. Eyes burning, Alex watched Meg race down the corridor. What the hell had just happened? One minute she'd been responding as if she couldn't get enough of him, the next his bollocks had been smashed up to his rib cage. All of his training with the MacGregors had not adequately prepared him for that particular move. But it was not one he'd likely forget. Ever.

Slowly, the pain ebbed. Had he frightened her? He must have. She was innocent. He shouldn't have rushed her. But one taste had nearly driven him over the edge.

He never would have imagined that such passion lay dormant under that innocent exterior. It amazed him that such a serious young woman could inspire such wickedly carnal feelings.

Her response had driven him half-mad with lust. Although inexperienced, she'd returned his kiss with eagerness and enough instinctive skill to make him forget she was so innocent. Her erotic little groans of pleasure had urged him on. But the tentative touch of her hands on his shoulders and the slight rubbing of her unmistakably hard nipples against his chest had been a potent aphrodisiac that proved impossible to resist.

At that point, he'd completely forgotten that it was merely a kiss of convenience to cover up his presence in the corridor.

No, he was lying to himself.

He'd forgotten about that the moment their lips touched. He'd wanted her since the first moment he'd laid eyes on her. And seeing her with Dougal had simply pushed him beyond endurance. He'd wanted to brand her with his kiss, to drive all thoughts of other men from her consciousness. To possess her in the most basic way.

But he'd never intended to take it so far. A few more minutes and he would have been doing a hell of a lot more than kissing her. He grew hard even at the memory. The honey sweet taste of her mouth and tongue, the pressure of her full breasts on his chest, the torture of her hips pressed against his rock-hard erection. He'd sensed her reaction when he'd moved against her. She'd liked it. She was ripe and so sweetly passionate. The urge to make her come had nearly overwhelmed him. Just the thought of rubbing her sensitive mound up and down his thick column over and over until she shattered . . .

He groaned. He couldn't even think about it. His was so hard, he could explode.

How had one small kiss progressed to such a passionate conflagration so quickly? A conflagration that had scared Meg enough to cause her to nearly make him a eunuch. He should have anticipated her fear. The force of their passion had surprised him. Somewhere between the moan and the knee he had lost himself in the heat, in the lust, and hadn't even realized that she might be frightened.

Hell, it even scared him.

Kissing Meg Mackinnon had been every bit as dangerous as Alex had expected. Meg made him think of things he'd never thought about before. Of a family. A home. Of a future that was not for him. One wee lass could wield the power to undo him. To make him lose focus—and if he wasn't careful, to destroy all that he'd worked for. His duty right now was to his brother and his clan, and to a certain extent to his dead cousins. A duty that was at cross-purposes to the type of man Meg needed to ensure the stability of her clan.

He might not approve her methods, but he should be thanking Meg for putting a stop to it. Indeed, it would be better if he avoided Meg Mackinnon altogether.

Like the black death.

Indeed, she'd already caused him enough trouble, including alerting the men he'd been spying on to his presence in the corridor. At least their kiss had prevented him from being discovered. And Meg's giggling had prevented further investigation, turning the men back to their meeting—albeit this time with the door shut.

Of course, he would apologize to her. But not right now. He still needed to learn when the ships would be leaving. He could only hope the king's minions were still discussing their plans. He was just about to slip back down the corridor when he heard more footsteps coming toward him from the direction of the hall.

From the shadows, he watched as a man crept slowly past the corridor and peered down the hall in his direction. Alex held perfectly still. It was dark, but he could see that the large, heavyset man was not a guest at the masque. He wore the breeches and jerkin of a guardsman. Seeing no one, the man continued on, heading in the direction where Meg had disappeared, not back toward the hall.

He felt a flicker of unease. There was something devious about the man's movements. Like Alex, he did not want to be seen. But there was more. Something niggled at the back of his memory. The man looked familiar. The realization hit him: He could be one of the men from the tavern. But he couldn't be sure; he'd never seen his face and had only a quick glance at the rest of him.

Alex looked back down the hall to the chamber where Lord Chancellor Seton and Secretary Balmerino were still meeting. An opportunity like this might not come again. He might never learn when they planned to leave, vital information if he and his kin were going to have any kind of chance of repelling the incursion. This was his sole purpose for being at court. Not to chase after some tiny stubborn woman and protect her from a phantom threat.

He knew what he *should* do. His head urged him back down the corridor toward the meeting. But another part of him, a deeper part of him, wouldn't let him go. Meg could be in danger. He just couldn't ignore the possibility that the two men were one and the same.

It might be ridiculous, but if something happened to

her, Alex would never forgive himself. Cursing the mess he'd managed to embroil himself in, he started down the passageway after Meg's would-be assailant.

But this was the last time he would put her before his mission.

Chapter 9

Meg's resolve had been torn to shreds by the events of the evening before. She felt an almost desperate need to see Jamie. To prove that kissing Alex had not changed anything and that she would still go through with her plan. She resisted the urge to press her fingers to her mouth for the hundredth time, still able to feel him on her lips.

She glanced at Elizabeth seated in the chair opposite her. They'd decided to spend a quiet morning in the salon after the "excitement" (if only Elizabeth knew) of the masque last night. Meg was glad of the short reprieve.

Holding her cup to her lips, she took a long sip of warm beef broth, peering at her friend over the rim. "Jamie should be returning soon?" she asked innocuously.

Not fooled for an instant, Elizabeth glanced up from the chess pieces she was organizing. "In a day or two. You're eager to see him?"

Meg ignored the hint of surprise in Elizabeth's voice. "I'm always pleased to see your brother," she replied firmly. "What was the urgent business for your cousin, anyway? Jamie was unusually vague."

Elizabeth shrugged. "I'm not sure. Something to do with ships for the king, I think."

Meg's brows gathered across her nose. "Ships? What for?"

"I don't know. But he did mention that he'd have to travel to Fife in a few weeks because the ships would be leaving. I'm sure he'll tell you all about it when he returns." Elizabeth studied her face a little longer. A wrinkle appeared between her brows. "Are you sure you are feeling well today, Meg? You look a little pale."

Meg shook her head. "I'm tired, that's all. Last night was—" She stopped, feeling the presence of someone beside her. She glanced up, startled to see Alex. How long had he been standing there listening to them? His ability to move so soundlessly was disconcerting. Not as disconcerting, however, as seeing him so soon after last night.

Color rose in her cheeks, realizing he'd probably heard Elizabeth's comments about her wan appearance. And Alex, unlike Elizabeth, knew the reason why. Their eyes met, and the memory of what happened between them rushed back to her consciousness full force. She lowered her lashes, not trusting herself to look at him for fear that he would read her turbulent emotions as easily as she read Latin.

The strain of the situation was wearing on her. Meg felt like a tightly wrought bundle of nerves. Always before she'd been able to manage the stress of her duties and responsibilities, but this was different. This was personal. Her emotions lay so close to the surface, at any moment she felt as though she could burst into tears.

It was horrifying.

Meg was not the type of woman who cried. Ever.

Tears, she knew, were a sign of weakness, of giving over to emotion. She'd always tried to solve her problems with logic. But there was nothing logical about last night. The truth was that Meg did not know how to solve this sort of problem. How could she forget about Alex MacLeod when each day he seemed more permanently imprinted on her consciousness?

So last night, for once, Meg's vaunted control over her emotions had lost to the powerful relief brought by a healthy deluge of tears. Tears that had begun to fall the moment she'd made it to the safety of her bedchamber and hadn't stopped for some time.

Never had she been so embarrassed. Her conduct had been outrageous. She'd responded to Alex as eagerly as a wanton and then lashed out, causing him real pain, when her own lack of control had gripped her in a moment of terror. Thinking only of escape, she'd reacted reflexively. What must he think of her? She owed him an apology, but she wasn't sure how to broach the subject delicately.

Why, why, why had she allowed him to kiss her? And how could she have succumbed so easily? When he'd kissed her, she'd lost the ability to form a coherent thought. She hadn't wanted to think at all. She'd only . . . wanted. She would never be able to look at him again without remembering precisely how it felt to have his mouth on hers, devouring her as if she were a delicious sweet. Meg's cheeks flamed. But it wasn't only the kiss. Never would she forget the erotic sensation of his hand on her breast and his arousal pressed firmly against her. Or of how close she wanted to be to him.

Grateful for small mercies, Meg had made it back to her room without seeing anyone. One look at her face would have announced her just-been-thoroughly-ravished state to all. She'd managed to clear away all vestiges of her tears by the time Rosalind and Elizabeth arrived to check on her.

According to her mother, when Meg didn't return to the hall, Alex had insisted that she check and make sure Meg had arrived safely in her room. His concern for her, especially after what she'd done to him, only sufficed to make her feel worse.

Meg was more confused than she'd ever been in her life. She had a duty to her father and to her clan. She thought of the unspoken plan hatched all those years ago. The plan that would ensure her brother would be chief and the clan safe from an outside threat. The plan that hinged on her choice of husband. Never had she thought it would be a sacrifice to fulfill that duty. But neither had she counted on meeting a man like Alex MacLeod.

He could ruin everything. How was she supposed to make the right decision if all she could think about was a man who was completely wrong for her?

Or was he?

That was the question that kept ricocheting around inside her head. She'd had her doubts from the first, and the more she knew of him, the more his reason for being at court did not make sense. There were too many things about him that simply did not add up. She wanted to believe that he was more than a mercenary who'd sold his sword and fallen out with his chief. But what if it was only wishful thinking on her part?

Her heart had failed her before; she would never forget how thoroughly she'd been deceived by Ewen Mackinnon. Alex was nothing like Ewen, but he was hiding something.

"I'm sorry to interrupt," Alex said. Meg looked up when he spoke to find him staring at her. "Your mother asked me to tell you that she will be delayed and unfortunately will have to miss your ride this afternoon."

Meg frowned, looking down at the gown she'd donned in anticipation of their outing. Her mother had been looking forward to riding in Holyrood Park. What had changed her mind. As if Alex could read her mind, he added, "I believe she is attending to Lady Seton."

Lady Seton could be quite demanding. Her mother had probably been conscripted into an afternoon of cards or embroidery. Lady Seton . . . *That was it.* The voice she'd heard last night had belonged to Lord Chancellor Seton. What had Alex been doing in that corridor?

Alex stood there, watching her with a strange expression on his face. Uncomfortable, Meg said, "Yes, well, thank you for the message, but as you can see, we were just about to play a game."

"Perhaps Alex would like to play instead?" Elizabeth asked smoothly, without a hint of a stutter.

Meg's pulse leapt as she shot her friend a chilling glare. She didn't want to be in the same room with him, let alone stare at him across a chessboard for who knew how long—well, probably not *that* long. But she didn't relish even a few minutes. So before he could respond, Meg interjected, "I'm sure Laird MacLeod is much too busy—"

"Thank you, Lizzie," he said, cutting Meg off. "I believe I could spare time for a game or two." His piercing blue eyes held hers, and Meg temporarily forgot everything but the deafening pounding of her heart wrought by the smoky intensity of his gaze. The intimacy they'd shared last night hung between them. Awareness settled low in her belly as she remembered the rough scrape of his chin against her skin, and the feel of his mouth roaming across her jaw, down her neck, and along her bodice, marking her.

She dropped her gaze. "You play chess?" she asked. Chess was not the typical warrior's game. It required exceptional skill, patience, and strategy. Intrigued, Meg wondered what type of player he might be. He was a leader, a man who liked to be in control. She assumed he'd play a straightforward attack.

Alex lifted one eyebrow, perhaps reading her surprise. "A bit."

Elizabeth stood up, relinquishing her chair to Alex with a grin of amusement. "I must warn you, Alex, Meg is an exceptional player. Virtually unbeatable."

Alex returned her smile. "I appreciate the warning, Lizzie. Although I would have expected as much."

Meg would have liked to murmur some maidenly words of modesty, but Elizabeth spoke the truth, better for him to have fair warning. She considered him from beneath her lashes. Alex was a fiercely proud man; she'd make sure to have care and not trounce him too thoroughly.

Assuming she could concentrate, of course. When he sat down, his large frame seemed to overwhelm the small area. The wooden chair where Elizabeth had sat now looked as if it had been made for a child. He moved, and a hint of spice wafted through the air, harkening back to the corridor. She remembered that intoxicating scent all too well and the way the masculine essence had enveloped her, drowning her in heat. Her body prickled with awareness. The space was too small. Too intimate. Too much of a reminder of last night.

And of how easily she'd succumbed.

Forcing herself to focus on the game, Meg reached across the board and nervously adjusted some of the ebony pieces that Elizabeth had been setting up.

Alex stopped her, circling her wrist with his strong fingers. Startled by the heat of his touch and the sensation rippling through her, Meg looked up into his face to see an amused glint in his blue eyes. "They're fine. I don't think it's necessary for the pieces to all face precisely the same direction."

Meg cheeks fired; she hadn't even realized what she'd been doing. Her penchant for orderliness was a great source of amusement to her mother and Elizabeth, and now, apparently, to Alex. But his smile could stop her heart. She responded with one of her own, realizing that she liked his teasing. Liked the fact that he noticed the small things about her.

"After you," he said, releasing her wrist and motioning to the ivory pieces set out before her.

She took a deep breath and studied the board intently. Though she was confident in her abilities, only a fool would dismiss an opponent without ascertaining something of his skill, so Meg paid close attention to his defense of her opening bishop's attack. After the first few moves, however, she relaxed. He was not a novice player but was also not a very sophisticated one, using a rather plebeian defense strategy against her attack. She'd already captured one of his pawns, and one of his bishops was in jeopardy. This shouldn't take too long.

He moved a pawn, and Meg noticed how his large,

battle-scarred hands dwarfed the carved chess pieces. She remembered exactly how gentle those callused warrior's fingers could be.

"You received a message from your father yesterday?" he asked, breaking her trance.

"How did you know about that?"

"Your mother told me last night." He saw the look on her face and explained, "I saw a man following you and didn't realize he was one of your father's captains."

Meg repressed a flicker of unease. Thomas Mackinnon had arrived yesterday with the missive from her father. Ever since she'd refused his suit, she'd felt uncomfortable around the man, but thankfully he would be returning to Skye right away. "Bishop—" She lifted her gaze, taking the piece. "Is that why you asked my mother to check on me?"

He nodded, and warmth spread over her. It was somehow comforting to realize that he was watching out for her. But why was he? "Do you still believe that the attack was not random?"

"There's always the possibility that it wasn't," he said, moving a pawn. "Until the men are caught, I would advise exercising caution. Better to be vigilant and safe than careless and sorry."

She tried to smother her growing excitement—he'd just left his knight vulnerable. This would be a quick game indeed. "Knight," she said, capturing the piece. She broke her concentration on the game long enough to appraise his expression. She still didn't see why anyone would want to harm her, but she trusted his judgment. "I suppose you are right. I will be careful."

"Good."

They played in companionable silence for a few minutes, and Meg was surprised by how natural it seemed. She could almost imagine countless evenings spent relaxing before the fire across a chessboard from Alex. For a moment the sensation was so real, she felt a pang of longing when it faded. But Alex was hardly a man to stay near the hearth. He was too much of a warrior. A fighter.

Though for a man who'd spent his life on battlefields, she had to admit that Alex demonstrated an unusual ability to adapt to his surroundings. Never would she have imagined the fierce outlaw who'd rescued her in the forest relaxing across a chessboard from her at Holyrood House. But never did she doubt that he was the same man.

The comfort of her surroundings, however, was short-lived. She could feel his eyes on her, lingering on her mouth.

"About last night—"

"I'm sorry," she blurted out, mortified color heating her cheeks. Meg, who was usually so direct herself, couldn't believe he'd brought it up without preamble. *Dear God, she hoped Elizabeth wasn't listening*. She couldn't bear to look at him. "I didn't mean to hurt you," she said in a low voice brimming with embarrassment. "I wasn't thinking, I was frightened, I simply reacted—"

"The fault was mine." He looked into her eyes. "You need say nothing more. I assure you that it will not happen again."

Something twisted in her chest. It was what she wanted, wasn't it?

The truth was that she wasn't sure anymore.

Alex moved his knight. Meg knit her brows. That was an odd move.

He leaned back in his chair a little, studying her. "I hope the news from home was not troubling."

Meg shook her head. "There are some matters that needed my attention, and my father wanted to know whether we would be returning in a couple of weeks as we'd intended." In other words, her father wished to know whether Meg had chosen a husband.

Alex understood. "Are you ready to return home, then? Have you made your decision?" he asked quietly.

Meg fidgeted with a pawn, betraying her discomfort with his bluntness. She peeked up at him, looking for some indication that her answer mattered. But his face was infuriatingly blank. "I thought I had."

He stared at her, mute, his jaw set in a firm line. He looked as though he wanted to say something, but instead he studied the chessboard, allowing the thick waves of his golden hair to fall forward, shielding his expression. She wanted to brush his hair to the side and force him to say something. Instead, he captured her knight.

Meg frowned, surprised to have missed that particular threat.

She studied the board, suddenly having the feeling that she had missed more than just the chess move. Why did she have the feeling that she was being played? That Alex was far shrewder than he had let on? She decided to put her theory to the test. "My father sought my advice about a tacksman who would like to pay a portion of his rents this year in barley instead of oats." Realizing her rook was vulnerable, she moved to protect it. "I told him it didn't matter."

"You should have told him no," Alex countered offhandedly. "It was a wet winter. Oats will fetch a higher price at market this year."

Which was exactly, in fact, what she'd told her father. His quick analysis impressed her. Alex took another piece, and Meg frowned. She studied the board, but it took her a moment to realize what she was seeing. Either it was a coincidence or he'd utilized a brilliant strategy that she'd never seen before. In a few moves, he could have her.

"Is something wrong?" he asked.

Meg swallowed. "No." She moved her piece, and he immediately moved his knight into position.

"Check," he said.

Meg moved to protect her king. Alex MacLeod was no novice, but she was not worried. She'd been suitably cautioned, but not outmaneuvered.

"Where did you learn to play chess?" she asked.

He thought for a moment, probably searching for just the right words that would tell her as little as possible. "Initially, I learned from my brother, Rory. We played together most evenings while growing up—too tired from our training to do anything else." He paused, clearly debating whether to say more. "And I played with my men for months when I was a reluctant 'guest' of the MacDonalds some years back. Of course, they would hardly give prisoners use of a chess set, but we managed to play thousands of games scratched out in the dirt." He lowered his voice so much that she barely heard him add, "I would have gone mad otherwise."

Sensing that he had just shared something important, and personal, Meg asked carefully, "Why were you imprisoned, Alex?"

His face darkened. She thought he was not going to answer, but after a few moments he spoke. "About four years ago, I was on the losing side of the battle now known as 'the Corrie of the Foray.' Many of my kinsmen were killed that day. I suppose I was one of the lucky ones. I survived, but only to be imprisoned in the dungeon of Dunscaith Castle." His voice sounded hollow, utterly devoid of emotion.

"I've heard of it, of course, it was the last great clan battle fought on Skye. I just didn't realize you . . ." She stopped when she noticed how hard his hands were gripping the arms of his chair. "How long were you imprisoned?"

"Three months."

Meg sensed that there was more, much more, but that he would not speak of it. At least not with her. But her disappointment turned to horror when she remembered something that had been needling her since the masque, something else that he had refused to answer.

"Alex?"

He turned and met her gaze. Their eyes held, and something strange passed between them, almost an understanding. He knew where her questions were heading.

Please let me be wrong this time, Meg prayed. But Dunscaith was a MacDonald stronghold.

Her voice was hesitant. "Alex," she said, and paused. "Is . . . that how you know Dougal MacDonald?"

His face darkened at the name. From the bright intensity of his eyes and the tautness of his mouth, she knew the answer before he replied.

"Yes."

Her heart dropped to her stomach with dreadful comprehension. Unknowingly, she'd allowed herself to be wooed by his jailer. No wonder he had seemed so upset to see her with Dougal. Meg thought back to the scene he'd witnessed. Dougal MacDonald had touched her. Yet another misfire in her inexperienced attempts to play the games of court.

"I'm sorry," she whispered.

Their eyes held a little longer, before he dropped his gaze. He nodded, apparently satisfied with her apology but indicating his unwillingness to discuss the subject further.

Despite his obvious aversion to talking about himself, Meg wasn't quite done yet. The knowledge that he'd fought for his clan only bolstered her belief that he was not what he claimed. She had to find out.

"Alex, what are you really doing at court?"

His eyes flashed with annoyance. "Didn't we already have that conversation?"

"I don't believe you."

His jaw clenched. "Leave it be, Meg."

But Meg could not heed the warning. "I've seen the way you watch everyone around you, and what does it have to do with being in that corridor last night at the masque?"

He moved his rook. "Has anyone ever told you that you have an active imagination?"

Meg countered his move by putting pressure on his remaining bishop. "No," she said, refusing to be deterred. "Now, answer my question."

"I came to court to find work, I went to the hall to get away from Dougal—as you now know, I despise the man."

"I don't believe that is all of it."

"Believe what you want, but it's the truth." He shrugged with such indifference that Meg knew she was on to something.

She shook her head. "No, it's not." Her eyes raked his face, searching for a crack in the mask. "But I'll discover the truth, don't you doubt it."

But her threat didn't seem to concern him. The corner of his mouth lifted in a wry smile. "Meg?"

"What?" She looked down at the board, and her mouth fell open. *Impossible.*

"Checkmate."

"I can't believe I missed it," her mother lamented an hour later. Elizabeth had just finished filling her in about Alex's unexpected coup.

Meg looked at her mother and shook her head. She was taking far too much pleasure in Meg's defeat. "It's just a game, Mother."

"Just a game!" her mother exclaimed with mock incredulity. "How many times have I heard you and your father go on about the game of kings? The great arbiter of intellect. 'You can tell much about a person by how they play chess,' " she mimicked. "Now will you admit it?"

"Admit what?"

"Don't be obtuse, Margaret. Why, admit that Alex MacLeod is the perfect match for you, of course."

"Simply because he beat me at chess? I'm not perfect, Mother, I do lose occasionally."

Though Meg spoke in jest, her mother sobered. "There is nothing wrong with not being perfect, Meg."

But there is, Meg thought automatically, thinking of her beloved brother. "Of course there isn't," she agreed.

Rosalind's perpetually smiling countenance slipped, becoming unusually grave. "You strive so hard not to fail, to always do the right thing. Only recently have I realized why. But you do not need to put so much pressure on yourself, Meg. I love both of my children, and so does your father—even if he doesn't always know how to show it."

Meg hoped so, for Ian's sake. But why did her father's love always have to be filtered by disappointment and conditions?

Meg walked into the small solar, seeing Ian seated at her father's desk, a quill in his hand, and his fair head bent over a piece of parchment. Dread crept over her as she realized that another lesson was taking place.

"No, Ian. Not like that," her father said, trying to be patient. "You've added wrong again. One merk is thirteen shillings, four pence. So the rent on twenty-four merks of land is . . ."

Meg could hear the helplessness in her brother's voice. "I can't do it, Father."

"Of course you can." Her father's voice was harder this time. "Try again."

Ian's face twisted with frustration. He tried again. Meg's pulse raced anxiously as he scratched out a few numbers on the parchment. She hated to watch him struggle. She knew he was close to tears, and her father hated when Ian cried. Braw lads of sixteen years did not cry.

"You remember, Ian," Meg jumped in. "You did it

perfectly yesterday." She bent over and broke down the equation for him. Ian could multiply and divide well enough, it was just figuring out what to do that could be overwhelming for him. In a matter of minutes, he said proudly, "Fifteen pounds Scots, six shillings."

Her father nodded, satisfied, but his smile was reserved for Meg.

Her mother didn't want to see the truth. Her father didn't know what to do with Ian. Meg had spent her childhood protecting her brother from his disappointment. Not allowing her father to feel the absence of an heir ensured that he would not focus on Ian's limitations. But Meg didn't want to talk about her father and brother. "You are making too much of this, Mother. It was just a game."

"But surely you must be reconsidering Alex as a potential suitor, Meg?" Elizabeth asked. "Any man who can beat you at chess must be an exceptional strategist."

Elizabeth's question forced Meg to acknowledge the truth. Initially, she'd discounted Alex, considering him too much of a warmonger who didn't possess the necessary acumen to deal with the king's men. But she'd been wrong. Behind the strong sword arm and impressive physique lurked an incredibly sharp mind. Sharp enough to best her at chess, employing a brilliant strategic defense to counter her aggressive bishop's attack. Meg hadn't just lost, she'd been routed. Moreover, her mother and Elizabeth were right: His undeniable skill impressed her.

There was much about Alex MacLeod that impressed her.

Her mother stood before her, arms crossed over her chest, looking remarkably pleased with herself. "I'm right, Meg. Admit it. Alex MacLeod would make a perfect husband."

Part of her wanted to agree, but the other part still wasn't so sure. There were too many unknowns. If only she could figure out why she was so drawn to him. "I'll allow that there is more to him than the hardened warrior I first assumed. But there is another problem—he isn't looking for a wife."

"He might not be looking for a wife, but that doesn't have to prevent him from finding one. And since he's arrived at court, he's made no secret of his interest in you." Her mother's gaze was full of tenderness. "You seem more relaxed with Alex. Less worried. Why, I've even seen him wheedle a smile or two from you." She shook her head with obvious dismay. "You would do well to laugh more, my love. I have warned your father that he demands far too much from you. You are too young to have locked yourself away from the pleasures of the world and devoted your life to the management of Dunakin."

"I enjoy what I do, Mother."

"I know you do, child, but I believe there is more to it than that."

Meg bristled uncomfortably, unsure of exactly what her mother might reveal but knowing that she did not want to hear it. Especially if it involved more talk about Ian.

"I hope you will listen to your mother, Meg," Elizabeth said as she moved toward the door. "I would like nothing more than to have you as a sister. But Jamie deserves to be loved."

Not giving Meg the opportunity to respond, Elizabeth closed the door behind her, leaving Meg alone with Rosalind. Meg felt a twinge of guilt. Elizabeth was right, Jamie did deserve to be loved. And Meg would see to it that he was.

She glanced at her mother warily.

"Don't look so defensive, love. I don't want to upset you; I'm only considering your happiness. I want you to laugh more and worry less. You take on so much to protect your brother. If I'd realized sooner why you pushed yourself so hard, I would have intervened long ago."

The unusual vehemence in her voice surprised Meg.

Rosalind shook her head sadly. "If only I'd been able to give your father more sons. I blame myself."

"There is nothing to blame," Meg said unthinkingly, wanting to comfort her clearly distressed mother.

But Rosalind cut off her denial. "I can see what you are doing even if you cannot. I know that you are only trying to protect your brother by taking his responsibilities upon yourself, and yes, I should have realized why you pushed yourself so hard a long time ago. The pressure of always being the perfect daughter is too much. You have repressed your own desires for your brother's sake."

"No," Meg exclaimed vehemently, "you are wrong, Mother. I enjoy the work I do. I want the responsibility of managing Dunakin for myself. It has nothing to do with Ian."

"You may have convinced yourself of that, but I believe it has everything to do with Ian. You will settle for a man you do not love, thinking that you are doing right by Dunakin. You have blinded yourself to everything except finding the perfect man to take the place that your brother will never be able to fully occupy." Rosalind sighed. She clasped Meg's hands and stared deep into her eyes. "But no one is perfect, Meg, including you. I hope you do not wait until it is too late before you realize that you have made a mistake and married the wrong man, for all the wrong reasons."

Meg hated being scrutinized; she only wanted to do what was right for her clan. Why did it have to be so difficult? She stood up and headed for the door, needing to breathe.

"Where are you going?" her mother asked.

"To put this riding gown to use."

"But it's getting late. Wait until tomorrow and I will go with you."

Meg gave her mother a reassuring smile. "I won't be long." Just long enough to get her mind back on track.

Chapter 10

It was well past midday before Alex neared the Sheep's Heid Inn. He'd taken a circuitous route from the palace to make sure he had not been followed. The meeting he'd arranged with Robbie couldn't have come at a better time. Thanks to Lizzie and Meg, the missive for his brother that Alex carried in his leather sporran now contained valuable information.

Originally, Alex had planned to ride out after breaking his fast, but he hadn't been able to prevent himself from checking on Meg first. He'd vowed to protect her, and it was his duty to see to her safety. Or at least that's what he told himself.

It was foolish, especially after his error last night in thinking that Meg was in danger. At first he thought his fears well-founded, when the man he was following led him toward the wing housing the ladies' bedchambers. Moreover, like the man Alex had seen in the tavern, this man was large and heavyset with red hair. As the light improved, Alex was able to get a better look at him. He was of middling years, with a blunt nose and a face that bore the unmistakable scars of a warrior. But just as Alex was about to detain him and question him about his purpose, the man joined up with a few of the Mackinnon guardsmen that Alex had ordered to keep watch on Meg and her mother.

They'd introduced him as Thomas Mackinnon, only just arrived from Dunakin with a message from his chief. Information that Rosalind Mackinnon corroborated only minutes later when she returned to her chamber from the masque. The man Alex had suspected of intending to harm Meg was actually a trusted Mackinnon guardsman—which made his desire to see Meg this morning ridiculous.

He couldn't explain it, but he needed to see her for himself. Perhaps it was better if he didn't try. But this time, his unreasonable concern for Meg was rewarded. He couldn't believe it when he'd walked into the solar and heard the information he'd been most eager to hear casually bandied about in conversation. Thanks to wee Lizzie, Alex now knew when the ships were leaving. Sometime in mid-August, the Fife Adventurers would set sail for Lewis.

And he would be waiting for them.

Alex approached the inn from the rear. He hoped Robbie hadn't had any problem finding the place; he wanted to pass on the missive and return to court as soon as possible. He didn't like the idea of leaving Meg alone. He would stay long enough only for his mount to be watered and to pass Robbie the wax-sealed note for his brother. The badge of MacLeod—the boar head emblazoned with the clan motto, "Hold Fast"—would prove to his brother that the carefully worded message indeed came from him.

The message should reach Skye well in advance of Rory's departure. In less than two weeks, Rory and Isabel were due to arrive in Edinburgh to satisfy the yearly obligation for the Island chiefs to present themselves before the Privy Council. Allegedly, it was to ensure their continued good behavior, but in reality it was a humiliating reminder of the king's new authority over the "uncivilized" Highlands.

Alex looked forward to their arrival. It would be the first journey for Isabel in some time, as she had only recently delivered their third child in as many years. His two small nieces and the newly arrived, much anticipated nephew would remain at Dunvegan.

With any luck, Alex hoped to have more detailed information to report to his brother when he arrived. There wouldn't be much time to formulate a plan of action if they were to beat the Fife Adventurers to Lewis, but Alex knew that whatever action Rory and the other Island chiefs decided to take, he would play an integral part. And this time he would not let his kin down.

Alex battled the inclination to leave for Lewis immediately. But he must not act precipitously. He would leave nothing to chance. There was time yet. So he would stay, waiting patiently for Rory to arrive so he could receive his orders and coordinate their plans. Until then, he would see what further information he could discover. Including what had brought Dougal MacDonald to court. Alex suspected that the arrival of a MacDonald at court was not a coincidence. If the MacDonalds intended to double-cross the Island chiefs, Alex intended to know about it.

And in the meantime . . .

There was Meg to consider. Once Jamie returned, Alex would forgo his temporary role of protector. Until then, he knew he'd have to tread carefully. He'd come dangerously close to compromising her the last time they'd been together. But it wasn't just his lust that he was worried about. Thinking back on their chess match, Alex realized just how easy it would be to grow complacent. He'd enjoyed matching wits with her. Far too much.

Dismounting, he glanced around the stable yard and was glad to see Robbie coming toward him from the stone-and-thatch inn. Except for a bit more dirt, the lad appeared no worse for the wear. He clapped Robbie on the back in greeting. "I see you've managed to stay in one piece."

Robbie grinned. "So far, my laird."

Alex lowered his voice. "Any problems?"

The boy shook his head.

"Good. We have much to discuss. But not here. Inside."

Robbie took the reins and led Alex's destrier into the stables. After putting the fear of God in the stable lads, he left them with specific instructions for tending the prized mount. They'd crossed the yard and were just about to enter the inn when Alex felt the unmistakable weight of eyes upon him. Someone was watching him.

He tensed and quickly scanned the surrounding countryside. The sight that met his eyes flooded him with a swift rush of anger—nay, with rage. A party of riders was heading for him, led by none other than Meg Mackinnon. He swore, causing Robbie to immediately reach for his dagger. Alex clenched his fists at his sides, trying to rein in his emotions. He recalled her earlier challenge: *I'll discover the truth, don't you doubt it.*

She'd followed him. And her stubborn foolishness could put his entire plan in jeopardy. *God's blood, he'd warned her. . . .*

Meg Mackinnon was about to learn that he was a man of his word.

This was exactly what she'd needed. As the imposing shadow of Holyrood House faded into the distance behind them, Meg and the party of guardsmen she'd brought as an escort wound through the copse of trees that banded the palace and headed deeper into Holyrood Park—the vast expanse of land that extended for hundreds of acres south of the palace. James V had enclosed the park only about fifty years ago, but for hundreds of years this land had been the hunting ground of kings. Now it was mostly green stretches of moors and glens with breathtaking vistas of dramatic rocky crags.

It felt like another world, yet she was barely beyond reach of the palace walls.

Meg took a deep breath, inhaling the freshness that surrounded her while relishing the rare moment of freedom from the rigidity of court. God, how she missed Skye. The quiet, the seclusion. This little piece of the Highlands tucked into a small corner of Edinburgh reminded her of all that awaited her at home.

Just as soon as she found a husband.

On that note, she decided it was time to return to the palace. Taking one last glance around, she caught a flash of gold shimmering in the sunlight ahead through a break in the trees. She could just make out the solitary figure of a man on horseback, riding toward a small building. Meg had to look twice just to make sure she hadn't imagined him. But the golden brown hair and tall, muscular form had become achingly familiar to her.

Alex. But what was he doing this far from the palace? Strange that he hadn't mentioned anything earlier, especially as he knew that her plans to go riding had been canceled. Unless he didn't want her to know. Meg debated for a moment—though in truth it wasn't much of a debate—and decided to follow him. She needed answers. Answers that would enable her to quiet the persistent voice in her head challenging her resolve.

Jamie would return to court soon, and when he did she wanted to be ready.

She and her guardsmen had just crested the hill behind the building when a tall, lanky man came out to greet Alex. Meg's eyes gleamed with satisfaction as she recognized the newcomer. He was one of the band of warriors who'd helped rescue her party in the forest. At the time, he'd struck her because of his youth and comparatively less fierce visage.

I knew it, she thought. *Let Alex try to deny it now.* But why had he lied? Why did he not want anyone to know it was he who'd come to their rescue that day in the forest?

Alex must have the instincts of a wolf. She had only just come into view, but he sensed her immediately. His head snapped around, and piercing ice blue eyes locked on to her. Even from a distance, she could feel the force of his anger. Anger that sent a shudder of trepidation reverberating through her body.

Which she promptly ignored.

Meg would not allow fear to get in the way of discovering the truth.

However, a bit of her bravado faltered under the ferocious onslaught of fiery rage. He really was quite menacing. She thought for a moment about returning to the palace, giving his anger time to dissipate, but she had a feeling he would follow her anyway. No, it was best not to show weakness, Alex would only smell blood. Stiffening her spine, she informed the guardsmen that they would take refreshment at what she now realized was an inn. Meg rode into the yard, pretending not to notice the fierce glare of the man waiting for her.

He looked different. It took her a moment to realize that he was dressed as he'd been the first time she'd seen him—in the traditional garb of a Highlander. He wore a fine woolen plaid of the softest blues and greens over a saffron linen tunic, secured at the waist with a thick leather belt and impressive dirk attached at his side. After weeks of being surrounded by colorful silks and satins, the *breacan feile* and *leine* that had fallen out of favor among the Lowlanders was a powerful reminder of home.

But it wasn't longing for home that was twisting her stomach in knots. It was the sheer magnetism of the man standing before her. Her mouth went dry just looking at him. Every inch the fierce, battle-hardened warrior who had rescued her, he looked big, strong, and heart-stoppingly male. It was hard to believe this was the same man who'd beaten her at chess a few hours ago. Perhaps it was that very dichotomy that drew her. And gave her reason to hope.

As she moved closer, she realized her error. Alex wasn't just angry, he was enraged. He strode toward her, every muscle of his body taut, taking the bridle in hand as if to forestall any thoughts of escape.

Gathering the reins of her courage, Meg lifted her chin and met his withering stare. "Laird MacLeod, what a surprise to find you here."

Alex didn't bother to respond; instead he turned to the young clansman at his side and said in a hard, clipped voice, "Robbie, take these men inside and get them some refreshment. Mistress Mackinnon and I have some things we need to discuss." His eyes fell on her, billowing her with heat. "In private."

When it looked as though her guardsmen were about to argue, Meg waved them inside, assuring them she would follow in a moment. She couldn't help noticing that the young warrior Robbie was gazing at her as if he felt sorry for her. As she watched them leave, a chill swept over her despite the warmth of the midsummer sun. Hesitantly, her gaze shifted back to Alex. Her pulse quickened. They were all alone.

Without a word, his hands circled her waist and he lifted her effortlessly from the saddle as if she weighed no more than a child. For a moment, she was pressed against him, and the familiar rush of pleasure softened her limbs. But she barely had time to savor the sensation before he'd set her firmly away from him, as if he didn't trust himself not to take out his anger on her person in an entirely different manner.

It shocked her to realize that the idea of his hot, violent passion didn't frighten her as it should.

His voice cracked like a whip. "In the stables. Now."

Meg bristled at his tone, digging in her heels. "Here will be fine."

A dangerous glint sparked in his eyes. "Either you can go on your own two feet or I will carry you there myself. But I don't think you will like how I do it."

Outraged, Meg pursed her lips together and walked as proudly as she could into the stables. She was relieved to see a couple of stable lads tending to a massive black horse that she'd seen once before. Her relief, however, was short-lived.

"Leave us," Alex ordered.

The lads took one look at him and scampered out as fast as they could. Chivalry was truly dead, she thought, watching them leave without a backward glance. As soon as the lads were gone, Alex rounded on her, his eyes pinning her to the ground. But he didn't touch her. She almost wished he would grab her arms and shake her; the dead calm on his face was infinitely more disconcerting. Unconsciously, she took a step back. "I warned you not to follow me. If you were a man, you'd be dead right now."

From the flatness of his tone, Meg did not doubt that he meant it. "Well, it's a good thing for me, then, that I'm a woman."

Apparently, now was not a good time for sarcasm. His eyes flared, and Meg could tell by the way the muscles twitched in his forearms that he was holding himself by a very thin thread. A very thin thread indeed.

"You test my patience, little one. Didn't your mother ever teach you not to play with fire?" His voice went deceptively soft. "You might get burned."

"You are making far too much of this," she said nervously. "I only thought to ride through the park, I had no intention of following you. But then I saw you, and . . . well, you can hardly blame me for being curious. You made no mention of riding today."

"I was not aware that I had to explain my comings and goings to you, Mistress Mackinnon."

Meg felt her cheeks burn with embarrassment. He was right, of course. He had no obligation to invite her along or inform her of his plans. Nor did she miss the formal mode of address. He was trying to put distance between them.

"You should never have left the palace," he continued. "I thought you agreed to have care until the men who attacked you are caught."

Was part of his anger because he was concerned for her safety?

"I brought an escort. Surely you would not see me chained to the palace for no good reason?"

His nostrils flared. "Almost being killed isn't reason enough? And I told you that I would watch over you. You should not have left without telling me."

A sugary smile curled her lips. "And if you had told me of your plans, I would have."

He took a step closer. "Don't push me, Meg."

She didn't like being put on the defensive. He had some explaining to do as well. "And what of you, Alex? Did you think that I would not remember your man Robbie?" She waved her hand toward his horse. "Or that terrifying beast over there? It was you in the forest that day. You *lied* to me. And I want to know why."

His jaw locked in stubborn silence.

Meg's emotions bubbled dangerously close to the surface. She wanted him to trust her. To give proof to the connection that had grown between them. She wanted some sign that her feelings were not the only ones in jeopardy. "What is it that you are not telling me?"

She took a few cautious steps toward him and gently laid her hand on his arm, feeling the tension coil under her fingertips. She stood so close, she could see the faint hint of stubble on his chin and the telltale pulse in his neck. The scar that crossed his brow seemed more prominent. And menacing. Yet she felt a strange urge to trace it with her fingertip.

"It has nothing to do with you," he said tightly.

"Then why can't you tell me—" Her voice broke. "Please, Alex."

Something in his expression shifted. The fury had been tempered by something that she could describe only as longing. She could see the tumult in his gaze. Deep inside, there was an internal battle being waged that she did not understand.

"Why can't you let it go?" His voice was strangely hoarse.

She couldn't tell him. She couldn't admit it even to herself. She couldn't let it go because she didn't want to make the wrong decision, and she'd begun to feel that the only right decision was standing before her.

"Do you really want me to?" she asked softly.

He knew what she was asking. She could see it on his face. She waited, not wanting to acknowledge how much his answer mattered. How much she wanted him to acknowledge what had grown between them.

"Yes, damn it. I want you to leave me alone."

Her heart plummeted. He didn't want her. Oh God, she was a fool. Chasing after a man who wanted nothing to do with her. Stricken, she turned away, not wanting him to see how much his rejection stung.

He swore. And before she realized what was happening, she was in his arms and his mouth fell on hers with a savage hunger that belied his indifference and took her breath away.

Meg was relentless, pushing him in a way that no one ever had before. Pushing him until he snapped.

From the moment she'd ridden into the inn yard, head held high with that adorable stubborn tilt to her tiny pointed chin, he'd been waging an internal battle. A battle between desire and reality. He wanted what he could not have.

It hurt just to look at her. The sun drenched her hair with flecks of gold light and flooded her translucent skin with a gentle pink warmth. Artfully arranged chestnut curls framed her moss green eyes to perfection. But it was her mouth that drove him wild. The memory of her honey soft sweetness laid siege to the fortress of his restraint.

Still, his anger held him in check. She'd followed him and interfered in his mission once again. He intended to be harsh, to ensure that she put an end to her foolish quest to discover his true purpose. With one wrong word, she could destroy everything.

But the hurt in her eyes undid him.

For a moment, he'd wanted to tell her why it was so important to him. Why he needed to do this. Why he wasn't for her. But for her own sake, as well as his, he could not embroil her in his scheme. A scheme that would brand him a traitor.

She thought that he was fighting for gold, but that couldn't be further from the truth. He was fighting for justice. For a way of life. For the land held by their clans for generations. But fighting was all that he knew how to do. He couldn't give her what she wanted.

But she'd stood there, achingly lovely, with hurt brimming in her eyes, and he'd reacted. With passion. As if he could wipe away the sting of his words with the force of his mouth.

At the first touch of her lips, he groaned, tasting the subtle sweetness that had been impossible to forget. Her heart fluttered wildly against his chest. He wanted to tame her, to kiss her into submission, to unleash the maelstrom of his passion, but his anger was immediately drenched in a flood of unexpected tenderness. He forced himself to be gentle, wooing a response with the soft urging of his mouth and tongue.

She relaxed and softened, melting right into him. His hand moved from her waist up her back to run his fingers through the silken web of curls tumbling down her back. It was even softer than he remembered. The subtle movement unleashed a beguiling scent of roses teasing his senses.

He moved his hand from her hair to gently trace the soft point of her chin, massaging with his thumb the frantic pulse below her ear. His fingers cupped her chin, tilting it back, coaxing her lips apart to explore the tender recess of her mouth, drinking in the honey moist taste of her.

Tentatively, her tongue reached out to meet his. Heat surged to his loins, filling him with a longing so intense, it should terrify him. But all he could think of was the delicate woman in his arms and how much he wanted her.

Her response grew bolder, and enticing little sounds escaped from between her lips. He recognized her building desire in the urgency of her movements.

Blood pooled hot and heavy in his loins. Alex fought to keep his passion in check, but he knew it was a losing battle.

She wanted him.

This sweet, willing surrender was the last thing he'd expected, burying his resolve under a blanket of white hot lust.

Her tongue drove him wild, entwining with his in a dark, delicious dance. She sank into him, pressing her body against his and clutching his shoulders as if she couldn't get enough of him.

He kissed her harder, wanting more, wanting to devour her very essence, but it wasn't enough. He wanted to feel her press up against him, naked, rubbing her breasts against his chest, circling her hips against his. Opening for him. He wanted her as mindless with lust as he was.

His mouth slid across her jaw and down the warm length of her neck. He was drowning in the scent of roses and smooth, baby soft skin. Her luscious round breasts pressed against him, too tempting to ignore. All he could think about was inhaling her, tasting her, touching her, plying all that soft, ivory flesh in his hands. Sucking her until she came apart in his arms.

But he knew he had to proceed cautiously, having care for her innocence—and for his bollocks. He remembered all too well how the force of her own response had terrified her.

Deftly, his hands skimmed over her tiny waist, stretched up along her stomach, and came to rest under the heavy curve of her breasts. He forced his pulse to slow, harnessing the sharp stab of desire. He kissed her mouth again, distracting her with his tongue as his hand finally covered her breast.

He groaned. God, she was lush. So achingly ripe.

She shuddered with desire, and Alex thought he might explode.

His need for her gripped him like a steel vise. He wanted to rip off the velvet gown that hid her nakedness and bury his face in her hot, fragrant skin. Biting back the lust, he gently rolled his thumb over her nipple, suffering another surge of pressure in his loins when she hardened immediately under his fingertips.

Her responsiveness taunted him, giving him a taste of her passion and hinting at the dangerously sensual creature hiding under a veil of innocence. His mind exploded with erotic possibilities. Of what he could do to her. Of what she could do to him.

She arched into his hand, silently begging and putting an end to his patience. He stroked her harder, feeling the excited flutter of her heart beneath his palm, lifting her breasts toward his mouth. He lingered along the creamy ivory skin of her bodice, teasing her with his tongue, kissing the sensitive flesh until she groaned. Only then did he slide his tongue beneath the fabric, flickering over the puckered edge of her nipple.

It was too much . . . it wasn't enough. With each taste of her, he wanted more; he had to have her.

He wanted to sink into her. To possess her. To put an end to this torment.

"Mistress, is everything all right?"

The sound of voices brought him harshly back to reality. It was her men coming to check on her. He jerked away, breaking the kiss. His breath came in uneven gasps as lust pounded through his body.

What the hell?

She looked just as dazed as he felt. It took her a moment to respond. "In here. I'm fine," she called out. Her hands went to her head as she attempted to put some semblance of order back into the curls he'd mussed. "I'll be right out."

Alex paced a few steps, raking his fingers back through his hair, more confused about what had just happened than he'd ever been in his life. One minute he was furious, and the next he was kissing her as if his life depended on it. That it very well might was something he could not consider.

She turned, presumably to leave, but he stopped her. "You will return with me." He would protect her. A hundred men wouldn't be enough to ease his mind, let alone the paltry few she'd brought along as escorts. "Ready your men, I will return in a moment." He would have to conclude his business with Robbie quickly. "And Meg?" She looked back at him. "This discussion is not over."

They rode in silence, the guardsmen she'd brought with her trailing behind. The heat of passion had faded, leaving Meg in a state of confusion. Alex claimed to want her to leave him alone, but then he'd kissed her—again. And not just any kiss, but a kiss of possession that branded her as his. A soul-wrenching kiss that had drained her with its emotional intensity, leaving her wanting more. Those moments in his arms, she could almost feel that he was hers.

Why was he trying to push her away?

She'd get no answers from Alex. The silence was deafening. They'd been riding for nearly half an hour and he'd hardly said more than a few words to her. She almost wished he'd resume their earlier conversation, as he'd threatened.

Was he still angry? She peeked out at him from under her lashes. She didn't think so. The taut lines around his mouth had softened. He looked glorious with the warm afternoon sun shining on his fair head, in stunning contrast with his deeply tanned skin and crystal-clear blue eyes. He was truly the most handsome man she'd ever seen.

From the way his eyes darted around, Meg knew he was on alert for anything unusual. Still, he seemed more relaxed than he'd been the entire time she'd known him. She suspected it had to do with being away from court.

"It's beautiful, isn't it?" she asked, indicating the breathtaking views of crags and a strange-looking flat mountain off to the west. "It's hard to believe we are so close to the palace."

Alex nodded in agreement. "Aye. That large rise over there behind Salisbury crags is called Arthur's Seat." He must have seen her look of confusion. "At one time it was called Archer's Seat. And you can see why—it looks like a ledge with an unobstructed view for as far as the eye can see."

"It's magnificent," she said wistfully. "It makes me feel not quite so far from home."

Alex broke into a wide smile, obviously appreciating her enthusiasm. Meg felt as though she'd been felled by a bolt of lightning. The radiance of that smile transformed his face. He looked charmingly young, revealing a glimpse of the lighthearted boy he must have been before life and war had hardened him.

"You miss Skye?" he asked.

"Don't you?"

"Of course," he answered, clearly taken aback that she would even question it.

"I miss everything about it." She sighed. "I miss the hypnotic roll of the water that fills every vista at Dunakin, the sounds of the pipers, the evenings spent around a fire listening to the stories of the *seannachie,* the smell of the sea, the sight of the *birlinns* bobbing on the loch, and so much more." She wrinkled her nose with a play-ful smile. "Even the smell of herring."

"All the symbols of our Island way of life that King James seeks to destroy," Alex said, not hiding his resent-ment. "Even our language is offensive to the king and serves only as further evidence of our barbarity."

"I fear that the old ways of the clans are coming to an end," Meg said, her voice tinged with regret.

England. Scotland's enemy for generations was now ruled by a Scot. Delicious irony, perhaps, but old preju-dices and old habits were hard to forget. And now the king had the means to enforce his policies against those he termed the "barbarians" of the Isles.

"Not if I can help it."

The fire in his voice caught her attention. She spun around to look at him. Anger consumed his whole body. This was not a man interested only in fighting. She gave him an appraising glance. He was much more involved in politics than he let on.

His response was typical of her countrymen. She un-derstood his frustration, but she also understood the re-ality of their predicament. She'd had this conversation with Jamie and Elizabeth countless times. "James is king of England now, not just Scotland. He has the strength of two governments behind him. Already the authority of the chiefs has been curtailed by the General Band. Whether you like it or not, Alex, there will not be much the chiefs can do to prevent change."

He looked at her as if she were a traitor. "How can you sound so philosophical, so complacent, about something so important? Don't you care about your home, about your people?"

His voice teemed with passion and conviction. But what did a mercenary care about justice or politics?

"Of course I do," she said evenly. "I love everything about our Highland way of life. But I'm also trying to be practical. It is not a matter of black or white. We must seek new solutions with King James or we can all end up like the MacGregors."

"What do *you* know about the MacGregors?"

Meg was surprised by the vehemence in his tone. He'd reacted as if she'd slurred him personally. "Enough to know that they are doomed. The king has stripped them of their land and even of their name. I know that they are hunted men forced to turn outlaw to survive." He was trying not to show it, but Meg could see that every muscle in his body rejected what she was trying to say. Her voice lowered to soften the blow of her words. "I know enough to understand that if we don't find a way to get along with King James, our own clans will suffer the same fate as the MacGregors. Aren't your brother's lands already forfeit?"

His grip on his reins tightened, turning his knuckles white. Clearly he wanted to disagree, but he couldn't. "Technically, perhaps. But King James will never hold Dunvegan."

"I hope you are right, for the Mackinnons' fate is tied to the fate of the other clans on Skye. If Dunvegan falls, Dunakin would also be in jeopardy. I don't want Skye to be the next Lewis, with the king attempting to colonize our land with Lowlanders."

"It won't be," he said flatly.

She'd barely heard him, but from his tone Meg realized there was something important that he'd left unsaid. Abruptly, Alex turned away from her. He was shutting

her out, trying to put the wall between them again. Whenever she felt they were starting to get close, he pulled
back. But not this time. She wouldn't let him. "For a man
so obviously passionate about his home, why have you
been fighting someone else's wars?"

He looked at her and shook his head. "You don't ever
give up." A smile hovered at the edges of his mouth.

She shrugged. "Where did you say you'd been fighting?"

His jaw fell in a hard, uncompromising line. By his
reaction, Meg knew she was getting close.

"I didn't," he said.

"Well, then, where were you?"

"Here and there," he answered vaguely, clearly growing impatient with her interrogation.

From the set of his shoulders, she could tell that she'd
pushed him as far as he would go. So she switched tac-
tics. "How long have you been away from home?"

"Almost three years."

Meg couldn't imagine leaving home for so long. "But
why?" she asked.

"I had to get away for a while."

"After your imprisonment?"

"Shortly thereafter." He sounded disgusted with himself for even talking about this. "After I was released, I
returned to Dunvegan for a while to stand in for my
brother, who was being held by Argyll at the bequest of
the king. The king was angry about the feuding between
the clans. Rory returned, and I left soon after he hand-
fasted Isabel."

Were the rumors of his falling-out with his brother
true? "But why did you leave?"

He shrugged. "It was time for me to get out on my own for a while. There were things I needed to do. I suppose I was restless."

Meg was beginning to understand. A man like Alex would not be content to live under another man's shadow. A leader in his own right, Alex needed to make his own way. But she felt there was more that he wasn't telling her. Something that was calamitous enough to drive him away from his home and family. And to keep him from her.

"And have you found what you were looking for?" she asked quietly.

He gave her a long, meaningful look. "No," he said. "Not yet."

Her heart fell to the floor. It was a warning. A not too subtle way of telling her to keep her distance, that there was no future for them. But from the dull ache in her chest, Meg suspected that it was a warning that may have come too late.

They entered the shadow of the trees, and the temperature dropped considerably. The heavy wool fabric of her gown, which had been too warm a few minutes ago, now felt quite comfortable. Although there were still a few hours of daylight, it was eerily dark; the soft orange rays of the sun had not the strength to penetrate the thick canopy of trees.

Meg sighed, disheartened by Alex's comments. She sank deeper into her saddle, tired and anxious to return to her rooms, both to rest and to consider what she'd learned. One thing was for certain, Alex was not simply the mercenary soldier he wanted her to think he was.

And with the way her heart skipped every time she

looked at him, discovering the truth had become imperative.

Alex didn't like being put on the spot, being scrutinized so carefully. He could sense her disappointment, but she wanted answers he just could not give her. "What about you, Meg? Have *you* found what you were looking for?'

She collected herself and said matter-of-factly, "Perhaps, but I have to be sure. The future of our clan is at stake; there is no room for mistakes."

He looked at her thoughtfully. "Your father seems to expect much from you."

"He trusts me." She sighed. "I always make the right decisions."

It was not said as a boast but was simply stated as fact. And it bothered him. "It seems like an inordinate amount of pressure to put on a young woman. From what I have heard, you practically run the clan lands already."

"There is no one else that my father trusts; most of the chieftains are old men. Those that aren't have not demonstrated any propensity to lead." She hesitated for a moment. "You know of my brother?"

He nodded.

"Of course you do," she said bitterly. "It is a small island, and people like to gossip. My brother will be chief, and I will be there to support him. As will my husband."

"What about for *you*, Meg? Have you found the right man for you?"

"It's all the same," she said tersely. "The right man for Dunakin is the right man for me."

He could sense her increasing anxiety, as if his questions dug deeper than she would like. But Alex realized that he was close to the truth, to the core of what drove Meg. "Are you so sure of that? What of your own happiness?"

He could see the color climb in her cheeks. Her eyes sparked with anger. "You don't understand."

He could see her resistance in the stiffness of her back and the tightness around her mouth. The façade of control had slipped. "Don't understand what, Meg?" he prodded gently.

She gazed at him with wide, glassy eyes. "I can't let them down," she said fervently. "They are all counting on me."

Alex hadn't meant to upset her. But he could see from the intensity of her response how important it was to her to do what was right. What was expected. And for some reason, that had become a struggle. He suspected he knew why.

A sound drew his attention to the bank of trees on their right.

His senses flared. He didn't like the feel of this at all. Something wasn't right. He held up his hand for them to stop.

"What's wrong?" Meg asked.

"I heard something." He paused, stone still, all of his senses honed to his surroundings. He moved his horse in front of hers, putting himself in the line of fire, and with a gesture of his hand ordered her guardsmen to surround her.

It was almost too still. The light had faded to near dark. They'd moved into the densest part of the forest, where the path narrowed to accommodate the enormous birch trees. It was the perfect place for an—

Suddenly, he detected the unmistakable whiz of arrows in flight.

Attack!

Chapter 11

"Get down!" Alex shouted, forcing Meg's head down moments before an arrow sped by, missing her by mere inches.

He breathed a sigh of relief, feeling as if he'd just had twenty years of his life shaved off. That had been too damn close. Later, he'd be furious with her for scaring him half to death. But right now he had other things to worry about—like how to get them out of this alive, which at the moment didn't look too promising.

He quickly assessed their situation.

Even though he'd anticipated an attack, the brigands, if that's who they were, had chosen a perfect spot for an ambush. Alex had sensed the danger, but too late to move them to safety. It was no conciliation that he'd been right about the threat to Meg, not when they would be in a fight for their lives in a matter of minutes.

One of Meg's guardsmen slid off his horse, an arrow protruding from his gut. Alex could do nothing for him. If he wasn't dead now, he would be soon. With two men left and little room to maneuver, he knew that he had only moments to make a decision or they would each be picked off one at a time.

The rush of battle hit him full force. His only focus

was to protect Meg and kill anyone who dared to threaten her.

He didn't need to look to know that they were surrounded. His first instinct was to ride hard and try to outrun them or fight his way through their position blocking the path. If he were alone, it would not be a problem. But with Meg he dared not risk it. Riding, she would be too exposed. He would have to take them down one by one, but not here.

From what he could tell, there were at least half a dozen men scattered around them. They had to get out of the open and draw in the attackers, taking away the use of their bows.

"Follow me," he ordered the men, quickly shouting out instructions. To Meg he said, "Keep your head down, and stay behind us." He knew she was frightened, so he made sure his voice sounded calm and controlled. He wished he had time to reassure her further, but every second they stayed out in the open they were vulnerable.

Heedless of the danger posed by the arrows, he plunged into the trees, hoping the archers would not be expecting a frontal assault. He was right. One of the men managed to get off another arrow, this one poorly aimed, before Alex cut him down with his claymore. One of Meg's guardsmen dispatched another. Meg's scream alerted him to the third. Alex whirled around, but not in time to prevent a powerful blow of the villain's sword from landing on his exposed left side. He barely acknowledged the pain, though the heavy weight of the blade had at the very least bruised a few of his ribs. Without thought, he sank his blade deep into the heart of his attacker, his reaction honed by years of training.

The threat from this side of the trees was gone. They would fight with no one at their back. Their situation was still precarious, but no longer desperate. Here, he could make a stand.

Knowing that their horses would only impede their movements and make them greater targets in the dense forest, Alex dismounted and ordered the others to do the same, getting them into position and giving them instructions. If he was right, he wouldn't have long before their attackers came to them. He had what they wanted.

He was agonizingly aware of Meg, and of the danger to her. But he couldn't allow himself to dwell on it. It would only distract him. And he needed all of his skills right now if they were to survive.

He looked around, searching for any place for her to hide. But time had run out; he could hear the other attackers moving through the woods toward them.

"Stay behind the tree," he said, pointing her in the direction of the largest tree he could see. "Use the horses for a shield if you must."

"But Alex—"

He could hear the tremble in her voice. "Don't worry, sweet. I won't let anything happen to you."

"It's not me I'm worried about."

Alex hadn't trusted himself to look at her, but he did so now. Her face was drawn and pale, and her beautiful eyes loomed large in her heart-shaped face. She was worried about him. Something inside him swelled. Instinctively, he reached down and cupped her chin, brushing his mouth across hers, ignoring the sharp twinge in his chest. "I'll be fine," he whispered. "Go."

He hated letting her go, hated separating from her, but there was no other choice.

He gestured to the men to be ready. Raising his sword high above his head, Alex let out a savage cry—"Hold fast!"—the battle cry of the MacLeods. The guardsmen followed his lead as the attackers came crashing through the trees.

There were more ruffians than Alex had thought. Perhaps another ten in addition to the three they'd already killed. Fortunately, they did not seem well organized. While they were busy shouting out instructions and getting into position, Alex started to even the score, wielding his claymore and dirk in deadly tandem.

None of the men looked familiar. Despite what they wanted him to think from the rags they wore, he'd already concluded they were mercenaries merely dressed as ruffians. Alex knew what an outlaw looked like. These men did not have dirt and grime sticking in every exposed crevice, seeping out of their pores, dripping from their unkempt hair. Their clothing might be rough and filthy, but the weapon that had struck him in the side was of good workmanship. But most important, these men did not have the unmistakable feral stare of hunted men. No, they were hired killers. And from their numbers, they'd sought to ensure that this time they did not fail.

But they hadn't counted on him. Alex dispatched the first two with ease.

Meg's guardsmen, however, were not having as easy a time of it. Two more ruffians came at him, preventing Alex from going to their aid. It took a few more swings of his claymore and strokes of his dirk, but the next two soon went the way of the first. Gazing around, he made a quick tally of the dead. One of Meg's guardsmen had managed to extricate himself from his attackers, killing one, but another had already come to fill his place. The other guardsman was not as fortunate. He lay prone in the dirt and underbrush with the dirk of the man he'd managed to kill before he fell still protruding from his belly.

Alex stared grimly at the fallen warrior. The attackers would pay. With their lives. Only four ruffians remained, and one of these men he recognized. One of the two men engaged in vicious battle with Meg's guardsmen was none other than the thin, sharp-featured man from the tavern. Despite his wiry build, he seemed to have some skill with a sword. Meg's remaining guardsmen would not be able to hold the two of them for long.

Alex felt no satisfaction in knowing that his suspicions had proved correct, only pure rage at the hired killer who would murder a woman. And not just any woman, but his woman, he thought with a fierce wave of possessiveness.

Alex would enjoy ending his foul life. But first he had to contend with the two remaining men now approaching him with considerably more care. They came at him from opposite sides. Alex smiled, knowing what they would attempt. He watched one man mouth, "Three, two, one . . ." As their blades descended, Alex spun with his blade high, blocking both timed blows with one precisely executed swing of his claymore.

The clang of steel on steel sounded the beginning of the end. Their strategy foiled, the attackers' next strokes were not as well timed, and Alex had no trouble blocking their blows. Quickly he assessed the relative skills of the men and concentrated his efforts on the stronger of the two, leaving his open side to the weaker one. Unfortunately, it was also the side that had taken the brunt of the blow earlier, and the villain managed to get in one strike on his ribs before Alex dispatched the other.

Gaze still focused on his man, Alex glanced out of the corner of his eye toward Meg's remaining guardsman. He'd managed to kill one of his attackers, but the hook-nosed man from the tavern had just dealt him a death blow. Alex returned the favor to his attacker and turned to face the man from the tavern. But something bothered him. He looked around at the dead littering the forest floor, searching for a body that would match the other man from the tavern.

Meg's scream cut through the still air, turning his blood to ice.

Too late, he'd found the man he'd been looking for. He cursed, realizing that while he'd been locked in battle, repelling the attack, the other man from the tavern had circled around his flank and found Meg.

Ignoring Hook Nose, Alex spun around and started toward the tree where he'd left Meg. But the scene that met his eyes forced him to halt in his tracks.

Rage such as he'd never experienced before coursed through him at the sight of the dirk pressed into Meg's neck and the light trail of blood trickling below it. He'd cut her. His response was visceral, every muscle in his body twisted with uncontrollable anger.

The memory of Dougal's evil smirk right before his cousins were gulleted flashed before his eyes. Alex would not let it happen again. Not to Meg.

An urge to kill crashed over him, so powerful that it must have been a remnant of his barbaric Viking ancestry. Everything went black, except for the clear vision of the ruffian, a man he recognized too well, holding the blade to her neck. Thomas Mackinnon. Her father's trusted chieftain wanted Meg dead. *What the hell was going on?*

"Let me go," Meg pleaded. "Why are you doing this?"

"Shut up, bitch," Mackinnon said. "This is all your fault. If you had accepted my proposal, none of this would be necessary."

So that was it. Alex watched the man so intently, he could see the hairs bend on his arm from Meg's uneven breathing. Not much ground separated them, but he dared not try anything with that blade so deathly close. He kept his gaze leveled on the attacker. He could not risk looking at Meg, seeing panic in her eyes. Panic that might paralyze him.

But what he saw in Thomas Mackinnon's gaze offered little in the way of reassurance. There was a hint of wildness in his eyes that bespoke a man who'd risked everything and knew it. Meg was alive only to get to Alex. Once Alex was contained, they both would be killed.

"I don't understand," Meg said. "What could you hope to—" She stopped as understanding dawned. Alex could hear the horror in her voice. "You want to be chief." Her eyes widened. "Tell me you didn't have anything to do with my father's illness—"

"I told you to shut up," Mackinnon growled. He pressed the dirk, and another drop of blood slid from Meg's neck. Alex could tell he was quickly losing whatever control he had on his restraint.

A cold rage settled over him, fueled by a bloodlust so powerful that he could taste it. "Let her go," Alex said.

It was not a request; his voice resonated with the promise of death.

Alex sensed Hook Nose moving toward him, and he beat him back with a fierce glare.

Thomas Mackinnon directed his venom toward his compatriot. "You fool. You said there were only three guardsmen. What is Alex MacLeod doing here?"

"He didn't ride out with her," Hook Nose faltered nervously. "You need not have interfered, I have everything under control."

"You should be thanking me, you idiot," Mackinnon said. "You would be dead right now if not for me."

Hook Nose studied Alex. "You look familiar . . ." Recognition dawned. "The outlaw." He turned to Mackinnon excitedly. "It's him. The man I told you about. Now you must believe me. I told you he fought with the skill of five men."

"I thought you said they were MacGregors?" Mackinnon snapped.

"They were," Hook Nose assured him. "My men recognized a good number of them."

Mackinnon looked at him sharply. "What is the brother of Rory Mor doing fighting with outlawed Mac-Gregors?"

Damn. Alex heard Meg gasp. Doubtless he'd have some explaining to do later. He took a step closer. "Let her go and you can have me."

"You are in no position to bargain," Mackinnon said. "Drop your weapons." He tightened his hold around Meg's neck, causing the dirk to press deeper into that delicate flesh.

He's a dead man.

"I'll put down my weapons, but lower the blade."

Mackinnon laughed. "And why should I do that?"

"A show of faith. How do I know you don't intend to kill us both?"

Mackinnon smiled, lowering the blade from Meg's neck. Alex breathed.

"Now your weapons," Mackinnon said.

Alex's dirk and claymore fell to his feet.

"Kick them away from you."

He did as ordered.

"Stop standing there and gaping, you fool," Mackinnon yelled to Hook Nose, who was hanging back, obviously hesitating to get within range of Alex. "Hurry up! Fetch the rope and tie him up."

Alex had to do something soon before the other man had a chance to secure him. But he'd need Meg's help. He had no choice; he'd have to look at her. Cautiously, he lowered his eyes to her pale face. She wasn't as bad as he'd feared. Her eyes were wide and glassy but lucid. Her lips trembled slightly. She was frightened but was holding her own. That innate look of control and confidence was less obvious, but it was still there. *Damn, he was proud of her.*

He just prayed that she would understand.

His voice turned soothing. "Everything will be all right, Meg. Just do what they say. Can you do that?"

She nodded.

"I want you to remember something, something that will help you. Can you do that? . . . Good. Think about the night of the masque when I kissed you."

Her eyes opened a little wider. Thomas Mackinnon's face flooded with rage.

"I want you to think about what you did to me—"

"Get the goddamn rope, Billy, and shut him up," Mackinnon spat.

Hook Nose, or Billy, had gathered the rope and was approaching, but very cautiously, eyeing him as if he were a wild beast. Alex had only a few more moments. He stared at Meg, begging her to understand.

Something flashed in her eyes. "I re-mem-ber," she stuttered.

"Whore. I'll give you a real man's kiss—" Mackinnon swung Meg around to face him and lowered his head.

"Now!" Alex yelled.

It was perfect timing. Meg jerked her knee hard into Mackinnon's crotch and quickly dove out of harm's way.

Thomas Mackinnon bent over, covering his groin, writhing in pain.

Alex turned crazed—as frenzied as a Berserker in battle. Bloodlust surged through his body. He pulled out the small dirk that he kept tucked in his boot and aimed it right for Billy's heart. He died with a startled cry on his lips.

Alex spun around to see Mackinnon hobbling toward Meg, his sword raised. Alex was going to enjoy this.

Sensing Alex's presence, Thomas Mackinnon turned, swinging his sword wildly at Alex. Alex swung his claymore in a high arc. Mackinnon met his blow, but he was no match. They both knew his end was a certainty. Alex could toy with him for a while, but Thomas Mackinnon wasn't worth his time.

With one powerful blow, Alex knocked the sword from his hand. Mackinnon didn't get the chance to pull the dirk from his belt. Alex had him pinned to a tree with the blade of his claymore.

"Please, I m-mean no harm to the lass—"

But the rest of his words were cut off as Alex slashed his dirk across Thomas Mackinnon's throat.

Dead men couldn't lie.

The attack happened so fast, Meg barely had time to think before it was all over. It wasn't until after, when Alex had scooped her up and cradled her in his arms, that shock gave way to an uncontrollable shaking—and the vivid recollection of the violence that had occurred in the midst of this deceptively tranquil setting. The forest floor was strewn with the bloody carcasses of over a dozen men, three her own. She mourned their senseless loss. Three more deaths to add to the recent losses would hit her clan hard.

Yet nothing could feel more right than being held by the man who'd saved her. Again. From the start, Alex had taken control of the situation with the swift, decisive command that she'd admired from the first. His incredible battle skills and calm under pressure had acted as a balm to her rising panic. He would not be defeated.

She'd been scared, but not terrified. Not until Thomas Mackinnon had surprised her from behind. At first she'd thought he was there to help them. Only when he'd refused to let her go did she realize her mistake. She still could not believe that he'd tried to kill her. She felt sick with the implications of all that her father's chieftain had done for ambition.

The terror that had eluded her during the attack rushed forth in full force once it was over. And Alex was there to be her rock, a steadying force merely by the solid strength of his presence. The callused hands that had taken life with such savage ferocity now stroked her hair as gently as if she were a newborn babe. He'd moved her away from the scene of carnage to the grassy bank of a nearby burn. After dampening the edge of his *leine* in the water, he carefully wiped the trickle of blood from her neck. She was lucky; she'd suffered nothing more than a scratch.

"Shush, love. It's all over now." His voice was low and soothing as he whispered words to calm her racing heart.

Through the wall of panic, her heart caught at the sweet endearment. *Love.* A sharp pang of longing hit her like a kick in the chest. *God, how she wished that it were so.*

He smelled of sweat and blood, but somehow it reminded her that she was alive. His voice and hands worked magic, easing her panic. She allowed herself the luxury of being rocked in his arms, relishing the security offered by his powerful hold. She burrowed deeper in his lap and tightened her grip around his waist.

He winced.

Her head snapped back to look at him accusingly. "You're hurt."

"It's nothing," he said, trying to brush away her concern.

But the fact that he was injured forced her back to reality as effectively as a hard slap. Meg was furious. "Why didn't you say something?" she said, moving out of his lap. "How could you allow me to carry on about a tiny scratch and not even mention that you were injured?" She knelt before him and began exploring his side with her fingers.

"It wasn't just a tiny scratch, Meg. His dirk was at your neck."

Meg ignored him. She didn't want to think about what she had barely averted, not when he was so obviously in pain.

He tensed as her hands moved across his tightly muscled stomach and back. He was not bleeding, and it didn't feel as if anything were broken, but she couldn't be sure. Carefully, she traced his ribs and the cut indentations of his muscled stomach with her fingertips through the *leine*. When her hand dipped low on his stomach, he made a sound and grabbed her wrist.

"I'm fine." His voice sounded pained, but this time with restraint. "Just a few bruised ribs, that is all." Their eyes met, and she could see the desire burning hot in his gaze. He wanted her, and the evidence was growing right before her eyes. She flushed, not with embarrassment, but with the knowledge that her innocent touch had aroused him so powerfully.

She wanted to touch him. To slide her hand along the sensitive flesh. To harness that strength beneath her hands. To revel in the wonder of being alive.

The air crackled between them. Temptation beckoned from the very depths of her soul. For a moment, Meg wavered on the edge of indecision. She wanted him. What was the point in denying it, or herself? Confronting her own mortality had made her yearn to experience life in the most basic way possible. The danger they'd just faced had stripped away everything but the fact that they were two people deeply attracted to each other. At that moment, nothing else mattered.

Desire stretched tautly between them. The dark intensity in his blue eyes bored straight through her. He held perfectly still, jaw clenched, his face an inscrutable puzzle of hard angles, every muscle in his body tense with restraint, awaiting her decision. One move would be all it would take, and his mouth would be on hers, erasing all memory of what had just happened.

The temptation was too powerful to resist.

So she succumbed to the moment, to Alex, and to the pull of desire that bound them in an undeniable way.

Having care for his injured ribs, she leaned over him, achingly aware of the warmth emanating from him and the long, hard muscles stretched out beneath her. Tentatively, she pressed her mouth against his.

It was all the excuse he needed. With a primal growl, Alex took hold of her, and Meg found herself rolled on her back, his body covering hers, and the full onslaught of his mouth returning her kiss with fervor.

"Your ribs," she murmured.

"To hell with my ribs," he growled. "Just let me taste you."

Meg complied willingly. His mouth was hard and demanding, brutal with need. It was perfect. She tasted his hunger and opened to him, taking him deeper as his tongue swept her mouth. He was holding nothing back, and Meg met the force of his desire with her own.

She'd been right. His kiss made her forget. His kiss made her feel alive, alive in a way that she'd felt before. As if every inch of her body were aflame. The passion between them consumed everything in its wake. There was no room for analysis or thought, only for the desperate cravings of their bodies.

She returned his kiss the way he'd taught her. Tentatively at first, and then with growing confidence, she matched the thrust and parry of his tongue stroke for delicious stroke. She couldn't get enough. The harder and deeper he kissed her, the more she wanted. Meg had succumbed, and she would do so not in half measure, but with verve, excitement, and eagerness.

This was dangerous. *Very* dangerous. She knew she should stop him, but it felt too good. She'd never dreamed that she could feel this way, that she could so crave a man's touch. She'd thought that she was not capable of this type of emotion, this type of sensation, this type of burning desire. But when he held her in his arms and kissed her, her heart flipped, her blood rushed, her pulse quickened. All she could think of was drawing nearer to the heat. Of being surrounded by this man.

Her hands explored the breadth of his wide shoulders and powerfully muscled chest. She wanted to touch every part of him, to feel his skin under her fingertips. She clenched him harder as the force of his kiss intensified.

Her frenzy seemed only to increase his own. Alex lifted his head, breathing hard, and the depth of emotion in his eyes took her breath away. It was desire, but also something deeper. Something that made her heart leap high in her chest. Something that she wanted to believe with every fiber of her being.

He watched her face intently as his fingers traced an invisible line down her side, allowing his thumb to slip forward over the curve of her breast. The nipple hardened under his touch.

Meg gasped as his thumb began to stroke small circles over the sensitive tip. She closed her eyes, allowing the warm sensations to crash over her as she gave herself up to his touch. Her entire body felt flushed and hot with pleasure. Vaguely, she was aware that he'd loosened the laces of her bodice and tugged the fabric down below the edges of her stays.

She guessed what he meant to do but made no move to stop him, remembering all too well what he'd done before. His mouth fell on hers again, holding her captive, kissing her with an urgency that gave proof of his intent. His lips and tongue trailed a path down her neck and bodice, perilously close . . . agonizingly close.

Meg held her breath as his fingers dipped below the edges of her stays and linen sark to lift out her breasts from behind their delicate confinement. She startled at the erotic sensation of his callused finger sweeping the sensitive, naked flesh. Her body turned liquid, and a heavy warmth pooled between her legs.

She heard his sharp intake of breath.

She opened her eyes. Her cheeks burned with embarrassment, suddenly aware that he was staring at her naked breasts.

"God, you're beautiful." His voice was tight and rough and held almost a touch of reverence. He outlined the swell of her breast with his finger, so feather soft that she wondered whether he was actually touching her or whether it was merely the strength of her own awareness. "So round," he murmured, emphasizing with his finger. His voice was deep and dark as molten lava, seeping into her consciousness. "So full." He moved to cup her, and Meg began to shiver, aroused by his observations. "So soft and creamy white." He lifted her closer to his mouth. She could feel the heat of his breath brush across her sensitive tip. *Oh God, this was torture.* His voice lowered. "With perfect pink tips." Meg felt a shudder go through her as his tongue flicked her nipple. "Mmm . . . so sweet."

She moaned, writhing in innocent frustration, more aroused than she'd ever been in her life. Every nerve tingled with awareness; she felt ready to jump out of her skin. He teased her already taut nipples, rubbing the rough pads of his fingers over the sensitive tips, then squeezing lightly. But it wasn't enough. Meg knew it wasn't enough. There was more. And finally, he gave it to her. His tongue circled her, and then his warm mouth closed over her.

Meg had thought herself not capable of mindless desire.

She was wrong.

He sucked her, hard. A needle of pleasure seemed to shoot straight to her heart. She pressed herself against him, savoring the sensation of his teeth and tongue as he pulled her deeper and deeper toward a blinding pleasure. A slow quivering pulsed between her legs, demanding attention. She wanted something; her body felt empty but yearned for fulfillment.

Dear God, she knew what she wanted.

She wanted him inside her. Filling her. Taking away the agony.

Instinctively, she knew that Alex would give her incomprehensible pleasure.

A firm hand dropped to cup her bottom as he nudged her breast erotically with his teeth, a nipping and sucking that drove her wild. She grasped for the safety of his shoulders to keep from fully collapsing. Meg was already addicted to the feel of him beneath her fingers. Through the linen of his *leine,* there was no mistaking the raw power of his impressive build. Her fingers explored every ripple, every muscle, of his powerful form. Alex was built for destruction. Every inch of him was strong and hard. His arms and chest seemed sculpted

from stone, the thick muscles chiseled, defined, and inflexible. *Warm steel.* He reminded her of warm steel.

Releasing her breast, he moved to take hostage of her
mouth again, kissing her with a dark sensuality that
would have shocked her senseless an hour ago but now
only thrilled her.

But then his hand slid under the edge of her skirt. Her
breath caught as his fingers worked their way up along
her calf, then thigh, then higher still.

She froze, and a moment of uncertainty broke through
the haze.

Meg could no longer return his kiss; she couldn't
think about anything other than his hand . . . and where
it was going.

"Trust me, Meg," he whispered against her ear, sensing her uncertainty. "I only wish to give you pleasure.
Nothing more."

She nodded hesitantly. She did trust him.

But nothing could have prepared her for the pure
burst of pleasure that hit when his finger brushed
against her tingling flesh. So achingly soft. Again and
again, he swept against her until she didn't think she
could take any more. She knew she should be shocked.
Surely, anything that felt this good must be a sin. But
held captive by this exquisite torture, Meg didn't care.

She writhed in sweet agony, almost delirious with
need. Craving pressure, she lifted her hips against his
hand, wanting it harder. He groaned and finally slid his
finger inside her, giving her all the pressure she needed.
Lost in the throes of nearly unbelievable ecstasy, she
grasped helplessly for something that hovered just out of
her reach.

Chapter 12

Alex watched, almost mindless with lust, as the flush spread high across her cheeks. As her breath hitched between her softly parted lips. As her back arched, delectable, pink-tipped breasts straining toward the sky and hips pressed erotically against his hand. She was going to come. For him.

Never had he seen anything so beautiful. He felt humbled just looking at her. She was so tiny and soft and sweetly feminine. An unfamiliar swell of emotion rose in his chest. He'd never felt like this before, moved beyond words by the significance of this moment.

He felt as if he'd been handed a precious gift. Never could he have imagined her soft surrender, the way she melted into him. And the honesty of her response. Meg's passion was like everything else about her, refreshingly open and honest. *And his.*

She was so close, writhing in innocent frustration, just as hot and desperate as he was. He bent over her, flicking his tongue against her taut nipple in perfect sync with the frantic rhythm of his finger. He nibbled her with his teeth, eliciting a fresh gasp of desire that shot straight to his already straining groin. He'd never been in this much pain. His body drummed with the need for release, but he didn't care. All he could think about was Meg.

His fingers slid over her dampness, feeling the swollen flesh under his fingertips. He ached to taste her, to bury his head between her legs and inhale her warm feminine scent, to lick and suck her delicate flesh until she came against his mouth.

He wanted to devour her, to explore every inch of this gorgeous woman who was about to come apart in his arms.

Her breathing was coming hard and fast. Soft little urgent moans escaped from between her parted lips. Her silky thighs squeezed against his hand.

"Oh, God . . . Alex . . ."

He could hear the sweet desperation in her voice. "Just let it come, sweet. I've got you."

She tensed as the force of her release hit her. He wanted to prolong her ecstasy, to make her remember this forever. Taking her nipple fully in his mouth, he sucked her hard as his thumb massaged her most sensitive spot, and she careened over the edge of sexual oblivion.

He felt a heavy thud of his heart as the soft cries of her pleasure echoed in his ears.

It wasn't enough. His need for this woman was too strong. He felt ready to explode—she was so ripe and wet, so ready for him. Blood pounded in his already burning loins, his passion dangerously close to spilling over. His entire body clenched with the effort at restraint. One touch, one innocent sweep of her hand, and he would be undone.

He wanted to sink into her, to cover himself in her heat. To bring her to a second orgasm as he thrust up high and hard inside her. To fill her with the hot burst of his seed.

To make her his.

No woman had ever done this to him, made him a twisted mass of dangerous cravings. The need to be inside her wasn't just lust, it was something far deeper and much more elemental.

The devil taunted him mercilessly, urging him on, urging him to take what was so innocently being offered. To relieve the pain, to plunge into her and spend himself in her innocence. She wanted him. He knew he could give her even more pleasure. *It would be so easy. . . .*

Her eyes fluttered open. An adorable sated smile spread across her face as she gazed at him with such wonder and trust that something inside his chest twisted.

And reality intruded.

What was he doing? He could almost allow himself to forget that she was a virgin. But as the haze of her orgasm lifted, he could see the reality of the situation coming back to her. Her gaze turned shy. Innocent. He sensed her subtle pulling away. The hesitation was back in her eyes.

Indecision teetered in the balance for one long heartbeat. But it was long enough to recognize the truth, damn it.

This was wrong. They'd gotten carried away by the intensity of the battle and drawn into the heady afterglow of survival. She'd been in shock by what she'd witnessed. He knew how vulnerable she was, knew that he should not take advantage of her in such a state, but her kiss had set off a combustion as powerful as fire on dry leaves.

His need for her was all-consuming.

But he could not delude himself that this was right. She deserved better than to be taken on a bed of dirt and leaves in the aftermath of a battle. She was a virgin, a gently reared lady who deserved to be showered with rose petals on a bed of silk. Who deserved much more than he could offer her.

Honor demanded that he stop.

Sweat gathered on his brow as the strain of holding himself back worked on him. Gathering the tattered reins of control, he rolled off her, staring blindly into the dark canopy of trees above them.

He felt stretched so taut, he jerked when she put her hand on his arm.

"Alex, is everything all right? Did I do something wrong?"

He heard the uncertainty in her voice.

"I'm fine," he said gruffly. He didn't trust himself to look at her, with her naked breasts still heaving over the edge of her stays.

"But you're in pain. Is it your ribs? Oh, why didn't you say something!" she exclaimed with alarm, immediately placing her hands on his chest, intent on ministering to his injury, but her touch only exacerbating the real source of his pain.

Sitting up, he grabbed her wrists, wrenching her hands from his chest. "It's not my ribs," he said through clenched teeth. "Just give me a minute."

Their eyes met, and he could see her begin to piece it together. "It hurt you to stop. Why did you? I . . . I know there is more."

So much more. His body wouldn't let him forget. He

wondered if he'd ever be able to forget what had happened here today. It was a sobering thought.

"Aye, but not here. Not like this." He swept aside a lock of hair that had tangled in her lashes, tucking it gently behind her ear. "It wouldn't be right." He stood up, intending to begin preparations for their return. After giving her a minute to adjust her clothing, he turned to help her to her feet.

"Thank you, Alex."

"What for?"

"For everything you did today. For killing those men. For being so honorable."

Alex felt a twinge of alarm. There was more than simple admiration in her voice. What damage had he done this day? He knew a woman like Meg would not give herself so freely, no matter how swept away with passion, unless . . . He couldn't think about it. Wouldn't allow himself the possibility. Wouldn't acknowledge the swell of happiness that rose in his chest. He was not the man for her. It was time to dispel her of her knightly imputations. "I'm not the man you think I am, Meg."

"Then who are you, Alex? If not the skilled warrior, the superior strategist, the honorable man."

I'm a man with a job to do.

He'd said enough already.

"Does this have something to do with the Mac-Gregors? Is what Thomas said true? Were you with the MacGregors all these years?"

"Leave it be, Meg."

She stared at him with wounded eyes. "You still don't trust me. Is that why you stopped?"

Hurt quivered in her voice, but he forced himself to ignore it.

Did he trust her? He didn't know. For a moment, before all hell broke loose, part of him had considered confiding in her. She was a Highlander after all; even her father was involved in his brother's plan. But something held him back. Her pragmatic approach to Highland politics, especially about King James's policies toward the MacGregors, had angered him. She was wrong. They couldn't stand around watching while their way of life was destroyed. They had to fight, practical or not. How would she feel about his taking a sword against the king's men?

And something else bothered him. Her close relationship with the Campbells. Jamie Campbell and his cousin Argyll were closely aligned with the king. Could he trust her not to say anything to her friends? Probably. But probably wasn't good enough, not with everything at stake.

"Trust has nothing to do with it," he said brusquely. "I stopped because your innocence is a gift that belongs to your husband on your wedding night."

It was a gift that was not his to take. No matter how much he wanted it.

He heard her sharp intake of breath. The urge to reassure her was powerful, but he held himself still. For a moment, he thought he saw tears brimming in her luminous green eyes. He ignored the sudden tightness in his chest. This was for the best. Let there be no illusions as to their future.

A gift that belongs to your husband. His words echoed in her ears.

Meg felt ill. The implication could not be clearer. It was not a position he intended to fill.

After the intimacies they'd just shared, his rejection stung. More than she'd ever dreamed possible. She knew he was not indifferent to her, he wanted her. What was holding him back?

She stared at him, praying for a sign, something to take away the sting of his words. Not knowing why, but knowing that it was vitally important, knowing that she'd never wanted anything more than she did at that moment. But he made no move toward her.

This was the reality, then. He didn't want to marry her.

And at that precise moment, at the moment of bitter understanding, Meg recognized the truth in her own heart. The truth that was so clear, she didn't know how she could not have realized it before.

She loved him.

Oh God, how could this have happened?

How could it *not* have happened? she realized. Alex was an easy man to love. Compelling in every way. Handsome as sin, a leader to admire, a skilled warrior, an impressive strategist both on and off the field of battle. But it was also how he made her feel. His strength gave her the freedom to feel vulnerable. Ever since she'd learned the truth about her brother, Meg had been the strong one. The one her father could always count on. It was a difficult façade to maintain, but Alex seemed to sense her strain. When she was with him, she felt strong, invincible. As if the challenges facing her weren't quite so insurmountable.

From the first, he'd seemed to see inside her. In his eyes she'd always felt beautiful, not the awkward girl at court who seemed never to fit in. Not once had he been put off by her blunt tongue; if anything, he seemed to admire her for it.

From the first moment she'd seen him, she'd sensed a connection. That connection had only strengthened the more she'd learned of him, and each time he held her in his arms and awakened her passion.

How could he deny it?

She waited for a sign that never came. The ache in her chest intensified. She would not cry. Not now. Later. Later, when she could sort out her thoughts.

Back straight, she turned, silently asking for his help lacing her stays and pinning her dress. And just as silently, he gave it.

Dougal MacDonald led the half-dozen palace guards through a scene of bloody carnage. He felt a surprisingly strong bolt of alarm before MacLeod stepped out from behind a tree, claymore drawn, shielding the object of Dougal's concern.

He breathed a sigh of relief. His bride was safe.

His gaze flickered over her. His eyes narrowed, noticing Meg's disheveled appearance and unmistakably swollen lips. He schooled his features into a mask of equanimity, though rage rushed through his veins. It was obvious what they had been doing. The bitch would pay for soiling herself. And MacLeod would die for touching her.

He should have rid himself of Alex MacLeod four years ago. Dougal didn't regret many things in his life, but not eliminating Alex MacLeod when he had the chance was one of them. Almost immediately, Dougal had regretted that rare display of mercy at Cuillin when he'd spared Alex's life. Although young, Dougal had recognized Alex's potential danger: Alex would demand vengeance for the deaths of his kin.

He did not usually leave such volatile loose ends.

But at the time, he'd been more concerned about Alex's brother. There was no question that Rory MacLeod would have avenged his brother's death. Dougal would have been a marked man. But Dougal now realized that he'd only traded one vengeful enemy for another.

But he didn't waste his time on regrets, not when they would soon be rectified.

The opportunity to take care of Alex MacLeod would materialize, and he would be ready.

"What are you doing here?" MacLeod demanded. Obviously, he'd noticed the palace guards, or Dougal felt certain he would have relished the opportunity to use the sword he had only now just lowered.

Dougal ignored him, addressing Meg instead. He was finding it difficult to look at her ravished face while hiding his anger, but he did his best to sound the concerned suitor. "When you did not return, your mother became worried," he explained. "I offered to ride out after you. I can see that it was a good thing I did. Are you all right? What happened?" He leapt down from his horse and started toward her.

"I'm fine. We were attacked," Meg said, and provided him with a brief description of what had happened.

To reach her, Dougal had to pass a number of bodies. He recognized one.

Stupid fool, he thought, stepping over Thomas Mackinnon. He couldn't pretend to be upset. He was glad to be rid of Thomas Mackinnon. MacLeod had done him a favor in ridding him of a man who'd outlived his usefulness. Initially, he'd planned to gain the Mackinnon's land through Thomas Mackinnon—a disgruntled man who valued his skills far beyond their worth. Mackinnon was only too happy to find a sympathetic ear in Dougal. But it had all changed once Meg had rejected her father's captain. Then, when Dougal had arrived at Dunakin, he'd changed his mind and decided to marry her himself. The change of plans had not sat well with Thomas Mackinnon, and he'd decided to take matters into his own hands. The fool could have ruined everything.

As he drew closer, Dougal noticed the awkwardness between the two. Maybe he was wrong. A bit of his anger dissipated.

"Come," he said, holding out his hand to her. "This is no place for you. Let me take you to your mother. My men will see to cleaning up this mess." He had to restrain himself from slapping her when Meg looked at Alex, as if begging him to disagree.

Alex stood immovable, making no claim. Dougal smiled, realizing that it must gall MacLeod no end to have her go with his enemy. He could only imagine how furious it would make him when Dougal announced their betrothal. Dougal had waited too long already to ask for her.

MacLeod was up to something. Something that prevented him from pursuing Meg Mackinnon, though it was clear he wanted her. Dougal knew the man, as well as any man would know a prisoner he'd watched over—and tried to break—for months. MacLeod was involved in something, and Dougal guessed that it probably involved the Isle of Lewis. Any resistance by the Highlanders to the arrival of the Fife Adventurers on Lewis would come from Rory MacLeod; and his loyal brother, Alex, would not be far behind.

He would bear watching. Any information Dougal uncovered was bound to be well rewarded by Seton. Being forced to pander to a man like Seton chafed. Lord Chancellor Seton treated all Highlanders with scorn, not discriminating between men of obvious civility like himself and useless scourges like the MacLeods.

But Dougal would smile and nod, acting the loyal cur, grateful for the meager scraps from the master's hand. It would be worth it in the end. The MacDonalds would be well rewarded by King James for betraying the Highland rebellion. Though Dougal didn't approve of King James's methods, he approved of his gold. Any hesitation Dougal felt about betraying his fellow Highlanders was tempered by the fact that it was the MacLeods who would suffer. And this MacLeod in particular.

"Thank you for your offer," Meg said. "But I would like to see to my men."

Dougal bit back his anger, knowing she wanted to stay with MacLeod. He smiled stiffly. "I'm sure MacLeod will see to it." He looked meaningfully at Alex, who didn't disagree, and then turned back to Meg. "Your mother was quite concerned. I really think you should come now."

Meg gave Alex one more pathetically heartbroken glance before she turned, reluctantly, to accept Dougal's assistance. "Very well, I'll go."

Perhaps Alex's rejection of the chit would work right into his hands. He would ask for her tonight, while she was still vulnerable. He would take her mind off Alex MacLeod. There really was no comparison.

Chapter 13

The gentle tinkle of laughter sliced across the din of the crowd, drawing his gaze like a fiery beacon to the woman across the room. Meg stood beside her mother, Elizabeth, Jamie Campbell, and a handful of other men, laughing at something one of the men had said. Her eyes sparkled in the candlelight with the warm effervescence of her laughter.

Laughter that stabbed like a dirk in Alex's gut.

Did she have to look so damn beautiful? Taunting him in a delightful concoction of white and pale gold that displayed all the womanly curves of her delectable figure. Curves that Alex remembered all too well. Soft waves of chestnut fell in beguiling curls down her back, emphasizing the snowy whiteness of her skin. Skin that had felt as smooth as velvet under his hands and tasted like honey. He knew he was staring, glowering actually, but he could not stop himself.

Jealousy ate at his resolve like acid.

He'd been like this all week. Anxious. Angry. Twisted into a tight ball of knots; feeling as though he were ready to explode. He told himself it was because Rory was due to arrive any day with the orders that would send him to the Isle of Lewis, but he knew the real reason was the beautiful woman holding court across the room.

Watching Meg be wooed by a bevy of suitors, knowing he could do nothing about it, was pure torture. This feeling of powerlessness for a man of action like Alex was both alien and unnatural. What he wanted to do was stake his claim in the most primitive way. Right now, he felt every inch the barbarian that Lowlanders claimed.

He knew he had no right to feel jealous. She needed what he could not give her: a marriage proposal. She had every right to look elsewhere. Why was he so damn angry that she would do so?

He tossed back what remained of his claret and slammed the empty goblet down on the card table with frustration. Nothing could calm the tangle of knots coiling inside him.

Not even the knowledge that he was doing the right thing.

But right or not, letting Meg go was the hardest thing he'd ever done. The memory of her face before she'd ridden away with Dougal MacDonald haunted him. The hurt. The confusion. The tender plea that tore at his conscience. He hated causing her pain, no matter the cause.

Nor could he get what almost happened between them out of his mind.

He couldn't forget the feel of her mouth under his. Of the soft silk of her breast. Of the honey dampness between her legs. And of the ecstasy on her face as she shattered in his arms. He didn't know how much longer he would be able to fight the overwhelming urge to take her into his arms and finish what they'd started.

If only it were simply about lust. But it was so much more than that. The feelings Meg aroused in him were like nothing that had come before. He admired everything about her. Her beauty, her intelligence, her frank honesty, her compassion, her drive. The confidence with which she approached everything. He wanted her on so many levels, each day that passed it had been increasingly difficult to remind himself why he couldn't have her. Forced to stand to the side as other men took the place that belonged to him.

Frustrated by the futility of it all, he tore his gaze from Meg and turned back to his card game. With Lord Chancellor Seton and Secretary Balmerino absent from tonight's entertainment, Alex had focused his attention on the Marquess of Huntly—his current opponent at maw.

"Pretty little thing, isn't she," the Marquess of Huntly said. "Rich, too, I hear."

Alex's gaze slid over his cards to the man across from him. The man who so far had yielded no new useful information. "Who?" Alex asked, feigning disinterest.

"The Mackinnon lass. I thought I saw you looking at her. I hear she's to marry young Campbell over there."

The news he'd been dreading burned a black hole in his chest. He fought to control his reaction. "I wasn't aware of the announcement."

Lord Huntly shrugged. "There hasn't been one. But I assume there will be in a few days. My daughter says it has been all but decided."

Bianca Gordon would know nothing about it, Alex assured himself. She would be the last person Meg would confide in. Speculation, that was all. Relieved, he loosened his hold on the cards, realizing he'd been crushing them.

"I heard you put on quite a display in Holyrood Park last week. My daughter can hardly talk about anything else."

Alex shrugged, knowing he had Rosalind Mackinnon to thank for spreading the story of his alleged heroics. He would have preferred to keep his part out of it. "Fortunately, I was there to lend my assistance."

Huntly shook his head. "Terrible, terrible thing to have happened to the poor girl. In this day and age, for a man to try to murder a girl for refusing to marry him. These barbarians in the Isles must be contained." Alex could feel him watching him closely, gauging his reaction. "Present company excluded, of course."

"Of course," Alex said.

Huntly gazed at him appraisingly. "I may have need for a man of your talents, if you ever want to put that sword to use."

Alex held perfectly still, well aware that Huntly might be hiring mercenaries to protect the Fife Adventurers. "I'll keep it in mind," he said, not wanting to appear too anxious.

"Do that," Huntly said, rising from the table. "Now if you'll excuse me, I'm afraid I have an appointment that cannot be delayed."

Alex stood up as Huntly left, his shoulders tensing when he heard a burst of fresh laughter. He didn't care that it seemed forced. His resentment intensified, especially when he noticed Dougal MacDonald at her side. Though she seemed barely to tolerate him, Dougal had made his intentions clear. Alex had been keeping an eye on Dougal, hoping for the opportunity to discover what he was really doing at court. Alex didn't believe it was solely to woo Meg.

"He's asked for her."

Alex turned to find Jamie at his side. The black expression on Campbell's face mirrored Alex's sentiments exactly. Nonetheless, even if they were in agreement about Dougal, Alex had been doing his best to avoid Jamie since his return from Argyll last week. Not only was Alex sure that Jamie suspected him of lying about his purpose in being here, there was also a subtle rivalry between the two of them that could not be denied. It was clear Jamie blamed him in some way for the attack on Meg in the forest, even if it was only for being the one to rescue her.

"She'll never accept him," Alex said finally.

"No, she won't," he agreed. He gave Alex an unmistakably challenging look. "Because she'll accept me."

Every muscle in Alex's body tensed. "I assume you have reason for your confidence?"

"I do. I know what she's searching for in a husband, and I'm her best choice."

Annoyed by Jamie's conclusions, even if they were accurate, Alex couldn't resist pointing out, "Not her only choice, perhaps."

Jamie didn't miss his meaning. "Stay away from Meg."

The words landed between them like a gauntlet dropped at Alex's feet. Alex lifted his gaze and met Jamie's hard stare with one of his own. He didn't like being threatened. By anyone. "Or what?"

Jamie did not back down, even though they both knew that he would be on the losing side of any fight between them. There could well come a day when Jamie would prove a challenge to Alex's battle skills, but that day was not now. If nothing else, Alex had to admire his courage.

"I have my suspicions about your true purpose in being at court," Jamie said. "Suspicions that I'm sure my cousin Argyll would find interesting. Of course, they are only suspicions, and as such I will be happy to keep to myself."

Alex smiled, though there was no amusement in the expression, only a warning. "You are more like your cousin than I realized. However, your suspicions and your attempts at blackmail are misplaced."

"Then you have no intention of making Meg an offer of marriage?"

There it was. The question that rose like a rock wall in the path of his destiny. It was the question that had come to haunt him.

Many times this past week he'd been tempted to ask her to wait for him, but he knew he could not. Hell, he could very well be dead in a few weeks. At best, he would be considered a traitor. That was how most Lowlanders would see him for aiding his kin, the MacLeods of Lewis, in their fight to repel colonization by the Fife Adventurers. Alex wasn't even sure that Meg wouldn't agree. She had argued for a compromise with King James with respect to his Highland policies; she seemed unlikely to support armed warfare against the king's men. A man who could soon be put to the horn was hardly the emblematic negotiator that Meg had in mind for a husband to better her clan's position with the king.

Moreover, Alex would not risk placing her in more danger. The threat from Thomas Mackinnon had only just ended. If it were discovered that he was helping the MacLeods on Lewis, a connection with him would be dangerous. Very dangerous. His enemies could decide to use Meg to get to him.

When he did leave Edinburgh, Alex would make sure that Meg's loyalty to King James was not in question because of a connection with him. It would be left to her father to determine how vocal his clan's involvement with the effort to repel the Fife Adventurers would be. The Mackinnon chief would decide what to tell his daughter. Alex would not do so for him.

But Alex acknowledged that his reasons went even deeper. He could not be the leader she needed for her clan, not until he put his past behind him. The demons of second-guessing haunted him unrelentingly. If he could only go back and change the moment when he'd refused to surrender to Dougal, his cousins might still be alive. But he'd defied Dougal, even when the battle was lost. He'd been filled with all the arrogance of youth, the sense of invincibility. And his recklessness had cost his cousins their lives.

Now he had the opportunity to make retribution. What kind of man would he be to turn his back on his kin, on those he'd let down before?

Alex looked Jamie straight in the face. "I have no intention of making Mistress Mackinnon an offer of marriage." He kept the bitter disappointment from his voice but was unable to prevent the uncomfortable tightening in his chest.

"Good." Realizing that he'd perhaps come dangerously close to pressing his luck, Jamie retreated from Alex and made his way back to Meg's side. Alex watched him with barely repressed fury.

Just then, as if Meg knew the direction of his thoughts, their eyes met. He felt a strange tightening that started in his core and spread through his entire body.

He knew she'd been watching him all week, confused by his sudden withdrawal. He didn't want to hurt her. But he could not give her what she most needed. It was better that she realize it now.

Turning away, he broke the connection. Every day—nay, every minute in her presence was a chink in his armor of resolve. Soon there would be nothing left.

He only had to hold out a few more days. But it was damn difficult, when every fiber of his being craved the one thing he couldn't have.

Out of the corner of his eye, he noticed Dougal slip out of the room. It was just the opportunity Alex had been waiting for. Any excuse to get the hell out of here before he did something he regretted, like storm over there, pull her into his arms, and kiss her until everyone in the room knew that she was his.

He tracked Dougal through the cool palace corridors in a direction that Alex quickly recognized. His instincts heightened as he realized this might be it, the proof he'd been waiting for. Curbing his excitement, he concentrated on not getting caught. Dougal checked behind him a number of times, almost as if he expected someone to be following him, but Alex anticipated his moves and quickly ducked out of sight. As he became even more certain of Dougal's destination, he was able to drop farther and farther back, minimizing his chances of discovery.

When Dougal entered the same room where Alex had previously spied Seton and Balmerino, Alex knew his instincts had proved correct. The MacDonalds were double-crossing Rory and the other Highland chiefs. Cautiously, Alex approached the room, sliding into the same uncomfortable niche he'd hidden in before.

"Glad you could join us, MacDonald."

Alex just caught the end of Lord Chancellor Seton's greeting, but he'd heard enough to discern the sarcasm in his voice.

"Gentlemen," Dougal said. "I apologize for the delay, Lord Chancellor, but it could not be helped. I wanted to make sure my departure from the hall was not remarked upon."

"Do you have reason to be concerned?" Seton asked suspiciously. His voice sharpened. "Have you been compromised?"

"No, my lord," Dougal replied hastily. "I just thought it prudent to keep an eye on the Highlanders that are here at court, especially Alex MacLeod. I don't trust the man."

"I'm not interested in your petty clan feuds, MacDonald," Seton said. "I leave the barbarians to you. Do whatever you think is necessary. If the man is a threat, remove him. As I've just been telling the others, the king will not tolerate another failure. All contingencies must be accounted for. This time, the Fife Adventurers will colonize the Isle of Lewis."

Alex realized Dougal had just been given license to kill him. He wondered how long he would take to use it.

"I've already begun going over the preliminaries," Seton continued. "I've received final confirmation that the colonists will be ready to depart as scheduled. What have you learned of the resistance, MacDonald?"

"We have nothing new to report," Alex heard Dougal

respond. "The chiefs have met to discuss the possibility of another attempt to colonize the Isle of Lewis, but there is no indication that they believe anything is imminent. Resistance, if any, is still much in the planning stages."

Alex knew he shouldn't be surprised, but even faced with such indisputable evidence—hearing it straight from Dougal's mouth—he still couldn't believe the MacDonalds' propensity for treachery. They had sworn allegiance to the other chiefs to help fight the king's efforts to plunder the Isles, yet here they were—through Dougal—betraying them all.

No doubt MacDonald expected to insinuate himself into the good graces of King James by feeding Seton information about the Highlanders' planned attacks. Rory would be furious to learn of their latest treachery.

But Lord Chancellor Seton's next words pushed aside all thoughts of the MacDonalds. "I want to be informed as soon as you learn of the Highlanders' plans. Any resistance to the Fife Adventurers' colonization will be crushed. King James has been clear in his directives. Our men have been instructed to use whatever force they deem necessary to root out the barbarians on Lewis"—he paused—"including slaughter or mutilation to discourage further resistance. The same will go for their supporters."

Alex couldn't believe his ears. *Slaughter* and *mutilation*? Seton's words sent a chill of foreboding straight to his bones. At that moment, Alex realized the full extent of King James's humiliation from the failed first attempt to colonize Lewis by the original Fife Adventurers. No doubt the mockery of his new English subjects had influenced this savagery. The English claimed that a king who could not contain a handful of barbarians was not fit to rule England. King James was taking no chances with this second attempt.

By empowering the Lowland Fife Adventurers with the power to exterminate the inhabitants of Lewis, the king had just sanctioned the mass murder of his own people.

Even the black-hearted Dougal sounded somewhat taken aback. "But, my lord, when the Highlanders realize what is happening, they will have no choice but to resist."

That's what they are hoping, you traitorous fool. This was no friendly colonization, it was a bloody conquest and the desecration of a people. Their people.

Seton's snort of laughter curdled Alex's blood. "Yes, they will, won't they?" Alex could almost envision Seton's smirk. "It will all be quite tragic."

Alex pressed his back up against the stone wall, trying to cool his rage. He took a deep breath. Resolve at last cleared the confusing cobwebs from his mind.

He had to see his mission through. He had temporarily lost his focus, lost sight of all that he'd worked for. Nearly undone by one wee wood nymph. But now that he was faced with such stunning evidence of viciousness promulgated by his own king, his duty was clear. Desire must come second.

There was really only one thing left to do. Fight.

He would leave for the Isle of Lewis as soon as Rory arrived.

And not look back at what might have been.

Meg watched Alex leave the hall, feeling the familiar curdle of disappointment. He'd barely spoken to her.

Each night she hoped it would be different, that tonight would be the night that he changed his mind. But tonight was no different from the rest.

The past week had been the hardest of her life. Forced to maintain an air of conviviality when inside her heart was breaking. Every moment of that day in the forest was branded on her consciousness. He'd awakened her passion and her heart. She wanted him to kiss her again, to touch her, to make her his in truth. And she knew he remembered it, too.

He held himself apart, but his eyes watched her every move with a possessive heat that sent a shiver of awareness down her spine. She sensed the anger and frustration building in him, but he made no move toward her. It didn't make sense. He wanted her, but something was keeping him from acting on those feelings. If only he would trust her enough to tell her why.

At the same time, she was almost scared to find out what it was. If what Thomas Mackinnon said was true, Alex had been fighting with the MacGregors. Alex was an outlaw—although she supposed it depended on one's perspective. It troubled her, but Meg knew that if he'd become an outlaw, he'd done so for a higher purpose. But she still didn't know what it meant as to his suitability as a husband and as a leader of her clan.

Had she given her heart to the wrong man?

Even worse, had she given her heart to a man who did not love her in return? Unrequited love, the fodder of poets and playwrights from time immemorial. And it had happened to her, to a woman who'd sworn never to fall prey to the dictates of her heart. Meg, the cold, hard pragmatist, had fallen in love.

She'd never dreamed that her heart could be at risk,

but it might not matter. She could not lose sight of her purpose in being here. She needed to find a husband, and time was running out. What was she going to do? She would never consider Dougal MacDonald's proposal—not after what she'd learned of him. Could she accept Jamie knowing that she didn't love him? That she loved another?

If only she could discover what it was that was preventing Alex from stepping forward. Then he would be free to marry her.

"Is everything all right, Meg?" Elizabeth asked. "You seem distracted."

Meg managed a feeble smile. "I'm fine, just a bit tired," she said. *My heart is breaking.* "I think I'll fetch us a couple of glasses of claret."

"I can go with you," Jamie offered.

But Meg had already moved away. "I'll be right back." She wanted a moment alone to clear her head. She knew her mother, Elizabeth, and Jamie were all concerned about her after what had happened.

It was still hard to believe that someone, a trusted captain of her father's guard no less, had been trying to kill her. Her mother had fainted upon finding out what her daughter had narrowly avoided and later sent a letter to Meg's father with the news of Thomas Mackinnon's treachery.

Meg shuddered to think what would have happened without Alex there. Twice now, he'd ridden to her rescue. The attacks on her life had made Meg realize that no matter how hard she tried, there were some things she simply could not do. Defending herself against half a score of warriors bent on killing her was one. But she also realized how ill equipped she'd been to recognize the danger. With his experience, Alex had identified the possible threat well before Meg even realized there was one. An invaluable skill for a Highland chief—or rather a trusted adviser to a Highland chief.

For a woman who'd been dependent upon herself for so long, it was startling to realize how much she liked the idea of Alex protecting her.

Alex seemed to have an acute awareness of everything around him. The prototypical warrior. Self-contained. Self-possessed. He didn't need anyone.

She felt a lump in her chest. *He didn't need me.*

As much as she'd grown dependent on him, it had become patently obvious that the reverse was not true.

She made her way toward the refreshment table but was forced to stop a few times along the way to exchange greetings. She'd finally reached her destination only to duck behind a column at the last minute to avoid Bianca Gordon. She was the last person Meg wanted to see right now.

Bianca had made it well-known this last week that if Alex was looking for a wife, he need look no further than the Marquess of Huntly's very willing daughter. Meg frowned, recalling that Alex had been playing cards with Huntly tonight. It seemed an odd pairing. And not the first time Meg had noticed Alex with some unusual companions. It was probably nothing. Alex would certainly never be interested in Bianca Gordon. Although excessively unpleasant, Bianca was undeniably beautiful. But Meg recognized the impatience hiding beneath Alex's smile whenever he was waylaid by Bianca. Bianca must have sensed it, too, because she took whatever opportunity she could to question Meg about her relationship with Alex.

Questions that Meg couldn't answer, even if she wanted to.

Standing to one side of the column, she was tucked neatly from sight of the occupants in the room without seeming to be hiding. Only the broad skirts of her gown gave her away. But ironically, since Rosalind had chosen a cream gown embroidered with delicate gold threads that happened to match the décor of the room, Meg didn't stick out too much. Good thing her mother had forbidden her to wear the orange gown again. There was something of the ridiculous in a grown woman having her mother pick out her clothes, but Meg had to admit that Rosalind had a flair for color and style Meg could never hope to emulate.

The derisive snort of her own name drew Meg's attention to Bianca's conversation. She hadn't meant to eavesdrop, but surely the pierce of that woman's voice could be heard clear across Scotland.

"Of course he's not interested in Meg Mackinnon," Bianca scoffed, and followed with a tinkle of pretty laughter. "As if the most handsome man at court could really be interested in someone like her. She's plain, far too serious, too learned by half, and she says the oddest things every time she opens her mouth. No maidenly modesty at all."

Her chest squeezed, surprised by how much it hurt to be dismissed so easily. But it wasn't the truth. Alex cared for her. She knew he did. She might not understand why he was holding himself back, but she knew that he was.

One of Bianca's companions spoke. "But he certainly seems to have singled Meg out for his attentions. I agree that it does seem an unlikely match, but you must admit that Meg's appearance has improved over the last few weeks."

"There wasn't much room for anything else." They all laughed. Meg's chest squeezed with each cruel giggle. "Even so, she can hardly be called a true beauty by any standards. Meg is merely a pale imitation of her mother. Mark my words, Alex MacLeod could have any woman at court. If he marries Meg Mackinnon, there is another reason."

Perhaps Bianca's cattiness might not have hurt so much if Meg hadn't thought the same thing many times herself. Intellectually, she knew that she had many other things to offer other than her appearance, but for a short while—in Alex's eyes—she'd felt beautiful. But Bianca effectively pierced the bubble of Meg's newfound confidence. She cringed when she thought of how much she'd enjoyed the improvement in her appearance over the last fortnight. Bianca was right, Meg would never compare with her mother—even with her help.

But Bianca's next words were not so easily dismissed.

"No doubt he's after her land. Her brother is an imbecile after all." Meg clenched her fists, her nails biting into her palms. She knew nothing about Ian. "If he can hold it, Alex would be the virtual chief of the Mackinnon lands at her father's death. I know some men who would marry a horse for less."

Meg's cheeks burned at the cruel comparison. *You have more land than I do,* Meg wanted to shout after Bianca as she flounced away, her puffy skirts crinkling along the way. *Why isn't he chasing after you if that is all he wants?*

Meg's heart pounded, hearing her darkest fears being bandied about court by the likes of Bianca and her friends. It hurt, quite a lot. Even knowing there was no truth to what Bianca said.

Alex wasn't Ewen or Thomas Mackinnon. He didn't want to marry her. He could have compromised her and forced her to marry him, but the fact that he stopped proved the honorable man he was. He wasn't after her land.

But Bianca's snide remarks posed a darker question, one that she thought she'd resolved. She shook with the wave of sudden self-doubt. Alex would never be the type of man to wrest control from her brother. He was ambitious and a natural leader, but he was no opportunist. He was honorable. Loyal. She knew it, despite what he wanted others to believe.

But had she just convinced herself of this because she loved him? Had emotions blinded her to the truth of his character?

No. Don't let that silly woman get to you, Meg, she told herself.

She couldn't be that wrong.

Chapter 14

Meg and Elizabeth had just settled to finish some embroidery in the small salon that used to serve Queen Anne's ladies-in-waiting when her mother entered with the most beautiful woman Meg had ever seen.

"Margaret, I have someone I'd like you to meet." Meg tried not to gape, but the woman was truly exquisite. Long red gold hair, pale skin, and . . . Meg blinked disbelievingly . . . dark violet eyes. "Isabel MacLeod this is my daughter, Margaret."

Alex's sister-in-law, Meg thought with amazement. They exchanged pleasantries, and Meg learned that Isabel and her husband, Rory, had arrived only yesterday. Meg was surprised she hadn't noticed her at the evening meal last night. Isabel MacLeod was hard to miss.

Isabel had seated herself next to Meg at the small wooden bench conveniently situated under a large window with a splendid view of the summer gardens. After a few moments, she said, "I've been eager to meet you."

Meg arched her brow. "You have?"

Isabel nodded, studying Meg with unabashed interest. "I've heard your name linked with Alex's more than once since I arrived, and I wondered at the woman who had finally captured my recalcitrant brother-in-law's heart. I wouldn't have believed it if I hadn't seen proof of it last night." When she saw Meg's confusion, she explained, "I was walking with Alex past the dining room when he saw you." Still grinning, she said, "I only wish his sister Margaret could be here to enjoy it with me, but her first child is due any day."

Meg's cheeks flamed under Isabel's close scrutiny. Her heart beat a little faster.

"You're wrong," Meg said quickly. "Alex and I are friends, nothing more." No matter how desperately she wished it differently. But if anything, Alex had seemed even more preoccupied and distant since that night two days past when she'd overheard that horrible conversation with Bianca. The conversation that still weighed on her despite her vow to ignore it.

If only she knew what it was that Alex was really doing at court. More and more, she thought it had to do with the MacGregors. She recalled his anger when she'd spoken of their plight with the king. Had he turned outlaw in an attempt to find some justice for the broken men? Was he at court not for a nefarious purpose, as she'd first assumed, but for a heroic one?

Isabel caught Meg's troubled glance. "Did I say something wrong?"

Meg shook her head. "No, of course not." She frowned, remembering something. "I'm just surprised to hear you speak so fondly of Alex. I'd heard rumors—" Meg blushed, realizing she'd spoken bluntly again.

Isabel returned her frown, appearing to weigh her words carefully. "Whatever is between Alex and my husband does not change how I feel about Alex. I will always care for him as a brother. I want him to be happy. And I sense he has found happiness with you."

If only it were true. She didn't want Isabel to see the

pain her words had inadvertently caused. Self-consciously, Meg turned her face to the window, attempting to dry the sudden dampness brimming around her eyes with the warm sunlight.

"You love him."

Isabel MacLeod was far too perceptive. Meg smiled wanly. "I'm afraid it does not matter. I must marry."

If Isabel was shocked by Meg's odd statement, her tone did not betray her. "Of course you must."

Meg turned back to face Isabel, her face impassive. "No, I mean I must marry *now*."

"I don't understand. Are you already betrothed?"

"No. But there are unusual circumstances. I have promised my father that I will have chosen a husband by the time I leave court."

Isabel's delicate brows knit together across her forehead. "Is Alex aware of this?"

Meg nodded. "And he's made it very clear that he is not interested in marriage."

Isabel bit her lip, looking a bit uncomfortable, as if weighing how much to say. "I very much doubt it is that he is not interested . . ."

"But something is holding him back," Meg finished for her.

Isabel nodded.

"Does it have something to do with the Mac-Gregors?"

Isabel looked at her sharply. "Did he tell you that?"

"Not exactly."

Isabel frowned, appearing to debate with herself about whether to say more. Finally, she seemed to come to some sort of decision. With a quick glance at Elizabeth and Rosalind across the room, she leaned in toward Meg. "What do you know of Alex's past?"

It took Meg a moment to comprehend what Isabel meant. "Do you mean about him being taken prisoner by the MacDonalds?" At Isabel's nod of encouragement, Meg continued. "He told me that he was taken prisoner after the MacLeods' defeat at the Corrie of the Foray. Although he did not say so, I got the impression that he took the loss personally."

"You're right. Did he tell you that he was the acting chief of the MacLeods at the time?"

Meg shook her head no, but understanding dawned.

Isabel continued, "The raid happened while Rory was away. He'd left Alex in charge for the first time. Alex took the loss to the MacDonalds as a personal failure—especially the deaths of his cousins."

Meg gasped. "I didn't realize. . . ."

"About twenty MacLeod clansmen lost their lives that day. Two close cousins of his from Lewis were brutally murdered right before his eyes."

Meg thought of the haunted look that she'd seen sweep his handsome features, his burning hatred of Dougal MacDonald, and the inner drive that she'd sensed but had not understood. "Poor Alex," she said, her heart breaking for him. "I knew there was something in his past that weighed on him." The death of his cousins under his first command was what drove him so relentlessly. "It explains so much," she said, shaking her head. "But it still does not explain his refusal to marry."

"Doesn't it?" Isabel encouraged.

Perhaps it did, Meg realized. If Alex felt there was still something he had to do. "Do you know why Alex is really at court, Isabel? Does it have to do with what you've just told me?"

Something distinctly resembling guilt flashed across Isabel's stunning face. "I've said too much already," she murmured dismissively. "But I do know that the loss of that battle weighs heavily on him. It changed him. In many ways, Alex is living in the past, trying to make up for his perceived failure that day." Isabel looked as though she wanted to say something more, but she held her tongue.

"But what can I do?"

"I don't know. You'll have to discover the rest from Alex. He deserves to find happiness. If there's any chance that he can find it with you—"

"You two look as thick as thieves at a fair," Elizabeth said, approaching them from across the room.

A quick glance over to Rosalind forced a smile to Meg's lips.

"I see your conversation is as enthralling as ever, Elizabeth," Meg teased, eyeing her mother napping peacefully in her chair.

Elizabeth laughed. "I think we may have missed the truly scintillating conversation. But I'll wager I can guess what—or should I say whom—you were conversing about." Elizabeth turned to Isabel and said, "Your brother by marriage has made quite an impression on my friend."

"I think it's mutual," Isabel said, returning her smile.

"I think you're right," Elizabeth agreed.

"If you two are finished speaking about me as if I'm not here, I believe I'm ready for that game of chess you promised me, Elizabeth."

Elizabeth ignored her. "Isabel, did Meg tell you about the game of chess that she—"

"That's enough for now, Elizabeth." Meg stood up and playfully pulled her smirking friend across the room.

Meg knew that she was only delaying the inevitable. She'd hear all about her prodigious loss to Alex yet again. But the teasing didn't bother her. Alex was a worthy foe—or ally, for that matter. She'd always thought of him as invincible. But in a strange way, learning about his past loss on the battlefield made him seem more human. The failure in no way diminished the man he had become, but rather explained it. The loss had framed his life. But had it overtaken it?

Talking with Isabel had only strengthened Meg's belief that whatever Alex was doing at court, it was for good. She didn't care who he was. Mercenary. Outlaw. It didn't matter. He was still the man for her. She knew the truth in her heart.

But Isabel had also made her realize something else. She had to do something soon or she would lose him.

But what could she possibly do to show him how much she trusted him?

Though Rory and Isabel had arrived only yesterday, to Alex it seemed intolerably longer. He had been anxious to advise his brother of what he'd learned but had been forced to wait until they could ride well away from the palace to preserve the damn pretext of a falling-out. Now that he'd confided in his brother, Alex was relieved to have unburdened himself, but at the same time he was uneasy, realizing that the time for him to depart court was drawing near.

Rory rode next to him in prolonged silence, no doubt considering the ramifications of the MacDonalds' treachery and King James's insatiable thirst for Highland bloodshed. His brother's reaction had been much the same as Alex's: shock followed quickly by anger and resolve. The grim set of Rory's chin and the tightness around his mouth told Alex just how determined his brother was to battle this last betrayal.

When they figured out exactly how best to do so, Alex would be on his way to the Isle of Lewis.

Alex brushed the sweat off his forehead with the back of his hand. But it was useless, he was drenched. The heat clung to him like a wet plaid. After a long day in the saddle, he was hot, tired, and in desperate need of a good dunking. The scorching summer sun crested high in the clear blue sky, reminding him of the last time he'd gone riding. In deference to that day, a handful of Rory's fiercest warriors trailed close behind them. With Dougal MacDonald thirsting for blood, they were taking no chances.

"You don't have to do this, you know," Rory said, breaking the silence.

Alex snapped his head around in surprise. That wasn't what he'd expected to hear. His gaze narrowed as he assessed his brother, not sure how to react.

Alex knew exactly what "this" meant—leave for Lewis. What he didn't know was *why* Rory would suggest that Alex abandon his plan to join the fight with their kin.

"Of course I do." If Alex's voice sounded sharper than necessary, it was because he wanted to make sure Rory understood just how important this was to him.

"I'm not questioning your fighting skills," Rory said,

knowing that was precisely the conclusion Alex had jumped to. A wide grin spread across his deeply tanned face. "I haven't forgotten the dunking I took on the lists a few years ago." He rubbed his shoulder. "Or the soreness of my muscles afterward."

Alex smiled, remembering their invigorating battle and Isabel's effective way of putting a stop to it. He'd had a few aches of his own.

Rory's hard blue eyes met his own. "You've changed in the last month, Alex. And I'm glad of it. I wondered whether you'd ever settle down long enough to fall in—"

"There's nothing—"

"Don't bother denying it." Rory lifted his hand from the reins, staving off Alex's denial. "You forget, I've been there myself."

Alex clamped his mouth shut. Rory was wrong, but there was no point in arguing with him.

"In fact, I think it's an excellent match and a golden opportunity for you. I wouldn't blame you if you were tempted to take it. You've risked enough here already. Our cousin Douglas can go to Lewis in your stead."

Alex could tell from Rory's voice that he was not convinced. They both knew that although Douglas was a strong warrior, Alex was the only one with the skills and experience necessary to help their kin—other than Rory himself. But because he was chief, there could be no question of his going. "You know as well as I do that I must go," Alex said. "I'm needed on Lewis. I want to finish what I started."

Rory's gaze intensified, but Alex didn't flinch. His fearsome brother hadn't been able to intimidate him in a long time. They'd been through too much together. But

Rory's continued scrutiny was uncomfortable all the same.

After a moment, Rory reached a decision. "You weren't to blame, Alex," he said gently, broaching the forbidden subject.

Alex flinched. His brother understood him better than anyone. Rory knew well why he pushed himself so hard. He turned away, focusing his attention on the rugged terrain of the grassy moors and rocky crags that surrounded them. Soon, the gray stone walls of the palace would come into view. Holyrood. What was once a guesthouse for the old Abbey of the Holy Rood, where a miraculous cross had appeared to King David I, was now a royal bastion of greed and deception.

"It could have happened to anyone, Alex. No one blames you."

The bloody image of his murdered cousins flashed through his mind. "But I do," he said to himself, hoping his voice was drowned out by the steady pounding of the horses. But Rory had the hearing of a hawk.

"There was nothing you could have done. There was nothing anyone could have done. Dougal MacDonald is a bloodthirsty cur, he was looking for any excuse to kill them. Getting yourself killed on Lewis won't bring them back."

"Don't you think I know that?" Alex said tightly.

"I just don't want you to make the same mistake I did. I almost lost Isabel for the sake of revenge."

The raw emotion in Rory's voice took the edge off Alex's anger. He remembered that long week a few years ago when Rory thought Isabel had betrayed him. He'd never seen his seemingly invincible brother suffer like that before and probably never would again. Rory and

Isabel were more in love than he ever thought two people could be.

He understood what had brought this unexpected halfhearted offer from his brother. Rory didn't want to be the one to force his brother to choose between love and duty.

"It's not the same," Alex said.

Rory lifted an eyebrow sardonically. "It's not?"

Alex shook his head. "No, I'm not the right man for her." His brother was aware of the Mackinnon's recent troubles, but Alex filled him in on the rest. "I won't put her in any more danger, and I can't be the man she needs to help her clan right now. I know how important it is to her to do the right thing by her clan. I won't ask her to sacrifice that for me. She's driven herself so hard over the past few years, I won't be the cause of her failure."

Rory gave him a wry smile. "Driven? Sounds like someone I know."

His brother's observation took him aback. "Perhaps," Alex admitted ruefully. They were alike in that.

"You're not being fair to yourself or the lass. Shouldn't she make that decision for herself?"

"That's not an option. Meg knows nothing about our plans." Alex deflected his brother's impending interruption. "And before you say anything, I have my reasons for not telling her. She's close to the Campbells, and if Argyll gets wind of this . . ."

All vestiges of humor vanished from Rory's face. "It could be disastrous. Argyll works for no one but himself. He's highly unpredictable, and if he decides it's in his best interests to inform King James of our plans, warding off the Fife Adventurers will be a much more difficult proposition—if not a losing one. Right now all we have is the element of surprise on our side."

"And we can't lose it," Alex finished for him. "I don't believe that Meg would betray us intentionally, but I will not take the chance that she lets something slip accidentally. And it's not just Argyll that holds me back from confiding in her. Knowledge of our plans and an attachment to me could put Meg in danger. I won't risk her safety." Alex held his brother's gaze. "I appreciate what you are trying to do, but it's not necessary. I know well what I risk, but it can't be helped."

Rory looked visibly relieved. "I'm sorry there isn't another way to resolve things with the lass, but I trust your judgment. Our kin need our help, and there is no one I'd rather send in my stead. You'll leave tomorrow night. There will be a boat ready to depart that can take you to Lewis. I'll take care of the MacDonalds, but the rest will be up to you."

"I won't let you down."

Rory turned to him and gave him a long look. "I never thought that you would, little brother."

Chapter 15

❖

Meg prayed this was not an enormous mistake.

She hesitated for a moment, contemplating the momentous decision she was about to make. If she went much further, there would be no turning back. What did she have to lose? Nothing, she thought wryly. Other than total disgrace and every ounce of her pride.

She was a fool to risk so much.

Still, she could not turn back while there was even a remote chance for happiness. When her happiness had even become important, she did not know. What mattered was that it had. Come what may, she'd decided to follow her heart and not her head.

So she continued on, winding through the unfamiliar territory, hoping that the maidservant's directions were accurate.

She pulled the hood of her cloak farther down over her head—she hadn't completely lost her senses—as she approached the gentlemen's living quarters, doing her best to avoid the curious stares of the servants she passed. Her features were well hidden, and she hoped it was enough. She'd made her decision; she'd have to live with the consequences.

At least there was a certain amount of logic to her plan. That fact should comfort her, as it always had before. But it didn't. Because if Alex did not listen to reason, she would be forced to play her final card. And there was not much logic to that particular part of the plan. And *that* fact made her nervous. Very nervous indeed.

If only she knew what to expect. But the riddle of Alex MacLeod was not an easy one to solve. Isabel's insight into Alex yesterday was at the core of what was pushing him away, but it wasn't the entirety. But Meg had made her decision. Whatever had happened to him in the past, it didn't matter. Meg believed in the man he was today. Enough to trust the future of her clan to him. For she'd decided to prove to Alex just how much she believed in him by offering him an alternative to whatever he was doing at court. One where his leadership and battle skills could shine.

Alex was the perfect man for her clan and the perfect man for her. She'd take the direct approach and tell him, and if that didn't work, she'd show him. First she'd appeal to his logic, then to their attraction. She bit her lip nervously. She hoped it wouldn't come to the latter. But if necessary, she would give him the ultimate proof of her love and trust.

It had to work. Rejection would be humiliating. Was this how men felt? she wondered, feeling an unexpected twinge of sympathy for Thomas Mackinnon. It was nerve-racking to put yourself in such a position of vulnerability.

She halted before a small closed door. His door. This was it. She took a deep breath, but the tumultuous pounding of her heart betrayed her unease. In twenty years, they'd probably sit around the hearth fire and laugh about it. She hoped.

Before Meg could change her mind, she rapped firmly on the door.

Nothing happened.

Her heart sank. What if he wasn't here? No, the maid-servant had assured her that he had retired for the evening. Meg drew up her shoulders and banged on the door.

The door burst open and slammed against the wall.

"What the hell!" he bellowed at the unknown person who had dared to disturb him.

Meg flipped back her hood and watched his face register shock as he realized just who had knocked on his door. His expression would have been comical if he didn't look so distraught.

His beautiful golden hair was tousled, his blue eyes tired, his face strained. He looked sad. Weary. But for a moment, before his face hardened, she saw a flicker of happiness at the sight of her. He wasn't indifferent. And the knowledge bolstered her courage.

But only for a moment.

Her eyes fell to his chest and widened. *Oh my.* It was a warm evening, and he'd removed his doublet. He wore a simple linen shirt and trews. A simple linen shirt that was opened at the neck, displaying a triangle of fine golden hair sprinkled across a broad, tanned chest plainly visible through the thin fabric. There was a raw sensuality to him that made her tremble with awareness, raising gooseflesh on her arms. The intimacy of the scene was hardly lost on her. Half-clothed. In his chamber. Alone. She hoped.

"You shouldn't be here."

She lifted her chin, tearing her eyes from the naked flesh revealed by his shirt. "I need to talk to you."

He didn't respond, but simply stared at her with a dark intensity that sent shivers racing up her spine.

Nonetheless, Meg took his silence, brooding though it was, as sufficient welcome and pushed past him into the room, immediately smelling the peaty aroma of whisky. Noticing the half glass on the table, she thought she could use a glass herself. But, no, she didn't want her senses muddled. His seemed as sharp as ever.

She glanced around, curious to view the lion's den. It was a small chamber, nowhere near as fine as her rooms. But she supposed the stark furnishings were adequate, if not luxurious. She ignored the rumpled bed. The rest of the room was surprisingly neat and tidy, with no personal items scattered about as she would have expected. Disappointed not to learn anything further about him from his room, Meg was nonetheless glad to confirm that he was alone—it would be impossible to do what she had to do with an audience.

"Why don't you come in?"

Meg frowned at his sarcasm and glanced at him again. His expression was hard and impenetrable, his body tense and watchful. He looked awfully forbidding, she thought, losing a bit of courage.

"You said you needed to talk to me?" he asked impatiently.

This was more difficult than she'd realized. She bit her lip. How to start? "I just wanted to let you know that I don't care what you are really doing at court. Whatever it is, it doesn't matter. I think I can offer a solution, one that will be beneficial to both of us."

Alex went still. If it weren't for the quickening pulse in his jaw, she might have thought he had not heard her. But he had.

He frowned. "What are you talking about?"

"An alliance—"

"Bloody hell, are you proposing to me?"

Meg blushed. At least he wasn't frowning any longer, she thought, looking at his expression of utter incredulity. That was a start. She took a deep breath and blurted out, "I suppose so. Yes. Whatever has happened in the past doesn't matter. I know you've helped manage your brother's lands before—"

"What did you say?" he asked sharply.

"Isabel told me about Rory's injury a few years back. She spoke of how well you managed Rory's lands." If the fabled Rory Mor had trusted Alex with his clan, it spoke much of Alex's abilities.

"What else did she tell you?" he asked, suspicion edging his voice.

Meg shrugged. "Oh, nothing much."

Alex folded his arms across his chest and glared at her, brilliant sapphire eyes hard and piercing. He was doing his masculine best to intimidate her. It might have worked had the bulging display of muscles straining against thin linen not set her mind on something else. Her mouth went dry. Unconsciously, her tongue flicked out to moisten her lips. He truly was magnificent.

"What else, Meg?" He took a threatening step toward her, enveloping her with the heady scent of whisky tinged with the heather and myrtle of his soap. Her pulse raced. The room felt even warmer and smaller. And teeming with raw masculinity.

She stepped back, and her leg came into contact with the bed. Though half tempted to fall and proceed directly to the second part of her plan, Meg grabbed the bedpost to steady herself. She forced her mind to focus on the task at hand, reminding herself that it might not need to come to that if he would listen to reason.

"Not much more than I already knew." Was that her voice squeaking?

"Meg . . . ," he warned, leaning over her, closer. She could feel the warmth of his breath on her hair. It sent a shiver of sensation down her spine.

She swallowed. Not from intimidation, but from the pure magnetism that radiated from him straight through her, warming her, engulfing her senses with heat. From his tense posture, she could tell he, too, was not unaffected by their closeness. The memory of what had happened in the woods stretched heavily between them.

"I know about your cousins," Meg said gently. Cautiously, she peeked at him from beneath her long lashes. Alex's controlled expression slipped, revealing his pain. She rested her hand on his arm. "Don't blame Isabel, she thought it might help explain some things, and it did. But why didn't you tell me?"

"I told you."

"Not all of it."

He stepped backward and turned away from her. "It was a long time ago."

"I know it was," she agreed, "but I also know that it still bothers you. Tell me."

He turned back to face her, meeting her hopeful gaze with a determined set to his square jaw. She could read it in the thin line of his lips, the shuttered look in his eyes: He still would not share his painful memories with her—and that hurt. But it was too late to turn back. He would learn to trust her.

"Meg . . ." he began softly.

From the look in his eyes, Meg knew what he was going to say. He was going to reject her. Again.

"I can't be the man you need for your clan—"

She clutched his arm. Perhaps she hadn't been clear? "Alex, I don't care about the past. I trust you completely. I trust your judgment, your leadership, your fighting skills. I trust you with the future of my clan. Is that not enough?"

"I'm honored, lass. More than you will know. If circumstances were different . . . but there are things you don't understand."

"Then tell me, help me understand."

"I can't."

"You mean you won't." Bitterness clung to her tongue.

"Very well, I won't."

It hadn't worked.

Words hadn't worked.

Her heart pounded and her pulse raced as she realized that the point of no return was fast approaching. Could she go through with it? Throwing herself at him like some common strumpet? Playing on their attraction? Seduction went against her normally forthright nature. It seemed almost . . . manipulative. She grimaced. Alex had left her no choice. She knew he needed a push. He cared for her, but something held him back. And she knew that if she did not try, she would never know. And living with that would be even worse.

There was only one card left to play. He'd thrown down the gauntlet.

To the winner went the spoils.

*   *   *

Alex knew the precise moment that Meg understood. He watched her beautiful green eyes cloud, the soft pink blush fall from her cheeks. He watched the pain of his rejection pinch her delicate features.

He hated being forced to hurt her. But what in Hades was she thinking coming to his room like this in the first place? Didn't she realize how dangerous this was? If anyone found her here, she would be ruined.

Damn Isabel for telling her about his cousins. He didn't want Meg's pity.

Marriage. The very idea taunted like a dream drifting just out of his reach. Marriage was something that he'd always thought would not be for him. But for the first time, he realized it could be. Regret came swift and hard. He was honored by her proposal and more tempted than she would ever know, but it could not be.

It was just like Meg to propose to him. Tenacious and straightforward no matter what. Coming here like this had taken some courage. But it also made everything more complicated. Had his life been anything else since he'd met her?

Conflicted didn't even begin to cover what Alex was feeling. One moment he was ready to jump on the next horse and race to the coast, eager to confront his future; the next he wanted to pull Meg into his arms and savor every precious moment with her. It had been like this ever since Rory and Isabel had arrived—when it had become impossible to ignore the fact that he must leave. And soon.

He should be proud of what he'd accomplished at court. He'd succeeded in the first part of his mission. He'd done what he came to do. But he took no joy in his success. Not when Meg had innocently become tangled up in his activities. He did take solace in knowing that the damage was not irreparable. Assuming he could stop himself from pushing her back on the bed and ravishing her as he wished.

By this time tomorrow, he would be on his way to Lewis. He was surprised that Rory had asked him to wait a full day. Alex had thought to be gone by now. He didn't know whether to be sorry or relieved. As his gaze slid back to Meg, he thought, Probably the latter. No matter how wretched he felt right now.

Where Meg was concerned, everything was in turmoil. A woman had never made him feel this way before. One thing was for sure: He would see that she never realized how difficult she'd made it for him to leave. He didn't want to give her false hope. Lord knew he didn't want to hurt her, any more than he wanted to say good-bye. But he had to do both.

She moved to the door. She was going to leave. But all he wanted to do was pull her back into his arms and wipe away the bruise left by his refusal with a kiss.

He forced his arms to remain by his side. Her back was to him, but he could see her fiddle with the clasp of her cloak. This was to be good-bye, then. His chest tightened. He forced his mouth closed, preventing the words from tumbling out to call her back.

He wanted her. But even if what she said was true, even if she did think he would make a good chief for her clan, Alex knew that he had to finish what he started. Rory needed him; there was no one else with his experience and skills. He had a duty to his clan and to his slain cousins to atone for their loss. And he would never put Meg in danger, physically from his enemies or from himself. An alliance with a traitor would be the exact opposite of the husband she'd hoped to find. No, it was better this way. Once he was gone, she would accept Jamie's suit. His stomach buckled with the blow of the thought of Meg with Jamie.

Her cloak had somehow slid off her shoulders and landed on a chair. And instead of opening the door to leave, Meg pulled the simple wooden latch across the door with a dull thud and turned to face him.

There was a strange cast to her face, determined yet vulnerable. She took a tentative step toward him. Slowly, her hands lifted to her hair. His breath caught. One by one, she pulled the pins that bound the thick curls, until the last one was gone and those beautiful chestnut locks tumbled freely down her back. Like a siren song, she shook her head, beckoning him to paradise. Or perdition. Alex was mesmerized by the shimmering waves of soft curls swaying in the candlelight.

He was growing very uneasy. And very aroused. His mind refused to accept what his eyes were telling him. His vulnerable little wood nymph was doing her best to look like a skilled seductress. It was utterly charming. And exceedingly effective.

"What are you doing?" His voice sounded ragged even to his own ears.

Her brow shot up, and a corner of her mouth lifted with amusement. "I must admit I'm new to this, but I'd hoped it would be obvious."

She continued her slow, swaying saunter toward him, until she stood right before him. So close that he could bend down and kiss the top of her downy head.

Suddenly shy, she peered up at him from beneath her long lashes. She reached up to place her hands on his shoulders. He groaned but forced his body to remain stiff and unyielding under her touch.

God help him, she was seducing him. His entire body clenched. He'd never expected this. Not from Meg.

"You need to leave," he said stiffly, then more adamantly: "Now." *Before it's too late.*

She shook her head and lifted her chin to look him straight in the eye, unflinching. "Tell me you don't want me."

Damn her, didn't she know how hard this was for him? How it had almost killed him to stop himself from taking her last time? How just being next to her filled him with a longing so intense, he didn't know how much longer he could stand not having her?

"I don't want you," he lied, his body pounding with desire.

She ran her hand up the top of his arms to circle around his neck, pressing her delicate body against him. Teasing him. He couldn't breathe.

"I don't believe you," she whispered, pressing a feathery kiss along his clenched jaw.

It hurt physically just to stand there, unmoving.

When he didn't respond, she pulled back, her expression an adorable mix of befuddled confusion. But Alex held firm under her gentle assault. She leaned closer, placing her hand on his chest for support, and brushed her mouth against his. The taste of her assailed him, drenching him with a slow-moving heat. Arousal swarmed his senses. He felt intoxicated, not with drink but with desire.

It took every ounce of his restraint not to take what she offered. He made a low sound, which was apparently all the encouragement she needed, because this time she kissed him harder, moving her mouth over his as he'd taught her to do. Her mouth was soft and unbearably sweet. He wanted to sink into her. To plunder the delicious cavern of her mouth with his tongue. He could have held out, would have, until she slid her tongue along the deep crevice of his mouth.

Damn her.

He pulled her into his arms with such urgency, he was worried that he might have hurt her. But she just mewled, like a sweet, contented little kitten. His head dipped and caught her quivering lips, lips that betrayed her nervousness. His chest tightened with protectiveness as he realized that she was not quite as confident as she seemed.

Instead of the hard, demanding kiss that his heated body craved, his mouth softened. Moving over hers, kneading her lips with his, persuading, opening. His tongue swept the inside of her mouth. She tasted so sweet, like warm honey. This was what he'd been dreaming of since that day in the forest. He couldn't get enough. Desire pulsed through him, urging him, taunting him, begging him to sate his desperate need. He was filled with it, his erection stiff and throbbing.

Soon, it would be too late to turn back. Lifting his head, breaking the promise of his kiss, was the hardest thing he'd ever had to do.

"I can't do this, Meg," he said, his breath harsh and uneven.

Her eyes were hazy with passion. Her pink mouth was swollen from his kiss. She'd never looked so beautiful. Lucidity finally broke through the haze. "I don't understand . . . don't you want this? I know what I am doing. I've never been more certain of anything in my life. You are everything that I need. Let me prove it to you."

Her faith in him pierced the shield encased around his heart. He believed her. A woman like Meg would not give herself lightly. She made him dream of things that he'd never allowed himself to imagine. For a moment, he forgot the shadow that had followed him for the last five years. This smart, beautiful woman believed in him.

His body wavered, but deep in his soul he knew this was wrong. He could not let her sacrifice herself, her future, her soul, for him. He would not be the cause of her failing her father. He knew how hard she'd worked to prove herself. Being here with him was a mistake. He couldn't give her what she needed. This had to stop. Here. Now.

"It won't change anything, Meg. I can't offer you what you want."

"I'm not asking for promises," she said quietly. "All I want is you."

Heart pounding, he unlaced her arms from around his neck, took her by her shoulders, and set her away from him. He tried to steady his voice as he said, "No. I don't want to do this."

She looked as though he'd struck her. Her eyes scanned his face, searching for any weakness. He forced his expression to stay hard, unyielding. He could almost see her mind filter through his words, analyzing what he'd said.

His heart wrenched as her face flooded with shame and humiliation.

"I'm sorry," she said, her voice trembling. "I thought you wanted . . . ," The words drifted away. Her cheeks burned scarlet, like two vivid handprints against a pale canvas. She could barely speak through the emotion strangling her voice. "No, it doesn't matter what I thought."

She flew to the door, gathering her cloak in one swift motion.

Hell, he'd made a mess of this. Alex grabbed her arm to stop her. "Meg, you misunderstand. It's not that I don't want you—"

"Please," she stopped him, precariously close to tears. "You don't have to say anything else." She tried to smile, but her lips trembled. "It's obvious that I jumped to the wrong conclusion." Her cheeks burned with humiliation. "Look at you. Look at me. I'm sure things like this happen to you all the time, women throwing themselves at you," she said with forced brightness.

Her wobbly composure broke him.

He swore, pulling her against him. He wanted to shake her for pushing him. Curse her for forcing this between them. Damn it, how could she doubt his desire? He took her hand and brought it between them, showing her how much he wanted her. "God, don't you feel what you do to me?"

Eyes startled, she nodded.

"You don't know what you are asking for, Meg. Go back to your room."

She shook her head and tentatively molded her fingers around him. Almost stroking him. He groaned as the dark sensations rushed through him. His stomach muscles clenched, and his cock pulsed with need.

"No," she said, refusing for the final time.

His control snapped. To hell with it. He'd tried to warn her. He was done denying what had been building between them from the first moment he'd seen her across the battlefield. The time for reckoning had come. She was going to learn just how much he wanted her.

He kissed her savagely, wildly. Finally unharnessing the violent passion that she aroused in him. He kissed her harder, punishing her with his mouth for what she was doing to him. For how she made him feel. For being the right woman at the wrong time. But if he'd hoped to scare her, he was wrong. Meg welcomed his fervor, returning it with her own.

There were no secrets left between them—or their bodies, at least.

She'd pushed him too hard. There was only so much torture a man could take. The warmth of her hand around him was it. Alex would not let himself think, even though a part of him knew *exactly* what this meant. Right now he was beyond thinking. His body craved hers, in a way that he had never before experienced. This was about possession. He moved with one purpose, to make her his.

She belonged to him. Forever. And somehow, nothing had ever seemed more right.

He wanted her.

Meg should be shocked by the intimate placement of her hand, but instead the proof of his desire seemed to shatter the final barrier between them. She wanted to feel him, she wanted to touch his body. To sever all secrets between them.

So she gave herself over to him, holding nothing back. She believed in him, trusted him. If he would not listen to her words, she would show him with her body.

The power, the vehemence of his kiss, told her what he could not. Her heart burst with pleasure. Passion that she did not know she possessed broke free.

The stubble of his beard burned her cheeks as his mouth slanted over hers. His hands pushed through her hair, forcing her head back to deepen the kiss. There was nothing gentle about his movements. But despite the raw energy of his passion, there was still something deeply tender in the primitive nature of his need. She, Meg Mackinnon, had shattered the mask of indifference. Her heart swelled with love for this amazing man.

She lifted her hand to rest on his sprawling chest, savoring the excited pounding of his heart under his thin shirt. *She* was driving him crazy, and it emboldened her like nothing else. Her hands roamed brazenly across his chest and back, tracing the hard edges of his body, pressing him closer, molding their bodies together as one.

His mouth moved across her jaw and down the curve of her neck as his fingers quickly worked the laces of her gown and stays. The beautiful emerald brocade gown that she'd chosen with such care to entice was soon lying in a puddle around her feet, until all that remained covering her nakedness was a thin sark.

His mouth lowered, moving down to the sensitive skin above her bodice. Deftly, he loosened the tie to bare her breasts.

"God, you are beautiful." He admired her with his hands, cupping her and then skimming down the curve of her stomach and hips like a sculptor. His mouth was achingly warm as he found her nipple. He sucked, and a needle of sensation shot through her body. She loved the brush of his rough chin against her skin as his tongue swirled and nipped, until each tip hardened into a tight bud. Molten heat flooded her body; her senses were drowning in desire. The area between her legs shivered and hungered, craving—no, demanding—fulfillment.

In her eagerness, her hand unknowingly grazed his waist, over the swollen round tip of his erection.

Alex flinched, sucking in his breath. Beneath his shirt, the muscles of his stomach rippled into taut parallel bands.

"Careful, sweet," he said tenderly, if unevenly, "or this will be over before it has begun."

Meg flushed. "I'm sorry."

His fingers lifted her chin, so he could look in her eyes. "For what? For making me want you too badly?" He smiled. "If you touch me, I will lose control. It is sometimes painful the first time for a woman. I want to concentrate on giving you pleasure." He paused, looking at her intently. "Do you understand?"

She nodded.

He kissed her again, and the brief poignant moment dissolved in the building storm of passion brewing between them. Deftly, he lifted her sark over her head. But before she had time to become embarrassed, he gathered her in his arms and carried her to his bed, laying her down almost reverently. The look in his eyes made her chest squeeze. Meg knew that she would never forget this moment. In his eyes, she saw the fulfillment of her dreams.

Though the summer evening was warm, she felt a sudden chill from leaving the protection of his arms. Little sensitive bumps appeared across her naked flesh, heightening her senses with anticipation.

"God, how I've dreamed of this," he said, lifting off his shirt and tossing it on the floor. His eyes moved across her bare skin, warming her instantly, burning a path from her head to the tips of her toes. "You are perfect."

She loved the huskiness in his voice. Meg hardly knew how to respond, her initial modesty eviscerated by his admiration and then by the powerful tanned chest and arms that blocked all rational thought. "So are you," she said. And he was. She would never get used to the perfectly chiseled masculine features or the sensual appeal of his powerful body. He was so much larger than her, so obviously male. His arms and chest were deeply tanned and smooth except for the thin triangle of golden hair below his neck. There was not one spare ounce of flesh on his muscled torso. He seemed ripped from steel without the bulk of most heavily muscled men.

His trews hung low on his hips, emphasizing the hard lines of his flat stomach. He sat on the edge of the bed and lowered his mouth to her breast, sucking until she arched against him and cried out. Smothering her cries with his mouth and tongue, he dusted his hand across her stomach, then lower.

She sighed, sinking deeper into the bed. Her body pooled with the hot memory of what he'd done to her before. She wanted that feeling again. Craved it. This time, he did not tease her but entered her gently with his finger, holding her gaze until her lids lowered and her head dropped back with the power of the sensations he wrought within her.

The rhythmic motion of his fingers drove all coherent thought from her mind. Her attention was consumed by the mastery of his hand.

He stroked her and stroked her until she writhed under him. Until her body grew slick with need. Until she felt the steady building toward the promise of the sweetest release.

*   *   *

Alex watched her eyes close as her head fell back on his pillow, tossing back and forth in sweet agony. He watched her body writhe with desire. His hand worked languidly between her legs, even as his own body cried out with urgency.

He couldn't stand this. He fought for every moment of her pleasure with the demons of his own desire. All he wanted to do was sink into the damp heat surrounding his finger. To thrust deeper and deeper, until her muscles tightened around him with the shattering ecstasy of her climax.

Almost. She was almost there. Almost ready for him.

He brought her to the brink with his hand before sliding off his trews and moving over her. His hands settled on either side of her shoulders as he propped up his chest and looked into her fluttering eyes. The beautiful, bewitching eyes of the woman he wanted above all others.

"It will hurt," he warned, his voice strangled. "But only for a moment."

Her eyes stopped fluttering as she fastened her gaze on his with sudden inquiry. Slowly, her eyes traveled down the ridges of his chest to his engorged staff.

Her eyes widened with shock. Even wet with desire, her innocent body could never prepare for a man of his size. Somehow she seemed to know that. "Trust me," he said.

She nodded. "Always."

Her heartfelt response humbled him. Alex moved the tip of his erection between her legs and resisted the sudden urge to make it quick. Even if it killed him, he would make this good for her. He pressed into her, inch by agonizing inch, going slowly, giving her body time to adjust to him. Sweat gathered on his forehead with the strain of restraint as the tightness of her body gripped him like an erotic glove. Nothing had ever felt this good. He wanted to close his eyes, throw back his head, and let the rhythmic sensations overtake him.

Not yet. He knew he was hurting her, but slowly her body opened for him. When he hit the point of no return, he hesitated. The full knowledge of what he was about to do, what he'd already done, hit him with a poignancy that he wanted to remember. The significance of this moment would be forever imprinted on his soul. He held her gaze, knowing that he'd never felt closer to any other person in his life.

Then, with one powerful thrust, he drove into her, plunging through her veil of innocence.

Meg Mackinnon was his.

Meg let out a cry that he covered with his mouth, seducing her passion away from the pain. The agonizing pinch of his entry dissipated into the tingling sensation of pleasure. Slowly, her body softened around him as she became accustomed to the feel of their joining. He was inside her. She reveled at the sense of fullness. Of the connection. Of how much she loved this man.

She sensed how hard it was for him to hold back. His muscles bunched along his shoulders, and his face was taut with restraint. Despite his obvious need for more, he desperately wanted her to enjoy this. His consideration tugged at her heart as nothing else could. Alex was harnessing all that power and strength for her.

Power and strength that had been revealed to her feasting eyes. His body was magnificent, as finely honed as a statue. A statue that radiated heat. The first touch of his hot skin under her hands was like pure magic. The granitelike muscles flexed beneath her fingertips as her hands trailed down his naked skin, exploring every inch of his back and arms. Just touching him aroused her.

And he sensed it. It was all the signal he needed. Slowly, he started to move. This was it. This was what she'd been waiting for. Yet she'd never imagined how it could feel. How the pleasure could rise and fall like a wave crashing on the beach. She could feel every erotic inch as his long, deliberate strokes drove her wild with need. Her nails bit into his arms as she fought to hold on. Her hips rose to meet him, taking him deeper. But soon it wasn't enough. This, whatever it was between them, could not be controlled. She wanted it harder. Faster. Deeper.

And God, he gave it to her.

His hand fell between her legs, and he caressed her gently as he plunged in and out. The pressure built until something in her broke, shattering, like thousands of shards of glass. Her legs wrapped around him, and her hand grabbed his muscled buttocks, driving him deeper.

With one last thrust, heaven found them both, releasing the tension that had built between them in a powerful burst of passion. Two souls tumbling together over the waterfall of tingling sensation. The emotions that ripped through her were so divine that Meg couldn't believe she had once thought she could live without love.

Gasping with wonder, she clutched Alex to her, her breathing short and shallow. His arms gathered her up in his protective hold, cuddling her body close to his. When their breathing returned to normal, he rolled to the side, one arm still resting across her naked chest.

He reached over and gently removed a strand of hair

caught in her lashes. A look of pure adoration lightened his features almost beyond recognition.

He stroked her cheek with his finger, and his expression grew tender. He seemed poised to say something. Meg wanted to believe that it would be significant to their future.

Her heart clenched, waiting.

But she would never find out what it was that Alex was going to say, important or not.

Because at that incredibly promising moment, when anything and everything seemed possible, the door burst open and Meg's life changed forever.

Chapter 16

"You bastard!" Jamie swore savagely. "I should kill you for this."

Alex immediately moved to block Meg from Jamie's view. Meg was only a second behind with the coverlet, lifting it up to hide her nakedness.

Alex's face hardened as he stared down his former friend. "You could try," he said with deadly calm. "But I wouldn't advise it. Especially after you've just barged into my room without invitation or without the courtesy of a knock."

"I was looking for Meg, and when her maidservant told me where she'd gone . . ." Jamie looked purposefully at the bed with a sneer. "Well, it seems I was too late."

"Have care, Campbell. Before you say something that I cannot overlook."

Some of Jamie's righteous indignation faded under the barely harnessed threat of Alex's rage. Alex should be the one issuing challenges, and if he hadn't felt guilty over the other man's jealous plight, he might have done so. He was furious at Jamie for bursting in on them and embarrassing Meg. His mere presence seemed to turn what they'd shared into something shameful and sordid. But most of all, Alex was angry at being forced to confront the reality of what he'd done before he'd even had a chance to savor the moment of contentment and bliss.

"Unless you want to bring the whole court down on top of us, you'll lower your voice and close the door."

Jamie looked as though he wanted to refuse, if just on principle, but after a quick glance at Meg's pallid face, he shut the now broken door.

In the same hard tone, Alex ordered, "Now, if you'll turn around for a moment, you can save Meg from further embarrassment."

Jamie did as instructed, turning away stiffly, giving them both time to dress. Alex slid off the bed, picked up his trews and shirt from the heap of clothing on the ground, and quickly clothed himself. When he'd finished, he handed Meg her garments, allowing her a moment to pull on her sark, then helping her as best he could with the laces of her stays and gown.

When her clothing had reached some semblance of order, Alex indicated to Jamie that he could turn back around. The quiet in the small room was deafening as they took turns staring at one another. Silent recriminations darted back and forth.

Jamie broke the silence. "So, it appears you've changed your mind. You'll be asking for her now?"

Everything went still.

Alex felt the consequences of his decision crashing down on him. Consequences that he'd been aware of but had hoped to work out on his own.

He knew what he had to do. Honor demanded it. The moment he'd taken her to his bed, the decision had been made. Even taken away by passion, he'd recognized it. Jamie's ill-timed arrival had only hastened his decision. But it didn't make it any easier to say the words. Nor did

he know what this would mean for his plans to go to
Lewis. He didn't want to put Meg in danger, and how
could he be the husband she needed if he was fighting on
Lewis?

How could he have jeopardized all that he'd worked
for these past five years? He thought of the hours spent
on the battlefield honing his skills, the years away from
his family and home, living in conditions not fit for a
dog. But most of all, he thought of his cousins and the
ill-fated decision that had led to their deaths. Must he
choose between Meg and his conscience?

This was exactly what he'd wanted to avoid. Alex
cared for Meg more than he'd ever cared about another
woman in his life. More than he wanted to think about.
Enough to know that marrying him would create problems for her. But there was no choice. He couldn't leave
her to face ruin, to face the disappointment of her father.

He blamed no one but himself, but he didn't like
being forced into anything, and certainly not like this.

Meg couldn't believe this was happening. One moment she was luxuriating in the single most beautiful
moment of her life, the next Jamie burst through the
door, discovering them in flagrante delicto. It all felt suddenly . . . wrong.

For a second, she thought they might come to blows.
These two strong men she cared so much about squared
off at each other with violent undercurrents running
between them. Meg hated to see them at each other's
throats because of her.

She wanted to say something to Jamie, to try to explain, but the words seemed to tangle in her mouth. He
wouldn't even look at her. Meg felt ill. She'd never

meant to hurt him. She cared for Jamie; he'd always been like a brother to her.

She knew what she'd risked in coming here, but she'd certainly never contemplated a nightmarish situation like this. A situation that had gotten that much worse when Jamie forced the answer to the question she'd most wanted to hear. But she wanted it from Alex. Freely given and without coercion.

Meg waited.

It was clear that Alex was waging an inner battle with demons she did not understand.

Her stomach twisted with apprehension. With every stretching second, she fought to hold on to the hope for the future that threatened to disintegrate into thousands of pieces at her feet.

Alex fixed his gaze on Jamie, refusing to look at her. "I do not need you to remind me of my duty."

Duty. The word ate a hole in her chest. She didn't want to be a duty. Meg could feel the resentment flowing between the two men, resentment that she feared would eventually extend to her.

Finally, Alex turned and took her suddenly ice cold hand in his. "Meg, would you do me the honor of becoming my wife?"

There it was. Her heart's desire.

His voice rang strong and steady, in the deep timbre that she loved. He did not hesitate or prevaricate, but Meg's chest squeezed painfully all the same. The proposal was sincerely given, but not his own. Not his choice. Not spoken with words of love, but compelled by his unfailing honor and nobility.

The truth nearly felled her. *He doesn't want to marry me.*

What could she have been thinking, coming here like this?

I've forced him to marry me, she realized. *But what can I do? I'm ruined. I have a duty to my family, to my clan.*

With his proposal, she had what she'd come for, but now she wished he'd turned her away. *He tried,* she remembered too vividly. Her cheeks mottled with mortification. Deep down, she'd honestly thought he'd wanted to marry her. She was wrong. And now they would both suffer.

A hot ball of tears lodged at the back of her throat and blurred her vision. She tried to smile, but it wobbled and fell into an awkward grimace. "I . . . I . . . yes," she finally managed. She was going to cry. She had to get out of here. "I must return to my chamber," she said overbrightly. With as much dignity as she could muster, she donned her cloak and headed for the door. With one last look at both men, she whispered, "I'm sorry."

"Meg," Alex said, moving toward the door. "Wait."

But Meg pretended not to hear him, dashing as fast as her tiny leather shoes would carry her down the cool, dark corridor.

Oh, hell, Alex thought, catching a glimpse of Meg's expression as she disappeared down the corridor. He turned to Jamie. "Well, that went well. Not exactly as I would have planned a proposal. What the hell were you thinking?"

Alex would make it up to her later, but it was obvious she'd needed time alone to get over the shock of what had just happened. He could understand the desire to be alone. But Campbell looked as though he had no intention of leaving.

"I never meant . . ." Jamie paused, seeming finally to realize what his rash actions had set in motion. By barging in here like this, he had compelled the very thing he did not want—Meg's engagement to Alex. "Damn." He paced around the small room, considering, looking at Alex occasionally as if he would read the answers on his face. When at last he stopped, the gaze that met Alex's wasn't friendly and might not ever be friendly again, but at least it wasn't twisted with hatred. "I knew something was different with Meg when I returned," he said. "She fancies herself in love with you. You took advantage of her."

Love? Alex felt as if he'd been struck. His whole body froze. Was it possible?

Yes. His chest swelled as he realized Jamie was right. Meg must think that she loved him. She would not give herself to a man if she did not believe that she loved him. And the intensity of his reaction told him how badly he wanted it to be true. The knowledge overwhelmed him. Humbled him. Thrilled him. And for a minute gave him hope. Having Meg's love was something he would cherish forever.

"Obviously, I underestimated you," Jamie continued. "You work fast. What is it? Money? Land?"

Alex's eyes narrowed. "Don't be ridiculous. It's not like that."

"It's not?"

Alex shook his head. "I told you the truth. I did not intend for this to happen."

"But you are not sorry that it did."

Alex thought for a moment. Jamie was right. He'd

tried to protect her by doing the right thing, but he
wanted Meg as his wife. "No, I'm not. For the manner
in which it happened, perhaps, but not that it did."

"You care for her." Jamie sounded stunned.

Alex didn't need to answer.

Jamie studied him with an appraising gaze, as if something that had bothered him finally made sense. "You
really do care for her. That is why you do not want to involve her in whatever you are doing at court." He held
up his hand, cutting off Alex's denial. "Don't bother. I
don't know what you are up to, but I'm sure it has nothing to do with finding work as a mercenary. I did a little
investigating of my own. Made a few inquiries. Seems
no one can recall an Alex MacLeod fighting as a mercenary with the O'Neill over the past few years."

Alex hid his reaction. He wasn't surprised that his
ruse had been discovered, just that Jamie had managed
it so quickly. He could take consolation that at this
point all Jamie had was suspicion. He didn't know anything specific. Alex knew that if he tried to deny it, it
would only make Jamie more certain. So he said nothing, neither agreeing nor disagreeing. "Think what you
like. My business is my own."

"Not when you involve Meg. Then it becomes mine."
Jamie took a deep breath. "It will not be necessary for
you to marry her."

"Of course it is."

"I will tell no one about what I saw tonight." Jamie
stood a little straighter. "I intend to ask Meg to marry
me."

Alex's fist clenched, ready to swing at Jamie's squared
jaw. He took a step forward. "I believe the lass is already engaged."

Jamie met his gaze defiantly. "Let her have a choice."

Alex fought to control the rage that swarmed his senses at Jamie's words. Meg was his. Every muscle in his body rejected the proposal, even as his mind realized that Jamie was right.

Jamie observed Alex's reaction but stood his ground. "Meg doesn't deserve to be put in danger," he continued. "If you are up to anything untoward, you will not involve her. You have to know that such a marriage would be the worst possible situation for her clan, and therefore for her. Unless you are willing to give up whatever you have planned?"

Alex didn't like hearing his own concerns bandied back at him by Jamie. He was honor bound to do two contradictory things: marry Meg and fight the king's injustice on the Isle of Lewis. His eyes narrowed as he studied his foe with part suspicion and part dread. Intuitively, it seemed, Jamie understood his conflict and was using Alex's conscience against him. Jamie knew that Alex would not endanger Meg unnecessarily, not when she could still come away unscathed. He pictured her face as she'd left his room. Well, relatively unscathed.

He clenched his jaw, biting back the refusal he desperately wanted to shout. But he couldn't, because Jamie was right. *Damn him straight to hell.* "After what you just saw, you know I am honor bound to marry her," Alex said. "I will not withdraw my proposal. It is her decision."

She thought herself in love with him. Alex knew Meg. If he confided his plans to her, she would make him into a damn hero and ignore the danger to herself. Part of him wanted to do just that, tell her the truth, placing the weight of the decision on her. She could have the facts and decide for herself, giving her a choice that he was fairly certain would result in his favor.

Could he marry her knowing that he would put her in danger when there was another alternative? A *safe* alternative?

Selfishly, he wanted to hold on to her now that he had her. But he knew he wasn't the best man for her.

Damn Jamie Campbell and his blasted proposal.

Alex would have to drive her away and give her no choice but to break the engagement. But it would have to look bad, giving her no choice but to turn to Jamie.

If there was a way to keep her from danger and stop her from making a mistake by marrying him, he would find one. No matter what the cost to himself.

Chapter 17

Alex need not have worried how he was going to convince Meg to break their engagement. The means to do so came to him.

And not a minute too soon. In a matter of hours, Alex's men would meet just outside the city gates to begin their journey to the Isle of Lewis. But he couldn't leave without resolving things with Meg—one way or another. He'd just finished breaking his fast and was considering seeking advice from his brother when the Marquess of Huntly approached him.

"Have you given any consideration to my offer?" Huntly asked.

Distracted, Alex had to think a moment before he realized what Huntly was talking about. Ah yes, Huntly had thought to hire him as a mercenary. As the need for Alex's pretense would be over when he left, the words were in his mouth to politely turn down Huntly's offer. Then, out of the corner of his eye, he saw Meg standing near the door. She must have paused just outside the door to the dining room when she saw whom Alex was speaking to. Alex pretended not to see her.

His mind worked quickly. This was it. This was his opportunity. He felt a sharp pang of regret for what he was about to do. Thanks to Huntly, Alex was effectively taking the decision away from Meg. Huntly had unwittingly given him the golden opportunity to strike her where she was most vulnerable—her brother.

"A bit," Alex answered. "What exactly are you proposing?"

"I'm not sure whether it would appeal to you. I am not at liberty to discuss the details, but I can say this: It might require fighting against other Highlanders."

Alex shrugged indifferently. But he was even more certain that Huntly was talking about fighting *for* the Fife Adventurers. The irony wasn't lost on him.

"Perhaps even against your brother," Huntly warned.

Was she close enough? Not taking any chances, Alex raised his voice. "No doubt you've heard that my brother and I do not see eye to eye on a lot of things. For the proper consideration, I might be amenable." He lingered on the word *consideration*. He dared not look at Meg to see if she was listening.

"You will be well paid," Huntly said. "A sword arm like yours would be highly valued for what we have in mind."

"Of course. But that is not the only consideration I was referring to." He paused at what he was about to do. *Forgive me.* "It seems I've recently come into some lands. Some considerable lands."

He heard a faint sound. The muffled sharp intake of breath. She was listening all right. His chest tightened as he realized the pain he must be causing her. Not yet engaged for a full day and he was already making claims on her land. But he was doing the right thing. The best thing for Meg. It was that knowledge that propelled him on, though each word he spoke pushed the dirk a little deeper in his chest.

Huntly looked surprised. "Oh?"

"Yes, Mistress Mackinnon has agreed to become my wife. As I'm sure you are no doubt aware, the situation is ripe with opportunity."

Huntly smiled. "So I was right. You did have designs on the lass."

Alex feigned a "you caught me" look. "She is tempting," he pointed out.

"Yes," Huntly agreed. "A very tempting morsel to an ambitious man like yourself. With the right support, you could be chief."

Alex paused, uttering the word that would seal his fate, driving Meg away forever and sending her right to Jamie. He tensed, his body fighting against it. He wished there were another way.

"Exactly," he lied. Meg *was* tempting, but for none of those reasons. But she would never marry him now. Not thinking that he meant to usurp her brother's position.

"And the consideration you refer to?"

"If necessary, when the time comes, a good word with the king."

Huntly gazed at him thoughtfully. "I will see what I can do. We are agreed, then?"

Hearing the gentle swish of skirts moving away from the door, Alex ventured a quick glance to see that Meg had left. He stood up. "I will think on it."

Huntly looked mildly surprised that Alex had not accepted right there, but he nodded as Alex walked out the door. His legs moved with the forced stride of a man going to his execution. He still had one thing left to do before he departed. It was time to talk to Meg. Or, he supposed more accurately, allow her to talk to him.

*   *   *

Meg had started the day with no more clarity of mind than she'd gone to bed with. She loved Alex and was convinced that he was the right man for her clan. Even knowing that he did not want to marry her, she couldn't disappoint her father and fail her clan by breaking the engagement simply because of her pride. There was too much at stake.

He cared for her, she knew he did. Surely he would come around . . . eventually?

With that thought in mind, she'd gone to break her fast, hoping to find him.

If only she hadn't.

She'd thought it odd to see him talking with Lord Huntly again. Not wanting to interrupt, she'd hung back, intending to wait until they were finished with their conversation.

Their voices carried right to her, as if set on a course straight for her ears. She'd been shocked to hear Lord Huntly's proposition to hire Alex and even more shocked by Alex's response. She must have misunderstood. Alex wouldn't fight against Highlanders—against his own brother—would he? The very idea was repugnant. Meg might take a pragmatic view of the problems facing the Highlands, but she would never condone taking a sword against her own people. But it wasn't the first time she'd questioned his loyalty. She recalled how she'd found him playing cards with a group of the king's men not long after he'd arrived.

What did she really know of his activities? She'd attributed a higher purpose to his fighting with the Mac-Gregors. But what if there wasn't one? Her heart started to pound.

Pounding that turned into a full-fledged hammer with what she heard next.

"I've recently come into some lands."

It didn't sound like him. This opportunistic stranger couldn't be Alex. There had to be some mistake. But it was the same golden head, the same strong, handsome features, and the same sensual mouth that had kissed her with such passion last night. She felt a moment of panic, waiting for what might come next.

"Ripe with opportunity," he said. She held the significance of a piece of fruit.

". . . you could be chief," said Lord Huntly.

And the response that had cut her to the quick: *"Exactly."*

No. She bent forward, clutching her middle as if the blow had been physical. She didn't want to believe it. Would never have believed it if she hadn't heard it for herself.

He might not want to marry her, but that didn't stop him from turning the situation to his advantage. He intended to challenge her brother's authority. The worst part was that he would undoubtedly make a fine chief. But not like this. Not by betraying her and ousting her brother.

Like Ewen Mackinnon before him, the boy who'd so cruelly destroyed her girlish dreams, Alex was just another man who wanted to use her for his ambition.

This didn't make sense. After what they'd shared? In his arms, she'd felt loved and cherished. He'd made love to her with such tender consideration. Was it all an act? *She'd thought . . .*

A soft cry strangled in her throat. *Oh God, she was a*

fool. A blind, lovesick fool. She'd thought he cared about her.

She'd been wrong. About everything. She'd put her trust in the wrong man. To think she'd worried that he was too much of a warmonger, without the necessary political acumen to negotiate with the king's men. He was wily enough all right—just not the way she'd intended.

He'd failed her.

No, that wasn't true. She'd failed herself. For she had no one to blame for this disaster but herself.

Meg was ruined, with no hope of finding a husband to help defend Dunakin. She'd failed miserably in the task she'd been given, and she would never forgive herself. She'd let her father down when he had trusted her where other men would not. What would happen to her brother? To her clan? How could she have been so selfish?

You are a smart lass, my Meggie. I don't know what I would do without you. Her father's voice echoed in her ears. Her heart wrenched to think of his disappointment. Smart, perhaps. But not smart enough.

She'd been duped. She'd known she was thinking with her heart and not her head, but she hadn't been able to stop. The signs were there, she'd just chosen to ignore them. So badly had she wanted him to be the right man. Meg had been deceived by a handsome face just like thousands of women before her.

And now she would suffer the pain of disappointment. Of letting down those she loved.

She'd risked everything for love. And lost.

It wasn't supposed to hurt this much, was it? The tight burning in her chest that constricted around her heart. She'd been disappointed before. It should be easier to weather the second time around. She'd been here before.

But she hadn't. Nothing could have prepared her for the anguish of Alex's betrayal. For the burning pain that seemed to consume her.

Breathe.

She wanted nothing more than to crumple into a puddle on the floor. To put her head in her hands and give way to the maelstrom of tears wailing inside. But somehow she found the strength to keep standing. It was a strength born of disappointment. She knew what she had to do.

Her back felt unnaturally stiff as she moved back from the dining room, her hands clenched in the cool silk of her skirts. She felt brittle, as if she could shatter into a thousand pieces with the slightest touch. She thought about retiring to her chamber or retracing her way back to Alex's room to wait, but she knew she had to do this now or she might not be able to do it at all. She entered a small antechamber not far from the dining room. They would have a measure of privacy, but the public nature of the room would keep her from falling apart. She'd already made a fool of herself.

She stood near the large stone fireplace, too anxious to sit, where she could see the steady stream of courtiers make their way from the dining room. She didn't have to wait long.

"My laird," she called to him as he passed by the open door.

At the sound of her voice, his head turned. Their eyes met, and the sharp pain that had just begun to dull knifed through her again, cutting off her breath. How could such beauty hide such treachery? The face that had first attracted her had grown more impossibly handsome as she'd grown to love him. Now with the mask lifted, she should see ugliness. But all she could see was the man who'd made love to her and looked at her as if she were the most beautiful, important person in the world.

Her pain was so palpable, she wondered if he could feel it.

"Meg," he said, taking a few steps into the room. "What are you doing here?"

She couldn't do this. Despair rose inside her, threatening to erupt.

No. She shook off the hurt. He would never know how hard his betrayal had hit. She'd never told him of Ewen.

Lifting her chin, she looked him straight in the eye. "I wished to speak with you." She waited for him to come closer. "Your noble sacrifice will not be necessary," she said with a hard edge to her voice that was surely not her own.

He'd caught the sarcasm. "I'm afraid I don't understand."

"Don't you?" She arched a brow. "You see, I've reconsidered. I'm afraid I responded to your proposal too quickly last night. The answer is no. No, I will not marry you," she repeated more firmly.

If she'd surprised him, he did not show it. But that was Alex, an impenetrable wall of granite. A warrior. A man who needed no one, least of all her.

His eyes bit into her with a hard blue intensity. "May I ask why? You'll perhaps understand my confusion after last night."

Her cheeks heated. "I've decided we would not suit after all."

He stood looking at her, as if waiting for her to say more. Finally he asked, "You will not reconsider?"

She wanted him to argue with her. To tell her she was wrong. To tell her all those reasons why they should be married. Her chest squeezed. To tell her that he loved her. But he accepted her decision with heartbreaking stoicism.

She shook her head. "No," she said softly, trying to mask the emotion shaking in her voice. Tears burned at the back of her throat. She couldn't hold on much longer.

He seemed to sense it and moved toward the open door. He glanced back at her one time, holding her gaze for only a second. For a minute, she thought she saw a flash of regret. Of pain so raw that it mirrored her own. "Good-bye, Meg. I—" He stopped. "Good-bye."

And then he was gone, leaving Meg feeling emptier and more alone than she ever had in her life.

Irony. Delicious at times, bitter at others. For Alex, this moment fit squarely within the latter. Just as he'd succeeded in driving her away forever, he realized just how deeply he loved her. At the very instant he'd destroyed any chance of a future with Meg, he finally, ironically, put a name to the feelings that had eluded him for so long.

Unfortunately, it had taken her broken heart to knock the truth out of him.

The truth hit him squarely in the chest as he watched her face him with that vulnerable pride and strength that had always drawn him. His own feelings became painfully obvious when each anguished emotion that crossed her face was mirrored—no, exceeded—by the agony he suffered inside.

Her eyes impaled him, her heartbreak written plainly across her delicate features, silently begging him to explain that which could not be explained. Ignoring that silent plea, refusing her comfort, was pure torture.

His poisoned arrow had struck her in her most vulnerable, protected spot: her heart. He knew how closely guarded she kept her emotions, hidden behind her confident, intelligent façade. She'd allowed herself to open up to him, trusted him, and shared the precious gift of her innocence, only to have her heart trampled.

He'd never meant to hurt her. The grief and desolation that haunted her face as he'd left the room fell like a cat-o'-nine-tails lashed across his shoulders. It took every ounce of his resolve not to go to her.

Although the realization of his love came suddenly, Alex knew that it had been there, staring him in the face, for some time. Perhaps from the first; even then he'd sensed something different about Meg.

But now he'd had a chance to explore the depths of that initial attraction. He loved her strange combination of serious and naïve, her no-nonsense efficiency, her practical approach to problems. She exuded confidence and capability effortlessly. He loved her compassion, her wry humor, her dedication to her friends and family. In truth, he loved everything about her.

Alex was in love with Meg Mackinnon and there was not a damn thing he could do about it. His sudden epiphany, while personally painful, did not change anything. He would still sail for Lewis, would still fight the

Fife Adventurers, would still put her life in danger if he involved her in his plans.

She would still be better off with Jamie.

Even if he could somehow repair the disaster that she'd just witnessed, it would not change their separate future. Letting her go, putting her happiness above his, was the most selfless thing he'd ever done.

He loved her, and she might even love him. But it wasn't enough. If they were two people alone in the world, with nothing or no one else to consider, he would find her right now and beg her to forgive him for his lies, making love to her until she forgot everything else.

But they weren't.

They each had people counting on them, depending on them. The only right, honorable thing for him to do was let her find her separate peace, fulfill her separate destiny. As he would fulfill his on Lewis.

Alex sighed, his breath pained. Anguish constricted his chest.

He just never thought he'd be forced to cut out his heart to save his lost soul.

Hours later, her tears at last extinguished, a soft knock on the door broke her reverie. "Meg, it's me." She recognized Jamie's voice. "I know you're in there. Please, I must speak with you."

Jamie was the last person she wanted to see. Well, second to last. But she also owed him an explanation. Assuming she could find one. She rose from her seat by the window and straightened her skirts and hair, knowing there was nothing she could do to hide her tearstained cheeks and eyes.

Slowly, she opened the door. "Jamie," she said in a

much weaker voice than normal. "I'm surprised you're here"—her eyes dropped to the floor self-consciously—"after last night."

"We're friends, Meg. Nothing has changed that. May I come in?"

She nodded, relieved that he hadn't said anything about her appearance. "Of course, if you want to. But I'm afraid I'm not very good company right now."

Jamie moved into the room and closed the door behind him. "I wouldn't disturb you if it wasn't important."

She nodded and led him into the adjoining parlor, a room that she usually found pleasure in. The neat orderliness was strangely calming. She glanced at a section of books in the cupboard: Seneca, Shakespeare, Sidney, Sophocles, Spenser, every book alphabetized and aligned perfectly. But she felt . . . nothing. Empty. She wondered if she would ever feel anything again.

There were two seating areas, one around a small fireplace and one near a small window. A vase of white roses was perfectly centered on a small table in the center of the room, two enameled boxes placed in front equidistant from the vase. She indicated for him to sit before the window, then took a seat next to him on the small bench.

Jamie took her hand in his, surprising her. Deeply embarrassed, she dropped her gaze to her lap.

"I need to apologize for what happened last night," he began.

Her head jerked up, and her eyes widened. "What are you talking about? If anyone should apologize, it's me. I feel horrible."

He shook his head. "Please, let me explain. I had no

right to barge into Alex's room. I was angry and worried about you. I regret that I forced the very thing that I'd hoped to prevent."

His kindness only made her feel worse. She'd treated him badly, and he'd been nothing but a friend to her. "Jamie, I'm so sorry—"

He squeezed her hand, cutting off her reply. "I'd be honored if you would consent to be my wife."

Her mouth dropped open. "You must be joking."

He bristled at her astonishment. "I'm quite serious. I would never jest about something so important."

"But, Jamie," she started, still aghast. "After what you witnessed, surely you can't want to marry me."

"I care for you very much, Meg. We share many of the same interests, we think alike." He smiled at her. "It is a good match, our families would approve. And nothing Alex MacLeod does can change that."

Meg couldn't believe it. She'd never dreamed that Jamie would still want to marry her. He was offering her the ability to salvage everything she'd worked for.

She studied his face, searching. "But do you love me?" she asked quietly.

"Of course I love you. I love you as much as I love my sister—"

"That's just it," she interrupted, a crooked smile on her lips. "Don't you see? I'm not your sister. Are you *in* love with me?"

A flush stained his cheeks. "Of course I'm in love with you, whatever 'in love' means."

"If you have to ask, you are not in love with me."

Jamie raked his fingers through his hair. "Meg, why is this so important? Our positions dictate that we marry where our duty lies. You have a duty to your father"—

she flinched at the blunt reminder—"to marry. A marriage tie with the Campbells is just what your clan needs. I can help Ian. I can protect your clan. I want you to have a choice. You don't need to marry Alex MacLeod. He's not what you think."

No, he wasn't. "I'm not marrying Alex."

Jamie looked taken aback. "But I thought—"

"I changed my mind."

"Good, then marry me."

"You don't have to sacrifice yourself, Jamie. I don't blame you for anything. I knew what I was doing."

"I assure you, Meg," he said stiffly, "marrying you would not be a sacrifice."

She reached for his hand. "Don't be angry. I meant no offense. You are a good friend, Jamie. You must think me terribly ungracious. To ask me to marry you after what you saw . . . Well, not many men would do that."

"Now is not the right time." He bent down and pressed a gentle kiss on the top of her head. "Don't decide right now. I'm confident that when you've had time to think over my offer, you will realize that it is indeed for the best." He cupped her chin with his fingers, forcing her to meet his gaze. "I do love you. I will make you happy."

Her eyes misted. She nodded, seeming to reach a decision. "You are truly a good friend, I don't deserve you. I must return to Dunakin. Perhaps on Skye things will seem more clear."

"Very well, then. Talk it over with your father. You will see that what I'm proposing is best, when you are away from here."

She knew what he meant. Away from Alex MacLeod.

Part Two

Chapter 18

Dunakin, Isle of Skye, September 1605

Three weeks was apparently time enough to fall *in* love, but not long enough to fall *out* of love. Meg had this unfortunate truth drummed into her head each morning when she woke, hoping this would be the day that she forgot about Alex, this would be the day she could get on with her life and put Edinburgh behind her.

She grimaced. Three weeks, three years, it didn't make a difference. She would remember. Everything. Every detail of those precious few weeks rolled through her mind as vivid as if it were yesterday. Alex's strength and natural command. The way he walked into a room and made every other man superfluous. The calm under pressure and immediate control he displayed in the midst of danger. The way he made her feel safe. But most of all, she remembered the exquisite pressure of his arms around her, the warmth of his skin heating hers, the way her heart fluttered when he kissed her, and the erotic sensation of him inside her. Filling her. Making her complete.

She tried to forget. Oh, she made a valiant effort to force him out of her mind by conjuring up the last image that she had of him, when he'd broken her heart and then simply walked away. But nothing could erase the haunting memories of love and passion before the betrayal.

She still loved the man she thought he was—even if that man had never really existed.

The shock waned, but not the pain. It would be a constant reminder of her mistake.

"What are you doing cloistered up here again, dearest?" Rosalind's chirpy voice startled her from her reverie.

Meg turned, meeting the worried gaze of her mother. "Enjoying the view. I love this part of the old tower. It's so peaceful up here, watching the *birlinns* cross the kyle."

"Tallying the daily profits, are you?"

Meg smiled. For hundreds of years, since her enterprising ancestor "Saucy Mary" strung a heavy chain across the kyle, the Mackinnons had collected tolls for boats passing through the narrow strait that separated Skye from the mainland. Tallying profits was what she should be doing, would be doing, if she could concentrate on anything other than . . .

She shook her head, clearing her mind. "No, not today."

"With Michaelmas approaching, I expected you to be huddled with your father somewhere." Rosalind approached the chair where Meg was seated. Her dainty fingers cupped Meg's chin, tilting her face gently. Soulful green eyes gazed at her with sadness. "What's wrong, love? You have not been acting yourself ever since we returned from court. I never thought I'd complain of such things, but I can't remember the last time I saw you read a book, balance a ledger, mutter about efficiencies or words that I've never heard before."

Her heart squeezed, thinking of Alex. "Perhaps I've been a bit more quiet than usual, but I've had much to consider." She tried to force a bright smile to her features. "In fact, I was just on my way to see Father. I need to speak with him about Jamie."

"Have you made a decision, then?" Rosalind asked warily.

Was there ever really a decision to be made? What choice did she really have? Nothing had changed since returning home: Either she accepted Jamie's proposal or she failed in her duty to her clan. Choice was illusory. She pushed aside the guilt, knowing she did not love him. Elizabeth was right: Jamie deserved to be loved, and Meg would do everything in her power to love him.

"I'll marry Jamie, of course."

Rosalind's face fell, and a mix of disappointment and distress pinched her delicate features. "Oh dear, dear," she muttered. "I'd so hoped . . . I'd thought perhaps Laird MacLeod—"

Meg stiffened.

Rosalind frowned, noticing Meg's reaction. "Just because I've not asked you what happened between you and Alex MacLeod does not mean that I don't realize that something did."

"I don't know what you mean."

"Margaret Mackinnon!" Rosalind stomped her tiny foot in what Meg realized was supposed to be emphasis. "Don't pretend ignorance with me. Why, we left court in such a hurry, I barely had time to change into my traveling clothes. And poor, dear Alys has never had to pack so quickly." She threw up her hands. "Wrinkled silks, crushed velvets, torn lace . . . anything could have happened."

"We were fortunate, indeed, to escape unscathed."

Rosalind's mouth twitched, but she otherwise ignored Meg's playful retort. "And if such haste was not bad enough, you barely spoke five words the entire trip home and your eyes were red and puffy for days. Really, dear, you should have let me put a cool posset over them to prevent those horrid black circles."

"As I explained, I felt ill and wanted to return home."

"Ill!" Rosalind made a sound of disbelief and rested her hands on her slim hips. "I may not be as learned as you and your father, but I do have the sense God gave me."

Meg's eyes widened with surprise. Had her mother just been derisive? Rosalind must truly be annoyed; she didn't have a derisive bone in her body.

"Please, Mother. There really is no need to discuss this further. There was, and is, nothing of import between Alex MacLeod and myself."

Meg whipped around to stare at her mother, who had just issued a most indelicate, unladylike snort. When she recovered from this latest shock, she continued, emphasizing the point: "I'm going to marry Jamie Campbell."

Rosalind shook her head. "But it was obvious to anyone who looked, Alex cares for you so much. Your father's health is much improved, surely you can wait—"

"It's over, Mother," Meg interrupted sharply.

Rosalind shot her a hard look in return, pursing her lips with obvious displeasure. "I've told your father . . . He's delayed long enough. He has something to tell you that might change your mind."

*   *   *

Curious as to what her mother meant, Meg lost no time and hurried down the stairs to find her father.

It didn't take long. The Mackinnon chief sat hunched over a stack of ledgers in the second-floor library of the old tower, two stories below the room she had occupied only moments before, massaging his thinning pate with his wrinkled fingers.

He glanced up as she entered the room. His short stature coupled with an impressive girth suggested a more jovial personality than was indicated by his serious visage. Meg supposed that in expression, if nothing else, she resembled her father.

Relief brought a slight turn to his lips, but it could not be described as a smile. It struck Meg how much older he looked after his recent illness. The poison had left its mark.

"Ah, Meg. I've gone over these accounts repeatedly—I'm worried about the amount of land held by wadset, and I can't find the entries for the north."

Meg leaned over her father and flipped through the thick stack of parchment.

"The entries are listed first geographically, then alphabetically by clansman, then by acreage, and finally by type of obligation, whether wadset or tack. Under each entry I've listed the date and method of payment, whether in grain, cattle, or silver. For each tack, you will see the grassum the clansman paid for the lease initially, then the yearly rental portion, again broken down by tack duty. The entries you are looking for should be . . ." Her finger traced the faint scratches of the quill down the page. "Right here."

" 'Tis so obvious, how did I not find it?" he said dryly.

Meg blushed, unsure whether he praised or jested

with her. She continued on, suspecting the former. Like her, her father appreciated thoroughness and attention to detail. "I've cross-referenced these entries in another ledger by wadset and tack. The total obligation for lands held by wadset are listed in that ledger. It should be easier to determine the amount from that. If you'll wait a moment, I'll fetch it for you."

The Mackinnon could only shake his head in amazement. "My dear girl, I don't know what I would do without you."

Meg felt a momentary swell of pride, but it was also a subtle reminder of her duty.

Rosalind blew into the room. "Tack, wadset! Who cares about leases and mortgages? Your only daughter's heart has been broken—"

"My heart wasn't broken." *It was ripped apart and torn to shreds.*

Rosalind continued on as if Meg hadn't spoken. "And all you can talk about is land! Lachlan Mackinnon, you've something much more important to discuss."

"What's all of this hysteria about, Rosie?"

Her mother shook her finger right under her father's nose. "Don't you 'hysteria' me. I warned you something like this might happen. You should have told her right when we returned, and now the poor child is about to sacrifice her everlasting happiness for you."

Her father sank back a little in his chair. A bit shamefaced, he turned to Meg. "What's this about, lass?"

"I've decided to write Jamie and accept his offer of marriage."

He nodded. "A good choice."

"Good choice!" Rosalind shrieked. "Have you listened to nothing I've said? Why, the girl is in love with

Alex MacLeod, and you have nothing to say but 'Good choice'?"

Her father sighed. "Meg's a woman grown, capable of making her own decisions. And Jamie Campbell is a powerful ally. What would you have me say, wife?"

Rosalind crossed her arms, positioning herself in a manner that demonstrated her every intention of digging in her heels. Meg barely recognized this controlling side of her mother. Although she knew they loved each other, Meg had always assumed that her father held the reins in the marriage. That there might be more to her parents' relationship than she'd assumed was vaguely disconcerting.

"I want you to tell Meg what you know of Laird MacLeod."

"I assure you, Mother, I'm not interested in hearing any more about Alex MacLeod—"

"Margaret Mackinnon, hold your tongue," Rosalind said sharply.

Meg dropped to a chair, mute, staring at the strange angry woman next to her. The same woman who hadn't even raised her voice when Meg used her best silver platter to slide down a snow-dusted Cuillin peak when she was eight or used her precious Flemish tapestry as target practice when she was eleven.

Her father looked equally unsettled. "Very well, dear," he said placatingly. "But, Meg, this must be kept in the strictest confidence. Only a handful of people know what I am about to tell you."

Meg nodded, perplexed by the unusual vehemence in his voice. She waited for him to continue, curious and a bit apprehensive about what this was all about.

He appeared to be weighing his words carefully. "Alex

MacLeod was sent to court at the bequest of the Island chiefs to discover information about the rumored attempt by the Lowland Fife Adventurers to recolonize the Isle of Lewis."

It took a moment for his words to settle in. The color drained from her face. "You mean that Alex was a spy?"

"In a manner of speaking, yes," her father answered. "Though nothing quite so dramatic. He was basically just to keep his eyes and ears open and see what he could learn. Given that he is the brother of a chief, and has been to court many times, we felt Alex's presence at Holyrood would not be seen by the Lowland government as suspicious. But it was also convenient that he had not been too tightly connected to his brother these past few years." He paused, clearing his throat. "Of course, not many people are aware that for the last few years Alex has fought with the outlawed MacGregors."

Meg stared dully at her hands, now curled into tight fists in her lap. She couldn't believe what she was hearing. She'd known that Alex had been up to something, had realized there was something he had not been telling her, but she would never have guessed that he was a spy. Not a mercenary at all. Nor apparently was he estranged from his brother.

Little oddities suddenly made sense: playing cards with Jamie in the room full of the king's men, his anger at the mention of the MacGregors and the Lewis political situation on their ride that day, lurking in the dark corridor . . .

Her stomach lurched. When they'd had their first kiss. Had he kissed her simply to cover up his presence in the hall?

"Tell her the rest," Rosalind said impatiently, obviously sensing Meg's distress.

Her father sighed and continued reluctantly, "The information that Alex uncovered at court enabled the Island chiefs to ready their assistance, secretly, to the MacLeods of Lewis. When the Fife Adventurers landed and occupied Stornoway Castle a couple of weeks ago, we were ready—in large part because of Alex." Her father seemed inclined to stop, but Rosalind nudged him along with a piercing stare. "And Alex has joined Neil MacLeod in leading the resistance on Lewis."

"Alex? Fighting on Lewis?" she echoed softly. She'd guessed what he was going to say, but it still came as a shock. Her mind was racing, trying to put together what she'd just learned with the conversation with Lord Huntly. Why would Alex be agreeing to fight for Huntly? *He wouldn't.* "But how? For how long?"

Her father shrugged. "He's been there for over two weeks, arriving just before the Adventurers. He probably left court about the same time you did. Neil and Alex have been organizing raids on the settlement at Stornoway, intercepting food and supplies meant for the Adventurers—wearing them down, much like last time. Small skirmishes thus far, but that will soon change."

"I knew he was up to something, I just never suspected—" She jerked back as if she had been slapped. The second betrayal hit nearly as hard as the first. Her father, the man she'd fought desperately to please, to convince that she could manage Dunakin, had not confided in her.

Acute disappointment formed a solid, bitter lump in her throat.

"Why didn't you tell me? Why was I not informed

that you intended to help the MacLeods of Lewis? How could you keep something so important from me?" She choked on her last words, unable to control the emotion strangling her voice.

Her father was in league against the king, and she'd been kept in the dark.

"You are many things, Meg," he said gently. "But you are not chief. That is a position I hope to hold on to for a few—nay, many more years to come."

Her father did not trust her.

"Lachlan, you are doing an atrociously poor job of this," Rosalind warned.

Her father glanced over at Meg, noticing her distress. "It's not like that, lass. I'm proud of you. You've acquitted yourself admirably in the face of difficult circumstances, with your brother . . ." He fiddled with some loose parchment on the table, flustered as he always was when discussing Ian. "Perhaps I rely on you overmuch. Your mother accuses me of demanding too much of you. I never thought so, but perhaps she is right. If you want to marry Jamie Campbell, do so because *you* want to, not because you think that is what I expect of you. Often the best solution is not the most obvious. Trust in yourself."

"Yet you do not trust me," Meg accused, still hurt that he had not confided in her.

"Nonsense. You must realize that you are not privy to all the decisions made around here."

In fact, Meg hadn't realized that.

"It was safer for you not to know. The fewer people who know of this, the better. We don't want to risk the king getting word of our involvement."

"I would never—"

Her father held up his hand. "I know that. If I'd known you were going to become involved with Alex, I would have warned you. And then when you came home, you spoke only of a proposal from Jamie. I wasn't convinced, or I refused to let myself be convinced, that what your mother told me about your feelings for Alex MacLeod were true."

Her cheeks grew hot. She heard her mother make a "humph" sound that said *I told you so.*

"If you wish to wait for Alex MacLeod to return before you answer Jamie, I do not object. But you must understand that the situation on Lewis is extremely volatile—and of course very dangerous. There is a chance—"

He stopped abruptly when Meg paled.

"I'm sorry, Meg, but I do not want you to suffer under any false illusions. Alex may not return. And even if he does, the king will hardly be pleased with him. With rumors circulating in London of a plot to overthrow the Fife Adventurers, Neil has already been put to the horn. The same could happen to Alex."

There were thousands of questions running through her mind. She didn't realize that she'd voiced them aloud. "What's the nature of our involvement? What chiefs are involved? Does the king suspect us? When do they plan to take the castle? What news have you had from . . ."

"From Alex?" Rosalind finished for her.

Meg nodded.

"We are in daily communication with the men fighting on Lewis. In addition to the MacLeods of Dunvegan and the Mackinnons, the MacDonald of Dunyveg, MacLean of Duart, MacLaine of Lochbuie, MacLean of

Coll, and the MacQuarrie of Ulva are all party to our plans. We have provided men and supplies, of course, but our primary aid is information. If the king suspects our involvement, he is not yet ready to move on his suspicions other than to forbid travel to the Isle of Lewis—which is why our messengers travel at night."

Meg took a moment to digest this latest information. Then she asked, "But what about the MacDonalds, are they not involved?"

"Ah, you noticed the omission of our mercurial 'friends.' Yes, they are involved. But the MacDonalds think they can straddle both sides by forming an alliance with the chiefs while secretly providing information to Lord Chancellor Seton. They sent a spy of their own to court, but Alex discovered who it was and we are feeding him false information."

"And who is this spy?" Meg asked, though she'd already guessed.

"Dougal MacDonald. Your mother said he was a suitor of yours at court?"

"Odious man," her mother said. "You never can trust a MacDonald. I never would have sent him after you in the forest had I known."

"None of us knew, Mother," Meg said consolingly. "But I never seriously considered his offer." Not after what he'd done to Alex. Refusing his offer of marriage had been easy; the hard part had been doing so politely. She turned back to her father. "With Alex no longer at court, how are the chiefs getting information from Edinburgh?"

"Spies. Informants. There are always people willing to talk for the right price. I believe Alex also recruited one of Seton's personal servants."

Oh no. No wonder he'd been so angry when he thought she was spying on him. "A maid, by chance?" Meg asked numbly.

Her father quirked his brow. "Yes, I believe so." He looked at her for a moment and then continued. "Rory MacLeod is still at court. He sends messages in duplicate, one to his brother on Lewis and one to me. It is my duty to keep the other chiefs apprised of the changeable situation."

"I believe Meg will be most interested in the latest missive you received from Rory Mor," her mother said.

Her father cleared his throat. "Yes, of course. The latest report of the next supply shipment two nights hence is the one we've been waiting for that should enable Alex and his men to take the castle and send the Adventurers running back to Fife." In case Meg missed the implication, he added, "If the MacLeods take the castle, this will all be over. And Alex will return to Dunvegan."

A hero, she thought. Despite his betrayal of her, Meg felt a wave of compassion for Alex. A victory on Lewis might help erase some of the pain of the loss of his cousins. She hoped so, for his sake.

Meg didn't know what to say. This new information had explained many things, but it did not change what he'd said to Lord Huntly. Or did it? He'd lied to Huntly about fighting for the Lowlanders. Had he lied about everything else? But why?

Her father stood up and began pacing before the large stone fireplace. "What I don't understand is why Alex would become involved with you, knowing the danger a connection with him would pose for you."

Meg didn't hear what he said next, because for the second time in the space of a few minutes she had been given a wicked jolt. *Danger.* Her mind worked quickly. *A connection with Alex would be dangerous.* He knew that. He also knew the danger he would face on Lewis. That he might never return, and if he returned, he might be imprisoned or killed. Had he known she was listening to his conversation? Had he merely been trying to protect her?

Her heart soared. A bright beam of sunlight broke through the oppressive darkness that had shrouded her soul since that morning in Edinburgh.

For the first time in three weeks, Meg allowed herself to hope. Perhaps when he'd finished his quest on Lewis, Alex would come for her?

Like an omen, a clansman shouted from the *barmkin* below, "A *birlinn* is approaching."

Her heart jumped. *Could it be?*

Chapter 19

Meg dashed to the window and peered down into the small *barmkin* above the sea-gate. She could just make out the figure of a man climbing swiftly up the stairs. He was certainly tall and broad-shouldered enough. . . .

Yet somehow she knew it wasn't Alex. Her heart plummeted as if someone had yanked a chain, forcibly bringing her hopes back to reality. Of course it was too soon—Alex was still fighting on Lewis.

She watched as the man jostled his way through the swarm of Mackinnon clansmen training in the courtyard. But even though he was partially concealed by the crowd, she easily made out the thick auburn hair of the new arrival.

"Who is it, Meg?" Rosalind asked, the excitement in her voice evidence that she, too, hoped for another.

" 'Tis Jamie," Meg responded brightly, trying to cover her disappointment.

Her father lifted a bushy gray brow. "Seems that decision might be pressed upon you sooner than you expected, daughter."

Meg steeled herself for Jamie's reaction, not sure what to expect. He'd changed in the past few weeks. He seemed older. Harder. "I'm sorry you had to travel all this way, Jamie, but I can't marry you."

His back stiffened, and his mouth drew into a tight line. "I'm afraid I don't understand. I thought you would welcome my offer."

He was angry and not a little surprised. In truth, she'd surprised herself. This was the second time that she had decided to marry Jamie and then changed her mind. Soon she'd have to add fickle to her ever growing list of character flaws. But she couldn't marry him, not when she didn't love him. And Elizabeth was right, Jamie deserved someone who did. Judging from his reaction, however, Meg suspected she'd hurt his pride more than his heart.

"I do," she assured him. "I appreciate it more than I can say. Marrying you would solve all my problems, but it wouldn't be fair to you."

"Fair to me." He combed his fingers through his hair, searching for an explanation, looking at her as if she were half-crazed. Perhaps she was. Jamie Campbell was not a man any woman would turn down lightly. But he was not the man for her. His eyes widened. "Good God, you're not with child, are you?"

Meg colored to her roots. She looked around the hall, relieved to see that they were still alone. "No . . ." Her voice faltered. "There isn't a child." Though she knew it was ridiculous, Meg felt a twinge of regret.

Jamie must have heard something in her voice, because his anger seemed to dissipate. His eyes raked her face. "Then why?" he asked gently.

She took a deep breath. He deserved the truth. "You are a dear friend, Jamie, but I don't love you, not the way you deserve to be loved, at least." She put her hand on his arm. "And I don't think you love me. Not the way I deserve to be loved."

"But—"

She stopped him. "I'm in love with Alex."

His eyes hardened. "But I thought you broke the engagement."

"I did."

"Then I don't understand."

Meg smiled wryly. "I'm not sure I do, either." How could she explain it to Jamie, when she couldn't explain it to herself? But if there was a chance that the conversation she'd overheard with Lord Huntly had not been true, she had to find out whether there was still a chance for them. Even if it meant waiting for his return. "I broke the engagement because I overheard Alex talking about marrying me as an opportunity to become chief someday. But I don't think it was true. I think he wanted me to think the worst of him."

"To protect you," Jamie finished for her. At her look of surprise, he added, "I'm aware of Alex's involvement on the Isle of Lewis, Meg."

So the "secret" was out. She supposed Alex had Dougal MacDonald to thank for that. "So if you know what Alex is doing, you can understand why he might want to shield me from a connection with him."

"Yes." Jamie didn't look surprised at all. In fact, he looked as though he knew more than he was letting on. "I wondered how he'd done it," he murmured, almost to himself. At Meg's questioning look, he explained, "I wondered how he'd gotten you to break the engagement so quickly. Alex knew of my intention to propose to you."

Meg's heart soared. "He did?" It made her even more

positive that Alex had been trying to drive her away. And she suspected that Jamie knew that as well. "What part did you play in all of this, Jamie?"

"None," he said flatly. "Other than to tell him that I thought you should have a choice in which proposal you accepted."

Her moment of elation faded. "Which he apparently decided not to give me."

Jamie gave her a long look. "He must really care for you to do something that he knew would make you hate him."

"Then why didn't he trust me with the truth and let me decide?"

A corner of his mouth lifted in a half-smile. "Perhaps because he knew you well enough to know that if you knew the truth, you would not walk away. You can be rather tenacious when you want something, Meg."

"So I've been told," she said ruefully. "But I still will have a word for him when he returns."

"That might not be for some time, Meg. And you must know that there is a very good chance that he will not be coming back."

Something in his tone sent a chill of alarm running through her. "What do you mean?"

"Even if the MacLeods of Lewis are successful in repelling the Fife Adventurers from the Isle, Lord Chancellor Seton's men know about Alex's involvement."

That wasn't all. Jamie was hiding something. She clutched his arm in earnest. "What else?"

He didn't answer right away. The depth of his struggle played out in the conflicting emotions crossing his face. Finally, he seemed to decide. "I only want you to be happy, Meg. Are you sure this is what you want?"

Meg nodded. "Please, Jamie, if you know something, you must tell me. I know you are angry with Alex, but you were friends once. I can't believe you'd stand aside and allow something to happen to him, not if you could prevent it."

"If it meant you would reconsider, I just might. Alex is fortunate indeed to have such a staunch defender." He paused, his eyes searching her face. "Very well, I'll tell you what I know. But for your sake, not his." He held her gaze. "One of the men fighting with Alex on Lewis has been ordered to eliminate both Alex and his cousin Neil."

"Dougal MacDonald?"

Jamie nodded, not surprised that she'd guessed the betrayer.

"But surely Alex knows of the threat from him and will be watching him carefully?"

"Yes, but Dougal knows he's been compromised. He's no longer pretending to take orders from the MacLeods. And he will have help. The next shipment will not just be supplies, as Alex thinks, but men. Fighting men. When Alex and his men are lured out to the shipment, Dougal and his men will close in from behind."

Meg blanched. Alex would be walking into a trap.

"Don't worry," Jamie said. "The next shipment is not until next week. There is plenty of time to get a message to him."

Meg shook her head, feeling the panic well inside her. "No. The report with the next shipment arrived last night. The shipment is supposed to arrive two nights hence."

"Damn!" Jamie swore angrily. "They must have decided to move it up."

Meg's mind was racing, her fear for Alex making it difficult for her to form a coherent thought. All she could think about was the trap he was walking into. She'd seen him fight, knew how skilled he was, but she also knew he'd die before he surrendered to Dougal. "I have to warn him."

"You can't. The king has issued a proclamation forbidding all Highlanders from traveling to Lewis. Besides, it's far too dangerous, your father will never let you go."

Jamie was right. But what choice did she have? She could tell her father, and he would send one of his men. But could she trust something so important to someone else? Meg knew the real reason. She desperately wanted—no, *needed*—to see him. To discover for herself whether there was a chance for them.

"I've made the short trip to Lewis many times. I'll be back before my father even knows I'm gone."

"I can't let you do that."

Meg gave him a hard, assessing stare. At that moment, he looked every bit as stubborn as Alex. "It's not your decision to make."

"Did you ever think that Alex might not want you there, might not appreciate your help?"

"What do you suggest? That I just leave him there to die? I'll warn him of the plot and return to Dunakin immediately. You're acting as if I'll be the only woman on the Isle."

"You're heading into a damn battle, Meg."

She took another look at his inflexible expression. "Please, Jamie, I need to do this. I have to see him. If it will make you feel better, I'll tell my mother where I'm going. She'll understand."

Jamie didn't look so sure. "Very well, if your mother agrees, I won't say anything to your father."

"Oh, Jamie, thank—"

"Don't thank me," he interrupted. "I'm going with you."

"That's not necessary—"

"Yes, it is. I can protect you. I should have guessed you would insist on going yourself. I'd go alone, but Alex wouldn't believe me."

Meg tilted her head to one side to study him. His body tense, his mouth clamped in a hard line. Consumed by her fear for Alex, she'd only just realized that by asking him what the king's men had planned, she'd put him in an untenable position. Jamie was obviously in the confidence of the king's men. And since he was loyal to his cousin, she could assume that at least nominally, the ever wily Argyll was involved with the Fife Adventurers' efforts to colonize Lewis. But Jamie was also a Highlander. And as such, the idea of Lowlanders stealing Highland land must be repugnant to him.

"Whose side are you on, Jamie Campbell?"

She didn't expect him to answer, but he did.

"Both."

Chapter 20

Near Stornoway, Isle of Lewis

Alex wiped the dirt from his eyes with the back of his hand and succeeded only in smearing it from one corner of his eye to the other. *God's blood, what I'd do right now for a bath and a fresh* leine. Three weeks of living in virtual squalor, with an occasional dunk in the salty sea loch to rinse off the caked-on layers of filth, had begun to chafe.

He was ready for this battle to end. And if all went as planned, it would—soon.

From his post along the rocky banks of Arnish point, the small horn of land that served as a perfect lookout into Stornoway harbor, Alex kept his vigilant watch. Weariness tugged at his eyelids, but his steady gaze swept back and forth across the water. Even with the full moon, it was dark as molasses out here, and since the mist had descended a few hours ago, the night was nearly impenetrable. The conditions, however, only contributed to the general sense of unease. His senses were flared on high alert, the threat of danger unnaturally ripe on an eerie night like this.

Normally, the anticipation of coming danger would invigorate him. But no longer did he draw overriding satisfaction from the thought of battle. No longer was it enough.

Fighting with his kin on Lewis should be the culmination of his ambitions. Leading. Making decisions in the heat of battle. Testing himself. Undeniably, the hard work and training of the last few years had paid off. With much smaller numbers than their foe, the MacLeods' precision attacks had seriously crippled the Fife Adventurers' position on Lewis. Soon, it would all be over and he would have the decisive victory that he'd sought for years. His kin would have their land, and Highlanders would have their justice against the machinations of a greedy and bloodthirsty king.

Alex should be ecstatic. Yet, inexplicably, success rang hollow.

Instead, all he could think about was Meg and how horribly he'd hurt her. He dreamed of her at night. He pictured her face at the most inopportune times during the day. He couldn't forget her gut-wrenching expression that morning, the heartbreak, the utter anguish. And during the long, lonely nights, he remembered all too well the erotic sensation of her body pressed against his. Even the mere thought caused his body to stir. He'd been too long without a woman, but from the moment he'd met her, she was the only woman who could sate his maddening lust.

For three long years, he'd lived and breathed nothing but battle. Now, however, something had changed. *He'd* changed. The all-encompassing drive for vengeance that had shadowed him unrelentingly since Binquihillin had quieted. No longer did the force of his single-minded determination snuff out everything else around him. For he knew what this battle had cost him.

He smiled sadly. Meg Mackinnon was proving to be as much of a distraction in her absence as she had been at court. Perhaps more so. The burning emptiness in his chest was a constant reminder of all that he'd lost.

Out of the darkness, the sound of footsteps drew his attention from his melancholy. The soft hoot of a short-eared owl identified the intruder as a friend.

"See anything?"

Alex turned to find Neil MacLeod, his cousin and current MacLeod claimant to Lewis, at his side. He shook his head. "No, but with the supply ship scheduled to arrive in a couple of days, I'm making damn certain there aren't any surprises. Dougal MacDonald is missing."

"Since when?"

"A few days ago. He didn't return from your last errand."

"Fool's errand."

Alex smiled, thinking of the various "missions" they'd sent Dougal on the past few weeks, all fraught with misinformation. "Yes, it was only a matter of time before he realized that we were on to him. But I don't want anything interfering with our plans to intercept that ship."

"And with it our best chance to take the castle."

"Aye," Alex answered. So far, it had been a delicate game of cat and mouse. They might not have had the fighting force to prevent the Lowland scourge from landing and taking the castle, but they'd had men enough to sink most of the Fife Adventurers' cargo. And with the help of Rory's spies, they'd prevented more food and supplies from getting through. With the MacLeods' constant raids, the Adventurers' stores must be dangerously low. "They need this shipment and will send out enough men to make sure they get it. We will take advantage of their desperation."

"You have a plan?"

Alex picked up a stick to scratch out a map in the rocky mud at his feet to illustrate his points. "I'll intercept the ship and divest it of its crew and cargo. A few of my men will row it through the harbor, and I'll circle around with the rest of my men to attack those waiting on shore from behind. At the same time, while the defenders are distracted, you will mount your attack on the castle."

Neil nodded, stroking the long hairs on his chin into a fine point. "It should work. You won't have many men."

"I won't need many. My men are well trained. I'll take a handful of MacLeods and MacGregors over an army of Lowlanders any day."

Neil laughed. "You're probably right." He looked back down at Alex's sketch, barely visible in the moonlight. "And with the castle considerably weakened by its defenders, it will be our best chance yet to take it."

"The 'colonists' are already demoralized. One more defeat should send the Fife Adventurers scurrying back to the Lowlands—for a second time."

Alex stood up, wiping out the plan with his foot. The two men stood in companionable silence for a few minutes, watching and waiting for the slightest disturbance in the rhythmic sounds of the night.

A sudden movement caught Alex's eye, the vague shadow of a boat slipping stealthily across the waves.

"Who the hell is that?" Neil asked.

"I don't know," Alex said, peering intently into the darkness. His hand reached over his back to grasp his

claymore. He was just about to give the signal for an attack when he heard the distinctive hoot of the owl. His
grip on his sword relaxed. A friend. As the *birlinn* drew
nearer, Alex recognized one of the Mackinnon's men.

He blinked and then rubbed his eyes again. He must
be more tired than he thought, because he could swear
that he saw the distinctive form of a woman perched
near the helm of the boat.

The *birlinn* drew closer. His pulse climbed.

No. Not just any woman.

Meg.

"I hope you know what you're doing," Jamie grum-
bled as the *birlinn* slid toward a small inlet along the
eastern coast of Lewis banded by a small horn, just
south of Stornoway harbor.

In truth, over the last few hours, Meg had questioned
the wisdom of her plan herself. Their "simple" journey
had been much more difficult—and taken far longer—
than she'd expected. The winds were light, forcing the
men to row harder than usual. But she refused to be dis-
suaded from her purpose.

She pulled her cloak tight across her chest to ward off
a sudden chill. The mist had descended without warning. "Of course I do," she said, lifting her chin stubbornly. "You worry needlessly. My mother agreed to let
me go, didn't she?"

"With the way you presented our wee errand, it's
hardly a surprise."

Meg's lips curved into a sly grin. "Can I help it if she's
a hopeless romantic? And I thought my analogy to the
heroic deeds of Roland was inspired."

Despite his somber mood since they'd departed Skye,

Jamie chuckled. "I never realized you had such prolific talent as a bard. You spun a tale so fanciful, I'm surprised you didn't cast blame on the fairies."

Meg shrugged. "No need to gild the lily. An allusion to a heroic journey interrupted by unrequited love and an ambush to rival that of Ganelon's for Roland did the trick."

Jamie shot her a look, wanting to challenge her use of the word *unrequited*. Instead, he shook his head and sighed deeply. "It's not Rosalind that I'm thinking about—it's Alex."

The thought of Alex's reaction to her arrival caused an annoying, and not insubstantial, shiver of apprehension to run down her spine. Despite her bravado, Meg couldn't guess how Alex was going to react to seeing her again, let alone to seeing her on Lewis. While she had recounted the dramatic rendition of her tale to Rosalind, Meg had found herself momentarily succumbing to the romance. She'd had more than one vision of reunited lovers falling passionately into each other's arms.

Realizing that such a turn of events was highly unlikely, if pleasantly diverting to contemplate, Meg suspected that Alex's initial reaction would be surprise. Then surprise would likely turn to annoyance that she'd traveled to Lewis in the midst of such conflict. But perhaps her worst fear was that he would be indifferent to her arrival.

The truth was that she didn't really *know* how he was going to react. And there was just enough uncertainty in her mind to make her nervous. What if she was wrong and he truly didn't care for her?

But she didn't want Jamie to realize that, so she squared her shoulders and said firmly, "It's too late for second-guessing. I'm sure Alex will be pleased to see me once he hears what I have to say."

"We'll find out soon enough." Jamie motioned to two men moving toward the boat. "Our greeting party awaits."

Meg squinted into the darkness, just able to make out the figures of two men. Two rather large men, but that alone was not significant in this part of Scotland.

"I suspect they are coming to greet my father's messenger." Though she might sound confident, the fierce hammering of her heart beneath the soft wool of her cloak betrayed her growing unease. The vague forms of the men on shore were beginning to take shape.

"You'll have to explain to me later how you convinced your father's men to agree to take us."

Meg shrugged. Her mother had told her who had taken messages to Lewis, the rest had been easy. "I didn't ask. You'd be surprised how far a wee bit of confidence and the uncompromising voice of authority will take you."

Jamie threw her an exasperated look. "I wouldn't be surprised at all."

But Jamie's sarcasm was temporarily lost on her. For standing not twenty feet in front of her, knee deep in water, was the man who'd consumed her thoughts for the last few weeks. The man who obviously—if the way her chest swelled with emotion was any indication—still held her heart in the palm of his hand. Meg bit her lip. The man who by the thunderous look on his face wasn't at all pleased to see her.

She gripped the wooden seat to steady herself and her suddenly jumpy nerves. She watched with growing trepidation as Alex forged effortlessly through the rough waters alongside the *birlinn*—heading directly for her.

The mist-shrouded moon bathed his features in an eerie light. Her breath caught. She felt a sharp pang. The face that had haunted her dreams was every bit as handsome as she remembered, yet infinitely more dangerous. Battle had taken its toll, and not just in the new scrapes and scratches that lined his face. He looked like a man who'd fought through hell and back, taking no prisoners along the way. His mouth was set in a hard, firm line, his stubbled jaw clenched and uncompromising.

Alex didn't say a word. He didn't need to. Rage radiated from every part of his body, evident in his harsh movements as he walked slowly, agonizingly so, toward her. She felt as if she were watching a fuse burn, just waiting for the explosion.

None of her romantic ruminations had prepared her for this particular reaction. No. This was not at all how she'd pictured their reunion. Something a wee bit less furious. Perhaps, she realized, indifference had its virtues. There was nothing indifferent about Alex's reaction to her arrival on Lewis. That fact should hearten her, but *this* reaction was altogether too extreme.

Meg's gaze flickered to Jamie for help, but his expression held little sympathy. This was her mess, she'd have to clean it up.

Finally, Alex was right next to her. She held her breath. The water lapped around his waist. His now wet *leine* clung to his rippled chest, molded to the rigid bands of his stomach, the muscles clenched not with passion but with an altogether different emotion. Rage. A whisper of fear made the tiny hairs at the back of her neck stand up, but Meg forced her eyes to his face.

Could one wither from the heat of a stare? Nonsense. Yet to her horror, Meg realized that she'd shrunk back in her seat. Enraged didn't come close to describing the fury blaring from his gaze. She'd never seen him like this.

Perhaps she should try to explain. "Alex, I—"

"Don't say a goddamn word. Not until we reach the shore. And then you better have plenty to say."

Meg flinched. He'd never spoken to her so harshly. Each word was uttered with steely precision. His voice was so fraught with anger that she almost didn't recognize it. She didn't understand. She'd taken a risk in coming here, yes, but nothing to warrant this extreme a reaction. "I—"

The look he gave her was blistering and cut off any inclination she might have of trying to make him see reason. His hands circled her waist and plucked her unceremoniously from her seat on the *birlinn*, as Meg found herself pulled roughly up against the hard, muscular chest that she remembered so well. After weeks of longing for such closeness, she yearned to sink against him and burrow deeper into his hold.

But there was nothing welcoming about the man who held her. He was drawn as tight as a bow—a bow that smelled warm and masculine and achingly familiar. Reminding her of all they'd shared, of how much she'd missed him, and of how deeply she loved him.

The wave of longing hit her hard. She hadn't realized how much she'd been holding out hope that he would be happy to see her. That he would take her into his arms and make her forget the anguish of the past three weeks.

But if anything, coming here seemed to have made

things worse. A pit of dread settled low in her belly. *Dear God, had she been wrong?* Did he truly not want her?

Alex had never been more furious in his life. She'd followed him. What insanity could have possibly driven Meg to the Isle of Lewis in the midst of a bloody war! He literally shook as he plowed through the waves toward the shore, cradling in his arms everything in the world that was precious to him. The familiar scent of roses drifted from her hair, a potent reminder of everything that he'd longed for these last few weeks—and everything that he could lose.

Meg. On Lewis. God, he felt ill. Didn't she understand the danger? If anything had happened to her . . . He could go mad just thinking about it. Alex had never felt more exposed, raw. Scared out of his bloody mind.

Every man had his breaking point, and Meg following him to Lewis, heedless of the risk, was his. He knew he was out of control, but he didn't give a damn. The moment her feet hit the rocky shore, he snapped. "What the hell are you doing here?"

Meg seemed to take umbrage at his tone and painstakingly adjusted her clothing, taking far more time than was necessary. Each second that passed was a testament to his herculean restraint. Alex clenched and reclenched his fists, waiting for her to meet his gaze. Finally, she peeked out apprehensively from under her long lashes.

The sweetly feminine movement nearly broke him. The moon bathed her features in soft light. His eyes gorged on her face, as if something exquisitely beautiful had somehow materialized from a dream. His heart ached. His body ached. God, how he loved her.

Seeing her on that boat had unleashed a torrent of emotions. When he'd first realized who it was, he'd felt a surge of joy. He'd wanted to crush her to him, to inhale her sweetness, to mold her body to his and feel her melt against him. For a moment. Until he remembered where he was. And then fear incited anger such as he'd never known.

"Obviously, I was looking for you," she said.

The inanity of her response only fueled the flames. He was holding on by a very thin thread, and she was talking to him as if she hadn't just shaved ten years off his life. "Have you completely lost your mind?" He took her by the shoulders, the frailty of her tiny form beneath his fingertips even more proof of her vulnerability. "Looking for me? You damn well better have a more pressing reason for coming here than that."

"Alex, you're shaking me."

He dropped his hands, stepped back, and stared at her, trying to rein in his emotions.

"If you'd stop yelling at me and just be reasonable for a moment, I'll tell you."

Alex didn't think he was capable of becoming angrier, but he was. Despite his wet clothing, his body blazed with heat. His voice lowered dangerously. "This is reasonable. But I'm getting very close to becoming unreasonable."

Meg blanched. "If you'll just let me explain . . ."

But her words were lost as Alex glanced over her shoulder at her traveling companion who'd just climbed up the shore. He didn't think he could be any more shocked than he had been at seeing Meg. But he was wrong. Jamie Campbell. He felt as if he'd been punched in the gut. She'd brought her damn fiancé with her.

"You brought Campbell? For God's sake, Meg, he's Argyll's cousin."

"Don't take your anger out on Jamie, he's only trying to help," she said.

Alex didn't miss the way she'd jumped to Jamie's defense. The dirk twisted in his chest. A dirk that Alex had plunged there himself. But it didn't make it any easier to stomach.

"I insisted on accompanying her," Jamie said stiffly.

"I'm sure you did." He looked back to Meg. "How could you do this? By bringing Campbell, you've risked all our lives." Her interference had risked his entire mission. The castle was nearly theirs, and with it the elusive victory he'd sought for years. Everything he'd fought so hard for was so close. Campbell could put everything in jeopardy.

"Jamie is not a threat, you should be thanking him."

He shot Jamie a look that could kill. *When hell freezes over.*

Meg took his arm. "I know you are angry, but I had to come. I had to warn you. There is a plot on your life. Dougal MacDonald has been given orders to kill you."

Given that Dougal had disappeared a few days ago, Alex couldn't say he was surprised. "I am aware of the threat posed by Dougal."

"I figured as much. But because of Jamie, we know how and when."

His eyes narrowed, unable to prevent the bit of jealousy, wondering how she'd persuaded Jamie to share this information—if indeed he could be trusted. "Go on," he said carefully.

"They are anticipating your attack on the supply ship, intending to surprise you with a new force of fighting men. While you are fighting off the ambush, Dougal will circle around and cut off your means of escape."

Rory's missive had made no mention of extra fighting men. If Meg's information was correct, Alex would have been seriously undermanned. He did not doubt he would have been able to escape, but it wouldn't have been without significant loss of blood.

Alex exchanged looks with Neil. Meg caught his glance, but he was in no mood for introductions. She wouldn't be staying long enough. He would have sent her back immediately, but there were only a few hours left until daylight. She would have to wait until tomorrow night. How the hell was he going to protect her and keep his hands off her for an entire day? It was going to seem like a bloody eternity.

"How do I know this is not a trap?" Alex asked, looking at Jamie.

"You don't," Jamie said bluntly. "But it's the truth."

Alex didn't know what to believe. "What do you get out of this, Campbell?"

He shrugged. "It makes Meg happy."

Jealousy tore like acid through his chest.

"Please, Alex—" Meg clutched his arm, her fingers singeing his skin. "Just take precautions."

He would. They would have to change their plans. Still, he couldn't believe she'd put herself in danger for him. Nor did it soften his anger.

Alex turned his anger back to Jamie. "I can't believe you allowed her to come here."

The look Jamie gave him returned Alex's anger in kind. "It wasn't my idea, but Meg was right, there wasn't time for anything else. You should be thanking her. Were it not for Meg, I might not have been persuaded to tell what I know."

Alex couldn't breathe. His chest constricted. *Persuaded.*

"Don't be angry with Jamie. If you are going to be angry with anyone, have it be me alone."

He was. How could she forget what had happened between them? It was what he'd wanted, but Alex didn't think it would be so fast. He couldn't stand here listening to the two of them together any longer. "Don't you worry about that, my wee crusader." He pulled her toward the copse of trees that hid their temporary encampment. "I've more than enough anger to go around."

He turned to Neil. "Don't let Campbell out of your sight."

"Wait!" Jamie shouted. "Where are you taking her?" He made a move to stop him, but Neil held him back.

"I'm just doing what the lady requested." Alex laughed, a harsh sound devoid of amusement. "I'm going to vent my considerable anger. On her, alone."

Chapter 21

Well, that didn't sound promising. This was not going the way she'd planned at all. Not one thanks. Not one tiny indication that he was glad to see her. Meg had thought he'd at least be appreciative of her information, if not pleased. Instead, he was stiff and unyielding and angrier than she'd ever seen him.

Angrier than he had a right to be. It didn't make sense.

When they'd trampled deep into the trees, well away from the men on the beach, Meg stopped short and shook off his hold on her arm. "I don't understand. Why are you so angry? I was only trying to help."

He looked at her as if she were daft and took a few deep breaths, obviously trying to control himself. "Because every minute that you are here, you are in grave danger."

The flatness in his voice belied any thought that he might be concerned for her. Meg's emotions felt frayed and precariously close the surface. "Why do you care?" she asked thickly. "I heard what you said to Lord Huntly. You don't need to pretend concern."

Nothing. No reaction. No denial. He couldn't even look at her. God, it hurt.

"This is no place for a woman. What I don't understand is why your father didn't just send a messenger? I can't believe he'd—"

Unconsciously, she bit her lip; it gave her away.

"Of course," he said, far more evenly than she would have thought possible given the present state of his temper. "Your father doesn't know you're here. How could you just up and leave like that, Meg?"

"I wouldn't trust something this important to a messenger. And I told my mother," she said defensively. "She knows I'm here."

"But it's your father who is going to strangle you when he finds out." He paused and said ominously, "If I don't do it for him."

"Don't be ridiculous," she said with a dismissive wave of her hand.

Her flippancy acted like a trigger. Alex pulled her roughly into his arms, crushing her against his chest. Meg felt the familiar rush of heat, the slow melting, the complete surrender of her body to his.

"Don't push me, Meg," he warned, his mouth achingly close to hers. "Not this time. You shouldn't have come here." His lips were white with anger, and the dark edge of his voice sent a shiver down her spine. But Meg didn't care. It might be reckless, but she liked making him lose control. At least it made her feel that he wasn't completely indifferent to her.

Her head fell back as she studied his face, trying to gauge the danger. If the black expression was any indication, it was considerable. Every inch of his incredibly hard body pressed against hers, ready to explode. Anger, frustration, and undeniable attraction sizzled between them.

All she wanted to do was lean up and kiss him, force

him to acknowledge what was between them. A sign. Anything to show that she was not alone in her feelings. But she knew that was probably the furthest thing from his mind. Meg had begun to accept the truth—she had made a mistake in coming here.

But his attempt to intimidate was not without effect. "Very well," she admitted. "Perhaps it was risky. But I was scared, I thought only to warn you. I needed to . . ."

"Needed to what, Meg?"

Had his mouth moved closer, or did she just wish it so?

"I needed to see you," she said softly, and dropped her gaze, unable to look at him—afraid he would see too much.

She was a fool. Why didn't she just admit it? She would have grasped at any straw to have the opportunity to find out whether the quick about-face that Alex displayed in Edinburgh was as it had seemed. But their reunion had not gone at all as planned.

Now, coming here seemed foolish. *She* seemed foolish for running after a man who didn't want her.

To make things worse, she was afraid she was going to cry. Meg was exhausted, hungry, and tired of being yelled at by the man she'd missed desperately the past few weeks. At any moment, she felt she might unravel.

Silence stretched between them.

Finally, Alex put his finger under her chin, forcing her to look at him. "But why would you need to see me? You're engaged to Jamie now."

Her brows shot together. "I'm not engaged to Jamie."

His expression darkened. "But Jamie assured me that he intended to ask for you."

"He did."

"And you refused him?" He was incredulous. For a moment, she thought she glimpsed relief in his eyes, but then he cursed. "God's wounds, what were you thinking?" he admonished her with a vehemence wholly unwarranted. "You can't refuse him."

Meg let out an indelicate snort of outrage. She lifted her chin to his and met his furious glare with one of her own. "I can, and I did," she said, not bothering to keep the bitterness from her voice. "Why do you care whom I marry? You did your *duty* and offered for me, even though we both know I came to you. Your conscience is clear."

His face was stony. "It's not about that."

"Then what is it about?" she said, unable to hide her frustration. "Why should you care whether I marry at all?" *You didn't want me. Only what I could bring you.*

"Have you considered what will happen if your father tries to arrange a match? You are no longer a virgin."

As if she needed to be told, when every minute in his presence reminded her of all they had shared. When all she wanted to do was move back into his arms and stay there forever. But it was clear that was not to be. Her back stiffened. "That is no longer your concern. Nor will my lack of virginity preclude my finding a husband. As you so astutely pointed out to Lord Huntly, my lands are enticement enough. But you can be sure I won't force a man to marry me who does not want me."

"Jamie wants you," he argued. "He's everything that you sought in a husband. He could make you happy."

Meg knew that was no longer true. She wanted to do right by her clan, and would. But Alex was the only man who would ever make her happy.

They stood so close, Meg could feel the tension flowing from his body. She yearned to circle her hands around his neck and melt against his heat. Had she imagined everything?

She had to know, no matter what the cost to her already ravaged pride. She rose on her toes and placed her hands on his shoulders, her breasts brushing against his chest. Her hips swayed into his. The massive evidence of his arousal made her shiver with anticipation. He wasn't indifferent. He wanted her in some ways that could not be denied. She rubbed a little closer, eliciting a groan that gave her courage. Her lips parted just below his, and slowly she flicked out her tongue to sweep across his bottom lip. Her heart pounded against his. She answered him in a whisper, just loudly enough for him to hear. "How could I be happy with Jamie? I don't love him. My heart belongs to another."

Alex swore, and with a sound that was half anguish, half fury, he surrendered to her sweet enticement. His mouth covered hers in a fierce embrace.

The first taste of him sent shivers of remembrance through her. This was what she'd yearned for all those weeks, this was what was real. She loved him, and nothing could feel more perfect. Bliss showered over her. Meg thought her heart might burst with happiness.

His mouth swept across hers, branding her with the heat of his kiss. Soft and sweet, his lips held hers in a possessive grip. His tongue slid into her mouth, taunting her with its suggestive rhythm.

Passion flared between them. All at once their movements took on a frantic urgency, and they tore at each other lest sanity take hold. Hot, fast, and absolutely perfect. One hand moved to cup her breast, the other held her bottom, as he ground her hips against his arousal in hot, circular movements. His erection throbbed against her stomach. She moaned, feeling a rush of dampness between her legs. Her body responded to the memory of his length thrusting inside her, of the violent release that had shattered her soul.

He leaned her back against a tree and trailed kisses down her neck. He pushed aside her cloak as his mouth sought the skin above her bodice. His chin scratched a gentle path, lower and lower. She arched her back, silently begging for more.

Her hands traced the blades of his shoulders, then roamed down his back, exploring the layered muscles. The weeks of fighting had only increased the strength of his warrior's body. He smelled of sun and sea, so wonderfully masculine. There was something raw and primitive about him that aroused similar feelings in her.

Desperately, she pressed herself closer, but it wasn't close enough. She wanted to feel his naked skin on hers, she wanted to feel the weight of that powerful body on top of her.

With a harsh sound, he broke the kiss.

He stared at her without saying anything, his expression unreadable. The hard rise and fall of his chest was the only indication that anything significant had just occurred.

"It won't work, Meg. Not this time. You won't change my mind."

"Why not?" she said, stung by his rejection. "I know you want me."

"I can hardly deny it. But passion isn't the issue."

Meg's heart broke. Again. Was that it, then? He wanted her, but not enough to marry her? Tears gathered behind her eyes. She had only one more question. "So was it true, then? What you said to Lord Huntly? Did you only agree to marry me for what I could bring you?"

She studied his face, looking for a flicker, a change, anything. With each second that passed, despair sank deeper into her chest.

He stood perfectly still. "What do you want from me, Meg?" His voice sounded so strange. Hoarse. Strained.

"The truth."

"You heard what I said. Why do you doubt it?"

"I thought that perhaps you meant to protect me." She hesitated. "I didn't want to believe what you said to Lord Huntly. Tell me that wasn't you in that room, Alex. Tell me I couldn't be so wrong."

His face remained impassive. She wanted to shake him. How could he just stand there and deny everything between them?

"Please, Alex." She clutched his arm. "I have to know."

"Does it really matter?" he asked, a hollow edge to his voice.

"How can you ask that? It means everything. I gave you everything." She took a deep breath. "I never told you that I was engaged once before."

She'd surprised him.

"I was sixteen and a fool. I came upon him making love to a serving girl in the stable, bragging about how he would be chief one day."

He swore. "Oh, Meg—"

She held up her hand and shook her head. "Don't. Don't feel sorry for me. It was a lesson I thought I'd learned. I trusted you with the future of my clan. I saw something different in you, Alex."

Alex turned away from her, staring out into the darkness. She'd just about given up hope when he spoke.

"I saw you outside the door."

"Then you knew I was listening." Her heart soared with the implications.

"I knew. I wanted to drive you to Jamie. I thought it was for the best."

"But why? I would have waited for you."

"Would you?" He laughed harshly. "You have a duty to your clan, you must marry. I doubt your father would find an outlawed son-in-law the proper choice. Just tell me one thing. Is there a child?"

"Would it make a difference?" she asked softly.

His jaw clenched. "Meg . . ."

She wanted to lie. "No. There is no child."

He let out his breath. She couldn't tell whether he was relieved or disappointed.

"Then nothing has changed. I am not the man for your clan, and you still do not belong here."

Meg didn't care. All that mattered was that she had not been wrong about him. But when she thought about the pain he'd put her through, she wanted to scream. Instead, she peppered him with furious accusations. "How could you have let me believe that? Why didn't you confide in me and give me the choice? Why didn't you tell me you were going to fight on Lewis?"

"The fewer people who knew, the better."

"That's what my father said," Meg replied bitterly.

"He was right. A connection with me would be dangerous for you. My enemies could use you to get to me. I also couldn't take the chance that you would allow something to slip—especially because of your friendship with the Campbells. And from some of our conversations, I wasn't sure you would agree with what I was doing."

"How could you say that?" Meg asked, horrified. "I'm a Highlander. Just because I recognize the difficult issues facing the Highlands doesn't mean I agree with the king's policies. I would never betray you or do anything to put my clan in danger."

"Does leading one of the king's men right into our camp not constitute putting us in danger? The fact that you brought Campbell with you proves I was right to be cautious."

Her cheeks burned with indignation. "Jamie risked much by helping you. You should be thanking him. I hardly think he'd turn around and betray you."

"Are you so sure of that?"

"He's the one who informed me of the plot on your life."

"And you believed him without question? Can you be sure that it was not a trick? His cousin Argyll is ever the opportunist. The Campbells would benefit greatly if Jamie could lead the king to us."

Meg felt horrible. How could he think that? Yet part of her knew he was right. The ramifications of her actions rained down on her. She'd never truly considered the possibility that Jamie would take advantage of their friendship.

She knew Alex was wrong in his suspicions but right in criticizing her for acting without thinking. "It's true that Jamie is loyal to his cousin, but he is also a Highlander. And he was once your friend. I am not like you, Alex. I do not see treachery in every shadow."

"It's my duty. Men's lives are at stake by my ability to see what lurks in the shadows."

Meg flushed. She knew he was thinking about his cousins. She hadn't meant it like that at all. Her stomach twisted. By coming here like this, she had thought to control the situation. She'd kept the information to herself, had not told her father of the situation. And now look what she had done. She'd possibly compromised his position on Lewis. How had it gone so wrong?

"I only wanted to help," she said softly.

Alex raked his fingers through his hair. *Damn.* He heard the shaking in her voice and knew she was perilously close to tears. He hadn't meant to be so harsh. The entire situation had him twisted in knots. He knew she'd thought only to warn him.

He did appreciate it, but he felt stripped of all his defenses when she was near. "You're right. I owe you my thanks. If what Jamie said is indeed true, we would have been greatly outmanned and quite probably trapped." He took her quivering chin in his fingers as she blinked away the tears that had been threatening to fall. "But that doesn't mean I think you should have taken such a great risk in coming here. Nor does it mean I trust Jamie. One day soon, he will have to choose a side."

She gazed up at him, her eyes wide and glassy. She looked tired and pale, but still achingly beautiful. And so damn alluring. The memory of their kiss surged through him, but he shook it off.

"You'll leave at sunset with your father's men. And not return. No matter what, Meg. Do you understand?"

She nodded. "And Jamie?"

"He'll leave with you, under guard until he is returned to your father. I'll write a missive to your father asking him to hold Jamie at Dunakin for a few days. It should all be over by then."

"And then what?" she asked, her eyes still focused on the ground.

He nearly smiled at the ability she had to cut to the quick. A myriad of questions wrapped up succinctly in one small, innocuous package.

"I don't know."

So much between them left unsaid. But he was glad she knew the truth. It made everything more complicated, but perhaps it was already. He couldn't prevent her heartbreak whether he'd driven her to another man or he never returned from Lewis. At least this way she would not doubt herself. Unknowingly, his poisoned arrow had struck too well. He wished he could take back everything he'd said to Lord Huntly. He'd meant to strike at her duty, not at an old wound.

He watched as she straightened her shoulders and lifted her chin, meeting his gaze. The soft glow of the moon cast deep shadows off the curve of her cheek. He knew what she was going to say and wanted to stop her. He opened his mouth, but it was too late.

"I love you, you know," she said softly.

There it was. Words that would be better left unsaid.

His heart clenched. He couldn't breathe. A thousand thoughts rushed through his head, thoughts of a future, thoughts of a family, dreams of happiness. There were no more lies left between them to camouflage the truth. With the secrets stripped away, the truth and all of its consequences lay bare before them. She loved him. But he wasn't ready to hear those words, not while he still had a job to do. Not until he'd laid the ghosts of his past to rest.

Overcome with emotion, he could manage only one word in response: "Don't." He pressed his fingers against her trembling mouth.

Her face crumpled.

He had to make her understand. "Not yet." He clasped her hands and pulled her up so that she stood before him. So lovely, so infinitely precious. Tenderly, he stroked the side of her face. "You deserve more than I can offer right now." His voice was laden with regret.

"How can you say that? I know you care for me. You cannot convince me that you don't."

He smiled crookedly, shaking his head at her unwavering determination. "I won't try. But right now, Meg, it's not enough. Your coming to Lewis only makes me realize how important it is that I finish what I've begun here."

"Even though you might die? If not at the hands of the Adventurers, then by Dougal?"

"Yes. If need be."

"But—"

"I promise I'll not go willingly. But"—he paused—"that is all I can promise right now."

"But why!" she cried, railing more at the injustice of the world than at him, he suspected. Her eyes sparkled with anger. "Why sacrifice your future for your past? You have nothing to prove to me or anyone else." She wanted to understand. "Tell me what happened to your cousins."

"There's not much to tell. You know most of it."

"But I want to hear it from you."

He felt the familiar resistance that occurred whenever this subject was mentioned. "Why?"

"I want to understand."

"Very well." He averted his gaze. "I was in charge. We had the advantage of surprise. I lost it."

"And your cousins?"

"They didn't have to die. I refused to surrender. My damned youthful pride cost them their lives." His voice grew tight. "I see that moment in my head over and over. If I could go back and decide differently . . ."

"Did you know what Dougal had planned?"

"No," he shot back. "Of course not."

"Then how can you blame yourself? You made the best decision you could under the circumstances. I know I was wrong to come here. Jamie warned me that you would not appreciate my interference. But it's not because I don't believe in you, Alex. There was no one else I could trust with such an important message."

"You *were* wrong to come, Meg. I know you only thought to help, but it's too dangerous for you here. It's too dangerous for me with you here."

He couldn't concentrate on anything with her so close. He was filled with such longing, to take her in his arms and cherish her love, cherish her body. Not focusing on the task at hand could be a deadly mistake. Her very presence on Lewis crippled him, putting him at grave risk.

The starlight seemed to catch the soft highlights in her hair. Unconsciously, he slid his hand over the smooth waves, weaving through their depths. Her very softness unleashed his desire. His body burned. He wanted to bury his face in her hair, rip off her clothes, and taste every inch of that soft skin. He wanted to make her tremble and come apart in his arms. If she didn't leave soon, he might forget the danger and give in to temptation. His voice turned hoarse with longing. "I can't think when you are near."

"Then don't," she whispered in the soft, seductive voice of an enchantress.

Her body sought his, her softness melting into his heat, teasing him with pleasure so acute that he began to shake. Despite the cool evening, sweat gathered on his brow. Blood coursed through his veins, and his erection throbbed unmercifully. Salvation waited only a hairbreadth away.

He stepped back, snapping the invisible pull. "I must. People are depending on me, Meg. Would you truly have me leave? Walk away from my kin when they are depending on me? What kind of leader would I make for your clan?"

She looked at him blankly, stubbornly refusing to acknowledge the truth.

He sank the knife of truth deeper. "Could you walk away from your clan, from your responsibilities? Would you have me do what you would not?" She looked as though she wanted to argue; the stubborn lass did not easily concede defeat. "This is what I do, Meg. I fight. What the king is doing on Lewis is wrong, and I cannot stand by and watch my kin be murdered without doing something." The call was just as much a part of him as Meg. He could not deny either. "I must do my duty to my clan, just as you must do yours," he said.

Her face collapsed when she understood his meaning. "But I can't marry Jamie." Tears glistened in her eyes.

And Alex was relieved that she would not. He still couldn't believe she'd refused Campbell. Shocked, but enormously pleased.

"Of course you can't," he said gently. "Not right

now." His fingers traced the contours of her mouth. "But you will marry if you must."

If I die. The words were left unspoken, but he knew she understood.

"Get some rest, there aren't many hours left before dawn." He whistled, and immediately a few of his men materialized out of the shadows. He urged her to go, watching as she faded into the darkness. Darkness that matched the deep abyss of regret in his chest.

Chapter 22

Bittersweet remembrance. Was that what awaited her for the rest of her life? Would Alex die and leave her with fleeting memories of a love that had barely been given the chance to spread its wings and soar?

Frustration tinged with resentment mounted inside her. The worst part was that she knew he was right. Alex couldn't leave Lewis, just as she couldn't leave her clan without a leader to help her brother for the future.

There was no other choice: Alex had to help his kin defend against the incursion of the Fife Adventurers. Nobility. Strength. Pride. None of those attributes would keep her warm at night. But Meg also realized that she would not love the man who was without them.

Not that it would make leaving him any easier.

Not when she knew now that he loved her. He might not have said as much, but she knew deep in her heart that he did. He wouldn't say so, couldn't say so. Not until he was free. Not when he might not survive. She understood that now, understood why he'd tried to push her away. But understanding did not bring her peace or lessen the hollow sense of unfulfilled longing gnawing at her soul.

She'd tossed on her makeshift pallet for an hour before deciding that there was only one way to calm her restlessness. She didn't have much time; it was almost dawn. And tomorrow she knew there would be little opportunity for further intimacy. He had a job to do, and she would not interfere. She'd leave tomorrow as he wished, but the night belonged to her.

Meg crept silently through the encampment of sleeping clansmen, careful not to disturb those who'd stayed behind to ensure their safe departure. Once away from the warmth of the fire, she shivered in the cool night air, wrapping the extra plaid she wore over her traveling clothes tighter across her shoulders. Though she tried not to think about how scary it was out here, in the dark, alone, the hairs on her arms and neck stood at attention. Her heart pounded. She followed the narrow path through the thicket of trees, where she'd watched Alex disappear earlier. Despite her unease, Meg realized she was lucky he'd offered to take the first watch—the first watch that had just ended. But he hadn't returned. That he'd probably done so to be away from her was immaterial.

What she had planned wouldn't work very well in a crowded camp.

The farther she retreated from the fire, the more she was forced to use her hands to help guide her through the dark maze of the narrow path. A branch scratched the side of her cheek. She gasped, more with surprise than with pain.

A hand over her mouth quickly smothered the involuntary sound.

Terror struck. Meg thrashed around, trying to break free, but her captor held her lodged tight against his body.

"Shhh."

She stilled, recognizing the deep timbre of that voice.

"Quiet. Unless you want a party of Lowlanders down on top of us." The warmth of his whisper so close to her ear sent a chill of awareness down her spine.

Meg nodded that she understood, and he relaxed his hold but did not release her. Now that her pulse had slowed considerably, she was able to recognize the familiar lines of the hard body behind her and the subtle erotic scent of sea and sun that clung to him like a warm blanket. Savoring his closeness—and not one to waste an opportunity—Meg sank deeper into the curve of his body, snuggling her bottom against his groin.

It was his turn to stifle a groan, but he did not loosen his hold. Danger must be near.

Meg listened, though not sure precisely what she was listening for.

Minutes later, it became clear when she heard the galloping stampede of a large party pass not fifty feet from where they stood.

After a tense few minutes, the intruders were safely away. Alex spun her around.

"What are you doing out here? Why aren't you abed?"

"I couldn't sleep." Meg ignored his furious expression. "Were they looking for us?"

He stared at her, eyes narrowed. Obviously, he was deciding whether to press his anger. Meg stood firm, meeting his gaze. There'd been enough anger between them. Finally, he answered her. "Yes, every few days they send out a scouting party."

"I didn't realize they would be so close."

He shrugged, unconcerned. "It's more of a nuisance, really. It forces us to move around, but they never seek to engage us. Not out here. Not on our terrain. Nonetheless, no matter how unlikely, we have to be prepared in the event they do decide to mount an attack."

Meg understood. "They keep you under surveillance, but prefer to fight with the castle behind them."

Alex nodded. "What strength they have is in their defensive position, and they'll not risk losing their best weapon by attacking our forces out here. Not without help. But had you alerted them to our presence, it would not have stopped them from trying to kill the both of us. You did not answer my question—why are you here?"

Meg blushed, grateful that he could not see her response in the darkness. She took a deep breath, reminding herself that this might be her only chance, and stepped closer. She stood just under his chin, forcing her head back to meet his gaze. "I wanted to say good-bye. Privately. There might not be an opportunity tomorrow."

He sighed and then said gently, "Meg, we've said all there is to be said."

"Have we?" she asked, boldly placing her hands on his chest. "I don't think so." He stiffened but did not remove her hands. Encouraged, she wove a lacy, seductive trail down his chest. Deliberately, she slowed when she reached the flat planes of his stomach. Brushing her fingers lightly across the layered muscles, she savored the way his body clenched under her fingertips. She teased him, stroking lower and lower, but not quite low enough.

He hissed between clenched teeth.

Meg smiled, her courage bolstered.

Her mouth touched his collarbone. She pressed delicate kisses along the lines of his neck. "I think we have more to say to each other, Alex. Much more." To emphasize her point, her hand dipped, grazing over the thick head of his erection bulging at the waistband of his trews. She wanted to circle her fingers around his length, to feel the thickness in her hands, to rub her thumb across the round head . . . but not yet.

"Damn you," he growled. His arms remained glued to his side, the powerful muscles in his arms flexed as he tried to control the lust she'd roused.

Her mouth moved to further explore his neck. Her tongue slid along the pulsing vein. *He was fighting for control all right*. She loved the taste of him, the same clean, slightly salty taste of the Skye sea breeze.

"I'm not a bloody saint, Meg."

Meg chuckled, pointedly gazing down to admire the size of his erection. "Thank goodness for that, it would be a waste." She licked her top lip hungrily. "An enormous waste."

Alex uttered a pained sound, obviously in no condition to admire her irreverent humor. "You don't want this," he said tightly.

If he only knew how wrong he was. Just knowing how powerfully aroused he'd become by her touch alone drove her wild. Desire pooled low in her belly, and her senses tingled with sudden expectation.

Meg eased the extra plaid from her shoulders, allowing it to drop to the ground. Tonight, his body would provide all the heat she needed. She stretched up against him and clasped her hands behind his neck, pressing the hard tips of her breasts to his chest. She played with the golden hair at the nape of his neck, still slightly damp from bathing. "I've never wanted anything as much as I do this," she said honestly.

He wrapped his arms around her, wavering. "It won't change anything," he protested, albeit weakly.

She pressed her fingers against his lips. "No promises, remember? I just need to feel you inside me. One more time."

The heartfelt simple plea was enough. The tension visibly drained out of him. She'd won, though in truth he'd not waged much of a war. There was a certain inevitability to this moment that neither of them could deny.

He kissed her, and Meg thought her heart would explode with happiness. The uncertainty that had drowned her the past few weeks dissolved into a distant memory. The beauty of this moment would be in her heart forever. She felt more alive, freer, than ever before. He kissed her with all of the emotion that he could not express. He showed her his love in the tenderness of his embrace, in the fierceness of his desire. He showed her every time their eyes met.

The kiss intensified. The exquisite taste of him made her shiver. His mouth was hot and demanding, his passion already inflamed by her seductive touch. She felt boneless, liquid, her body heavy with desire. She'd not thought it possible, but their passion had grown even more intense and overwhelming. There was a tender poignancy to this moment; this was a mating not just of their bodies, but of their hearts.

He made love to her with his lips and tongue. The rush of pleasure hit her hard and fast. With each rhythmic stroke of his tongue, her heart raced with anticipation. He wooed her and teased her with his tongue, driving her frantic with need. A conflagration of emotion so pure and powerful, it took her breath away.

The warmth between her legs spread through her body like wildfire. His erection pressed possessively against her abdomen as his tongue slid in and out of her mouth, driving her mad with desire. She wanted him inside her. Filling her. Thrusting deep and hard until her body shuddered around him. Her body dampened, priming itself for his powerful entry as her hips rocked against him, seeking the exquisite pressure only he could provide.

She ached to feel his hands on her, in her, stroking, but he still had not touched her. She knew that he was holding himself back, trying to control the swell of passion that threatened to storm and overtake them both.

A soft moan escaped her parted lips when his hand finally cupped her breast. Over the fabric of her gown, his thumb rubbed against her swollen nipple. It wasn't enough. She wanted to feel the rough calluses of his hands branding her skin. She pressed against his hand. No more pretense left between them. She wanted the pleasure that only he could bring her. She wanted everything.

Alex lifted his mouth from her soft lips and smiled— a sly, predatory grin that should have warned her. "Not so fast, my sweet. I'm going to use every last minute of darkness."

They both knew that it might have to last a lifetime.

Her breath came quick as he knelt and spread her plaid over a small patch of moss. "I wish I had a better bed to offer you."

"It's beautiful," Meg said.

And it was. Nature's own bower beneath the trees. Though making love with Alex anywhere would feel like paradise.

When he finally seemed satisfied that he'd made the makeshift bed as comfortable as possible, he stood up and began to work the laces of her gown. Piece by piece, her clothing was removed until she stood naked before him. She shivered as the cool night air hit her flaming skin. Resisting the urge to cover herself, suddenly shy, she peeked up to gauge his reaction.

He looked at her ravenously, like a starved man being offered a feast. His eyes glowed with admiration. "You are beautiful."

And strangely, for the first time, Meg truly believed it was so. Who would not feel beautiful with this fierce warrior looking at her with such aching need?

When he reached out to touch her, his finger grazing the curve of her breast, Meg thought she might fall to the ground. Her legs had turned to jelly. It wasn't enough. Couldn't he see that he was torturing her? Her body shuddered with need.

"Your breasts are magnificent." He reached under to cup her, weighing their fullness in his hands. Her ivory flesh flowed over his tanned fingers. "So large and round, yet your nipples are so small and pink. I'll never forget how sweet you taste."

She closed her eyes, allowing the heat to wallow through her as his words dragged her down into the dark blanket of bliss. Bliss that wrapped around her, drowning out everything but the pleasure.

With a wicked grin, Alex leaned down and flicked his tongue across her hard tip. "Ummm. I'm not sure that's enough." He buried his face between her breasts, allowing his jaw to scrape against her sensitive skin. He blew across each nipple, his warm breath fueling the fire.

His tongue swirled over her nipple, and she trembled

with anticipation. She writhed in sweet agony, arching her back against his teasing mouth.

"Alex!" she moaned.

"Tell me what you want."

She wanted the agony to end. For a woman rarely at a loss for words, she could only manage to choke out an insufficient, "You."

It was enough.

At last his mouth enveloped her breast. Her fingers dug in his back as he sucked, pulling her harder and harder toward release.

Alex mustered restraint that he did not know he had. God, she was perfect. Melting against him, so soft and pliant. So honest in her passion. He couldn't believe the good fortune that had brought Meg to him. He was done fighting fate. Meg in his arms, surrounding him, was meant to be. Honor had a place, but it wasn't between them.

She was shaking with need. He knew he was torturing her, but he didn't care. When she'd touched him earlier, teased him, the blinding haze of incomparable desire descended over him again. His blood pumped through his body, and the pressure building in his groin was nearly unimaginable. He wanted to thrust himself deep inside her, diving into that warm heat, and succumb to the all-consuming need for her that threatened to steal his soul.

One thing held him back. He loved her, and he had to show her how much. Over and over. With every minute etched in his memory.

His tongue swirled around her nipple as he sucked. Reveling in the sweet honey taste of her skin. His mouth trailed down her stomach as his hands sculpted her curves, from the swell of her lush breasts to her tiny waist and narrow hips. He'd forgotten how small she was, how precious and delicate. His hands seemed so large and rough in comparison.

His mouth dropped lower. She sucked in her breath.

He knelt before her, his hands cradling her small round bottom. She was so smooth and soft, so sweetly hot. He slid his tongue along the satiny skin of her inner thigh, teasing. She trembled and made a tiny sound. Her delicate feminine scent flooded his senses, filling him with a fierce craving.

Perhaps she'd guessed what he was about to do.

"Alex, what—"

He cut off her question with a small flick of his tongue, tasting her, savoring the sweet essence of her pleasure. A more potent aphrodisiac he could not imagine. She was so soft and achingly wet for him. He was rock hard, his cock straining against his stomach.

She froze, undoubtedly shocked, and made a sound of protest.

"It's all right, Meg. Trust me. I want to taste every inch of you."

His tongue flicked her again, probing gently against her delicate skin. The shock of his intimate kiss soon waned. He teased her until she trembled. He pulled back, and she made another sound of protest, this one different. "Do you still want me to stop?" He kissed her softly again. "Tell me, Meg."

Her hips pressed toward his mouth. He breathed softly against her. "Tell me."

"God, no."

He entered her with his tongue and felt her shudder of absolute surrender. She made a sound so low and sweet, filled with such satisfaction, that his chest squeezed at the pleasure he was giving her. He wanted to hold on to this moment, to prolong the ecstasy, to make the night last forever.

Her body tensed, and he knew how close she was to shattering. His mouth covered her, sucking, devouring, taking her hard and deep. She cried out, arching her back and pressing her hips against his mouth.

God, she was sweet.

Her release came hard and fast. She muffled her scream with her hand as her body pulsed against him

But he wasn't done. Not when he'd been waiting so long to have her. He was unrelenting, needing to stake his claim to her in some primal way. Sobs of pleasure racked her body as he forced her to a second orgasm hard on the heels of her first.

She'd never looked more beautiful. Naked, with her chestnut curls tumbling down her bare shoulders and her ivory skin gloriously rosy with passion. Her red lips were parted and slightly swollen from his kisses. Her eyes were heavy from the exertion of her release, the soft green still fuzzy with desire. Eyes that stripped him to the core.

"I never dreamed . . ."

Alex quirked his brow, trying not to smile. "It pleased you?"

She shot him a sharp look. "From your expression, you know very well that it did. You look altogether too pleased with yourself." Her pretense of seriousness faded under a saucy grin. "But I suppose it is well deserved."

He brushed aside an errant curl that had tangled in her lashes, grinning. "Your pleasure is mine."

She returned his smile, but then a curious spark appeared in her eyes. Her gaze traveled over his face, down his body, and lingered appraisingly on his erection. Heat drenched him. Just the weight of her eyes on him made him hot and hard as a damn rock.

What was she thinking with that naughty little glint in her eye?

The smile slid from his face. He knew how quickly her mind worked. His pulse hitched and then broke out in a full race when a slow, sensual grin played across her lips.

"Now it's my turn," she said. "I wonder if I can make you beg?"

His whole body tensed, not daring to hope.

She lifted his *leine* over his head. The admiration that flooded her gaze would normally make him hot, but he was already on fire, consumed by the sensual promise of her words. Her hands splayed across his chest, running over the ridges of his muscles, on a fiery path to his stomach. Her fingers traced the taut bands, but she didn't tarry long. He noticed the slight shake to her hands as she unbuckled the leather belt that secured his plaid, but it was nothing to how he was shaking inside.

He helped her as she pulled off his trews and boots, leaving him every bit as naked as she, and then stilled, waiting for her reaction. Waiting as her gaze settled lower. . . .

Her eyes widened. "My." She looked at him hesitantly and then bit her lip. "This might be more difficult than I realized. You're a large man, aren't you?" She blushed. "I mean, all over."

He managed to nod. *Yes, damn it. And getting excruciatingly larger by the minute.*

She reached out to touch him, circling him with her

hand, her soft, delicate fingers pumping him slow and easy as he'd taught her.

She was killing him. Sweat gathered on his brow as he tried to think of anything but spilling his seed in her hand. Only the promise of an even darker torture held him at bay.

He groaned and his stomach clenched, but he did not make a move to stop her innocent exploration.

With one finger, she traced a delicate path up the long length of his staff from root to tip, rolling her thumb over the head and sliding a small bead of liquid through her fingers, as sensual a movement as the most accomplished jade—but infinitely more enticing by its innocence.

Holding his gaze, she lowered herself until she was kneeling before him. It was the single most erotic moment of his life. Only inches separated her mouth from the heavy head of his cock. Just the thought of her tiny red lips stretched around him, taking him deep into the warm recesses of her mouth, filled him with nearly incomprehensible heat. Her hand reached out to cup him, and his bollocks tightened in her hand. He was on fire, every inch of him a sensitive trigger to the touch.

"Meg—" His voice cracked with what was supposed to sound like a warning. If she wanted to make him beg, she was succeeding. She was torturing him. Paying him back every bit for the teasing he'd given her. This woman could bring him to his knees.

She positioned her mouth inches away from him and parted her soft, moist lips. Her hands moved behind to hold his buttocks. "I wonder . . ."

His eyes sparked black with passion, and his jaw clenched tight. The vein at his neck twitched. *Damn her.*

She'd turned him into a quivering mess. She was well aware of how badly he wanted her to take him in her delectable little mouth.

"I wonder," she continued, "if you taste as good as you look."

"Oh God, Meg . . . ," he said with a guttural moan.

He beaded again, and her wicked tongue flicked out to taste him. "Mmm," she murmured.

His legs nearly buckled.

She laughed wickedly and traced a path with her tongue that her finger had forged up the long length of him.

He swore and groaned, running his hands through the soft silk of her hair, silently begging. Finally, she gave it to him. Her tongue swirled around the top of him, and slowly she closed her mouth over him.

Alex lost the power to think. He'd died and gone to heaven.

Her mouth drew him in, deeper and deeper. Milking him long and hard, stroking him with her mouth and tongue. He wanted to come so badly, he fought the overwhelming urge to thrust and explode deep in her mouth.

With a small groan, he tore her mouth from him. He'd had enough of this exquisite torture. Breathing hard, he framed her face with his hands and lowered himself to his knees to face her. She looked like a debauched angel. His chest tightened with emotion, and a wave of incomparable tenderness swept over him. He'd never felt so close to anyone in his life.

Slowly, he lowered her onto the waiting plaid. After settling his hips between her lean legs, he eased her open with his fingers, stroking her body from its own sated slumber of exhaustion until her hips rocked against him again.

Tiny whimpers sounded from between her parted lips. Her head tossed back and forth, a look of wild abandon transforming her features. She was close. And so was he. She began to moan, loudly this time, and he covered her mound with his hand, putting even more pressure against the surging violence of her release. He cupped her as she writhed in pleasure against his hand. Right before she crested, he plunged deep inside her, filling her to the hilt in one smooth movement.

Tight, unbelievable heat surrounded him.

He closed his eyes and thrust, urging her sensitive, tingling flesh to crest again. Sweat born of forced control gathered on his chest and brow as he tried to be careful, she was so small.

"I won't break," she whispered, reading his mind. "Don't hold back. I want all of you, Alex."

Damn her, she didn't know what she was asking. But her luminous green eyes saw right through him, forcing him to reveal every dark, tortured part of him. The place no one had ever seen before. Something in him broke. He was out of control, raw, exposed. All that was left was his primal need for her. The all-consuming fire that raged inside him that only she could douse.

So he gave it to her, driving in hard and deep. Grinding and thrusting with all the savage emotion that she'd wrung out of him. He gave her everything. Everything but the promise of a future. And she met his dark strokes with a plunder of her own, holding his gaze, raking his soul of its secrets.

She knew just what she meant to him.

He felt the pressure building, knowing that he could

not hold on much longer. He looked deep into her eyes, silently seeking . . . acceptance. Something almost sacred passed between them. A reflection of a love so pure, it dissolved the last shadow between them.

A wave of unbelievable euphoria crashed over him as he came, the sheer force causing him to let out a deep roar. Her own cries met his own. Again and again his body clenched with release, shooting his seed deep inside her as they crashed together in a perfect storm.

Meg thought she must have died. She couldn't move if her life depended on it. Never had she felt so completely drained and yet so completely fulfilled at the same time.

Alex collapsed next to her. She managed to curl up next to him and rest her head on his chest, listening to the fierce pounding of his heart. He wrapped his arms around her and pulled her tight into the curve of his body.

Neither of them spoke. Words seemed wholly inadequate.

Never could she have believed that her body was capable of expending so much energy and experiencing so much ecstasy. Four times he'd driven her to paradise. She didn't think she could handle that again.

The horror of the thought stopped her heart. There might never be another time. He'd warned her, but she'd never expected . . . this. What had just happened between them was cataclysmic, but it hadn't changed the fact that she would leave on the morrow.

She closed her eyes and concentrated on the powerful beat of his heart. She wanted to savor this moment, make it last forever.

Tomorrow would come soon enough.

Chapter 23

They'd made love again, in the crisp early hours of dawn, as the first rays of light penetrated the darkness of night. Perhaps it was wrong, knowing the uncertainty of their future, but Alex could no longer fight what was between them or his own need for her.

He woke her with a kiss, rousing the slumber from her eyes with the gentle persuasion of his mouth and tongue. The fierce, hungry passion of the night before transformed into the languid, sensual exploration of lovers. Naked, limbs entwined, he caressed her velvety soft skin until she heated under his touch and then stroked her with his fingers until she arched against his hand, her lovely full breasts straining to the sky.

He circled his tongue around her nipple, pulling her with his teeth and lips until she writhed beneath him. She was so damn sweet, her response eager and honest with an intensity that matched his own.

He entered her slowly, watching her face, wanting to remember the pink flush of pleasure that spread across her cheeks as she took him into her body. Gripping him tight, until he dissolved in heat and sensation.

He stilled for a moment, savoring the sensation of being buried deep inside her, of filling her, of being joined together in God's heavenly embrace. He held her gaze and pushed deeper, shuddering with a wave of pure tenderness. The look in her eyes stripped him to the core. He couldn't move, wanting to preserve the moment, wanting never to forget how it felt to experience perfection.

He drew out slowly, lengthening his stroke, building the rhythm gently and then with increased urgency. When her eyes closed and she started to come, he let himself go, surging hard against her until he sank into her full hilt and came with a violence that shocked him. It was the most profound climax of his life. Drawn slowly from the deepest part of him, his entire being consumed by the force of his love for this woman.

It was the most beautiful, bittersweet experience of Alex's life. He cradled her in his arms with all the tenderness of a man who'd been given his heart's desire, only to realize that he could lose it in the amount of time it took an arrow to fly or a sword to fall. He wished it could have lasted forever, but not even the force of his considerable will could hold back the sun from its determined rise.

Reluctantly, he let her go, sending her back to her pallet before the others woke. Though he doubted they were fooling anyone. Jamie, he was fairly sure, knew exactly where Meg had spent the night. In his old friend's gaze, Alex read censure, but also reluctant acceptance.

The hours passed quickly. With the battle looming, he and Neil had spent most of the day planning a new strategy of attack. He kept Meg within his view at all times. When occasionally their eyes would meet, he knew she was remembering, just as he was, but there was little time for conversation. What had needed to be said had been said last night. Their future, if any, rested in God's hands now.

He loved her more deeply than he'd ever thought possible. But something kept him from telling her. Perhaps he thought it would be easier for her to move on if he did not return. Or perhaps it was because when he told her he loved her, he wanted to be free to do so.

When it was time to load the *birlinn,* he ordered Robbie and two of his most trusted warriors to accompany the party of Mackinnons. He could not spare them, but neither would he take any chances with Meg's safety. Meg objected, but he would not be gainsaid.

Finally, it was time.

She stood to the side on the rocky shore, alone, watching the men load the boats. Alex approached her, steeling himself for what he'd been dreading since the moment she'd arrived. Saying good-bye.

When he looked at her face, the ache in his chest tightened. She was trying to be brave, but her eyes gave her away. Wide and luminous, they reflected the depths of her fear in the glistening shimmer of unshed tears. He knew her strength, but she looked so heartbreakingly fragile, it took everything he had not to wrap her in his arms and soothe her fears. But he knew he could not.

God's breath, he had no intention of being killed or taken prisoner. Or of losing, for that matter. He'd fought too damn hard for this moment. Every warrior knew each battle could be his last. He never dwelled on it but accepted it as a price of the life he'd chosen. But never had Alex had so much to live for. And he was just as aware as she was that they might never see each other again. He shook off the morbid reminder. He would not let that happen.

He wanted a life with Meg. To protect her. To ease her burden. To help her clan. His throat tightened. To hold their first child in his arms. He wanted that more than he'd ever wanted anything in his life. But he had to finish what he'd started. While there was a breath left in his body, he would fight against the king's injustice. And deep down, he knew he could not have the life he wanted to have with Meg until he'd put the past behind him.

He stood before her, taking her hands in his. They were shaking slightly and cold, despite the warmth of the morning. "It's time, lass."

The color slid from her face. The flash of panic in her eyes hit him hard.

"Let me stay with you," she pleaded.

He stilled. She was killing him. Didn't she know how difficult this was for him? He didn't want her to leave, either. He wanted never to let her go. But he'd weighed the risks, and it was far more dangerous for her to stay. He shook his head. "No."

"Neil's wife is here, as are many of the other wives," she protested.

"They have no choice; this is their home. Their battle. It's not yours."

"I don't care," she said fiercely. "I don't want to leave you."

And I don't want you to leave. It would tear out his heart a second time to send her away. "But you will," he said in a voice that did not bode argument.

She held his gaze, pleading with her eyes, but Alex would not be persuaded. Not in this. He wanted her safely away. Only then could he focus on the task at hand.

"Come," he said, leading her toward the boat. "It is time." He was relieved when she followed him without further objection.

His feet felt like lead; each step claimed a little of his heart. He helped her into the boat and looked at Jamie. "I appreciate what you did for us," he said, realizing he'd been remiss. "Thank you. I know what it might have cost you."

Jamie nodded.

"Take care of her," Alex said.

"I will," Jamie answered. "Until your return."

Alex turned back to Meg. His eyes scanned her face, trying to take in every last detail. He wanted to memorize everything about her, from the spattering of freckles on the bridge of her nose to the golden light that sparkled in her green eyes. She was so tiny and yet so enormously precious.

Night was falling, and the wind had just begun to pick up, carrying with it a stray lock of her hair. Unthinkingly, he tucked it behind her ear, allowing his thumb to stroke the soft curve of her cheek. She pressed her face into his hand.

"I'll see you . . ." Her voice fell off, and she started to cry. Softly. Bravely. In a way that broke his heart.

The tightness in his chest was almost unbearable. Each tear that fell ate a bigger hole in his heart. Heedless of those around, he kissed her gently, but with a sharp poignancy that could not be denied. His mouth lingered for a moment, savoring the taste of her, wanting to remember it always.

Finally, he lifted his head. Tilting her chin, he looked deep into her eyes. "You will, my love. Soon." He could not doubt it.

The boat pushed away. Her hair blew wildly around her face in the wind. Tears fell unchecked down her pale cheeks.

He wanted to turn away but forced himself to stand and watch, though the pain intensified with each minute that she slipped farther away. *To safety,* he reminded himself.

If only they'd met at a different time. Before his life had been inextricably entwined with the fight to free Lewis. Before the series of events that had been set in motion that day long ago on the corrie in the shadows of the mighty Cuillin mountain range, when his cousins had lost their lives.

His jaw locked as he fought the swell of emotion as Meg vanished from his view. *Soon, my love.*

It was time to put the past to rest.

Chapter 24

Fortunes were made on luck and perseverance, and Dougal MacDonald had both.

The sun had all but disappeared beyond the western horizon. Night was falling fast, and with it came the gray veil of mist that would aid Dougal in his plan tonight, preventing those on shore from seeing what was happening at sea. He smiled. Again, luck.

There was just enough light left to make out the activities taking place on the rocky shore below him. From his vantage point hidden in the trees that lined the southern point of the inlet, he watched Margaret Mackinnon and her clansmen climb into the waiting *birlinn* and prepare to push back from shore.

Ironic, he thought. Their ship was going out, yet his had just come in.

By sending the Mackinnon chit away with the messenger, Alex MacLeod had unwittingly given Dougal the means to salvage a nearly disastrous situation.

The king's men had been increasingly impatient with his inability to provide them with any useful information. The MacLeods had kept him so well contained, he couldn't even direct the Fife Adventurers to the rebel encampment.

Dougal hadn't expected Alex and Neil MacLeod to

discover his perfidy so fast. The first time, their false information had successfully prevented him from arranging their capture, making him look like an idiot before the king's men. The second time, he'd been sent on a fool's errand while Alex intercepted a shipment of supplies. It was then that Dougal knew he'd been discovered.

He should have taken MacLeod out at court when he had the chance. But Dougal had been in a precarious position. He couldn't do so without betraying himself, limiting his usefulness on Lewis. Now that he knew the MacLeods were on to him, it was no longer a concern.

Alex had forced him to choose sides. And Dougal had done so. The rewards offered by the king were too hard to refuse.

Knowing he would not get any information from the MacLeods, Dougal had realized he'd have to find it on his own. So he'd focused his efforts on intercepting their messengers. Who would have guessed that the next messenger would also bring Meg Mackinnon?

Now he would have them both—Alex and the Mackinnon chit.

The bitch had refused him. Even three weeks later, he still couldn't believe it. And now with the knowledge of his perfidy surely spread throughout the Highlands, he doubted that she could ever be persuaded to accept his offer of marriage. Which was why he'd been doubly lucky today. Once he had her in his possession, her acceptance was immaterial.

She must fancy herself in love with the bastard. Her rejection of his offer had only made Dougal more determined to get rid of Alex. And Meg Mackinnon would be just the means he needed to bring Alex MacLeod to his knees.

Impatient, he turned and vaulted onto the powerful stallion waiting beside him. He enjoyed breaking spirited animals, just as he would enjoy breaking Alex MacLeod.

He'd done so before; unfortunately, he'd not finished the job.

Now it was only a matter of time. And Dougal could be a patient man, a *very* patient man. The reward would be well worth the wait. He'd serve his chief by helping the Fife Adventurers defeat the MacLeods, and he'd finally have the means to take care of an annoying loose end from his own past.

He galloped toward the *birlinn* of armed MacDonald clansmen who waited just on the other side of the small inlet, sniffing deeply of the morning air. There was nothing like the promise of a good hunt to stir a man's blood.

I will not fall apart, Meg vowed. Even though she felt as though her heart were being wrenched out of her body and torn to bits. The *birlinn* pulled farther away from shore, and the tall man standing immovable at the water's edge melded into the shadows of the falling night. Not willing to let him go, Meg kept her eyes locked on the place where he stood, wanting to hold on to him for as long as possible. Her chest squeezed with longing. She understood why he was sending her away, but it did not make their parting any easier.

She straightened her spine, refusing the urge to curl into a ball and give way to the desolation ripping her apart. She would be strong, a worthy mate to the courageous, honorable man who'd won her heart. Every bone in her body resisted leaving Alex, but she would do her duty, just as Alex must do his. She was proud of him, and she would not shame him by doubting him.

"He'll be fine, mistress."

Meg turned to Robbie, who sat protectively to her left, Jamie on her right. She'd tried to argue against the need for Robbie and the other warriors accompanying them, but Alex had been adamant. It made her feel all the worse for coming to Lewis. She was only too aware that she had left Alex even more undermanned. She wiped the tears from her eyes with the back of her hand and took a deep breath. "Indeed he will be, Robbie."

Meg believed in Alex, completely and without reservation. He was the fiercest, most skilled warrior she'd ever seen. If Alex and Neil MacLeod could block the supplies and reinforcements from reaching the castle and create a diversion, victory would be theirs. And Alex would come home to her. They would begin their life together. It was that knowledge that held her together.

She pulled her *arisaidh* more firmly around her shoulders. The mist had descended like quicksand, swallowing everything in its ethereal hold. The salty wind was cold and damp as it blew across her nose and cheeks. At least it would help speed their journey. Now that they'd parted, Meg was anxious to return home. The sooner she was home, the sooner Alex would come to her.

After some time, Jamie broke the silence. "Are you all right?"

No. There was a dull, empty space in her chest that would not be gone until Alex returned to Skye. But Jamie did not need to hear that. "I'll be fine," she said instead.

Jamie took her hand and gave it a friendly squeeze. "I

would have done the same thing as Alex, Meg. It's not safe for you to stay on Lewis."

She managed a wobbly smile. "I know."

They were quiet for a few more minutes before Jamie spoke again, this time to Robbie. "Look over there," he said, pointing behind them.

She could tell by the agitation in his voice that something was wrong. She looked over her shoulder and noticed that a *birlinn* had suddenly appeared out of the mist and was rapidly closing the distance between them. A much larger, faster, more heavily manned *birlinn*.

Immediately, she understood the reason for Jamie's concern. Something about the way the boat pursued them set her already frayed nerves on edge. That reaction was exacerbated in the next few minutes as her clansmen made an initial attempt to evade the other boat, shifting directions—only to find that their pursuers had done likewise. No matter how fast they rowed, the other *birlinn* moved at a purposeful, almost menacing clip directly toward them.

A smattering of dark spots appeared out of the mist. In horror, Meg watched as dozens of arrows began to land with horrible precision in the water around them.

There could be no doubt. They were being hunted. But by whom? Had the king's men found them out? Would her father's men be imprisoned? Dear God, what would happen to Robbie? If it was discovered that he was a MacGregor, he would be hanged. Meg's heart stalled. They couldn't be caught.

Another spray of arrows headed for them. Jamie's hands on her shoulders forced her down. "For God's sake, Meg—get your head down!"

Her heart pounded, but she didn't have time to panic.

In the sudden commotion of a shared purpose, every effort was put into trying to evade their pursuers. The endless blue vistas of shimmering sea suddenly seemed the enemy. There was nowhere to go. They could not outrow the other boat, and they were cut off from retreat back to Lewis.

Her men gave it a valiant effort, but in the end escape proved futile. They were simply outmanned. When an arrow landed with a thud in the back of one of her clansmen, Meg knew she had to put an end to it.

"Stop. There's nothing we can do."

Jamie turned to her. "We can try—"

"They'll kill us all," she said, shaking her head. At least this way we have a chance. Maybe they've made a mistake."

He nodded and repeated her order for the men to hold their oars.

It seemed to take an eternity for the other boat to reach them. They waited in seeming unison of tense apprehension as it neared.

A grappling hook was tossed over the side of their *birlinn,* and slowly their boat was pulled alongside their attackers. Close enough to make out the occupants. Meg let out an audible sigh of relief. Not the king's men. These men wore plaids. They were Highlanders. Perhaps it *was* only a terrible mistake.

Her relief, however, was short-lived. A chill ran down the back of her spine that turned her blood cold. She recognized one of the men.

No. There was no mistake. They had indeed been hunted. At that moment, she almost wished for the king's men. Because the man who'd captured them was none other than Dougal MacDonald. He stood at the helm with his arms crossed, a smug smile twisting his handsome features. The expression terrified her; she knew well what he was capable of.

He noticed Jamie, and his smugness quickly turned to anger. "What are you doing here, Campbell?"

"I would ask the same of you," Jamie said, rising to stand. With the waves tossing their small boat around, he had to spread his feet to keep his balance. "My cousin will not be pleased to hear of your impertinence."

Dougal flushed. "These men are rebels," he said, indicating Robbie and Alex's other men. When Alex's men looked as though they wanted to protest with their swords, Meg shook her head. Dougal would only delight in the opportunity to kill them.

"These men are guarding a woman who is seeking to return home," Jamie said. "Leave now, MacDonald, before you do something you will regret."

Dougal stared at him, furious, as he considered what to do. Meg knew that Jamie's presence had complicated things for him. Making war on the Highland rebels was one thing, capturing the cousin of the Earl of Argyll another. His eyes narrowed as he called Jamie's bluff. "I think it is you who should reconsider, young Campbell. I have been authorized by the king to detain all rebels. If you oppose me, you are opposing the king. And I think your cousin would be surprised to see you with these men. Perhaps you'd care to turn them over to me instead?"

They were trapped. By bringing Jamie along, Meg had put him in a horrible position. She took his arm, forcing him to meet her gaze. "I'm sorry, Jamie. There is no use in opposing him. It will only make things worse for you."

Jamie knew he was caught, but he wouldn't give up. "Mistress Mackinnon is not a part of this," he said. "Do you use a woman to win your battles now, MacDonald?"

Dougal shrugged, refusing to be shamed. "It is regrettable, but I will do what is necessary. The lass will be my trump card. The king will not care how the rebels are defeated, just that they are. Besides, the king will hardly concern himself in a matter between a man and his *wife*."

Meg gasped. "Never!" She would die before she married Dougal MacDonald.

Robbie and Jamie moved to protect her at the same time, using their bodies to shield her from Dougal's vile glare.

Dougal's face darkened. "Have care, Mistress Mackinnon. I am prepared to forgive you much, but do not try my patience." Meg shivered at the coldness in his eyes. "You do not want to anger me."

"You bastard!" Jamie growled. "You will not involve her."

Dougal's amusement fled, turning to annoyance. "You are hardly in a position to be issuing orders. I will do what I must. Alex MacLeod has proved exceedingly difficult to kill. If need be, Mistress Mackinnon will prove an irresistible lure."

Meg's heart sank. *No.* She could not be the instrument of Alex's destruction. *Dear God, what had she done?* She should never have come here.

"What are you planning to do with us?" she challenged, refusing to cower before such filth. She might be terrified, but she knew if Dougal sensed her fear, it would be like the scent of blood to a vulture.

Dougal sneered at her bravado. "I'd say that all depends on you, my dear."

Meg quickly learned what Dougal meant. He would have killed Robbie and the other men when they'd landed back on Lewis, but he spared their lives at the last minute when Meg agreed to marry him. As long as she did what he wanted, the men were safe.

Dougal MacDonald repulsed her; the very idea of marriage to him was repugnant. They both knew she'd agreed only under duress, but Meg suspected that Dougal enjoyed toying with her. Taking sadistic pleasure in manipulating her to his bidding, in watching her panic as he'd held the blade to Robbie's neck, in making sure she knew that she was his prisoner and that he was in control. Meg thought of Alex's imprisonment all those years ago in a MacDonald dungeon at the hand of this man and couldn't imagine what he'd been forced to endure.

It gave her insight into the rage that drove Alex. Dougal MacDonald was a man to inspire vengeance. Anger could be a great motivator, as Meg had learned. It was anger that had propelled her over miles of rugged terrain without complaint.

They'd camped last night in the woods well south of Stornoway. Meg had been too frightened and anxious to sleep, though she soon wished she had. Today had been a nightmare. They'd walked for hours, skirting well clear of the MacLeods as they headed north just past Stornoway to a rocky ridge above the northernmost section of the harbor. They'd stopped, finally, but it would not be for long.

Since their capture, Dougal had kept her separated from the others and well guarded, leaving her no opportunity to escape. He knew as well as she did that even if Jamie or the others could have escaped, they would not leave her behind.

Sitting on a rock, resting her aching feet, Meg wanted to weep with exhaustion and frustration. She swept a strand of hair from her face, feeling the dirt and grime of the long day sitting on her skin. But she knew that it would get much worse before this day was done.

As soon as Alex appeared below, Dougal would make his move. Using her.

Meg would never have told Dougal anything that might put Alex in jeopardy. And he must have guessed as much, because he focused his persuasion on Jamie— this time using her as the pawn. Meg begged Jamie not to say anything. Dougal wouldn't kill her, not until he'd married her. But when he'd held the blade to her throat, Jamie had told him what he knew—which, thankfully, wasn't much. She was glad that they were not privy to all of Alex's plans. Though when Dougal realized he'd lost his attempt to take Alex at sea, it had forced him to use her as his sword.

By coming to Lewis, Meg had unintentionally given Dougal the very opportunity he'd been waiting for. Meg knew as well as he did what had happened to Alex's cousins and how much Alex blamed himself for their deaths. Dougal would give Alex another chance to surrender, this time with her as his bait.

She would be the cause of Alex's death. For even if Alex surrendered, thereby saving her life, Dougal no doubt intended to kill him. Alex would know that, too, but it wouldn't stop him. And it wasn't just Alex's life at stake. If Alex didn't do his part, Neil MacLeod would be walking into a death trap at the castle.

Because of her, the entire rebellion could fail.

Chapter 25

Alex and his warriors approached Stornoway harbor from the south, keeping as close to the tree line as possible to avoid detection. As they neared the crags bordering the northernmost section of the inner harbor, he signaled for his men to halt and ready themselves for battle. From this vantage point, he had a direct line of sight to the sea-gate of Stornoway Castle and of the harbor below it.

He kept vigilant watch of his surroundings, wary not only of an attack, but also of keeping an eye out for the return of Robbie and the other men he'd sent with Meg. They should be back at any time, and he would need them. There was no cause for concern . . . yet. But all the same, Alex would be relieved when they returned and confirmed that Meg was safely ensconced at Dunakin.

Meg. God, how he missed her. Her coming to him on Lewis had changed so much. With no secrets left between them, the distraction that had plagued him since he'd departed Edinburgh had lifted. Now he could focus his full attention on the battle, knowing that the woman he loved was waiting for him.

When his work was done.

The battle he'd been waiting for was finally upon him.

Justice would be theirs. For his kin. Both living and dead.

He felt excitement rushing through his blood as it always did before a fight. This was when he was at his best, when clarity of thought and unity of purpose drowned out everything else around him. The challenge invigorated him. Each battle was a test not just of strength, but of strategy and cunning. Of courage and of honor.

Today was the culmination of years of training and months of preparation. Their plan was simple, as the best usually were. Simplicity minimized the opportunities for something to go wrong. But timing was everything.

It was a three-pronged attack. At sea, trying to capture the supply ship, as they'd originally intended, would take too many men. They knew this now because of the information Meg had brought them. Instead, they hoped to delay it—and eventually, if they were successful, prevent the ship from landing at all.

Two *birlinns* of sixteen MacLeod clansmen stood ready just offshore, awaiting his signal to attack the supply ship as it entered the outer harbor. Alex's guardsman Patrick MacGregor would do his best to keep the ship busy while the land phase of their attack began. Except for his brother, there was no man Alex trusted more than the fearsome MacGregor.

Alex had handpicked a small force of men that he would lead in the attack against the castle guards coming out to meet the ships. They would be outnumbered, but it was nothing they hadn't faced before. At the same time, Neil and his men would lay siege to the castle, hoping to hit it hard when it was not as heavily defended. In doing so, Neil would be leaving his flank vulnerable. If anything went wrong, and the guardsmen were able to return to the castle too soon or with more men, Neil and his men would be trapped. To complicate matters, they also had to watch for Dougal trying to outflank Patrick at sea.

The MacLeods' strength would be significantly divided, but they would have the element of surprise. It would be enough.

Alex scanned the sea again. It was near dark, but he could just make out the white of a sail in the distance. He ordered his men to wait for his signal. He kept his gaze focused on the castle. Waiting. Any minute . . .

The sea-gate to Stornoway Castle opened.

Every inch of his body was trained on the small stretch of land between the castle and the harbor, where the sixty or so men had begun to descend the stairs of the sea-gate and march toward the four waiting galleys. There wasn't much time; Alex and his men had to attack before the Lowlanders could embark in their ships. He raised his claymore, ready to give the signal that would send his men galloping down the hill toward the unsuspecting soldiers.

This was it. The moment he'd been waiting for was upon him. It was time to put his demons where they belonged, in the past. And win the day for the MacLeods of Lewis.

The sound of stomping hooves from behind stilled his hand. He was just about to proceed anyway and lower his hand when a voice rang out.

"I wouldn't do that if I were you."

Alex recognized the voice and then the face that halted not twenty feet behind him. Dougal MacDonald.

The rush of hatred hit him hard, but he would not allow it to interfere with the task at hand. He cast his gaze down to the soldiers making their way toward the boat. Nothing looked amiss. But he knew Dougal well enough to know that he was up to something. Whatever it was, it wouldn't work. Alex was no longer a boy of eighteen.

He would not be defeated. Perhaps it was fitting that his nemesis should arrive to witness this moment.

Dougal led a dozen or so of his men through the clearing, forming a semicircle around them.

Alex's eyes narrowed at the implied threat, but he felt a vague inkling of trouble. "Don't interfere, MacDonald. You're outnumbered." He indicated his own score of warriors, waiting for his signal to careen down the hill. "Surrender now and you won't have to die."

Something in Dougal's expression bothered him. He looked too confident, like a man holding an unbeatable hand. Alex's uneasiness spread. Dougal wouldn't challenge him like this unless he was damn sure of the outcome.

"It's not I who will be surrendering, MacLeod. You see, I need but one person to defeat you."

Alex stilled. *No. He couldn't . . .*

Dougal turned, motioning for someone to step forward.

Out of the darkness from behind the trees, the tiny familiar form broke into view. Meg. Spitting-fire angry with a knife pressed to her throat by one of Dougal's men. Vaguely, he was aware of Jamie and the other men behind her, bound, their wrists tied with rope.

The ground shifted under his feet as the memories collided with the present. *Not again.*

"Alex, don't listen to him. He won't kill me, it's just a trick—"

"Shut up!" Dougal shouted, striking her hard across her cheek with the back of his hand. Meg's head rolled with the blow.

Alex let out a strangled sound and leapt forward to attack—stopping only when he saw MacDonald's man press the knife deeper against Meg's neck.

A red haze clouded his vision. He forced himself to breathe, forced his pulse to slow. He needed his mind to clear, he had to think. His gaze fixed on Meg, but out of the corner of his eye, Alex noticed that Jamie and Robbie had also leapt to Meg's defense.

"Stay out of this, Campbell," Dougal warned.

Alex couldn't speak. Icy fear gripped his throat. He was staring at the knife.

"Well? It's your decision," Dougal said, gloating.

Just like four years ago, Alex thought. Dougal had re-created the scene for maximum effect. Would it be Meg who was gulleted before him this time?

Alex was trained to lead. To make decisions. To make the hard decisions.

Just not this decision.

Could he surrender, saving her life, knowing that in doing so, he'd be forced to sacrifice so many others who were depending on him?

Alex eyed the castle guardsmen on shore who were fast approaching their boats. There wasn't much time. If they reached the boats, he'd fail. Patrick and the two *birlinns* of his men would be too far outnumbered in a battle on water with both the men from the castle and the new recruits. The Lowlanders would return to the castle with reinforcements, and Neil would be storming into a death trap.

He made his decision.

He lifted his claymore and swung it in a wide circle, the signal for his men on land and at sea to attack. They obeyed, their trust in him absolute. With a fierce battle cry of "Hold fast!" the men surrounding him rode off, thundering down on the unsuspecting castle guardsmen loading onto the boats. Leaving Alex alone to fight Dougal and his dozen warriors.

The battle to take Stornoway Castle had begun. Without Alex.

Meg dared not breathe.

As the piercing scream of the MacLeod war cry rang in her ears, she knew that any breath might well be her last. Not that she was ready to die. She prayed that Alex had a few more tricks up his sleeve.

She was so proud of him. She knew what this decision had cost him, but it also proved the man he had become. A leader willing to do what was necessary for the protection of his people, no matter the personal cost. Never had she been more certain that this was the man she wanted to help lead her clan.

Dougal's stunned expression indicated that Alex's defiance had surprised him.

"Apparently, I overestimated the chit's worth to you," Dougal snapped.

"It's not her you want," Alex replied calmly. "It's me. I'll surrender, but not until I am assured that Mistress Mackinnon is safe. Allow Campbell to take her away and I'll go with you."

"No!" Meg gasped, understanding exactly what he was doing. Dougal wouldn't take him anywhere. Alex was bargaining his life for Meg's.

"Fine," Dougal agreed. "Release the lass. Campbell, take her."

The nameless MacDonald clansman released his deadly hold on Meg's neck and then, using the knife he'd just lowered, sliced through Jamie's bonds.

Meg tried to pull away, wanting to run to Alex, but Jamie reached out to stop her.

"Don't, Meg," he said under his breath. "You can't help him."

She didn't care. "Alex, don't. It's a trap—" Despite his words, she knew that Dougal had no intention of letting them go. The moment Alex was dead, they would be hunted. Alex was giving his life for nothing.

"Enough," Alex cut her off harshly, refusing to look at her. "Jamie, do as he says, get her out of here." He slid off his horse and divested himself of his weapons. One by one, they fell to the rocky ground.

He glanced down toward the shore, where his men battled the castle guards. Despite their smaller numbers, the MacLeods appeared to be holding the advantage. A rider galloped back and forth along the beach with a torch. She followed his gaze as two *birlinns* headed out to sea. His mouth curved with satisfaction. Meg understood. His plan was succeeding, so far. But they needed him. By giving himself up to Dougal, he was risking everything he'd fought for—and failure. It was the ultimate proof of his love, but never would she have wished for such a noble sacrifice.

Jamie tried to lead her away, but her legs wouldn't move. Not until . . . Finally, their eyes met. His face was a mask of strength and resolve. Her heart squeezed. *Oh God.* He knew. He knew that Dougal would never take him prisoner, would never let him live. But he wanted to give her a chance, no matter how slim. He was giving his life for her.

A hot ball caught in her throat. She couldn't stand this. "Please," she choked. "Please, don't do this—" *I don't want you to die. Not for me.* Her voice broke. "Don't make me leave you."

He looked back to Jamie. "Take care of her, Campbell. I love her," Alex said softly.

I love her. The words rang in her ears. Pain and happiness gripped her heart as he so simply spoke the words she'd been longing to hear. Tears spilled from her eyes. What should be the happiest moment of her life was instead one of utter desolation and anguish. How could this be happening? He'd given her the greatest gift of her life, his love—but at the cost of his life.

"Alex," she cried softly. He heard the soft plea in her voice and met her gaze, but only for a second. Long enough to glimpse the intensity of emotion tempered by regret. Then he turned away.

"Get her out of here," he said to Jamie. "Now." Alex and Jamie exchanged a look, and Meg could see the vestiges of the longtime friendship they once had shared pass between them. Jamie nodded in understanding, took her arm, and forcibly dragged her away.

Her mind was going in a thousand directions as something close to hysteria descended over her. This couldn't be happening, there had to be something they could do. She couldn't just leave him to die. Unarmed. Slaughtered at the hand of a coward.

*I just found him. Please don't take him from me.
I need him.*

"Touching. Not that it matters," Dougal taunted. "Not where you are going."

She froze, knowing well what he meant. A sudden burst of strength enabled her to break free from Jamie. She spun around, just in time to see Dougal pull out his dirk.

"*No!*" A guttural cry tore from the depths of her soul.

What happened next took mere seconds, though it seemed to unfold in horrifically slow motion.

Meg didn't think. She ran straight toward Alex as Dougal's arm began its downward stroke. *Not enough time,* she thought as she leapt, intending to knock the dirk from Dougal's hand. But she missed.

Unable to stop the pendulum of his swing, Dougal plunged his dirk into flesh.

Her flesh.

She felt the sear of the blade, the sharp knife of pain, and then . . . nothing.

Surrounded by Dougal and his men, unarmed, and with his own men already down the hill, Alex knew there was a good chance he was going to die. But he wouldn't go down without a fight. Dougal's eyes were bright with excitement. He raised his dirk high above his head, and the silvery blade caught a beam of moonlight and flickered like a silvery reaper.

He prayed he could hold Dougal off long enough to give Meg a chance to escape. He heard a scream and knew that his prayers had gone unanswered. But he could not look away from the glittering blade.

Grab his hand, he thought as the dirk began to fall.

A movement from the corner of his eye distracted him. When he realized what she was doing, it was already too late. Meg had jumped in front of him. Alex had managed to knock his arm but couldn't get hold of Dougal's hand. *The blade. Oh God. The blade.*

Not Meg. Take me, goddamn you! It's supposed to be me.

She collapsed into a puddle at his feet, Dougal's blade protruding from her side.

A sound of rage tore from him.

His first instinct was to drop to his knees and gather her in his arms. His next was to kill. He knew he could not help her until Dougal was dispensed with, so he reached for the nearest MacDonald clansman, wrapped his arm around his neck, and snapped it while relieving him of his blade. Dougal's face had gone white as he stared in horrified awe at the sight of Meg slumped on the ground, but he'd recovered long enough to pull his claymore from his back, intending to finish the job on Alex.

It was already too late.

In one continuous motion, Alex plunged the dirk deep into Dougal's heart. Almost without thought. After years of waiting for revenge, the moment of Dougal's death was remarkably anticlimactic. And insignificant given the magnitude of what vengeance might have just cost him.

He couldn't look at her. Not yet. Not until he could help her. And to help her, he had to take control of the situation.

He tossed a blade to Jamie, who released the others. And in a matter of minutes, with three more MacDonalds dead, the rest of Dougal's men surrendered.

But Alex was already kneeling at Meg's side. Her eyes were closed and her face pale, but the worst part was how still she was. Terrifyingly still, like a little crumpled doll. This couldn't be happening. He wouldn't allow himself to consider the possibility.

He gathered her in his arms, pulling her against his chest and pressing his mouth against her brow. The faint scent of roses still lingered in her hair. "Oh, Meg—" His voice cracked. "Why?" Despair, incomparable grief engulfed him; weighing on his chest like a stone.

It took him a moment to realize that her velvety skin was warm, blissfully warm, and her even breathing tickled softly against his cheek. Relief swept over him. He buried his head deep in the warmth of her hair. Thank God. She lived.

Carefully, he laid her down to better examine the wound. A small circle of blood surrounded the dirk, enough to make his blood run cold, but not as much as he'd feared. The blade did not look deeply embedded. His attempt to deflect the blow had likely saved her life. Hands shaking, he slid the blade from her side. She continued to bleed, but the removal of the knife had not increased the flow of blood. Not realizing he'd been holding his breath, he exhaled.

"Campbell, find me something to stanch the bleeding."

Jamie hurried to do his bidding. Until he returned, Alex did the best he could with his plaid. The wound didn't appear life threatening, but he would take no chances. He'd ministered many battle injuries over the past few years, but none with such personal significance.

Robbie had returned after securing the MacDonalds,

and Alex ordered him to find Ruaidri, one of his older soldiers. He wasn't a healer, but he was the best they had until Alex could get Meg to the village. A quick glance down the hill told him that his men were holding their own. So far, the plan was unfolding as they'd intended. For his part, he couldn't leave Meg. Not until she was safe.

Jamie was at his side in seconds with a remarkably clean-looking drying cloth. Alex quickly fashioned a pad and secured it with a piece of linen torn from his *leine*.

"Is she going to be all right?" Jamie asked.

"I think so," Alex said. "But until she wakes—"

He stopped as her eyes fluttered open. Beautiful green eyes—surprisingly lucid beautiful green eyes—met his. "What happened?"

Alex could have wept for joy. Her voice sounded marvelously strong. He knew he shouldn't jostle her, so he resisted the urge to enfold her in his arms again and kiss her senseless. Instead, he smoothed the hair from her brow. Not wanting to remind her of what happened, he answered her question with one of his own. "How do you feel?"

His question seemed to snap her back to the present. Her face lit with joy. She lifted her hand to cradle one side of his face, rubbing her palm across his stubbled jaw. "Alex, you're alive . . . I was so scared."

He dropped a kiss on the tip of her nose and smiled, his eyes growing suspiciously damp. Emotion locked in his throat. Everything was going to be all right. "Aye, lass, I was scared, too." *More scared than I've ever been in my life.*

Her adorable little nose wrinkled. "All I remember is running and the dirk . . ." She looked down at her side and blanched. "Oh."

"Why did you do it, love? God, Meg, you could have been killed." The full force of what might have happened hit him hard again.

"I didn't stop to think, I just reacted." She gave him an adorable little shy smile. "I love you, Alex. I couldn't let him kill you because of me." The smile broadened as she remembered something else. "And you love me."

"Aye, you heard that, did you?"

She nodded.

"More than my life."

She squeezed his hand, tears glistening in her eyes. "Say it. Please."

Alex looked deep into her eyes. "I love you, Margaret Mackinnon. With all my heart."

He pressed his mouth gently against hers, needing to taste her, even if briefly. He felt her immediate response as she opened her mouth for him, melting against him in sweet surrender.

Hearing Ruaidri approach with Robbie, Alex broke the kiss. How the lad had managed to find him so fast, Alex didn't know, but he was grateful. He moved aside to allow the older man to examine Meg, though he held her hand the entire time. Needing the connection. He couldn't stop touching her, assuring himself that she was going to be all right. That she wasn't going to die.

After a few minutes, Ruaidri stood up. "It will need to be stitched, and I suspect she'll be weak for a few days, but with a proper poultice the lass will be fine."

Alex sighed with relief. It was the first relaxed breath he'd taken since Dougal had appeared with Meg.

When he thought of what she'd done, risking her life for his, he was moved beyond words. Humbled, awed, and now that he knew she would be all right, not a little bit angered. But *that* discussion, he would save for later. Now, he just wanted to carry her away from here.

Meg was floating on a wave of pure euphoria, feeling nothing but the strength of Alex's love. The searing pain in her side seemed strangely detached, almost not her own. Everything was going to be all right. Alex was safe. Dougal was dead, and she . . . well, she had everything she ever wanted. The perfect man for her *and* her clan.

Alex slid his arm under her back and started to lift her. She winced at the sharp reminder of her injury.

"I'm sorry, love. This might hurt, but I need to lift you up to get you on my horse, all right?" When she nodded, he added, "Put pressure on it like this." He moved her hand over the pad he'd fashioned as a bandage. "It has stopped bleeding for now, but tell me immediately if it starts bleeding again."

"I think I can stand," she offered.

"No."

He looked so charmingly worried, she decided not to argue. It was too wonderful being cared for so lovingly. Gently, Alex lifted her and bundled her in his arms. She pressed her cheek against his thick quilted cotun, the tiny plates of metal cool against her cheek. She wanted to stay in his arms forever. And she could when . . .

All of a sudden it hit her.

"Alex! The battle. Is it over?"

He shook his head. " 'Tis just begun, love."

Her stomach lurched. Her own need to have him near

her, holding her, warred with the knowledge of what she had to do. She knew how important this was to him. Knew precisely what was at stake. Knew the men who were relying on him. *It wasn't over.* No matter how tight she wanted to hold on to him, no matter how much she needed him, he wasn't hers—yet. Her chest squeezed as she forced the words from her mouth, releasing him. "You must go to them. Your men need you. Jamie can take me to the village."

"My men are well trained. I'll not leave you. Not until I see you to safety."

"But it might be too late—"

His expression turned obstinate and forbidding. "Don't argue with me, Meg. Not about this. You could have died."

Something in his eyes stopped her. The raw emotion. The hint of lingering fear.

"But I didn't," she said softly. "Promise me you'll go—"

"I will. As soon as I am assured of your safety." They'd reached the area where his horse was tethered. Meg listened proudly as Alex gave orders to his men. His quick decisiveness and utter command never ceased to impress her. Most of the men he sent to help those battling the castle guards. A few of her father's men who'd accompanied her on the *birlinn* were to keep watch over the MacDonalds, and Robbie would ride to Neil and explain what had happened.

"Is there anything I can do?" Jamie asked.

Alex nodded. "Ride ahead. Find a healer and have her come at once to the inn."

Carefully, he handed her to Robbie while he mounted

his horse. She felt a fresh stab of pain at her side but smothered her cry, not wanting to alarm Alex. Soon, she was settled before him, happily ensconced against the protective wall of his chest.

The ride to the village did not take long, but Meg wasn't feeling so well. She felt queasy and unbearably weak. But she forced herself to be strong and fought the nausea rising in her throat. She realized that her wound had opened and blood was seeping from her side, thankfully well hidden under her *arisaidh*.

It was getting harder and harder to keep her eyes open. She was so tired, so horribly tired. Her eyelids felt so heavy. Her dreams beckoned, tempted. No, there was something she had to do. One more thing before she slept.

She felt a prickle of alarm, knowing she was losing too much blood. But she dared not say anything to Alex. If she did, he would never leave her. And he needed to do this. Needed to help his kin, or the past would always haunt him.

"How are you feeling, my love?"

Awful. "Fine. I'm sure it looks worse than it is," she said, nearly exhausting what little strength she had left to make her voice sound normal.

"We're almost there."

A few minutes later, they found the inn and an available room. Alex had just finished laying her down on the bed when Jamie followed with the healer, a short, roundish woman of indiscriminate age with graying hair and a pleasant face. Meg relaxed immediately. The woman gave off an indisputable air of capability.

Alex relayed what had happened, and the woman,

Mairi, bent over Meg to begin her examination. Meg was starting to panic, which the woman obviously mistook for embarrassment, and she quickly shooed the men out of the room.

Meg flinched as she started to peel back the sticky layers of clothing, using a knife where necessary to cut the seams.

Mairi gave her a hard look. "Why did you say nothing? You've lost a lot of blood."

"Please," Meg begged. "You must do something for me." She knew she sounded desperate, bordering on hysterical. "You must tell him that everything looks fine. He'll never leave . . . please."

The woman frowned disapprovingly and shook her head. "If you are sure that is what you want?"

Meg nodded furiously. "Yes. Please. It is very important."

"Very well." The healer opened the door, and Alex immediately entered the room.

"I will stitch the wound to stop the bleeding. All she needs is rest," Mairi assured him.

"See?" Meg said brightly. The relief in his eyes gave her a burst of strength, and she managed a smile. "I'll be fine. Go now."

He bent over her and kissed her hard. Meg drank in the taste of him, wanting to grab on to him and never let him go. Did he sense her desperation in the fervor of her response?

"You're sure?" he asked, looking uncertain.

"Of course I'm sure. I'll be here when you return."

"I'll be back as soon as possible." He looked to Jamie. "Send for me if anything changes."

His lips pressed against her forehead, his arms

squeezed her tight, she heard him whisper something, and then he was gone.

Through sheer force of will, Meg refused to give in to the dizziness and the weight that hovered over her. Not yet . . . the door slammed. A horse galloped away. A few more minutes . . .

Only then, when she was assured that he was truly gone, did the blackness envelop her.

Chapter 26

Stornoway Castle fell, but not without a struggle. It was two days before Alex walked through the castle gates with Neil and savored the victory that had taken two long days of constant fighting, and four years of preparation, to achieve.

He was filthy, sore, and exhausted, with a dozen new cuts and bruises peppered across his scar-ridden body, but he was happier than he'd felt in years. To Alex, it felt as if a great weight had been lifted off him.

It was done.

The Fife Adventurers had been sent scurrying back to Edinburgh. His kin once again held Lewis, and justice had prevailed. At last the ghosts had quieted. The deaths of his cousins had been avenged.

He couldn't wait to get back to Meg. To the woman he loved. And to his future. There would be problems—not least his precarious position with the king—but he was confident they would find a solution. Together.

The smell of blood permeated the morning air, drawing his attention back to the present. He gazed around the courtyard, at the slew of bodies littering the dirt, and shook his head with disgust at the prodigious waste of life.

After leaving Meg at the inn, Alex had arrived just in

time to help his men defeat the last of the castle guards. Using the defeated guardsmen's boats, he and his men had joined Patrick in the battle at sea. Unable to land, and under constant attack, the ship had retreated, leaving the castle severely underdefended. Despite their assured defeat, those who remained in the castle had refused to surrender, necessitating the further loss of life.

He had just set about seeing to the removal of bodies when a rider stormed into the courtyard under the portcullis. Alex's mood changed in an instant when he recognized the man. It was the messenger from the village who'd brought news of Meg from Jamie. And he was obviously in a hurry.

"For you, my laird," the man said, handing Alex a missive.

Alex scanned the letter, and his stomach crashed to his feet. *No.*

Meg begged me not to write you, but I've waited as long as I dare. Come quick. Fever has set in. I fear . . . do not delay.
J.

Neil must have read something in his expression. "What's the matter?"

Alex had already started to run for his horse. "I have to go."

Meg woke with a strange heaviness crushing her skull. She opened her eyes and quickly closed them again. Bright sunlight filtered through a small window, flooding the room with light and splitting her head in two. Wincing against the offending sun, she made a sound of pain.

Her hand was immediately enfolded in a strong grasp, and she felt the warm, calming presence of someone at her side. The same strong presence she'd felt in her dreams. The same strong presence that had called her back while she floated on the calming sea.

"Thank God you're awake."

Alex, she realized. Why did his voice sound so strange? Raw, almost desperate. She frowned. What was he doing here? He'd promised to go to Neil. Jamie had sworn not to send for him.

More cautiously this time, she opened her eyes. It wasn't a dream. He was there, at her side, so golden, so radiantly handsome that it was almost difficult to look at him. She blinked and looked again. Actually, he looked as though he'd gone through hell and back. His eyes were bloodshot, he looked exhausted beyond measure, and his face was strained and bruised with barely healed cuts—

Her eyes snapped open.

"Oh God, Alex, you're hurt!" she exclaimed. She tried to sit up, only to slump back down on the bed when her head exploded in pain. She fought the swift kick of nausea.

"Shhh," he said gently, pressing a damp cloth on her forehead. "I'm fine. A few cuts and bruises, nothing more. Don't try to sit up."

"But why are you here? Why aren't you with your men? What's happened?"

He smoothed her hair over the top of her head and rubbed tiny circles at her temples, immediately soothing the pressure in her head.

"It's all over."

"What!" She shot up, only to crumple back onto her pillow again. Perhaps he was right. Lying down seemed a good idea. "But when? How?"

"Stornoway Castle is ours. The battle went much as planned. Without reinforcements, the castle fell within two days."

She scanned his face, taking in every inch of him, noticing every cut on his beloved face. Aside from needing sleep and a shave, he looked well enough. "And you are not hurt? Truly?"

"Barely a scratch," he assured her, stroking her cheek with the back of his finger.

Meg sank back into the pillow, relaxed. "I'm so proud of you. I know how much this means to you."

"Aye, but it's nothing compared to what you mean to me."

Meg tried to smile, but a sudden burst of pain caused her to grimace. "I'm sorry, I seem to have a horrible headache."

He pressed a soft, soothing kiss on her temple. "I'm not surprised. You've been ill." His voice dropped. "Very ill."

"I don't feel ill. Except for the headache." She wrinkled her nose. "And perhaps a little hungry."

"The fever only broke last night. You've been unconscious for four days."

"Four days!" That took her aback; she must have been worse than she realized. She glanced over at the plaid strewn across the bench before the fire. And this was obviously where he'd spent every minute of those four days. No wonder he looked so tired.

He bowed his head on her hand. "Oh God, Meg. I

didn't think . . ." He lifted his head and looked at her fiercely. "I thought I was going to lose you. Twice." There was an undertone in his voice that hinted at something far more serious that she'd realized. "Don't you ever do that to me again. You should have told me you were bleeding. How could you not let them send for me?" His voice thickened. "I was so damn scared. You'd lost so much blood, and when the wound festered you didn't have the strength to fight the fever."

Seeing how distraught he was, Meg felt a strong pang of guilt for what she'd put him through. She'd known she was ill, but not deathly so. His hair had slid forward across his eyes, shielding his gaze from her view. She reached out and tucked it behind his ear. The look in his eyes humbled her. Never would she doubt this man's love for her. She fit her hand around the curve of his whiskered jaw. "I'm sorry. But I knew you would not leave otherwise—"

"Damn right I would not have left," he said gruffly. "Don't you understand what you mean to me? You are everything. Never doubt that. My place is with you, only you."

The emotion in his voice tugged at her heart. She understood exactly what he meant, because she felt the same. Contrite, she slid her arms around the back of his neck. "And you are everything to me."

He sank into her, his mouth covering hers with a groan. He kissed her with such hunger that she soon forgot all about the pain in her head. Her body softened, warming under his solid masculine strength. She opened her mouth and his tongue found hers, deepening the kiss. She felt the force of his fear for her in the raw desperation of his kiss. A kiss she returned with all the emotion she'd been holding inside while he battled for his clan. She grabbed his shoulders. He was so strong and hard, and she loved him desperately. The power of their passion swept over her, sending a shudder of desire rippling through her.

He tore away with a curse. "God, I want you."

She gave him a suggestive look, sliding her hand slowly down the taut bands of his stomach.

He clasped her wrist before she could circle him in her hand. "Not now, you jade. You need to get back your strength. There will be plenty of time for that."

She smiled. "How much time?"

He took her face in his hand, rubbing his thumb over her chin. The look in his eyes made her heart catch. "Forever," he promised huskily.

She was so deliriously happy, it almost didn't seem real. "'Tis really over? The Fife Adventurers are gone?"

"Aye, it will be some time before the king dares try that again."

Meg sighed. "But he will try again."

Alex nodded. "It seems inevitable. He'll not give up on the promise of riches to be found in the Isles." Alex, too, it seemed, had recognized that change was coming. But she knew that he would never stand by and allow injustice. Alex was a Highlander, a warrior. And she wouldn't have it any other way. He was the perfect man to help lead her clan into the future. Her brother's position would be safe.

She frowned, realizing not everything was behind them. "But what will happen now? The king will be furious with you." Panic bubbled in her chest as the reality of the situation intruded. "You'll be imprisoned." The words wouldn't come to her mouth. "Or worse."

"Nothing is going to happen," he said soothingly, stroking her hair. His mouth curved into a wry grin. "I suppose we have Jamie to thank for that."

"What do you mean?"

"Through Jamie, Argyll and my brother have brokered an alliance. Argyll has agreed to intervene with the king. It seems I am to be forgiven. I'm a free man."

She couldn't help it. She popped up and threw her arms around him again, burying her face in the warmth of his neck and hair. Her heart swelled, and tears streamed down her cheeks. "It's really over."

He laughed, a low sound that warmed her to her bones. "Aye, love, it's really over. There is only the future to look forward to."

Meg felt as if the last vestiges of the past had dissipated from her consciousness. They were free. "Our future," she said. "Together."

But rather than echo her sentiments, his expression was oddly somber. "What is it, Alex?" she asked. "What aren't you telling me?"

"Rory has rewarded me with the lands of Miningish."

"That's wonderful," she said, knowing how important having his own lands would be. Nonetheless, she was disappointed. She'd hoped he might be speaking of their future. Together. But something was wrong. Something that he was holding back. Her heart stopped cold. Would these lands prevent him from marrying her?

His voice grew thick with emotion. "You had me so worried, Meg—" His voice broke. "When I think of all that I might have lost. How could you not tell me?"

She was genuinely confused. "What are you talking about? I apologized for not telling you that I was bleeding."

"Yes, but I'm talking about the babe."

Meg's brows shot up to her forehead. "What babe?"

He studied her face intently. "You didn't know?"

She shook her head, stunned. "But I thought . . ." Her hands went to her stomach, still perfectly flat. *Could it be?* She'd had some bleeding around the time of her menses, it had been unusually light, but she'd just assumed . . .

"Mairi, the healer, thinks sometime around May Day."

Still at a loss for words, Meg nodded. A child. Their child. It was almost too much to comprehend. A warm glow radiated from the deepest part of her. She thought her heart would burst with happiness. To think that she carried a part of Alex inside her.

"I've sent for your parents and brother, Rory and Isabel, and my sister Margaret and her husband, Colin. We'll be married as soon as they arrive."

Meg couldn't hold back the smile, even though it hurt. *Married. A child.* Everything was going to be all right. Her future couldn't look more perfect.

Alex was looking at her expectantly, probably wondering whether she'd take umbrage at his edict. But Meg knew when to surrender. Her mouth twitched. "Do I get no say in this, then?"

Alex grinned and leaned down to press a kiss to her lips. "Absolutely none at all," he murmured against her mouth.

Meg didn't mind at all. After all, she'd accomplished what she'd set out to do: finding the perfect man for Dunakin.

And the only man for her.

From the first moment he'd broken through the trees,

rescuing her from the hands of certain death, he'd claimed a part of her heart. Now he held it all.

"I love you," she said. "And if you're wondering, that's a yes."

His finger swept the side of her cheek, and their eyes met, soul to soul. The gentle teasing of the past few minutes was replaced by a look of heartfelt earnestness. "And I you, my love. Marry me, be mine, forever."

"Gladly." And she kissed him with all the promise of the future.

Historical Note

In the end, the Fife Adventurers tried and failed three times to colonize the Isle of Lewis. Unfortunately, the MacLeod victory on Lewis was short-lived. Neil Mac-Leod was eventually captured and hanged in 1613. The Mackenzie of Kintail married the last of the Lewis "Siol Torcuil," sons of Torquil, branch of the MacLeods and obtained lease of their lands in 1610. So disappeared the Lewis branch of the MacLeods.

Alex MacLeod was held responsible for the MacLeod defeat at the Corrie of the Foray, the last clan battle fought on Skye in 1601. About the time of my story, Alex was rumored to be fighting on Lewis. It seemed plausible that he might be trying to redeem himself for his earlier loss.

Dougal MacDonald is loosely based on Donald Mac-Iain 'ic Sheumais, a kinsman of the MacLeod's bitter foe, the MacDonald of Sleat. The MacDonald of Sleat played a significant role in the first book of the trilogy, *Highlander Untamed*. Donald MacIain was a renowned warrior and bard for the MacDonalds, and his arrival on the scene of the battle at Binquihillin after its start was reported to have wrought great havoc on the MacLeods.

Although most of the characters in this story were actual historical figures (the primary exceptions being Jamie and Elizabeth Campbell and Rosalind Mackinnon), the love story is pure fiction. But Alex MacLeod of Miningish and Talisker did wed Margaret Mackinnon, daughter of the Mackinnon of Strathardale and sister of "Ian the Dumb." Alex and Margaret had at least two children, William and Norman.

For more information, please visit my website at www.MonicaMcCarty.com.

Looking for more sexy Scottish adventure?

Turn the page to catch a sneak peek at the
next pulse-pounding book in the
Highlander series

❖

*H*ighlander
*U*nchained

❖

By

Monica McCarty

They hit another bump. Flora held her breath as the carriage perched sideways for a long moment before settling back down on all four wheels. When it came to a sudden halt, she thought they must have damaged something.

"I'll have the coachman's head for this—"

But Lord William Murray's threat was lost in the deafening thunder of horses and the sudden burst of loud voices coming from outside.

Her pulse shot up in an explosion of comprehension. An attack!

From the quizzical expression on his face, it was clear that William had not yet realized what was happening. He was a Lowlander to the core—a courtier, not a fighter. For a moment, she felt a stab of frustration, then she chastised herself for being unfair. She wouldn't want it otherwise. But clearly, in this situation, he was going to be of little help.

She could hear the sporadic clash of steel against steel moving closer. They didn't have much time. Grabbing his arm, she forced his gaze to hers. "We're under attack." A shot rang out, punctuating her words. "Do you have anything? A weapon of any sort?"

He shook his head. "I have no use for weaponry. As you can hear, my men are well armed."

Flora cursed, not bothering to curb her tongue.

His frown returned. "Really, my dear. You mustn't say such things. Not when we are married."

Another shot rang out.

She bit back the sarcastic retort that sprang to her lips. Married? They might not be alive in an hour. Did he not understand the desperation of their situation? Scotland was rife with brigands that roamed the countryside. Outlaws. Broken men without clans who weren't known for their mercy. Flora had thought there would be some protection in staying close to Edinburgh. She was wrong.

Lord Murray was exhibiting the arrogant obtuseness characteristic of many courtiers—the confidence that rank and wealth would protect him. But a few muskets would not stop a Highland sword or bow for long. They needed something to defend themselves with.

"A sword," she said urgently, trying to mask her impatience. "Surely you have a sword?"

"Of course. Every man at court carries one. But I did not want to be bothered with it at my side during the journey, so the driver strapped it to the box with your gown. I do still have my dagger." He slid the blade out of the scabbard at his waist and offered it to her. From the heavily jewel-encrusted hilt, Flora could tell that it was intended for adornment and not battle. But the six-inch blade would suffice well enough.

From the awkward way he held the blade, as if it were

distasteful, it was obvious he didn't know how to use it. "I'm afraid I don't have much experience—"

She did. "I'll take it." Flora slid the dagger into the pocket of her cloak right before the door swung open with a crash.

And everything happened at once.

Before she could scream or make a move to defend herself, she was plucked roughly from the safety of the carriage into the viselike hold of a man. A very large man. Who from the feel of him was as strong as an ox.

She gasped from the force of being brought up hard against the granite wall of his chest. Laid out against him, the full length of her body was plastered against hard, unyielding stone.

Dear God, no one had ever dared to hold her like this. She'd never been this aware of . . . anything. Her cheeks burned with indignation and from the sudden blast of heat that seemed to radiate from him. He'd wrapped his arm around her waist and pressed it up snugly under the heavy weight of her bosom, making her deeply conscious of the rise and fall of her breasts against his arm. Although she was not a small woman, her head tucked easily under his chin. But the worst part was that with her back to his chest, her bottom was pressed directly against his groin.

Instinctively, she rebelled at the closeness. At the intimacy of being molded against the hard-muscled body of a filthy villain.

Except that he didn't smell filthy at all. He smelled of myrtle and heather, with the faintest hint of the sea.

Furious at the direction of her thoughts, she turned her outrage on her captor. "Get your hands off me!" She struggled to wrench herself free, but it was useless. His arm was as rigid as steel. Though he was only restraining her with one arm, she'd barely moved an inch.

"I'm afraid not, my sweet."

She froze at the lilting sound of the burr in his voice. A Highlander. His voice made the hair on her arms stand straight on end. It was almost hypnotic. Deep and dark, with an indisputable edge of steel.

Her blood ran cold. The direness of their predicament had just grown markedly worse. Highlanders had the morals of the devil. Unless she could think of something, they were as good as dead.

Repressing the impulse to struggle further, Flora stilled, feigning submission, giving herself a moment to appraise the situation. The night was dark, but the full moon softly lit the wide expanse of moorland, enabling her to see just enough—or perhaps too much. Because what she saw wasn't good. They were surrounded by about a score of powerful-looking men dressed in *breacan feiles,* the belted plaids of the Highlands, all brandishing enormous two-handed claymores. To a one, their faces were hard and uncompromising. These were fighting men, warriors.

But they did not bear the hungry, feral look of hunted men. Glancing down, she noticed the finely spun linen shirt of the man holding her. His plaid was also of fine quality—soft and smooth to the touch.

If they weren't outlaws, just who were they and what did they want?

She didn't intend to stay and find out. Every nerve in her body clamored to break free, to escape from danger. But her options were few.

The handful of men whom Lord Murray had brought as an escort were greatly outnumbered, and from the looks of things, they had given up without much of a fight. She saw a few muskets and hagbuts scattered at their feet, although most still held their swords.

But surrender was not in Flora's nature. *Especially* to barbarians. And she had no doubt that these men were Highlanders. If their speech hadn't given them away, the manner of their dress left no doubt.

"What do you want?" Flora recognized the haughty voice of her betrothed. "And get your filthy hands off her."

Lord Murray had been pulled from the carriage behind her and was being restrained by a fearsome-looking Highlander. His size, piercing blue eyes, and shock of white blond hair left little doubt of his Viking ancestry.

The brigand gave her a moment's pause, leaving her to wonder whether the brute holding her was equally as formidable. Perhaps she was glad she could not see him; she was frightened enough as it was. Her heart was beating so hard, she was sure he must feel it.

"Take whatever it is you want and leave us," Lord Murray added. "We are on important business this night."

The man behind her stiffened, and Flora realized why. She'd never noticed the tinge of condescension that threaded through William's speech until now.

"You are hardly in any position to be issuing orders, *my lord*," her captor said with unveiled contempt. His arm tightened possessively around her middle. "But you are free to go. Take your men with you. I have everything I want."

The blood drained to her feet as his meaning became clear. *Me. He means me.*

William would die before he allowed a barbarian to

take her, and Flora couldn't be the cause of his death. Nor would she contemplate what the villain might do to her. Her gaze darted around frantically as she tried to come up with a plan.

"You can't be serious. Do you know who we are?" William paused. "Is that what this is about? Do you intend to ransom her?" He laughed scornfully, causing the man behind her to stiffen further. Flora wished William would be quiet before he got them all killed. "You'll wish for a simple hanging if you take her. You will be hunted like a dog."

"They'd have to catch me," the brigand said flatly.

From his tone, it was obvious he thought it impossible. This was no typical brigand, Flora realized. She could tell from his voice and his facility with Scots, the tongue of the Lowlands, that he had at least some education.

A glint of silver coming from the rear of the carriage flashed in the moonlight like a shimmering beacon. There it was. Her chance. She only hoped that William's men would be ready.

William had started issuing more threats. It was now or never. She hoped the man holding her didn't notice the sudden spike in her heartbeat.

She prayed she remembered what to do. It had been a long time since her brothers Alex and Rory and her cousin Jamie Campbell had taught her how to defend herself.

She took a deep breath and stomped down as hard as she could with the wooden heel of her shoe on the brigand's instep, causing him to loosen his hold just enough. In one swift movement, she slid the dagger from her cloak, spun, and thrust the blade deep into his stomach.

But he'd turned slightly, and the blade sank into his side instead.

He let out a pained curse and fell to his knees, grabbing the handle of the dirk that was still in his side.

Horror crept up her throat; she'd never stabbed a man before. She hoped . . .

Nonsense. The brute intended to kidnap her . . . and worse.

She turned around long enough to see the surprise on his face. A face that was not what she expected. A face that made her hesitate. Their eyes locked, and she felt a strange jolt. *God's breath,* he was the most ruggedly handsome man she'd ever seen.

But he was a villain.

She turned from the wounded man and leapt toward the carriage.

"Fight!" she yelled to Lord Murray's gaping men.

Lunging for the flash of silver she'd glimpsed, she prayed, letting out a sigh of relief when her hand found metal and she pulled Lord Murray's sword from the box.

Her daring had spurred the men back into action. The fighting began again in earnest.

Escape. She couldn't let them take her. Perhaps if she could make it across the moors, just a few hundred yards to the edge of the forest. She turned to look for William and was relieved to see that the man holding him had made a move toward his injured leader—for she had no doubt that the man she'd stabbed was the leader—and then found himself engaged in a sword fight with one of William's men. After tossing the sword to William, she pulled him behind the carriage. "We have to run," she whispered.

He stood frozen, looking at her with the strangest expression on his face, a mixture of awe and revulsion.

She tamped down her rising irritation. He should be thanking her rather than gaping at her as if she were a Gorgon. "Look, we don't have much time." Not giving him an opportunity to reply, she pulled him toward the moors and started to run toward the line of trees that loomed in the distance like an oasis.

But freedom was fleeting. She hadn't taken more than a few steps onto the heather before she was brought down from behind, landing hard against the ground with the full weight of a man on top of her. Her breath slammed against her chest.

She couldn't move. Or breathe. Heather, dirt, and twigs pressed into her cheek, and her mouth tasted dirt. She didn't have to look; she knew who it was just by the feel of him.

He wasn't dead.